The Erkeley

A novel

Michael W. Thomas

The Erkeley Shadows

Michael W. Thomas

ISBN: 978-1-7384043-2-2

Front cover artwork by Ilco Rietveld

Swan Village Reporter

Dedication

To all the Canadian towns out and back along this trail—and to what remains of the Erkeley.

Acknowledgements

The author would like to thank the following:

Lorna Tracey and the late Jon Silkin at *Stand Magazine*. This novel began life as a short story, 'Taking Pete Wiznuk Out', which was a finalist in *Stand's* International Short Story Competition, 1997.

Stephen Theaker at *TQF Magazine,* in which the opening chapters of this novel first appeared (*TQF* 68, Autumn 2020).

Polly Stretton and Tony Judge for guiding the novel skilfully up the Amazon.

Ted Eames for his excellent artwork.

'Untroubling and untroubled where I lie' is taken from John Clare, 'Sonnet: I Am' (1845).
'Another time has other lives to live' is taken from W.H. Auden, 'Another Time' (1940).

Preface

The Erkeley Shadows has had its fair share of
lives. It began as a short story, 'Taking Pete
Wiznuk Out', which was a finalist in *Stand
Magazine*'s   International   Short   Story
Competition, 1997. I might have left it at that: a
compact tale with a small number of key events,
Jonathan Parry as the sole significant character
and Police Officer Will Apland in a walk-on part.
But it kept circling back. At some point it was
suggested to me that I could develop Will's
character further. So the story became a novella
and Will's role was somewhat enlarged. Unlike
Jonathan,   however,   he   still   didn't   have   a
significant   back-story.   Questions   remained
unanswered. What had Will's life been up to that
point? What made him tick? And crucially, what
was it in his history that drew him into the story
that Jonathan had left for the world? And so the
novella became this novel. As Jonathan's tale
unfolds—all those carefully written pages in that
bulky folder—Will's fascination with it deepens.
Initially telling himself that the tale will offer a
diversion, something to keep him warm, so to
speak,   while   his   family   are   away   for   a
Hallowe'en weekend, he gradually unearths what
he thinks are parallels between this stranger's
history and his own—with results which, if acted
on, will be shocking indeed. By the end, Will is
thinking and planning in ways that are wholly

out of character. Or are they? And what should be made of the tale that sets him on this path?

I lived in Canada for many years, drawing on my experiences for the novel's several settings. I should add that I'm no Jonathan Parry, having, I like to think, a more equable relationship with the world. That said, though, perhaps there is a Jonathan in many of us. It only needs a twist of happenstance—an episode here, a revelation there—for him to emerge. I hope not. But no doubt Jonathan hoped the same, before the events in *The Erkeley Shadows* announced themselves and slowly, balefully wove themselves together.

Michael W. Thomas, Summer 2023

Contents

Saskatoon Star-Clarion, Friday October 30th:
The body of a man was found in an apartment on Cumberland Avenue South early Wednesday morning. His identity has yet to be made public but he is thought to have been a European landed immigrant living alone. There was no sign of disturbance. The alarm was first raised by his upstairs neighbour, who had spoken with him through his door a couple of times but received no response to further attempts. The involvement of a person or persons unknown is not suspected.

1

Will was about to go off shift. The station was quiet for a Saturday afternoon so the one-off arrangement with Smeets had turned out okay. Will had needed a break from the streets. Patrols attracted trouble on the weekend. Through the window he could see the last stragglers being exited from the City Library. He smiled. There was Grace Popescul holding open the door as she'd done forever. The lady had a way with her, no doubt of it. When he was twelve he'd tried bribing everyone in his grade to return his overdue books. At last Dad had driven him downtown, frog-marched him into the lobby, nodded at Grace and gone to wait in the car. He'd been left with her wrath and what felt like the whole province's population looking on. Man, she didn't look a day older than when she'd torn those strips off him. But of course she was older

1

and so was he and so it would go on. Except for this Cumberland Avenue guy.

Smeets had jumped at the chance to take Will's place with Terry M. He needed to be out in the weekend city in the way Will didn't. Old Smeets had been truly antsy since Wednesday, when the pair of them had discovered the guy. Then Terry M had arrived. There'd been a break-in at a store in Market Mall and Terry was heading back along Cumberland when he saw the car…just in time, in fact, to catch the tail-end of Smeets's usual performance. Will had been Smeets's patrol-pal often enough. He knew the theatrical drill and the Cumberland episode was no different: Smeets stepping backwards, arm flung up, treading hard on Will's toes (Will really should charge him for replacement boots), crying, 'Whoa, you don't want to see this'— whether this was a bloodied drunk or a bunch of stolen white goods.

But there'd been nothing to see, not of the kind they were trained and seasoned to expect. Still, Will had to hand it to Smeets: there was something about the place, the feel of it, that justified his antics. Terry M had agreed and he had absolutely no time for vibes and auras…just secure the scene of crime, report, turn things over to superiors and forensics. But what crime had there been? No break-in, nothing even forced. The lady upstairs said she might have heard something the night before, but she was a devil, she said, for falling asleep with the TV on so it could as easily have been from some late-repeat soap. Nothing looked disturbed...yet everything felt that way. The guy was on the bed, calmness itself, as though he'd decided on a moment's lie-down and just zizzed off. College type, they thought at the time, and enquiries had quickly located his place of work. A prof at the uni, it seemed.

And yes, Smeets had tried to be his usual upfront self when he arranged the swap with Will but he'd still looked spooked, a little wilder than usual about the eyes: 'That smell', he'd said again, like he had in the apartment, like all of them had. It didn't seem to come from any one place. They'd eased open the walk-in closet, they'd looked under the bed. Nothing. It was as though the guy had had a visitor, maybe more than one, anyway someone who wasn't crazy about washing. An ancient smell, Smeets had said, prompting Terry M's usual roll of the eyes. But old Smeets, he'd pressed on. A smell from down the ages, he insisted. Will always let the pair of them indulge their routine: 'No, no, hear me out' from Smeets, 'Give it a rest, Asimov,' from Terry. He just liked to listen to their hooey. And maybe Terry's counter-suggestion was right, maybe the guy was long overdue a trip to the laundromat, though the place had a shared washer and dryer. Ok, so maybe he couldn't work them...profs, eh?

And now, lying in clear view on the front desk, what had been bagged up and brought away from the place: a folder, not that much bigger than a book but with wide rings, its light-

3

blue cover splashed here and there. Coffee, apparently. No sign of old Clance, of course, the most reluctant desk-sergeant in the province. Barysko had headed up the case and didn't you just know it? Evidence left around for anyone to read or make off with. A note on the bag said that the lab was done with the folder and DeConinck would be taking it for onward dealing. Like Barysko didn't know where DeConinck's office was, like he couldn't manage the few steps from his own desk. Will smiled. Onward dealing. Barysko just loved his management courses, those buzz-words waiting for him to take them home and love them.

Will looked about—Old Clance must be on a two-cigarette break—and picked up the bag. He'd seen enough goodbye notes to last him forever, but this one beat the band. Sort of fitted with the vibe in the guy's apartment. He waited. Still no Clance loping back to the front desk and, amazingly, no troubled citizen bursting in from the chilly world outside—where Grace Popescul was still at the library door like a patient Noah waiting on the last beasts to get out and get on with it. Without thinking he slid the folder into his bag. He was taking a chance. God knows, Barysko could do a Grace Popescul when he suspected rule-bending. Ah, but he was off at some junket in Regina till Wednesday and DeConinck had been drafted into that Cluff Lake murder case way up beyond La Loche. Meantime, head honcho at the station was

4

Murray, whose sole concern was keeping his door shut.

Besides, Will was hooked. Goodbye notes were often heat-of-the-moment affairs and you could only guess at how awful those moments were. This folder said time and determination. Anyway, he was alone this weekend. Mags and the kids were doing Hallowe'en with the in-laws up at North Battleford, Will having promised them a trip to the lake in lieu of doing his own ghoulish routines. They were wearing a bit thin now, he thought. No, had been told, by both his kids, along with an affirmation that Nanna and Gram Rundberg were so much better at the scary stuff, more inventive—Gram especially. Weird, huh, dad? And them both so old. Like, older than you, even.

Quick dinner, scotch, a call to North Battleford, a carefully-inserted question about possible dates for Gram Rundberg's operation, confirmation of the return bus. Then the rumpus room.

Old Clance was just lumbering back as Will left. For the look of it, he lifted his bag, tapped it and said, 'Just some stuff, Clancy. Have it back on Monday.' Old Clance looked at where the folder had been. He might have realised what Will had taken but he just said, 'Have a good one,' shrugged and pulled a sheaf of other business under his nose.

*

Twenty minutes later Will crossed the road to the liquor store and 7-11. All he needed for the evening was a half-block from home. And a half-mile, maybe, from where the dead guy was found. That was part of his curiosity. Like doctors and psychiatrists, police were meant to leave cases go at a proper time. There'd be others along; they were gathering while you wrapped up the present one. But sometimes you couldn't help it. While you were going on living, others on adjacent parts of the grid weren't. Why was that? What brought them to their stopping-point?

He met Ernie Lester going through one of the liquor turnstiles and the old man greeted him as he had last time, as he would till mid-March at the least: 'Mean weather, Will.' But yes, it was getting that way. The day before, Mags' mom had phoned to say the cold was January-bad up there, they'd had the first fall and it might get fierce at the weekend. It would be lovely to see her daughter, her grandkids, but should they come up? Sometimes the ploughs could be late getting out. What if they couldn't get back? When the kids heard her questions (he and Mags really should remember when to cut the speaker-phone), they protested at the first and whooped at the second. Will had sealed it: 'Weather is weather,' he told Mags. 'Can we deny them your dad's Bela Lugosi?'

'Hey, Ernie,' he said now, lifting a basket from the pile. 'Yes, shaping up real mean.'

He'd skip dinner, he decided back home. Scotch and snacks would do. And there were still

6

some of the kids' Thanksgiving treats wrapped up in the fridge. Amazing, he thought, taking what he needed down to the rumpus room. Most times such stuff didn't stand a chance. He and Mags were forever on at them about wolfing. A weekend with the olds, of course, and they'd come back twice as bad. Plugging in the phone, he made the call. All good in North Battleford. March, Gram's operation might be, or April. These things, they took so long. Nanna was just getting everything fixed for the tricking and treating. No major snow, yet. As Mags spoke, Will pictured all the jump and hurry at his in-laws' house, then saw the guy again on his bed. A silent room. But not serene.

Duty discharged, he unplugged the phone, got all his sustenance about him and opened the folder on his knee.

2

The rings were set to burst open. Man, this guy had just flowed or maybe worked and worked his story so it would say just what he wanted. Hell of a note. Neat, the writing, old-fashioned careful. Will could appreciate that. This was the last thing the guy had real control over. You couldn't hover in the air to check how your body was being dealt with or if your funeral came up to par. Briefly he felt guilt at taking it. Ah, but Barysko had said the tests were all done and, despite his briskness shtick, he lived in a blur much of the time so wouldn't remember that he'd left it for any Joe to gawp at rather than handing it straight to Dave DeConinck. Anyway, you never knew what happenstance HQ would throw at you. Will might not have been on the case at all and now might be the only time he'd see such a labour of love, or of something, as this folder. In truth, he felt like one of those characters in an old story, a smoking-room guy out of Dickens or whoever, about to listen to some other guy's tale, uninvolved, able to reflect while swishing a glass of…he topped up. Was that mean…just the vicarious doo-dads? No: he wanted to get close in to the guy, to know what had turned him from someone who could, say, lift a liquor basket from a pile into a body on a cold day. He wanted to know why his own ways of dodging the darkness—haring about with the kids on ski-doos, staying too long at barbecues—didn't work for everyone. There: you just couldn't let that stuff go sometimes and perhaps any doctor or therapist would say the same. He wondered if he should glove up to turn the pages—he always had a pair or two in his case—but decided against, swallowed a treat and focussed:

*

I thought I'd go batty (the guy began) if Mum said it once more: 'Just think, Jonathan—cross-country ski-ing and that kind of lacrosse they do and all sorts.' I couldn't care less about sports at the school I was leaving; a new country wouldn't make any difference. She didn't say much else to me that summer and nor did Dad. Evenings found them surrounded by all that paperwork, except when we did the rounds of goodbyes— Macclesfield, Kettering, Builth. Aunts and uncles full of awe and nostalgia and speculation, saying the same things over and over till I'd have given anything to grow skis and vanish: 'All that space, Jonathan, all those mountains—bigger than Snowdon, some of them, easy.' 'You could say goodbye to someone on the prairies and still see them walking off an hour later. You try it, lad.' 'I was in Winnipeg just after the war. Should have stayed. I was that restless.' Uncle Sid, the Kettering Sid, not the Builth one, ruffled my hair: 'Well, young 'un, give my love to Rose Marie and the Mounties. They always get their man.' That's true. They will again, this man, though not quite how Uncle meant it.

I tell a lie about Dad. He did say something to me that summer: 'Turn off that blasted *Good Night, Midge*. I can't think straight.' He never explained *Good Night, Midge*, though he sang it. He was always singing, stuff from the war, ditties about pumping ship and *The Rodney Renown*. So I assumed that *Midge* was more drollery of the ocean wave. He sang it to the start of *Three Blind Mice*—or to put it another way, the way he so much objected to, the start of 'All You Need is Love', which pretty well melted on my turntable. Not their best single but, for me, their most magical, probably because of how they recorded it, at the end of 'Our World', the first global TV hook-up, which went out one

Sunday night and wound up at Abbey Road. John, Paul and George were perched on bar-stools with those mikes like Skyrocket lollies. John chewed gum as he sang.

I had to placate Dad. He controlled the electricity, which he wasn't above cutting off to dramatize a point. Most of the time, though, he was hunched over forms or the telephone, or arguing with Mum about how to word some reply to the Consulate. Always 'The Consulate', never the Canadian Consulate or the High Commission of Canada. Both of them handled the word as though it were 'Eden' or 'Xanadu.' And it was, to them, especially whenever Mr Walden, Dad's prospective boss at Manitoba Power, entered the picture. Communications from him were beyond sacred. He'd interviewed Dad—both of them, in fact—in London, an experience which, going by Mum's star-struck account, made an audience with the Queen seem like a quick nod in our local pub.

Of course I didn't accompany them either to see Mr Walden or breathe the Consular air with its intimation of big horizons just beyond the reception desk. Odd, that always seemed. You'd have thought someone in the immigration chain would have wanted to check that they weren't smuggling a weirdo, a human virus, into the unsuspecting former dominion. But there it was...they farmed me out to neighbours when they went off to swoon before officialdom, usually the Butlers, who did their own bit to prepare me for the big leap by presenting me with a calf-bound copy of Longfellow's *Poems,* inscribed 'Read *Evangeline* and *Hiawatha.* That'll set you up. Mr. and Mrs. Arthur Butler.' An evacuee in my own street, I wondered if anyone on the Canadian side actually knew of my existence. Actually...was it a big con and were my parents secretly planning to meet Rose Marie and the Mounties as a childless couple, having arranged for another family's latchkey to hang around my neck, a state of affairs I'd only discover when, coming back home one day, I found that it wasn't home any more but a bunch of blank windows? Did my future actually hold, say, the rotund figure of Uncle Sid—the Builth one, not the Kettering one—with his carpenter's plane in one hand and my apprenticeship papers in the other?

But that theory faded as the summer went on. My parents were not play-actors. Even acting out love was a bit of a strain. And Mum sort of put things straight when she said, 'You'll have to say goodbye to that pair, Hunter and Forbes. Far better lads where we're going.'

Bevvo Hunter was with me when I bought 'All You Need is Love'. We rode our bikes all round Bilston one fabulously scorching Saturday, the day after the single came out. Banged our handlebars against the window of 'Timothy's Electrical Supplies', the only decent record shop around, and burst in. I had my ten-shilling note at the ready. Bevvo made straight for the 'on-off' knob of a Dansette Hi-Fi (*separate speaker available for full stereophonic*

11

effect—I knew, I had one) and started flicking it, making the pin-head light flare and die till Timothy the elder yelled, 'You can pack that in for a kick-off.' Fiddling with a tank-sized telly, he had his back to us. Bevvo was in awe of his telepathic powers and always made a point of tampering with something to check they were still in trim. Timothy *fils*—a mix of acne, crooked teeth and his father's shirtiness—was behind the counter, advancing himself in the business he would inherit. Bevvo leaned across: 'Awl Yuh Need is Lerv, Baby,' he drawled, channelling his beloved Presley. Such devotion in that era would have created severe image problems for lesser boys, but Bevvo carried it off with a defiant swagger. 'Last one,' sighed Timothy *fils* disdainfully, reaching behind him and taking my note. He liked Mel Torme, poor soul.

Gordy Forbes fettled telescopic cigarettes. Bevvo and I shot straight over to his house that afternoon. His mum and dad were out for the day, fussing round his newlywed sister in Cannock. Within minutes of our arrival, the French national anthem, all cod-pompous brass and frilly drum-roll, was blaring out of his player and we were into *Good Night, Midge.* Gordy, meanwhile, was exhibiting 'Polaris' for our admiration, three roll-your-owns gummed together. French windows open wide, he and Bevvo demolished it.

Gordy's musical loves were different again. His brother-in-law, a merchant seaman on

Pacific runs, had long since introduced him to post-surf California. Neither the Grateful Dead nor Jefferson Airplane were ever far from his player and, like mine, his father enjoyed playing God with the mains. That afternoon, the Airplane's *Surrealist Pillow* album succeeded the Beatles: 'Cool stuff, man,' drawled Gordy, informing us that, as soon as circumstance would allow, he was off to 'Frisco.

'Wankers, all that lot,' condemned Bevvo.

'Elvis was in grade school with my granny, man,' returned Gordy. 'Only she got through'— and their routine scuffle was on, through the French windows and up the lawn.

I neither scuffled nor smoked but I loved their exuberance, their flirtation with delinquency. A sub-contractor, you might call me, leaving all the madness to them. Others would have barred me from their cabals, but Bevvo and Gordy indulged me. And we had things in common, not least our attitude to school and the hard-men gangsters among our peers, whom we were convinced would sink into rubbishy lives. That wasn't our plan. There was my prospective departure for a start, which I think invested me with a kind of glamour in Bevvo and Gordy's eyes. And—I may as well set it down here—Gordy did in the end make it to the West Coast and Bevvo settled in Normandy. So when my mother predicted a better class of companion for me in Canada, I thought that wouldn't be true. More my luck, I felt, to be stuck with the likes of Pete Wiznuk.

Pete Wiznuk was a gouge in the pattern of life. With a busby-cap thatch and a pinched and ratty face, he patrolled the school playground, endlessly fomenting trouble. His height was unlikely to break five-two and I think he knew it. Accordingly, he employed two low-browed minders, Cadman and Bell, to finish off his aggravation. Creeping up on you, he'd blow his nose on your blazer; turning, you'd find the other two hideously filling your gaze. Just before you hit the deck you'd glimpse Wiznuk clapping and gurgling well out of harm's way. His upturned nose would poke at the air, his bushy eyebrows would go crazy, reminding me always of those tales where a dummy comes to life and terrorises its ventriloquist.

Certain boys they avoided, my friends included. Bevvo, in fact, had once cheerfully walked over Wiznuk's face, stilling that twitchy nose for the rest of the day. I was not so blessed. Again and again the asphalt swung up to meet me when Bevvo and Gordy weren't around to intervene.

Inevitably, when my departure for Canada became known, Wiznuk and his apes came tumbling after me with redoubled zeal. They would of course wait till Bevvo and Gordy were absent, usually at some break-time club. Wiznuk would dance round me, hand pummelling mouth in a demented war whoop filched from a hundred dodgy westerns, and the ground and I would be as one. I did fight back, but three to one make infallible odds: 'Johnny Canuck, Johnny

14

Canuck,' Wiznuk would shriek, pretty-polly style. The impoverishment of his taunts incensed me more than anything else. Was that really his best shot? Cadman and Bell should have charged him for their muscle to make up for it. God knows what he'd grow up like. No...God can only assume, on the evidence of his thirteen ratty years.

*

Man, oh man, thought Will, this is one verbal guy. Pages in and he's still on the same summer. But he knew he was thinking that for thought's sake. The picture was taking hold in his head, nothing fudged or skimped. He ate the treat he'd been holding since the Timothy's Electrical bit.

3

On the last Tuesday of term, Gordy waxed romantic:

'Hey, let's come back here tonight, man. Mooch round the Erkeley after hours. Souvenir for you, Jon, golden memory: hanging loose, Erkeley-wise.'

He and Bevvo laughed. The Erkeley ran all around the school, almost, but was bounded on one side by a residential lane leading up to the main road. It must have been as impressive as Cannock Chase once, all ridged and hollowed. But houses had clawed most of it away and now it was a wide-ish bracket of pylon scrub with a few copses. On the far side of the school, its ridges had been conquered by interwar council-houses of small, black-brown brick. Opposite the near side stood a row of perky Sixties detacheds, declining from the main road with the run of the lane, curving past the school gates till they joined others of their kind in a flaky village-green arrangement. Shanty shacks, we all called them. What remained of the Erkeley would probably outlast them. The Timothys lived in one.

We had on occasion decamped to the Erkeley during lunchtime, risking detentions for the sake of Gordy's ingenious cigs. I had never ventured there of an evening: never wanted to. The Erkeley meant school, from which I naturally scarpered as soon as possible. But this school would vanish from my life in four days' time. Demob happiness was upon me, along with the notion that the adventure would make a great memory-snap, me and my best friends mucking about in the place that had brought us together— a rebuttal of Mum's sniffy notion that better friends were waiting across the sea.

We met there at seven that evening. If I'd wrecked the house before leaving, my parents wouldn't have noticed. Mr Walden and the Consulate had both written on the same day— God and Santa speaking as one. The table was awash with fresh paper-work. As I left the house, I wondered if their absorption would persist in other forms once we'd emigrated. Not for the first time I felt the pinch of loneliness foretold in that huge land with its miles of wheat and snow.

But the sight of Bevvo Presley and Gordy Airplane banished all that for the moment.

'And the hunt begins,' announced Bevvo. This meant a scavenging spree round the Erkeley. Bevvo was fascinated by *Going For A Song,* that wacky TV programme about antiques. I felt sure that, one day, he'd barge onto an episode unannounced with a bag of non-antique tat. Gordy and I had heard his mother berating him for the boxes of rubbish that were already poking out either side of his bed. 'I'm sure your two friends don't go in for that silliness,' she'd said, looking at us. His two friends had kept silent with a polite smile. You just didn't abet adult point-scoring.

Gordy said he knew which house was the Timothy lair. Should we pop up at their window first, gurning away, dishing out the heart-attacks? Bevvo said no: if Timothy *père* saw us we'd be chased up the lane 'and it'll be sayonara to this boy's treasure-hunt.' Maybe on the way home, he added. So we left the lane and started picking our way across the Erkeley.

'And here we go!' shouted Bevvo, holding up what looked like a decanter stopper. 'A guinea's worth right there.'

Already sculpting a cigarette, Gordy snorted: 'Mental, you are, Hunter.'

'A penny if you're lucky,' I corrected, chuffed to be adding to the mood, and then there was a fourth voice:

'Ahtside for physical jerks, vest and plimsolls at the ready!'

17

'Ah, good evening, your worship,' said Bevvo and we all looked round at a scraggy tree some yards off, tilting over a pond in a parody of country charm. Sprawled against its trunk, the worship thus addressed heaved himself onto one elbow: 'Mine, that is!' he called, pointing unsteadily at the stopper in Bevvo's hand.

He probably didn't have a clue what it was. Old Tafler, dubbed the Lord of Erkeley, had inhabited that ground forever. In school, estimates of his age ranged from seventy to two hundred. Mythology also said he'd known no other home—had probably been born on the Erkeley—but he survived somehow. From a classroom window you could sometimes just make him out heading to the council estate, where he'd do the rounds of the dustbins. Kind souls there were known to see him all right in bad weather. But he made himself scarce when everyone was pouring into and out of school and for sure he never crossed the road to the detacheds. The lane was like a cliff-edge to him; the shanty shacks, as distant as Mars.

Bevvo good-naturedly lobbed the stopper at him. If Tafler did know its purpose, it was more use to him than to anyone. Bottles of all shapes were often discovered in the grass, announcing his residency like spoor. But there was no harm in him. Besides, back then, it wasn't automatically assumed that tramps were bred to violence.

We skirted the pond towards him. Gordy, still working on his über-ciggie, made a low bow: 'How sleeps your worship these days?'

Tafler shook his head frantically: 'That Jez Wallings has been again. I don't like him. Comes all the way from Penzance just to mess me about. I haven't got his wireless, never seen it, I don't like him.'

It was a safe bet that, like most else in Tafler's world, Jez Wallings either didn't exist or was lost in another time and place. One lunchtime we'd come across him staggering about, crying the name to the bony trees. A gunner, maybe, Gordy had theorised, last seen in the chaos of a Normandy beach. It had been enough for the three of us to style ourselves Wallings' Waifs and Bevvo and Gordy had gone through a phase of using the name on new exercise-books, adding it to team lists on notice-boards, considering detention and extra homework a paltry price to pay for keeping the faith.

Bevvo and I bowed also, wondering what was in the bottle which Tafler, now sort of upright, was trying to plug with the wrong end of the stopper. Bevvo was just leaning down to him, making flipping motions by way of guidance, when Tafler dropped the bottle, jerked back and lowed like a cow:

'Midges!' he cried, slapping both his ears. 'Sea midges! He stuffs them in my head, that Wallings, when he comes at night. Penzance midges. Ahtside for physical jerks. I don't have his wireless.'

But they weren't midges. No midge could have caused the gash that now opened up round Bevvo's ear. We spun round in the direction of the council-houses. Spaced apart, three figures were pelting off their ridges towards us, one raising his hand, flexing a catapult which, even at that distance, looked hugely monstrous. 'Bloody good shot,' breathed Gordy, impressed despite our friend's wounding. We knew damn well who they were but I couldn't for the life of me say what had compelled them to take Bevvo and Gordy on. Had one of them passed near Gordy when he made his suggestion about tonight? Was the idea to turn my memory-snap from golden to black and blue?

Bevvo biffed my arm: 'Royal send-off you'll be getting.' Oblivious to the mess his ear had become, he charged after Gordy to meet the common foe, swerving and hunching as the catapult was again hefted and discharged. I followed nearly on all fours, my stomach in torment, fresh accusations about the malign Wallings in my ears.

Between the ridges and us were two huge hollows, big enough, Bevvo had frequently asserted, to hide everyone at the school. As we ran we saw the three figures slide down the nearer one and out of sight. In the art of true surprise, the trio were clueless. Their old routine on the level playground was as slick as they got. Easy-peasy, then, to pile in on top of them but impossible to tell if they were packing anything besides the catapult.

Which they were. The first in, Gordy just avoided Cadman's lunge with a Stanley knife. Bell had wire twine ready-wrapped about his wrist and tried getting it round Bevvo's neck. He succeeded only in snagging his injured ear, opening the gash further, and Bevvo went at him in bellowing rage. Last in, I stumbled between the grappling pairs, my eyes full of thrashing arms and legs, my head ringing with obscenities. I couldn't see the catapult. To begin with I thought that Pete Wiznuk was in there somewhere, too, and when I realised that he wasn't I saw that the situation at last gave me the chance to face him one-to-one: a thought which hit me just a second before the fear that he was about to jump me from behind with who knows what hardware. Accidentally treading on Gordy's leg, almost giving Cadman a fatal advantage, I spun round to see a pair of heels slithering up out of the hollow. Wiznuk the brave—or was his intention to draw me off? The idea that he might actually want to go at me face-to-face, far from the protection of his cavemen, and that he might have had the idea before I did, incensed me. That he thought he could take me on, all nought-feet-nought of him...that his brain had whirled faster than mine...intolerable. I scrambled out of the hollow.

By the time my eyes could focus, Wiznuk had reached Tafler's tree. I started running, the screams of the hollow-battle receding in my ears, replaced of a sudden by shattering glass. Wiznuk was half-crouched, swaying, as oblivious to

21

Tafler as the tramp was to the world. As I approached I saw the catapult sticking out of his pocket, but he made no move on it. His hands now cradled the neck of the bottle he'd smashed. Tafler was still bemoaning the spite of Jez Wallings's midges, his lament an eerie counterpoint to Wiznuk's taunts:

'C'mon, Johnny Canuck.'

'All over me at night.'

'Johnny, Johnny, useless Johnny.'

'Tucking in like I was lumps of meat.'

'Attaboy, Johnny, c'mon, c'mon.'

'Buzzing my ears off.'

The rat lunged, slashing a Zorro-sign in the air. At once I regretted giving chase. Nought-feet-nought and alone he might be but I had no idea how to manage the neck of that bottle. But out of Tafler's sodden ravings came a guiding word: 'He's left them to work me over, bloody Penzance midges—all of 'em left.' Elsewhere on the Erkeley you could find firm enough paths with ease as long as you knew where to look. It was sort of like Conan Doyle's Great Grimpen Mire that way. Round Wiznuk, though, the ground was especially perilous. Anyone dashing near Tafler's tree could yank his foot off in a minefield of dips and clefts. But the gleam in Wiznuk's eye said that, whatever care he'd taken in getting to where he was, the ecstatic anticipation of cutting me had driven it from his mind. 'He's left them,' wept Tafler now, prompting me—and left I went, toes sliding carefully, two, three yards. At first Wiznuk stayed put, brow furrowed, stretching his bottle-arm as if it were a crook to yank me back, but soon I was right out of lunging range and of course he couldn't have that. He leapt to his right, completing the chess move I'd set up, his ruinous shoes landing on the rim of a serviceable crater, swinging up as he fell back. I thought that, once I was in, I'd have to stamp the bottle-neck out of his hand but in his shock he'd flung it nearly at my feet and I scooped it up as tenderly as an antique buff on *Going for A Song* handling a Queen Anne locket.

As I came up on the crater he twisted to face me. Beautiful, the evening sun, catching the dark glass of the neck. Old gold, you might call it. In the distance there were fewer cries of battle now and I recognised most of them as my friends'. Maybe they were punching the cavemen out in the old-fashioned way, maybe they now had the knife and the twine. Peering over, I thought Wiznuk's body would split, bursting as it doubtless was with cries for help which he couldn't release and which anyway would go unheard. Little ratty thing, eyes pin-heads of terror, mates bested and useless far behind. As I'd never done in gym lessons, I sprang from a standing start...got one cry out of him, anyway, a pig-squeal followed by a long, failing sigh which, weirdly, sounded like my mother when, looking for something but not saying what, Dad messed up a newly-sorted pile of papers. I lifted the bottle-neck clear and held it over his eyes, moving it like a dowsing-rod. There was some commotion far off, feet thudding into the distance. They were the only sounds. After that, the bottle-neck's was the only movement.

Minutes later I cleaned the bottle-neck in Tafler's pond and dried it with fistfuls of grass, finishing off with my handkerchief. Laying the neck down, I pocketed the handkerchief for later disposal, washed my hands in the pond, tore up longer tufts to make a sling for the bottle-neck and pitched the lot into a nearby patch of stalks. The neck swished as it went through them, the tufts staying tight enough round it. And all the time Tafler serenaded the coming night with more sea-midges and his innocence in the matter of Jez Wallings's wireless.

Then I ran—back onto the lane, past the school gates, down to the last of the detacheds round their sad little village green. Beyond them was Erkeley Walk, a permanently muddy path enclosed by ancient walls and overhanging trees, a relic of the days when the Erkeley had its own stately pile. Rising parallel with the school lane, it met the main road further down and without warning: the Headmaster was forever on at us not, not, not to use it on the way home. Some did, I didn't but now was different. Mud became a fringe of cinders became the main road and a van climbing the hill to Sedgley just missed me, as did a car barrelling the other way, my way. Two horns echoed the Head's embargo but I didn't care—down and down I ran till I reached *The Jolly Waggoner* at the corner with Brook Street and collapsed under the pub's sign. Home was my only thought though others were trying to get in and I swiped them away like Wallings's midges. I'd just pulled myself upright when I heard my name from up the road. Bevvo and Gordy were racing at me, bigger and bloodier by the second.

'You fairy,' called Bevvo, 'bogging off like that.'

'You and Wiznuk, you're two for a pair,' Gordy wheezed. 'S'pose you just said *boo* to each other and took off.'

It turned out that, having sent the cavemen packing into the sunset, they'd raced off the Erkeley further up, by the top of the main road. Pointless, they'd reckoned, to ask the Lord of Erkeley if he'd seen Wiznuk or me. They too got a long *parp* from an accelerating car.

After some minutes of rasping breath and glowers, they started their walk home. I trailed them.

'Shame,' I said finally, 'we didn't do what you said, Gordy.'

Silence.

'You know, jump up at the Timothys' window, scare the daylights out of them. That would have been....' I sighed. Why had I started talking? A step or two further on, Bevvo swung round: 'God help you with the Red Indians. They'll have you scalped, no messing.'

'Ye're jus' an asshole, baby,' drawled Gordy— some line from the Airplane, perhaps, or more likely Frank Zappa. For a second I was minded to reply in kind: I'd heard enough of Gordy's favourites, I knew lots of lines, I could pretend to love them too. But it was all I could do to keep walking.

4

I'm no stranger to sleeplessness now, but that night was the first time. I went through next day underwater. People spoke to me but their words were melting echoes. One word forced its way in, though, clear as the school bell: 'Wiznuk', on everyone's lips. With the end of term so close, serious schooling done, speculation was unbound in every lesson. Each teacher would reprimand us, direct us back to whatever thin pass-the-time diversion they'd concocted till the lesson bell went and we were out of their lives for another year. But then the murmuring would resume, and rise, till the little rat's image flitted between the desks.

At lunchtime the police arrived and Bevvo, Gordy, Cadman and Bell were summoned by the Head. Inevitably, Wiznuk's creatures had been waylaid running and screaming onto the council-estate. Stopped, questioned, bereft of their tiny leader, they'd spilled all about the fight, and that brought my friends into the picture. I didn't touch my sandwiches. Huddled tight in a cloakroom corner, I wondered why I hadn't been hauled in with the rest.

The school's reputation was Mr Vesey's sole concern. Beyond ritual duties, you hardly saw him about. Everyone was convinced that, after the home-bell, he sat on in his study, hands and feet sprouting roots, and so he remained, a self-pinioned Gulliver, unthinking and unmoving till next day brought its first arrivals. Bevvo, Gordy and I imagined him on the rare occasions when someone left his door ajar, staring in bewilderment at the institution beyond, then swallowing a handful of magic pills to jerk him back to the here and now and his role in it. But circumstances alter cases. The scrapping foursome had despoiled the image of the school. That the incident had happened outside school time was neither here nor there. For most of the year, Bevvo, Gordy, Cadman and Bell sported the school badge with its owl and its turret, its motto, *Sapience and Duty.* No matter that, on Bevvo's and Gordy's badges, the owl was black-eyed and on crutches, the tower was blasted from Stuka-fire, or that Cadman's and Bell's were half-torn. Sapience and Duty had been cast aside. For Mr Vesey, that was abominable. Even Wiznuk came second, though the Head obligingly pretended otherwise to the police.

I learned all this, or a version of it, from Bevvo and Gordy in the afternoon break. I was so happy that we were back on speaking terms, though anyone passing might not have seen it like that. I'd been there the night before, so I had to be brusquely clued in. They didn't reveal what penance if any had been handed out to them or the other pair. Finally, at the start of the last lesson, I was sent for.

'Parry,' sighed Mr Vesey, using my name as an introduction and a command to be seated. The two policemen, one in uniform, one plain-clothed, smiled at me.

'Hello, son,' said the plain-clothes man. 'Bit of a do last night, eh?'

The other one's smile intensified: 'Boys being boys, sir.'

'Yerrs,' murmured Mr Vesey as though, despite their being half of his bread-and butter in the school, he'd happily arrange for boys to be boys in another dimension. The plain-clothes man pursed his lips:

'Boys being boys, constable, with a pretty desperate arsenal. We're still mopping up from Harry Roberts and his shenanigans'—a reference, this, to the murder of three policemen in London the previous August—'and I'm not happy about the message that sends out to any trainee desperadoes, whatever their game is.'

'Yerrs,' offered Mr Vesey, frowning, probably wondering if Harry Roberts was an old boy who'd gone off the rails. I'd heard the name all right, on the very few occasions I'd steeled myself to accompany Bevvo and Gordy to a Wolves match the previous season, when the North Bank supporters were in full throat: *Harry Roberts is our friend, is our friend, is our friend, Harry Roberts is our friend, he kills coppers.* I worked my knuckles in the palm of my hand. Having expressed his professional distaste, the plain-clothes man now tilted his head to me in a manner not unlike Uncle Sid, the Kettering Sid, not the Builth one:

'Still,' he murmured, 'that's not our business here, eh, son?'

I knew I'd be out of my depth with any policeman not on telly, but I really couldn't figure what was going on here. From being all hanging-judge, the plain-clothes man now sounded solicitous. Perhaps his comments on Roberts were meant to be a secular take on that religious *Ten To Eight* slot on Home Service radio, which quivered in my ears each morning as I got myself sorted for school. He was handing me a homily on right and wrong for my future use. Desperately wishful, I anticipated further guidance. Don't get drawn towards wrong 'uns, lad, you look a decent sort, you've got your whole life ahead of you. Yes, perhaps they'd already concluded that there was no connection between the Erkeley battle and why they were here, or no connection that involved me. Perhaps their enquiries had cooled to a bit of professional top-and-tailing, which was why I'd been brought in last. For form's sake. Oh, perhaps a thousand things. My thread of speculation, taut from lack of sleep, now snapped. Again I worked my knuckles.

'If you could just help us out, son,' the plain-clothes man continued. 'We've spoken to your mates and had a good long natter with Mr Vesey here. All we need now is what you remember, from when the three of you met up.'

I knew I'd get a deluxe sigh from Mr Vesey. There I was, mouth open, unable to coax a sound. Never a favourite of his, I possibly ranked alongside Wiznuk or even lower. He sat steepling his fingers before his mouth, being all sphinx-y, as they're probably taught at Headmaster school. His attitude hardly helped when I did get going, but then the constable said 'Easy, son, easy, take your time,' and that steadied things. A little. Knowing that the first part would concur with what Bevvo and Gordy had said, I lingered over particular details— Bevvo's discovery of the stopper, Gordy's question about whether Tafler was sleeping well—as a way of showing that I loved the truth. But I alone could see, looming like a thundercloud, the point at which my tale would part company with theirs, just as I'd left them to it with Cadman and Bell. One of Mr Vesey's ludicrous pot-plants caught my eye as I got to the bit about scrambling out of the hollow after Wiznuk. How I wished I could shrink to an atom, slide down its stem, begin some new, unimaginable life—'untroubling and untroubled', as some poem in a forgotten English lesson had it—in that little lump of soil.

Mr Vesey saved the day. Down went the steepled fingers and now he was assembly-tetchy. It was clear that, in his view, I had no further light to shed. I was just describing the heels on Wiznuk's shoes—dawdling with details again—when he said, 'Yes, yes, Parry, the others said that you must have got out after him. And then?'

I expected some sighs and throat-clearing from the policemen, intimating that his job wasn't to do theirs. But they just waited, smiling as before. At this, without thinking and dead out as I was, I managed what I've done a thousand times since, diced the facts and picked my morsel: 'Then, sir...then I ran. Ran and ran, sir, like the wind.' And I described my route ('Oh, that confounded Erkeley Walk,' Mr Vesey murmured), inventing the colour of the Sedgley-bound van that nearly did for me.

Mr Vesey made that pinch-of-snuff face we all knew so well. I could tell what he was thinking: loathsome though the whole business was, I could at least have shown some oomph and taken Wiznuk on. From his repertoire of disdain he produced his smell-a-silent-fart *ewwfff,* but the constable leaned forward and patted my arm: 'It's all right, son, it's all right.' Mercifully, the plain-clothes man nodded agreement. The relief made me feel as though I'd slept like a top. An actor's life for me, I thought. Meanwhile, Mr Vesey was shaking his head, wondering how I would last five minutes in adult life, advising that I discard my sheep-like manner forthwith. His words, burnished from general reprimands dished out in assembly, were smooth, elegant, but essentially the same as those Bevvo and Gordy spat out by *The Jolly Waggoner.* He looked briefly at the policemen.

The plain-clothes man gave the faintest nod of the head:

'All right, Parry, vanish, vanish.'

As I reached the door, the constable said, 'Good luck in Canada, son.' For a second I expected his voice to morph into Uncle Sid's, the Kettering one, as he urged me to give his love to Rose Marie and the Mounties. Love. There'd be little of that hereafter and if there was, I wouldn't be able to hang onto it. I thanked him, which sent Mr Vesey's shooing hand into overdrive. The end-of-school bell sounded as I climbed the stairs. Bevvo and Gordy plunged down past me. Back home I phoned them both and was told they weren't around.

Sadly, another sleepless night followed. I went over the afternoon's interview, trying to hold onto the relief I'd felt, but it wasn't having any: 'Fresh air and bags of it, that's what you need,' counselled Mum at breakfast, while Dad maundered about in search of some mislaid health certificate. The fresh air could wait: I needed a proper all-clear. It was waiting at school. Wiznuk's name had disappeared from the classroom gossip to join its owner in the fiery holes. In its place was Tafler's.

The police had taken him in for questioning the previous night. He was as well-known to them as to us. They, too, had probably thought him harmless and perhaps their investigation was initially based on that assumption. Something must have changed all that—the bottle-neck, maybe, retrieved from the nearby stalks? I can't imagine what happened down at the station. Probably, to begin with, those present were treated to dire warnings about Cornish midges, the unwisdom of dropping into Jez Wallings's orbit, as the Lord of Erkeley was bundled through the main doors. I can imagine that he remained as clueless as ever throughout. Maybe he looked about him and wondered how and why his tree and his pond had changed so weirdly. Going by the school chat, though, there must have been something else. At some point in the small hours, after all the insistent questioning, when he was back in the holding cell, his sky must have cleared. If this was what the Erkeley had become, there was another place he had to find, where midges and wirelesses gave way to lovelier shapes, sweeter music.

His name and fate wouldn't have been everywhere if one of the caretakers hadn't had a mate who had a son who was on shift at the police station the previous night, and caretaker and mate didn't take the drive to work in turns: 'Thought they were supposed to strip 'em of everything in custody,' muttered one dinner-lady to another, walking by my class just before lunch while our pass-the-time activity was life-drawing on the grotty little terrace by the labs. 'Likely they did,' hissed the other, 'and he still found a way. Guilt, see? He couldn't live with the guilt.'

On the Friday, Mr Vesey cantered through the last assembly of term in his usual style. He mentioned the Wiznuk affair, devoting just enough time to it to block any charge of heartlessness and adding a fragmented homily about Tafler:

'The path of life, everybody. The path of life. We are all of us just a step away from'—a shuffle of papers—'from…just one ill-advised'—nose-scratch—'school, are you with me?'

He offered brisk good wishes to departing members of staff, to people going off on a couple of school trips that summer and lastly to me: 'Parry of 2 Alpha is quitting us for Canada,' he rushed, his tone between boredom and distaste as though he were announcing renovations to the toilets. It was common knowledge by then but one or two folk wished me luck and then we rose for the school hymn. I neither joined in the opening verse nor really heard it. I was thinking of the Head's mangled words about paths, about ill-advised…steps, I guess his itchy nose stopped him saying. Yes, they were a swine, those missteps. Who knows what you'd fall backwards into and what, once prone, you'd see looming at you. Or not. Like a bottle-neck. Shivering theatrically as if throwing off all the past up to that moment, I prepared to join lustily in with wherever we were at. Then I noticed Gordy. He was in the row in front, a bit to my left. Turned almost fully round, he was staring hard at me. Beside him, Bevvo turned too but just till I saw his profile. He rubbed his chin and they both turned back.

5

Will refilled his drink, selected another Thanksgiving leftover and set it down. He took a turn round the rumpus-room, reminding himself that he really must sort out that one leg on the pool-table. That's what you got for letting two healthy young bodies clamber over it, pirates on the Spanish Main. Making to sit down again and continue, he didn't do that either. Instead, drink in hand, he went upstairs, pulled on a jacket and went out onto the back porch, where he breathed the air deeply. Mean weather, Ernie Lester had predicted, as per. But something was brewing to the north. You could tell from the extra cinch of dryness.

This guy as a kid in that place, wherever it was. Check it out? There was an atlas someplace, belonged to his dad, from the days when England gave pink to the world. Shrugging, he considered what he knew about England. All the usual stuff of course, real and unreal. The Queen, who'd visited Saskatoon a couple of years earlier. He was on route patrol—no problems, barring a few over-eager line-rushers. Cricket, or baseball in a trench as he thought of it. Saskatoon's very own cricket club was up at the Forestry Farm Park and Zoo. Smeets and Terry M were enthusiasts and he'd been up with them a time or two. Yeah, he got it and he got all the fussiness about cricket whites and recliners and tea, saw that that was all part of it. He'd maybe take another shot over to the Park in the summer, if only to watch Smeets bowl what he called his killer googly, which sounded like something you'd run a guy in for possessing or selling photos of.

The Beatles, of course. This folder guy surely loved them. And boy, Uncle Gary, his dad's younger brother, he was all hot to see them when they hit Vancouver. Late '64 or early '65. An unholy ruckus, that caused. Old Gary, he had his backpack ready in the wardrobe till Granma Apland moved him to the small back room on account of it had a lock and just a skylight, not a sash window he could slide up easy in dead of night. Still he'd made it somehow…well, got as far as Kamloops, where a copy of the *Vancouver Sun* told him the show was sold out and plans for an extra one had been scuppered because of the Fab Four's tight schedule. Bad planning, Uncle G—but that was him all over. Go for it, never mind details. Onto the next thing and the next. He was a food-wolfer, too, like the kids, leaping up from the table when everyone else was still on their mains. He'd had to hitch back from Kamloops and that was what gave Granma and Grandpa full-on conniptions, more than if he'd got into the gig and yeah-yeah'd with a bunch of out-of-it girls (the other pull, of course, perhaps more than the band). Dad got a pasting, too, for aiding and abetting ('Which I never did'—Will recalled the way his dad had strung out the words all butter-wouldn't-melt, then winked). Should've been old hat by now, The Beatles, but their influence kept hanging in there. Someone was probably still ready to lay down a pile to get the survivors together. And, well, good tunes. That 'Hey, Jude'. Sweet.

Stepping back into the hall, he stared at his breath on the window of the inner door and took a sip. Then there was the non-real stuff. 'The name's Bond, James Bond', he drawled. Man, his father-in-law could do that just right, Connery, Roger Moore, what's-his-face that lasted just...two of the movies?...one? Ah, he could do them all, Stan Laurel, Richard Burton, Sellers, Hitchcock. Probably doing Hitchcock all tonight on the Hallowe'en rounds, delighting his grand-kids, scaring them to death and so delighting them even more. *Gud Eve-ding.* Plenty of Christopher Lee, too, all the Hammer Horror cheesiness. Yeah, and *Carry On Screaming.* That Kenneth Williams. *MMnneer, stop messin' about. Abaht,* that was it, *abaht.*

And the movies of Mini-cars done up in bad-trip paint flying past their Houses of Parliament, some babe grinning and waving out the skylight with.... He stopped and, frowning, pulled off the jacket and went slowly back downstairs. Houses. Far as he could tell, England, the real England, was just a bunch of houses. And in some small part of the bunch, from a scrawny piece of land, this story had emerged. Here was this regular kid who had only gone and...no, he chided himself, settling down again, swallowing the discarded treat. Don't jump ahead, don't be an automatic cop. What was the point of reading the stuff if he immediately got all hanging-judge over...what was that word the guy had used...a misstep?

Missteps came at him from all sides in his work, in statements he took or had to corroborate in court. A farewell like this guy's, easy as long as a Shakespeare, it wasn't about to boil down to *I'm so nice and happy but now I must go.* Let him say his say. He was owed that much.

6

The end of term was my last contact in England with either Bevvo or Gordy. Over the next fortnight, while my parents ran round in circles and Uncle Sid, the Kettering one, turned up to help in ways he didn't specify and instead spent two days tippling, I phoned my friends times out of number. I always got their mums or, in the evenings, their dads, and the excuses were irritatingly plausible: Bevvo was out at summer soccer training he'd just signed up for; Gordy was staying with his sister and brother-in-law; vaguely, they were just 'out.'

'He's not well, Jonathan Parry,' snapped Mrs Hunter once.

'Oh, I'm sorry, Mrs. Hunter. Was it an accident at soccer?'

'Yes, I'm coming,' she called into the obvious silence beyond her phone. 'You'll have to excuse me.'

I wondered at this unavailability—worried about it. Ok, they might still be disgusted at the sorry sight I presented by *The Jolly Waggoner* that Erkeley evening, interpreting it as the last straw in a friendship which they saw as increasingly pointless, a slur on their credibility. A coward, I'd be out of the picture soon anyway and Canada was welcome to me. For teenage boys, though, two weeks and more was a hell of a long time to stay disgusted. You left that sort of thing to girls or adults, who, from what I could tell, happily worked in terms of months, years. If they didn't see any point in even a modest rekindling of friendship, couldn't they at least come to the phone and manage their own truth or lies? Ducking out on that hardly gilded their triumph in the Erkeley battle. Even just a 'See you, then, all the best', for the sake of just saying it, wrapping up the connection?

Or had something clicked with them? Was that the reason for Gordy's scrutiny of me during the last assembly, Bevvo's profiled intimation that he was thinking, thinking? Or did the penny drop in a later confab? All of that was much on my mind during the week I didn't phone them, couldn't, when we were on holiday in Dawlish. The Lammas Chase Hotel, it was, run by an ex-colleague of Dad's who'd sort of done his own emigration thing, leaving rush hours and productivity graphs and becoming his own boss. Why my parents didn't cancel I have no idea. One of their holdalls was filled with all the Canada stuff and they simply spent the week exchanging their hot phone for the hotel's. I was largely left to mooch about the town, the thronged beaches, the lanes and woods above the hotel. Scenarios filled my head and they were nothing to do with Mum's hopes that I'd make proper Canadian friends and spend all my free time skiing or playing baseball. The sleeplessness returned. I half-expected a police visitation, my name called from the door of the hotel dining-room during the evening meal, everyone looking up and suspending their cutlery-clicks.

But the law left me free to mooch and it didn't haul me in for another grilling when we got home. I didn't bother trying Bevvo and Gordy again; bit by bit, sleep returned. In any case, bigger events took over. Soon we were off, to be welcomed by Toronto immigration officials with sunshades pushed back on their heads and, a while later, the leisure-suited Mr Walden, all smiles and questions about the old country— Norfolk, his folks were originally from, Downham Market, but hey, don't worry, he knew that was a hike from where we'd lived, he wasn't about to ask if we knew any Norfolk Waldens; he knew his geography, he wasn't a Yank (a shove to Dad's arm). The days before our departure are pretty much a blur to me now, though I do remember another bit of Mum's sagacity, about my recent purchase of *Sergeant Pepper's Lonely Hearts Club Band*: 'Jonathan, you should leave that for Mr and Mrs Butler's Kevin. Complete waste of money—they've got different voltage over there.'

So life changed. Or stopped and started again, which is how I preferred to see it. Sheer distance—from my old home and in my new country—made what had happened seem more and more unreal. For sure any summons from the police in Worcestershire could get through— Interpol and all that, or even the dispatch of a couple of dogged officers, maybe the ones I'd found waiting in Mr Vesey's office. But for no particular reason, I felt better able to deal with the prospect, surrounded as I was by lakes, by wheat fields, by seemingly inexhaustible space. You could fit a hundred Erkeleys into any Winnipeg park. And anyway, I told myself, if the heat was on, I could always disappear...crazy, I know, a thirteen year-old boy, a suburbanite, thinking he could just melt into the land. But this wasn't, I realised, just a daft notion, unlike my fleeting dreams back in England of one day becoming good at, or even really interested in, football and cricket. I felt I really would give it a go if the law came after me, imagining a life pugnaciously opposed to the tight little confines of England, a life in which, growing up fast and ever more confident, I took on casual work, farm to farm or wherever, cash in hand, no questions asked, making enough to hunker down out of sight during the winter. Bit by bit, in my head and my heart, I wasn't who I had been. Call it a teenager's callousness, but I even prided myself on what I'd done that evening, seeing it as a great thumping step on from what Bevvo and Gordy had managed in the hollow beyond Tafler's tree. Later, of course, I had cause to regret that. Deep cause. For now, though, those two shrank, as did Cadman, Bell, Mr Vesey, my relatives, till they seemed like the plastic soldiers in cellophane you dredged up from cereal boxes.

Time passed and no summons arrived from across the water. I had less and less reason to consider assembling a special backpack for boots, hard-wearing shirts, a map of the Prairie provinces, or do any gripping or rubbing exercises which, I assumed, would harden my hands. And my new life brought chances aplenty to aid my reinvention. Happily, dreamily, I took on the role of mascot at my high school in Winnipeg, playing up to the image of emissary from Swinging England. My classmates goggled as I told them I was related to Ian Stewart, keyboardist and founding member of the Rolling Stones, who exited before they really took off: 'He's from Kettering,' I said, which sent them scurrying for their atlases. Thinking about it, I should have got some of the Geography teacher's pay for upping their knowledge of Britain. It would of course have been easy to blow it, to claim kinship with one of the Beatles or the Animals, one of the familiar Stones. But that would have been pitching it too high. As it was I nearly made a mistake, practising George Harrison's autograph with a view to transcribing it to my copy of *Sgt Pepper*. Only just in time did I remember that they'd stopped touring over a year before, so the autograph couldn't have been a stage-door squiggle. The alternative explanations would have been mind-bogglingly messy. Did I bump into him in India or on Haight-Ashbury? Was my pa in their inner circle, like that dentist who'd given George and John their first LSD? No, best to go for a lesser light. And as it was, discovering that Ian Stewart was actually from Fife, I had to shift pretty quick with inventing a new branch of my rellies and concocting a tale about their move to Kettering. 'The Stewarts weren't there long,' I added to later queries. I got away with it.

In the end, if I thought at all about Pete Wiznuk and that evening at the Erkeley, they seemed like something out of those dramas my Mum watched back in England, *Armchair Theatre, Play for Today.* You could see the whole thing as a social-conscience effort— modern youth, a generation innocent of war and spared National Service, lacking any channel for their darker energies but, above all, cosseted and bored. As for Tafler...well, yes, I was still sort of niggled. But I quickly developed a strategy for turning him off in my mind so that, instead of his shambling frame and wild eruptions, there was briefly the white noise that sounded when tv programmes shut down for the night in the country I'd escaped. I guess my mascot-status helped there. I mean, how could the boy I was turning into have anything to do with violence and duplicity in English suburbia? Still, deep down, I needed to say a proper goodbye to Tafler. So I was mightily relieved when, heading for my room one night, I heard Dad out in the kitchen, talking to Mr Derksen from next door. They were batting around a news item they'd heard that day, about the latest phase of the US

Rolling Thunder offensive in Vietnam. Mr Derksen quoted some general or Washington politico who'd used the phrase 'collateral damage.' 'Ah, yes,' said Dad, 'those numbing words from the days of Hitler'—and he orated its definition.

That was it. That was what the Lord of Erkeley had become after my loving disposal of the bottle-neck. Regrettable...inevitable. In my room, I whispered, 'Jez Wallings. Sea midges. I don't have his wireless. Collateral damage.' And I laid poor Tafler to sleep.

7

Call it all up. Build the picture. Will repeated the words under his breath and then aloud.

The pool-table, the easy chairs, the tv, the huge plastic bucket with baseball bats and mitts, the other huge plastic bucket of old toys whose disposal might or might not cause screaming fits—one by one they vanished. In their place Will saw the lane, school gates to the left, detached houses to the right. Further up, the lane rose, the school fence ended and the Erkeley began, all that poor grass, the odd tree or two, one of them Tafler's, the big puddle of a pool. A bright evening, sun going on and on. A warm snap for an English summer, a break in the rain, their national element. Beyond all of that, over towards those council-houses...housing projects, Will assumed...the whoops and hollers of the fight. The one with the antiques bug and the one with the kooky cigarettes are starting to win. Will strained his eyes and he could just see them, blurred bodies thrashing up over the lip of that hollow and dropping down again. They could be cartoons, Popeye and Bluto, Wile E. Coyote and whoever's nailing him now. But this is kids playing grown-up, trying on dad's shoes. Rage and vengeance and sheer cussed strength, as absolute as that.

Now pull back again. What's here? Will saw the tree, the pool and the tramp. What did the guy's folder say and what's to add? The tree some way in from the sidewalk on the school side, Tafler leaning easy against it—or is he still up on his elbow from when he told Bevvo to give him the stopper? No, he slapped at his face after that, when the sling-shots came. Did a shot really hit him then? If so, that Wiznuk could've got the jump on William Tell. Anyway, he jerked back, the folder says, so he'd have been down on his haunches at least. Ok, so have him lean easy against the tree. He deserves comfort. So, foreground, then, the sun's on the pool, the tramp's giving out about Wallings. Behind him, Parry is someplace towards the tree and Wiznuk is right by it. For just that moment you could be looking at an old photo. Games in the twilight. Parry's a dorky kid, well, he makes out he is, but here's a piece of sublime cool. He's maybe scared of wetting his pants but he's an operator too, he selects one of Tafler's dumb words...left, left. Chance is opportunity. He steps left, and at that moment he's way older than the sluggers in the hollow behind him.

Parry moves and Wiznuk can't glass him from where he is so he has to follow Parry's line. Pull back a tad more and from the sidewalk you could see them going deep to your right. The little rat vanishes into that hole. Like a ballet, the way the folder tells it, and chancy again. What if Wiznuk's shoes had gripped and he hadn't toppled? Is what happened what happened? There's only the folder to go on, only this story, but the way the words tell it, they just can't believe their luck.

The fight over in the hollow is getting to its end with a few last whoops and hollers from Bevvo and Gordy, but that's just landscape now. Stay on the foreground. In goes Parry. The distant fight fizzles out and sounds rise from the hole by the tree—more than two young bloods just giving each other a standard whupping. If there was no hole, the sounds would carry better and maybe Bevvo, Gordy—hell, those other two as well—would have run across. But if there was no hole, the rat might have done what he meant—he was waiting crouch-steady with that piece of glass, he knew how to sway—and Parry would be cut...or worse.

Let the other sluggers go, they've done their bit. Now the words in the folder surely do believe their luck. All that careful post-op stuff. Parry cleans the bottle-neck, makes that sling of grass, hoicks the whole lot away where it can't be found. The words love that. But what do you know? It can be found, it probably is, and of course the old tramp's handily in situ because he doesn't know anywhere else. Still not hurting a flea. Here's proximity so here's incrimination. Poor jerk might as well have held his hands out for the cuffs.

Will eased back in his chair and thought about the school lane, the ways across that treacherous grass, muddy Erkeley Walk leading to the main drag. He imagined Parry imagining the same. But now he invented a further scene where the boy forgot all that and went further down his new path. So he grabs Tafler by the scruff of the neck and dunks his head in the pool. Poor feller's a souse…wouldn't need to be too deep or take too long. All that waking-up in the young guy's head and hands, the ecstasy of violence, Will could see it speeding him on. He jerks Tafler's head back—no ghost-midges doing that now—and leaves the tramp flat by the trunk of his only home. If that had happened, the story that went into the world would be that guilt had done for Tafler long before any cop turned up.

It wasn't that way but it could have been. Will had broken up enough teen-fights to spot the point at which the blood cools, the raging man hides again behind the kid's face. Parry was unobserved. If things had been different, he could have mixed the rage and the cool a bit longer. Will looked back at the last thing he'd read: *In my room, I whispered, 'Jez Wallings. Sea midges. I don't have his wireless. Collateral damage.' And I laid poor Tafler to sleep.* Oh boy, he thought, you do yourself a disservice, Jonathan. You changed before you got to this country. You laid your boyhood to sleep back there by the tree. Never mind any goodbye ritual to Tafler: that's just a kid tidying his room under pressure. Who's to say that, a moment longer as what you'd become, you wouldn't have done like I pictured?

But no. Here's fear, here's the push to survive. I see your buddies heading up to the main drag by that other track way beyond where you are, running back into their usual selves. You'd best be gone, boy, with that thing at your heels, that new darkness. Go, scoot, down through that muddy old Erkeley Walk, play chicken with the traffic (was it at the back of your mind that you should end it too? Ok, no, just more fear…I'll give you that). Now get yourself all crumpled by that public-house, ready for your buddies' contempt. And however the folder tells it, you take their sneers on the chin. There are other things to think of. You've opened a door and the wind's too high to shut it.

Another treat, another top-up. As Will was about to lift his glass and the Erkeley scene was dissolving, Mark appeared in his mind's eye. For a moment there was a weird flashback: the hummocky ground, Tafler's tree and, in front of them, that broad, blond-thatched face, full as ever of his younger brother's sass. And the bottle-neck.

8

After Winnipeg I enrolled for a degree in Art and Design in Ontario. I'd been good at Art since England, Technical Drawing, too: better than Bevvo or Gordy, one or other of whom was always asking for homework tips. I was of use that way. So, playing to strengths they never had, I had the chance to take myself yet further away from them. And not just that: I could have stayed in Manitoba for my studies, Winnipeg or Brandon; most of my classmates did. But the preoccupations that had consumed my parents during that last summer in England persisted in other forms. Dad's job at Manitoba Power was bigger and wider than I'd thought, insofar as I thought of it at all. He was often all round the province, initiating or signing off new projects. As for Mum, soon after we arrived she wangled work as a reading assistant at grade schools in Winnipeg's South District before getting her provincial licence as a proper teacher. I admired that: she bucked expectation—not for her the round of coffee mornings and good cause drives, though something like that came in the wake of the posts she landed. I did artwork for the odd event at her schools, Nativity specials, summer fetes—once a gaudy backdrop and trimmings for a talent show. From what I remember, she wasn't unpleased.

But it all meant that we drifted further apart, my parents and I, beyond the usual teenage thing. While I didn't have knock-down, drag-out arguments with them, I didn't feel either that there was a family bosom into which I could burrow if needed. As in England, I was just there. I remembered the evening I headed for the Erkeley: how my exit could have brought the house down and they would have just sat on, dust in their ears and rubble down their necks, poring over whatever the Consulate or Mr Walden had just written. It was like that in Winnipeg when I left for school each day or to hang out with friends on the weekends. I guess I could have contrived to go splendidly off the rails to test their parental bond or even just their powers of observation. But I was as disinclined to do that as I was in the days of Bevvo and Gordy. Anyway, my mascot-status ('Hey Jonathan, say stuff.' 'Hello, blokes.' 'Do the pears thing.' 'I'm a-goin' up the apples and pears to see the God forbids, fab, gear') absolved me from rebelling without a cause. So after high school it didn't seem strange to, as you might say, leave our house in Crescentwood one evening and walk over eleven hundred miles to Windsor. Maybe a glint of interest came into my parents' eyes: never mind the Art bit, sonny...the Design, now that could get you seriously earning. But they never said. Viability assessments for machine upgrades, lesson plans on the seasons or the Roman world—the tables in our house were as thickly cluttered as they'd ever been during that Erkeley summer.

In the spring of my final degree year—with a Master's lined up to protect me a bit longer from the cold winds of the world—my Dad was killed in a plant accident up at Nelson River. I had to do some fancy dancing, rescheduling the submission of two major term papers and, more crucially, altering the date of my end-of-degree exhibition, on which admission to the Master's crucially depended. I wasn't in the best of moods when I flew back to Winnipeg at the end of March, a situation unimproved by finding out how much I hadn't been told. For a start, the rellies were there *en masse*: not just for the run-up to the funeral but also, it seemed, for an unspecified stretch of time after. And if their behaviour on the day of the funeral was anything to go by, one purpose of this lingering stay was to lay hands on my shoulder and whisper, 'You look after your Mummy, lad.'

Mummy? When had I ever called her that? She'd never expected it, nor had Dad and nor, when I was young, had any of this lot. But I was apparently meant to see her that way now, the mother gazing eternally, soulfully at her little boy on their twig of the family tree. Uncle Sid, the Kettering one, was particularly urgent in his use of 'Mummy'—particularly lachrymose, too, weeping out the entire provincial stock of hard liquor, as far as I could see, till I expected it to jet from under his turn-ups and all over his brogues. I remembered his ruffling my hair back in that Erkeley summer, his insistence that I convey his love to Rose Marie and the Mounties. For a long time after, I thought I'd got the point of the gesture, one which he was expressing on behalf of everyone: a new start, lad, a blank page, you go off to that young country and make it your own. Now, with the 'Mummy' bit, they were winding me back into something that I'd never felt. Interestingly, the Builth Uncle Sid, the carpenter, to whom I'd fleetingly feared my parents would abandon me, was the least intrusive of the lot. A remote man, I remembered him as, seemingly forever on the point of inventing some new law to lay down. But before the funeral and on the day he mainly smiled and nodded at me, equal to equal, as though I were one of the Manitoba Power mourners, on hand to talk in low, official tones about the corporation's position vis-à-vis an employee's death. When push came to shove, though, Builth Sid fell in with the rest.

The shove was the other thing I hadn't expected. Not for Dad an urn-burial here in Transcona Cemetery. Mum, or the rellies' committee, had apparently determined on a last transatlantic hop with his ashes, all the way to Gornal Wood Crematorium, where another ceremony awaited him and a plot to go with it. It became clear that the rellies were hanging about after the funeral to help Mum ready herself for this second phase—save Kettering Sid, who, at least honest about what he saw as the best use of his time, stayed plastered. Mob-handed they'd come, as a muffle-drum escort they would return. But it was also assumed, without a word passing between me and any other body, that I too would make the journey, clutching tight to Mum's arm

52

to get through what the rellies called our dark days. But in my estimation, and however slowly and painfully for Mum, the days were meant to get brighter under their own steam. She didn't need all of them crowding in to become herself again...or anyway the self I thought I knew. But maybe that was what they didn't want of her. Anyway, the ghoulish replay at Gornal Wood wouldn't help at all.

All this just wasn't on. I'd allowed four days for the funeral, not on a whim but because, adding in a further five days after my return to Windsor, I'd be able to submit the first of the two term papers on the new deadline agreed with my prof. I'd told Mum this on the phone before my return and, while I could guess what was claiming her thoughts, her heart, it seemed like she understood. It was a different situation in Crescentwood. For one thing, it was impossible to get her on her own. The rellies filled every available space, ready with their shoulders should she need to wilt. I never saw her in clear outline: always there was a hand or two looming in, squeezing her arm, patting her back. The rellies were changing the very air of the house and, with it, the history of our patch of the family. No longer was it assumed that I should make the most of a new life (and how new was it, anyway? We'd been there nine years. What did they really think I'd done with all that time? Stayed thirteen?). A big sad something had happened and I was now to revert to a position I didn't accept and had never understood.

Finally I did speak to her. It was the day after the funeral and the Gornal Wood plan had been outed. We hovered awkwardly together in the conservatory while the rest of them milled about the kitchen, absorbed in flight itineraries and documents from the officials back in Gornal Wood. Dear God, had it been ordained that this whole family should exist merely to shove bits of paper around on suburban tables? Again I repeated to her, as softly as I could, my need to get back to college, get that first term paper in, get weaving on the second and see this and that person about planning my exhibition displays. I heard myself adding that I'd go over at a later date: visit Gornal, see that everything was ok, do the rounds of the rellies. That hollow promise clenched my stomach but right now I could live with it. She drew herself up, then threatened to totter, her eyes for a moment just whites in her head: 'You what?' she asked as though I were broaching something new and bizarre, as though she didn't know me but thought I might be a door-to-door salesman pushing his luck.

Instantly Auntie Irene, Builth Sid's wife, was at her side, eyeing her up and down, goggling at what she seemed to regard as the prospect of a second death, another plot at Gornal. Like a marionette breaking up, Mum was steered to the comforting sound of page kissing page at the kitchen table. Minutes later, Auntie Irene was back with the appalling Nicky, her eldest daughter, whom even as a kid I remembered as a wild-eyed feaster on tragedy and upset. Her own son, Craig, was several years younger than me and I used to dread his visits. For him, the world existed to be screamed at and broken and he didn't care what shape it took—say, my record-player, my books, toys long unused but still loved. 'Our Cray-igg,' his mother would say in dumb adoration, 'aww, he's a terra.' Luckily he'd been interned with Nicky's mother-in-law during this visit.

'What's-this-Jo-na-than?' Auntie Irene said now, parting out the syllables as a Scrabble player with a top score might press home each tile. I kept my explanation brief, making clear that this was something between Mum and me alone.

'Not-at-a-time-like-this-look.' Auntie Irene presented her piqued-deity face, another vivid memory.   'Pull-ing-to-gether-is-what-it's-all-a-bout. Fa-mi-lee-look.'

'Blood, Jonathan,' Nicky got in. 'Thicker than water'—an all-weather saw of hers from way back.

'They-been-gol-den-to-you-Jo-na-than, mum-an-dad. Gol-den to ev-ry-one.' Auntie's final words turned everything airless. In the hour of tragedy, she seemed to say, all the family had turned into Mum and Dad's children. I had an image of them as my brothers and sisters. For a moment I couldn't breathe.

A sob broke in on us from the kitchen. Turning to face each other, my interlocutors offered a moment of profiles, synchronised headshakes, before they retreated to swell the attendance upon Mum.

Between then and my return flight I spent as little time there as possible. On the day of the flight, they all made an expedition to the travel agents to double-check things for which, it seemed, a phone call or black-and-white details on the kitchen table were inadequate. Nothing further had been said to me. I was positioned as Everyman, hanging between heaven and hell. Would I come good or not? From the living-room window I watched them go. Propped between Builth Sid and Irene, Mum's head lolled slightly. Suddenly I felt great anger. Mum had been a wife and was now a widow. But she was also the sharp, forever-organised teacher who did wonders for even the most unpromising kid, who could pull a knockout Christmas pageant out of the hat like a rabbit—and could do again, all of it. But would she? Once more I feared that, after her own true grieving, she wouldn't be allowed to find her way back to herself. I saw each gesture, each hand on her arm and shoulders, as covert disablement. Riding at her waist, a bit of paper protruded from her handbag. A tissue? The flight details for her and me? A script concocted by her escorts?

I'll give them this, though: as they got into the hire-cars, no-one glanced back with a 'You'll come to a bad end, young master' look. Accidentally classy restraint. Once they were gone, I retrieved my bundle of clothes from behind the sofa, packed my holdall, put the mourning-suit back in its zipper-bag, pinned an envelope with the rental cost to the plastic and took off for my own plane.

After that, nothing was the same. The very notion of my having a family turned vague, hard to credit, even weirdly jokey. But I got everything sorted for the end of my BA degree, even emerging with distinction for my exhibition, and the Master's was secure. That summer I spent in Windsor, getting work as a support instructor on intersession and summer school courses. One of the Art and Design profs was off on a sabbatical for the following year and a friend and I reached an agreement to house-sit for him and his family. They had a cat which we never saw but the regularly emptied food- and water-bowls indicated that these two strangers hadn't scared it off to death by starvation; a tankful of exotic fish, too, which initially made us blench until the prof said that a friend of his, an expert, had a key and would stop by to see to them as needed. It was a good summer. Goodish. The weather was kind, there were regular trips over the border (once down to Chicago to see the Grateful Dead at Soldier Field—a surprise gift from friends for wrapping up my degree in some style. I was in it for the whole buzz of the thing, keeping to myself my opinion of the band, which hadn't changed since England days. But they were ok, and I didn't think of West-Coast devotee Gordy once during the concert); and I had my first serious relationship, a bank-teller at Windsor Credit Union whom I'd met at an off-campus party. To round things off, I was offered a Teaching Fellowship for my first Master's year, potentially renewable. Ok, it meant running a freshman course, plus other bits and bobs that might arise at the whim of the department, but it was extra money and, given the modest terms of the house-sitting arrangement, I might even start to save.

Jim Kloes, my housemate, was an all-round good thing. We'd really only got to know each other in our Honours year. He was a History major and both of us had been roped in as undergrad assistants, doing occasional gofer work for profs in our departments—research, mainly—on a nickel-and-dime basis. You could say that our overlords had been monitoring us as potential Masters material. But we first bumped into each other at the initial meeting of *Arundats*. Unionisation was all the go and the university's Graduates Association, which a bunch of us would be part of the following year, was pretty feisty. So it was that an Honours guy in Geology (from Luxembourg, I think) came up with the Arts Undergrad Assistants...Body? Collective? Arundats actually sounded Luxembourgish to me, to Jim too, but as we both admitted that first meeting, what did we know?

Strictly, it was a load of us taking over a big table in the Sidebar Motel downtown once a fortnight, mainly to kvetch about the mismatch between how much the profs were making us do and how little they were paying us for doing it. There were some pretty heated wing-dings, though. Bicentenary-fever was all over the USA that year, moving some of the blow-in American undergrads to say—mainly as a wind-up but in one or two cases for real—that it was high time that Canada did the decent thing, rolled over and became the 51ˢᵗ State. During one of these uncourteous exchanges the bar-staff nearly showed us the door. That, in fact, was the meeting at which, with a puckish wink, Jim really sealed our friendship. Clapping a hand on my shoulder, he broke in with 'Bullshit, bullshit, bullshit. How about we all turn history upside down and team up with this bloke's old club again? Pretty smashing, hey?' At least it shut everyone up for all of a minute.

Then, too, Jim and I took the same elective course, a rider to our Honours degree paths, 'Socrates and his World.' For Jim that wasn't that much of a stretch, since his historical interests were decidedly pre-modern though, weirdly, he had a thing about the lives and fates of Bismarck and Anne Frank. But the Dark Ages were his focus and, with each passing day, the Master's thesis he'd have to write in a year's time, once his coursework was done, took ever more crystalline shape.

I had little idea what the Dark Ages were all about and anyone similarly uninformed would have said that it sounded just right for Jim. Usually he made out like a clear light had never shone anywhere on his life. He just couldn't handle this, that or the other, he said. Things were either a bummer or about to be. His shit

59

defied him to get it together. He came from just outside St Eleanors, Prince Edward Island, and was fond of playing up to the stereotype of the nation's smallest province:

'Only thing you see moving there are trucks and trailers of potatoes. Spuds, yeah? We live on the suckers, we're made of them. Man, we're spud-tastic.'

Would my connection with Bevvo Hunter and Gordy Forbes have developed in any way like this if I'd stayed in what Jim called my old club, if Mr Walden and the Consulate and the Erkeley hadn't happened? I'd thought about that and the more I thought the more I doubted it. That evening, the way they froze me out on the walk home from *The Jolly Waggoner*...if it hadn't been that it would have been something else: lower-level, yes, but...not even a particular something, maybe, just a time when they and I found we were at the end of things to say. Maybe there would have been some manufactured episode or a blurting from the heart. Me telling Gordy that his West Coast bands were crap? I wouldn't put it past me now. Thinking about that stuff one time, I found another line of something or other wafting back from the days of Mr Vesey and Wiznuk to join 'untroubling and untroubled where I lie.' More modern, this one, I think: 'Another time has other lives to live.' Perhaps that was it, sort of. Another time has other friends to know. I'd known enough since I came over here. Some had veered towards closeness while others had stayed, to mutual satisfaction, at

'How're ya?' Now, with the Master's degree extending my days of refuge and a damn nice house to spend its first year in, here, first and foremost, was Jim.

In terms of his beliefs, his sentiments, what you saw was always what you got: no stratagems, no angling for a special effect. He had a sincere notion that the Master's was just an inconvenience for me, that they should have let me sail straight past it to a doctorate: 'Dr Jon,' he'd growlingly call me, 'The Night Tripper'— cheerily confusing me with Mac Rebennack, aka Dr John, the New Orleans pianist and singer, a firm favourite of his (and, in time, mine); insisting that, in some weird way, my scholarly chops reflected the funk style that Dr John had birthed. 'You the man with the gris-gris, Dr Jon', he'd say, and to be such became my devout wish. A gentle soul, Jim, a deeply affable presence. I felt sure that, if he'd been with me way back there, he'd have found a way to neutralise Wiznuk and his apes without lifting a finger.

'Bit of an accent there?' was the first thing she didn't say. Maybe it was after an Arundats meeting or maybe a general bunch of us were seeing out a Friday night with beers and talk about movies or predictions on how the Toronto Argonauts and Hamilton Tiger-Cats would fare in upcoming football fixtures, or their hockey counterparts, the Senators, the sainted Leafs. (I surprised myself with a love of listening to all this. Ok, the rules and stats were beyond me, as they had been for soccer and cricket, but I treated it as a conversation course in a language both impossible and seductive. Now and then I even threw in something remembered from English soccer commentaries on *Match of the Day,* a tv fixture for Dad back then: some multi-purpose saw whose idiocy stuck in my mind while I was walking through the living-room. Sometimes the company would frown at my attempts but more often the words would drop right in and produce 'Yeah, Jon, that's pretty much the way of it.' My lobs, it seemed, gave me a not half bad score-rate.)

Anyway, all the chat was cut short that Friday night when some friend of a friend leaned over our table and hissed 'Party!' like they were pulling a strand of gum. Some while later I found myself lugging a six-pack through the door of a huge house out near Malden Park, taking in the swirl of smoke, laughter and the alternating sounds of The Eagles, Dr Hook and Silver Convention. Jim wasn't with us that night and in fact everyone I'd arrived with shortly vanished. Disconcerted—I liked at least one buddy at hand when making landfall at a party—I shouldered through to the kitchen, opened one of the beers and, in my confusion, opened another:

'Someone's on the toot,' she said. She'd been shouldering in the opposite direction but she stopped and eyed the bottles in mock-amazement.

'Oh…yes, I didn't mean to…would you like one?'

A smile of slow radiance, a tilt of the head and a raised glass: wine? whiskey?

'I'm good, thanks.' She widened her eyes. 'Some house, hey? So, how do you know Ray?' Her head kept its tilt. Strands of auburn hair fell loose. Blue-green eyes? Guys aren't supposed to notice such things. Maybe it was their clearness that fascinated me.

During the next few minutes I improvised. As far as that went, something of the sweaty boy in Mr Vesey's office returned, but I soon told him it was way past his bedtime and sent him home. How do I know Ray? Oh, must have met him…where was it…a match, maybe, or—

'Jeez, why wouldn't you? He knows more about the Argonauts than they know themselves.'

I'd hurdled that one nicely, it seemed, with space to spare. The lovely smile again…but then came,

'Are you in Ray's line too? Aluminum sidings?'

This was a hurdle too high—up in the peak mists, really—but I didn't want to launch into details about being a college-guy. I knew by now that there wasn't the town-and-gown garbage you got back in England—so many people here had done something, however brief, beyond high school—but, well…I think I must have qualified my answer with 'I'm afraid' or some other deprecation.

'I love Edward Hopper.' She made a silent toast, perhaps in honour of the bars and bottles that turned up in Hopper's work. Here was a problem. I didn't know much of his work but what I knew I didn't like; he struck me as a hungover Norman Rockwell. Here we go, I thought ungallantly: I'll have to nod and smile and study the crest on my beer bottle while she praises nighthawks and figures sitting naked and disconsolate on afternoon beds. But she swerved right past those and, with delicate precision, introduced me to the world of Prospect Street, Gloucester, Mass and a guy shutting up shop for the night at a remote gas station:

'I keep coming back to that one,' she said. '*Gas*. It's like a lot of his. You think things into a picture, you know what I mean? You're sure they were in there when you last looked but when you come to look again, they're not. And yet they are. Does that make sense?'

Now I did nod, vigorously. For me, one of the joys of art was the way an artist might invite you to complete the picture. Once you'd done it, added something that you felt should be there, it was never not there afterwards.

'The deep woods beyond the gas station,' she was saying. 'Except there aren't, not for sure. But there are, and there's something in them. There are trees along the other side of the road with that blue above...velvety, you know, end of the day. There's light in the sky, even, just a smidge further over. But below the tops there's dark amongst the green and it makes the green look not friendly. You can see trunks behind trunks going along. Further off they start fading just to black. The gas station lights don't reach them.

Ok, rationally, it might be just a wide verge of trees. But the lights in the station are…well, not real soft but not harsh either. They make it look like the station's trying to be a safe place, kind of, a refuge. So you immediately think, well, has to be a refuge from something, so it must be a refuge from the woods going back and back. Especially in that twilight. There's this little piece of human activity going on, the guy checking the pumps, and over the road there's nothing that wishes him well. So your brain puts the deep woods in because…because what's the whole damn opposite of someone going about his legit business? The scary woods. I see that line of trees and I see whole acres of the things, like as if the painting's 3-D. And what-all might be in there? A robber might be the best of it. I look at that painting, I never don't feel that robber.' She cocked her head. 'I'm one crazy lady, right?'

'I think you talk more sense than all the experts…well, most of—' Damn it. Why choose now to go for a limp qualification? Too many bloody term papers, too much of the *X avers although Y counsels caution* research. But 'Thank you, sir,' she said. I'd never been twinkled at before…though I wasn't as keen on what came next:

'And the road in that painting, it's like a river, a ravine, you couldn't imagine the gas guy crossing it…'

I had to stare hard at the crest on the bottle's label. It wavered and sharpened over and over while, in my head, Tafler stopped looking across the school lane to the detached houses, turned round and retreated to his own land, where he sank effortfully down beside his tree. *Collateral damage,* I reminded myself. What? Was he making to get up again? No. Just changing position, perhaps to free a bottle from a remote pocket. He vanished behind the label's crest.

'I must have a closer look at that painting,' I managed.

'Oh, you must. That's a beauty, *The Mansard Roof.* Helped put him on the map.'

What Mansard Roof? How many other paintings and titles had whizzed by during my Tafler episode? And here was another one, *Laurie Becker.* I didn't know Hopper went in for portraiture of named subjects but then I realised she'd just told me her name.

'Lo-lo, we're out of here.' A tall blonde girl was pushing through to us. 'Oh, hi.'

'This,' said Laurie, 'is…?' Again the cocked head and a frown. I told them.

'Bit of an accent there?' queried the blonde, cocking her head too. Just in time, I didn't. Ah, well, at least the old observation had come from someone who wasn't in the process of enchanting me.

'Awful sorry,' Laurie said. 'Debs and me, we're up with the larks tomorrow. Our branch is part of a charity day at Malden Park. Stupid clothes, styrofoam dollars on our heads.'

'Dollars?'

So I learned that she and Debs worked at the Credit Union and where they'd be tomorrow on Malden Park. Yes, I said, of course I'll come along. Sounds great...better than lonely gas pumps.

'She been bending your ear about Eddie What's-his-face?'

'You, Deborah, are for sure an ignoramus.'

Two winks at me: Debs' wink said I love pulling her tail, Laurie's said she's my best friend.

After they'd gone I wondered why I hadn't. I ventured to the hallway, peered into a couple of rooms, made out one or two of my gang. But they were deep in their own conversations, harangues, whatever, and they didn't see my wave. Retreating to the kitchen, I took one last swig for the road. Why had I bought the brand I liked least? A quick and necessary grab, really: if we'd left the Sidebar any later the liquor store would have been closed. So I was happy enough to hear 'Say, buddy, hope you don't mind but can you spare a beer?' at my shoulder. Not so happy to turn and find I was looking at Pete Wiznuk. Ok, the face had a pencil moustache, the hair was longer, but the nose was small and sharp, the features looked like they should always be twitching and the eyes were shiny with malevolence. Except that they weren't. That was me adding to the picture. Even so, after saying 'Sure, there's another three or four in that box' and being thanked with a cuff to the arm, I was relieved to think that I'd probably never see the guy again. But he did call 'Thank you, sir' when

I left the kitchen, as Laurie had said after her guided tour of *Gas*, so that sort of righted things and Wiznuk obligingly fell back into his Erkeley hole.

An advisor and a guide, diligently filling in the gaps in Laurie's knowledge of art. An insouciant reference-dropper—you might know the sort of thing: 'You may want to read Bill Brewer's reconsideration of Jan Stewer's appraisal of Peter Gurney (the Younger).' A lip-purser when her enthusiasm cut itself adrift from the evidence. I was none of these things and didn't care to be. After she'd rid herself of her charity togs next day we went to a pizzeria on Tecumseh, then back to her apartment where we drank, talked and laughed. Midweek I met her after work and we went to the movies, passing on *The Omen* and *Logan's Run* for the fabulous rubberiness of Walter Matthau's face in *The Bad News Bears*. The following Saturday was her place again. Again we talked and laughed but hardly drank at all. Sunday was high in the sky when we woke and made love again.

To be with her was to move beyond the gas pumps in my modestly-lit world, to cross the road and find, in amongst the black trees, a world that asked nothing more than that I take it as it was. I met her friends, among them the wonderfully garrulous Ray, and she met a few of mine; turned out that another of her interests was jewels and finery from, oh, aeons ago, so Dark Ages Jim was in his element. With her friends, I took up my stance on baseball mounds on

Sunday afternoons and was joshed and encouraged as I imitated a man swatting flies with a crowbar, looking almost as stylish as the no-hoper kids Walter Matthau was trying to bring on. Debs approved of me. The whole thing—the talks, the parties, Laurie—felt like a health cure, a natural widening of my vision.

But there was a wind at my back, sometimes so cold that I felt I was wearing nothing but a surgical gown. A thousand miles-plus back west, a woman was going about a singleton life amid the lawns and mailboxes of Crescentwood. Phone-calls home were terse. In the old saying, I felt like the goalie who keeps getting the ball passed back to him. A visit home towards the end of August found me helping her to sort Dad's stuff out in an atmosphere given over to the hum of the fridge and the whoosh of passing cars. Why had she left it so long? Well, yes, you never know how long it'll be before you can face such things, but I guessed it was also imposed penance for my no-show at Gornal Wood—which featured amid the fridge-hum and the fleeting cars in such remarks as, 'Nicky's Craig's doing ever so well. Looking at the armed forces after school. Big lad now…right beside me, he was, as we went into the Gornal chapel'; or, 'Kettering Uncle Sid is fading…he needed propping up at Gornal for the laying to rest. I felt for him every step he took. Just like me when we went to the airport to fly home. Marvellous, the stewardesses were, helping me up the gangway, arranging my rug. On the flight back here, too.' Which I hadn't trekked from Windsor to meet.

I felt like someone on the eve of bankruptcy, sitting comatose while a kindly but despairing advisor tried to make sense of all the bills. One particular bill, my hollow promise to go over to England, fluttered everywhere about the house. Trying to ignore it, ignore everything, I came back with questions about her upcoming school year. Just a bit to go before the start, eh, Mum? Back doing great things. Bet you can't wait. Would you like to teach a different grade sometime?

'Oh, all that,' she'd sigh, as if considering a social function she'd give the world to avoid. On one occasion, fierce and out of the blue, she said, 'Not a patch on England, the education here'— then, straight at me, 'a Master's here, you know, it's only like a Bachelor's there.' I thought back to my hopes of parental enthusiasm when I headed east for my BA: how they, or at least Dad, might approve of the Design side as a smart earner. But at best there'd just been thin smiles of the if-that's-what-you-want variety. Mum's outburst now was a long-delayed judgement. And what she said about Master's degrees just wasn't true. Still, that was me told…and, behind the words, told yet again of my image in the family as an uncaring deserter.

Christmas passed on giving joy to my bit of the world. I was hoping to bring Laurie to Winnipeg but several things conspired against. She never missed her family's traditional

Christmas at Kenora, a wonderfully Germanic affair by the sound of it, all Glühwein and Lebkuchen. I would have loved to join them—I loved Caspar David Friedrich and that would surely have been good for a verbal canter as the wine took hold—but a stark, woodcut image of The Crescentwood Widow sat in my head, so no go. And anyway, before that, an exploratory phone call to Mum at the start of December was ominous. The notion of my bringing Laurie back prompted a reaction which reminded me, jaggedly, of the way she'd said 'You what?' the day after Dad's funeral, when I'd secured my few minutes' audience with her and told her—reminded her—I couldn't stay, much less fly over for the Gornal do. Her voice was ice but for a moment, in the static silence, I'd hoped it would melt a bit, at least enough for a grudging 'Do-what-you-like'. Only later did I realise that, for her, bringing a girl increased the potential threat of a future all my own, which looped me back to Kettering Sid ruffling my hair that Erkeley summer and wishing me a grand life among Rose Marie and the Mounties—a wish that, however sincere at the time, counted now for nothing.

As that Christmas took its course, the fridge-hum grew louder. Outside, the cars ground down more sharply on fresh snow. I went for a beer or two with old Crescentwood friends and, once, an acquaintance from high school. But things had changed there, too. I'd been away and they hadn't. Some of them had taken local courses and gone into local work. Fair play to them but with each meeting, under the lights of bar or diner, they looked a bit more like ageing Bevvos and Gordies. My mascot status had long gone, forgotten alongside my dodgy claim of kinship with Ian Stewart. Now the fandom was replaced by 'Man, your English punk stuff. All over the goddam radio. What is that shit?'

Christmas Day was a matter of old movies on tv, my surreptitious top-ups and, at lunchtime, the quiet exchange of presents. *Worcestershire Past and Present,* said the book of photos and drawings I unwrapped.

'Oh, now,' I said, stamping immediately on any memories it might evoke, 'this might give me some good ideas for the course I'm teaching'— lingering on the last word as if I were waving a big card of identity.

'Well, if it helps your little job,' murmured Mum, smiling stiffly at the matching hat and scarf I'd got her, laying them aside without trying them on. Then, 'This came for you', and an envelope with my name on it slid onto my side-plate. It turned out to be an enclosure with something Mum had received from our old neighbour, Mrs Butler.

'Great,' I tried to mean. 'At least it got here for Christmas.'

'Came a month back.'

Mr and Mrs Butler had been just there when I was a kid, part of the adult furniture, and I could take or leave their son Kevin. But they were ones who mostly took me in whenever Mum and Dad went to bend the knee to officialdom in London.

And as I read the enclosure after lunch a warmth spread through me such as my family life had never gifted.

'I sent this to your Mum,' wrote Mrs Butler, 'as she said she wasn't sure about your address but then she's had a lot on her mind bless her. Sorry we didn't see you at your father's ceremony. But you must be proper busy. I have to say'—I swallowed, waiting for a brickbat in the style of Auntie Irene; instead—'good luck to you Jonathan if you like where you are and you've found what you want. Your mother said you might be popping back and if you do Mr Butler and I would love you to call by—stay if you like. And Mr Butler says did you ever read the Longfellow book we gave you and that Evangeline and Hiawatha? He knows Hiawatha by heart heaven help us and between us it gets my goat when he starts in on it so I hope you haven't memorised it to drive some poor Canadian lady up the wall. Kevin's doing well he and Marlene have their second on the way so yours truly is doing the fond granny-to-be routine all over again but that's alright as they only live out Trysull way so not too far. He's had a promotion at the furniture showroom which is great but you could have knocked me down with a feather when he told me because this country is going down the drain fast no-one's working you stay where you are Jonathan you're well out of it. Another thing I should say (I've made a "list" here of what to write honestly my memory that's age that is Jonathan) is that I heard on the grape-

vine about those two you used to pal about with
Bevan was he called? and that Gordy.'

The warmth vanished. I turned away from the
page.

9

As did Will. Time to take another five elsewhere.
Leaving drink and treats, he went through from
the rumpus room to the garage. Boy, but the
place needed sorting out. There was barely
enough room for the truck and the ski-doos. All
around the walls the kids' bikes, cables, hose-
lengths and what-have-you brushed against the
vehicles like craziness. Boxes and crates of
forgotten contents demanded a squeeze-and-
limbo routine when you wanted the ski-doos. If
they went ahead and bought that car from Mags'
PTA friend—Shirley? Shelley—they'd need to
thin the stuff out for sure. But it was nice and
warm in there—that extra insulation from Terry
M's buddy had worked a treat. Resting against
the truck's hood, you might almost think the
engine was only just turned off. Will did just that
and thought of families. Famn damilies. People
talked about death and taxes, but family was the
other big uncertainty. Maybe in years to come
some boffin might tweak it so, somehow, before
you even got to being a twinkle in an eye, you
could choose what kind of people you wanted to
end up with. For now, though, you came down
the chute and there it all was, waiting for you.
First you were helpless. As you grew up among

your folks and then started your own family, you got to be not so helpless. You gained some kind of position. Your opinion counted for more, maybe lots. Or a lot at first then less, then just a matter of humouring you, then nothing. It all depended on what was happening, day by day, month by month. As for that, the cards were being re-dealt all the time. But there you were, as a kid or a father, a mother, trying to rub along, staking out territory, giving and taking—mostly without even thinking about it. Unconsciously reminding yourself that these people weren't strangers, that you owed them and, if you were half-decent, they counted on you.

He thought about his own family. Mom, dad, his Uncle Gary, Aunts Paula and Therese, his sisters and brother. It had been a clear run through up to now, mainly. No-one had gone incommunicado for permanent, his sisters hadn't stolen each other's boyfriends growing up. He felt closer to some of them than others but that was just the way of it, and even now he'd sit down with any of them any old time. Innocent words, yet they made him press hard on the hood and he felt it bulge down and spring back up. Again there came that weird vision he'd had at the end of his mental journey through time and space to that Erkeley evening. Here was the blond hair again, the I-dare-you-not-to-adore me grin. Brother Mark. Here again was the neck of that smashed bottle. But now it seemed to float teasingly over Mark's head, his own head, like someone was waving candy at trick-or-treaters.

Who wants me? the neck said. Who wants to use me?

Trick-or-treaters. He guessed that was causing the dull thuds from upstairs. Jeez, take the front door off, why don't you? And now, impatient stabs at the bell, making the chimes sound once and stop, twice and stop, and then string out like a toy siren. Then nothing. As though willing himself out of a bad sleep, he tried to get rid of what his mind had been at. Yes, he'd sit down with Mark, too. Why wouldn't he? Leaning away from the truck, he shivered. Terry M's buddy's insulation didn't seem such a wise move now. Or was the furnace on the fritz?

No, it was breathing and humming the same as ever in its little realm between garage and rumpus room. He stood looking at it and tried to take his thoughts in hand.

He and Mark had never had a massive bust-up. Maybe that was the problem. The only real family bust-up was when Uncle Gary, unpredictable as ever, upped and pretty near sold the family holdings just east of Lloydminster. No preamble, no discussion and the first anyone else knew of it was when some rep from Alsask Grain got hold of dad's name and phoned him to ensure that he was officially part of the deal and check some discrepancy in the acreage stats. Big fat news to everyone, not least the Raskobs who, quite rightly, thought they could go on farming the spread indefinitely if the rental agreement stayed good. Will would have been what? Fourteen, fifteen? He'd stood in the dining-room doorway when, after repeated and increasingly wild phone calls, dad finally got Uncle G to come on over, sit down and tell him what the hell he was playing at.

Fifteen, yes—the eldest, the older son. Following dad's lead, glowering when he glowered, turning all thunder-browed with him. Mom was hovering, looking ready either to throw a bucket of water over the men if they started whaling on each other or dish up more sandwiches, on the assumption that courtesy to her would restrain them while food and good crockery were about. The girls weren't there. They'd been sent to play with friends. Even if they had been there they wouldn't have been. It was for him, the eldest, to practise the glower and thunder-brow, to learn the ropes of displeasure over family betrayal, adult transgression.

Not that it was completely his gig as it should have been. Mom's indecision between water-chucking and sandwich-dishing had to take a third course, gurning and shooing at the doorway. Because who kept looming, vanishing at mom's scoot-scoot gestures, looming again? Who should have been away like the girls? Would have been except that he was probably between friends? Each time Will glanced side-ways, the blond hair looked wilder, the grin stupider:

'You shouldn't be here,' he'd whispered on the back of one of mom's scoot-scoots.

'Oh and you should, big man?' Mark had a way of combining his grin with a swoony back-tilt of the head, a way of saying I'm one big pain in your keister and you can do zip about it. Its effectiveness depended on his ability to read situations and that was disturbing—sharper than anything mom, dad or even ducking, diving Uncle G could manage. Really, some smart medic should have reached into his head and pulled it out. He could see, the idiot, that the two men were in strenuous confab, that the wire between them was pulled tight as tight. Any kids' ructions would have put them back at square one, Uncle G laughing like a drain, dad crying out that this was serious, dammit! Then their whaling would have started for sure. Thinking about all that now, Will recalled an Australian teacher he'd had in grade school and her sure-fire line when anyone did the old mad hand-wave to be chosen for everything going: *Well, well...there's no show without Punch.* For Mark, it was all the sweeter to be Punch when his older brother feared he couldn't move a muscle without looking ridiculous or risking 'Aw, don't do that to your little brother' from some or other party. And if older brother was caught in a squeeze as now—mom's agitation, Punch getting more and more into it with each moment—that was sweeter still.

Finally, dad's eyes had flickered to the door. He still had his end of the wire tight but part of his attention was edging out, like the smidge of sunset that girl, Laurie, was going on about in that painting. Mom saw and did that grown-up thing at Will, the pursed lips and juddery shoulders that could mean all sorts...*What did I tell you to do? What did I tell you not to do?*—or, as now, *Do something!*

At that Will hauled Mark away but Mark knew that, brother to brother, he held all the cards. Will had wanted to stay put uninterrupted as per official permission, do his threshold-of-manhood turn in support of dad. And he hadn't acted wholly off his own bat: mom's agitation was a demand for action mixed with annoyance that it was so tardy. Mark sensed Will's feelings, the shame spreading inside him and how it weakened his bouncer routine. And mom, of course, was the punch he led with:

'You had to rely on her, hey, Willie Willie? She had to give you the prod.'

At times like this Mark would make real young, break down his words, miss off letters as though he was a ghost-kid in a chiller film or humouring what he pretended was Will's sad level of smarts. He might have said something else then. Will couldn't remember, didn't want to, and anyway he cut it off by pushing him out the back door to join the trash. At the last second Mark cried 'You're not besting me, Willie' and fought back—and dammit he could. You had to catch him right, pin his arms, dodge his feet. Sometimes he was like a cat whose rage made it a tiger. Will did remember, though, that as he got the right purchase on Mark's neck and thrust him out, his head just missed the door-post. He should have yanked that head back, lined the post up and thrust again.

Oh, come on. That's long over. Forgetting to close the rumpus room door, Will went back to his chair. Ancient history, he told himself, but he nearly downed his glass in one go. Lookit, you're supposed to be a smoking-room guy out of Dickens, remember? Following this Parry guy's tale, a tale from another world, with you all nice and comfy, taking in the ups and the downs, raised eyebrow here, tsk-tsk there.

But hey, what was that? Footsteps, he realised, vibrating away from the front stoop up ahead. Another thwarted trick-or-treater, probably. Now he could hear the furnace clicking and changing its breath. There was something he hadn't heard before, something in its sound like a thread running through its usual hum. Damn, it wasn't going to give them trouble, was it? Not with winter coming on?

With a huge effort, Will got himself back into his Uncle G's tale. He'd returned to the dining room just as uncle's money troubles were coming to light. Dad's wrath turned to looser exasperation at a prodigal brother and his secret foolishness. Ok, he didn't reach out and ruffle Uncle G's hair—for a while after he could have cheerfully wrung his neck—but mom was able to replenish the sandwiches without fear of wreckage. And the debacle sent dad back to take a good look at the Land Titles and letting particulars for the Lloydminster spread, and he found handsome leaks in the whole arrangement. So the story that made itself up over time was that Uncle G had done dad a quirky favour. He was back in the fold and his money troubles were addressed, in the form of a bank account that he couldn't touch or maybe even see till the last cent was paid off. And everyone went back to the usual round of visits, seasonal whoop-ups, odd little fallings-out and big hugs to end them.

And Mark went on being Mark. Will hadn't thought for years about his carry-on that evening. If someone had asked him about his Uncle G, if he'd been in anecdotal mood with Terry M or Smeets, he'd have just told the tale of the Lloydminster land and Uncle G's fecklessness without remembering his brother's intervention…or if he had, without even feeling the need to add it as a bit of wacko comedy. And it wasn't so different from how Mark had acted a hundred other times. But now it had got out of its box, threatening to turn the main event of that remembered evening into fuzzy background.

Ah, but things were fine now. Mark was all set up in Nova Scotia doing…what was he doing? Will realised that he could never get a handle on it. Corporate work was as close as he or their sisters had ever heard. It had been the same when he'd lived in Fredericton—'legal support' was the pat answer then. Will frowned. Man, he'd left Fredericton in a hurry. First they'd known of it was when his sister Annie rang round everyone from Vermont. She hadn't tried Mark in ages…no-one had, it turned out…and his phone was dead. Then she'd written and her letter was promptly returned. But someone must have got a gander at her address label because shortly after that she received a frankly sinister letter noting her attempts to make contact with Mark Apland Esquire and requesting that she let the sender know if she got lucky; meantime, the sender would continue with his or their own efforts at same. Two, three summers ago, that was, but it wasn't till the Christmas that they all got change-of-address details in cards from Antigonish. They never got to the bottom of the business. The rest were hoping that Will would step in but, boy, he'd tried that before when Mark and Holly were going through their stuff. That was bad…and their twins were—what?—only a year old then?

No, dad wasn't about to ruffle Uncle G's hair that evening when it all came out about the land. But suddenly Will had an image of Mark breaking free of his hold, bounding across the room and doing just that. Dodger to dodger, apprentice to sage. Will wondered if his brother would make good on his eternal promise of a trip back west. There hadn't been a whole clan reunion for an age now. Topping up, he realised that he was thinking as family. But right now, how much did he really want to see Mark? As he raised his glass, he heard the furnace's new, weird little noise again. Wheedling, it sounded like, as though it were trying to say *Willie Willie*. Or maybe *Johnny, Johnny Canuck…c'mon, Johnny.*

Will picked out another snack. Take a good step back, he advised it. Families…not his, not a lonely English kid's…the generality. Other families managed things differently because they had different things before them. The Balzers, now, on the next block. Who needed tv or radio when you had them? Every last disputatious move in their lives was on show for everyone. Fighting or making up, their brouhaha was strictly public. Why they didn't live outside permanently and have done with it, he didn't know. He'd nearly asked them more than once, when their neighbours up and down the block, unable to bear any more, came demanding respite. Now and then, he'd had to intervene officially, mostly when he and Terry M or Smeets were on their way back from something else and got the call. He preferred it if Terry M or Smeets got out and took the lead but that wasn't always allowed to happen. Well, he couldn't just skulk in the car and soon enough one of the neighbours would spot him and guilt him back to his duty. His hope was that having Terry M or Smeets do the questioning would somehow convince the Balzers that they were getting bigger and bigger on the radar, turn them back into regular humans. The hope had yet to come good and might never, even if he had Starsky and Hutch along.

Anyway, domestics weren't a favourite in his job. What the Balzers offered, though, was more an arena sport out of control. Anything could set them off but mainly it was old man Balzer and poor little Patty, the youngest daughter, the only one left at home. The others were long gone, having done their time at the firing post. Man, you could chart the progress of Patty's love life from Walt Balzer's grandstanding. You'd see her running for the bus or to the corner for a ride and you just knew that old Walt had tracked her from the porch and down the front path, cussing and deploring, louder and louder, till he was stationed on the sidewalk, ready with the final lungful: 'Army and Navy clerks are no-goods'…or, 'When I say ten o'clock, missy, I do not mean dark-thirty' (like she'd ever be late)…or, most apocalyptic of all, 'Don't you be bringing shame back to this house' (like she ever had or would). If you were minded to step out and witness Walt in full torrent, you'd see Mrs B, five foot zilch to his six-three, pulling at him on the sidewalk like a toddler trying to uproot a tree.

'She knows what I mean,' he'd say, brushing Mrs B off. She'd take Patty's part, and why not? The kid was a sweetie, had babysat for Will and Mags several times and the kids loved her. But Mrs B had to reason with him and that meant raising her voice to match his, even drown it, which was defeat every which way and doubled the nuisance. It drove Mags crazy, especially now the kids were asking what mad Mr Balzer meant by no-goods and shame. One day, she predicted, little Patty Balzer would come racing past with a suitcase and she for one would not blame her one bit.

But then you'd see the three of them in town or just driving by and everything was tranquil. It was just that they, or specifically Walt, needed to get up on the stump for a regular hour and give out to the nation. And deep down he probably knew that Patty would never get silly with a guy, as sure as she knew that he knew. All well and fine, but the neighbours couldn't be expected to console themselves with a piece of pop-psychology whenever Walt blew up. Either he had to control himself or something more far-reaching than a couple of cops would be coming their way. Phil Stobbe, right next door to the Balzers, had already started muttering about a pal who knew a pal who could do a neat eviction.

Families...turning out as they turn out, settling for what they are. Which kind of brings us back round to...Will went back through to the garage and plunged his hands into the all-sorts box he kept on the workbench, remembering to close the rumpus room door when he returned with paper and pen. If he'd found a note-book in the box he could be flipping it smartly open now, feeling professional, on the beat in the warmth of his own home. At work or wherever, he liked to write things down. That way he could keep good hold of something helpful or see it for the dead end it was. Resting the paper on his chair-arm, he wrote *Jonathan Parry could have done with brothers and sisters*. Was there something in that? Well...start with the facts: Jonathan just didn't have them. Did he compensate with imaginary siblings? His folder didn't say. But would he have wanted the real thing? Loner though he was, it might have helped. Look at his family: a tribe of aunts and uncles, the way he was telling it, crowding him like moms and dads from every which way. Now the cousins. The only one who really figured here was that Nicky: another mom—always had been by the sound of it, no need for a kid of her own. That line of hers when Aunt Irene bore down on him—'Blood, Jonathan. Thicker than water'—she'd had that drilled into her or happily drilled it herself. He'd said it was her party-piece. Ok, let's say he had several cousins. Nicky must have stood in for them all—how he saw them, how they treated him. As for her kid, he was just unhelpful news for Jonathan, plus he was way younger. Similar ages might have led to something better, an understanding, a liking, but by the time this Craig was capable of all that, assuming he was, Jonathan had long gone. Chance ruled him out, then, if nothing else did. Shame about the one Sid, the carpenter. Jonathan sounded scared of him early on but the man treated him with some respect at the funeral...might have done even more if his looks and nods had come to words. But there was a line to toe and carpenter Sid had to get alongside the rest.

Will looked up. There was a toe-line for every family...every family he'd known, anyway...and you might have to step up to it daily or yearly or just once in your life. You couldn't tell with toe-lines. You couldn't tell why or when a family might want to chalk one and maybe they couldn't, not fully...not till after, maybe, when they had to make usable sense of a thing, figure out the story to go with it. Uncle G had jumped right over the Apland toe-line—made like no such thing existed—but a tense evening and mom's sandwiches had brought him back, him and his debts and his hooey. The Balzers, you could say, had their own line. Suppose Walt grew tired of his cockcrowing...maybe Mrs B and Patty would be on at him, asking if he were ill or had lost all respect for the Balzer way. As for Jonathan: Will pictured the Parry toe-line as a group photo from the early 60s. Black and white or that queasy colour some home snaps had then. Whichever, the kid was smack in the middle in short-pants uniform. All round him a forest like in Laurie's take on the Hopper: tallness and breadth, light-stoppers with big hands, one on each of Jonathan's shoulders. The one kid. What he needed was a kinsman his age right next to him, taking his share of the controlling hands. Someone who might whisper to him, look, if the olds backed off, we could shrug together. Someone who cared to get what Jonathan was all about. Someone kind.

So, Bevvo and Gordy. His brothers, then, in any way? You heard kids fooling around with 'brother' and 'sister,' their way of saying someone was a super-pal or would be welcome to come and tip a real sibling out of the basket and take over. He'd found such a brother himself—Billy Acton in grade school; inseparable they were, in the back yard, the park, trouble. (And he really had wanted Billy to relieve Mark of his duties. Billy and Mark had met just the once. In big-guy mood, Mark had laid into him without any provocation, Billy had given as good as he'd got

87

and Will had glowed richly for days.) Even as a kid, though, you knew calling someone brother didn't make it the real deal. It was like that rash of mock-weddings all the kids staged when Charles and Diana got married. Maybe there was a wish to make it really real, in some kid's mind anyway, but you all knew that you'd go home unmarried, with the same family as when you left the house that morning.

Will doubted that the brother thing had ever come up, could ever, with Jonathan and his pals. There was the age thing for a start. They were guys just into adolescence so declarations of the heart were out. As for their friendship…flicking back through the pages, he found particular passages and nodded. They thought he was ok. They didn't mind him and that came out as liking, so they had him along. There was stuff in common. But then, too, he'd stuck his neck out, said he was better than them at Art and such, helped them out. And helped with other things? Will got that feeling. So the smarts were his additional ticket in and, for him, that was good enough. He wasn't into antiques or cigarette-sculpture, he never led the pack. He just appreciated their regular-guy behaviour and they appreciated that. Maybe more than they knew sometimes? It was no big show of buddy-ness but Gordy didn't have to suggest the trip to the Erkeley that evening.

Ok, so…would Jonathan have wanted brothers and sisters? 'No,' said Will aloud and raised his glass as if toasting the solution to some defiant formula. He was an only and would have stayed that way in a baker's dozen. Billy Acton, now, he was an only but he dealt with people as you did when you knew sibling ways. Schoolyard games, sleepovers, he had the give-and-take thing. This guy didn't. He wrote that down, adding *wouldn't want it, his world precious to him.* For several minutes he flicked back through the pages till he found the day after the funeral again, with that Aunt Irene's dressing-down: *In the hour of tragedy, she seemed to say, all the family had turned into Mum and Dad's children. I had an image of them as my brothers and sisters. For a moment I couldn't breathe.* Inching his paper up, he wrote *Idea of Auntie and the rest as his sibs—gross! Any real sib would have turned out just like them? Plus doesn't feel he really exists in their eyes. Dad's dead, mom's in pieces, they all walk through him to deal with that. Invisible man.*

Will made a face. All this was on the level, right? This was really the guy's life as he'd lived it. What choice had he, the smoking-room guy, but to accept that? Sure, there was always embroidery—the world was full of tale-tellers, his job showed him that every day—but the last bit of your life would be a weird time to sit down and make up a story. Anyway, if he didn't accept the guy's word, he'd need to have statements from everyone else to set against it. Corroboration—the eternal nightmare, so often like trying to complete a jigsaw with bits from all over. People had their own take on things and their own take was gospel. That collision in Nutana a couple of weeks back, top of Broadway Bridge...good old Five Corners, someone was always getting pranged there. He and Smeets had been quick to the scene and of course you had the usual routine, the few witnesses who'd apparently been well placed to see what happened and then the crowd who just wanted to be part of the latest jolt to civic peace. Going over the statements later, though, it seemed the reliable eyes and the passing extras just mixed themselves up. On paper, the collision ranged from a slight disagreement with the sidewalk to midnight apocalypse. He could just imagine a pile of sheets at his feet, each headed 'The Jonathan I Knew', fighting it out to get their version on top. Their cries would fill the rumpus-room: 'I was there! This is him!' But he just had the one contender, from the guy himself. Just the one story...which had reached some jinxing lines in a letter from England. Will found where he and Jonathan had abandoned Mrs Butler and he was about to resume. Instead he thumped the chair arm. Dammit, why had Mark left Fredericton in such a hurry? And the family left in the dark, like it was some superior screw-up whose complexities he'd be wasting his time to explain. A slow deep breath, another swig and treat. Mark. Jerk.

10

It was nearly dark when I read the rest of what Mrs. Butler had to say. Me and the sitting-room armchair with the standard lamp behind it: a circle of light, bright enough at the centre but weakening as it spread outwards till it gave up at the tv screen, the few spines on the bookshelf, the subtle spaces where Dad's things weren't. Mum was next door at the Derksens'. Egg-nog and Christmas Day chat—reminiscences, perhaps, about when we first arrived, the failure of initial attempts to blend with our new world, the usual things we had to get clear (pavement for road, sidewalk for pavement, 'I'll call by early' not 'I'll knock you up'). They might rehash my terror at my first day of high school, how Dad had to prise my hands from the banister. Or I mightn't figure at all. Whatever, she'd be gone a while and I'd hear her crunching back past the curtains. For a comfortable spell, I was the last man on earth.

Coutances, Bevvo had settled in, down the coast from Cherbourg ('I found our Kevin's old school atlas to give the spelling a special check'). Married, Mrs Butler had heard ('A little French madam oooh la la'), and whoever had told her said he had a kid, possibly two. As for Gordy, he was in San Francisco, in 'something to do with the pop scene Jonathan', making me speculate on whether his brother-in-law had influence beyond just bringing those records back from his merchant travels—whether he had in fact changed career and settled there with Gordy's sister. Probably not. Gordy and Bevvo would have landed on their feet anywhere they chose— and Gordy had been deep into his music. From nowhere the memory returned of that afternoon at his house when he and Bevvo scuffled on the lawn and my copy of 'All You Need is Love' gave way to the Airplane's *Surrealist Pillow*. 'Wankers,' Elvis-loving Bevvo had called the West Coasters and even now, after my friends' generous treat the previous summer, the Grateful Dead at Soldier Field, I seconded that. 'Wankers,' I said aloud, though less to compound his opinion than to hear a word that had passed no lips around me for years and years. I imagined Gordy wowing all the residual hippies at the intersection of Haight and Ashbury with his crazily-fettled cigarettes, chock full of this and that with a token wad of tobacco. Even as I thought that, a bud of ice in my chest told me what was coming. One by one the memories reared up in reverse: my Bachelor's exhibition, the ugliness round Dad's funeral, the high school mascot years, the lonely lanes above the Dawlish hotel on that last, pointless holiday in England— till, once again, there was Gordy in the final assembly, staring hard at me from the row in front, and Bevvo's profile and the way he rubbed his chin before turning from me for the last time.

Again the questions and speculations came fast but I stood my ground. They weren't going to get me like those memories just had. Questions...speculations...for years they'd been a comfort, a duvet to go with lemon-and-honey and daytime tv during a cold. I loved considering things because I could preen myself on what a clever lad I was, going all round the houses, nothing left unturned—nothing finally resolved, either, which was part of the comfort (well, Jon, at least you gave it a go, eh?). But now, under the standard lamp in that silent room, perhaps…just perhaps…I finally did a bit of growing up. At any rate, I stared at a possibility—even fettled it, you might say, like Gordy with his cigs—and didn't back down.

They really did know what had happened and they'd told no-one. Of course, interviewed by the police and Mr Vesey, they'd stuck to the truth of what they did, like I almost completely had, but now it seemed that they'd honoured an unspoken pact with me. Why? Because, despite their sneers as we walked home from *The Jolly Waggoner*, they wanted to give me a clear run to Canada? Because they couldn't get their heads round what stopping me would mean? Because at that age death was still unreal to us, stuck as we were in the limbo years between accepting 'Your grandad's gone to the angels, love' or some such and knowing the hurt of irreversible absence? Or more banally, because Wiznuk was a tosser and, to be honest, who'd miss him?

Yes, I'd wondered what they knew, or didn't, in the first weeks of that summer holiday, had some pretty bad times in consequence, especially since I couldn't get hold of them. But that was a different me, scarcely formed, caught between

93

terror at an official knock on the door and a hazy gratitude that Canada was about to dematerialise me from that world, that evening, the neck of that bottle. And yes, even when we got here I feared the long shadow of PC Plod falling on me and felt he only properly gave up when, fortuitously, I overheard Dad and Mr Derksen discussing the Rolling Thunder offensive and the words 'collateral damage' rose on the kitchen air, becoming the scrap of prayer I used to bury Tafler with Wiznuk.

'He's not well, Jonathan Parry'—I could hear again Mrs Hunter's snappish tones when I made one of my many attempts to speak with Bevvo. If he and Gordy had told, there'd have been a hell of a lot more to deal with than the irritation of a hard-pressed parent and I'd be dealing with it still. So they'd become men with a terrible truth in their hearts: a truth that, really, was nothing to do with them. We were together that evening, sure, but not for what it had come to mean to me. Never mind that now. They'd still lived with the evening in their own ways, and then, when they could, they'd dodged the past and found themselves new lives, new places. They'd got clear of the tree, the pond, the hollows. I recalled my feelings when they didn't answer or return my calls that summer, how my bafflement at their silence had turned to contempt; and how, when we got over here, I even preened myself on leaving them behind at their humdrum Erkeley scrap—leaving them in every sense, taking my part in it way beyond a ruck in a hollow and on to its logical end. Now, getting up, leaving the circle of light to fix a drink, finding my way back, checking the curtain-gap for any sign of Mum's return, sitting down again in that steady glow, I saw myself as the lucky one, lifted out of it all while still a wet-eared kid: the selfish spaceman who, knowing that there's only enough oxygen for one on the homeward flight, gets up the ladder first, locks down and zooms, knowing but not caring that his two buddies are waving their arms laboriously in the dying atmosphere below, silently screaming.

But pacts have two sides. A horror rose in me as though, right now, in a winter as cold there as here, I were being lowered into Tafler's pond. I didn't ponder anything technical: possible consequences even now for Bevvo and Gordy, terms like accessories after the fact. They didn't even cross my mind. Only Jeff Cordingley did.

Dad knew him through the Derksens. Mr D had brought him over at least once: a tall man, blond—to my young mind, a Texan. He was quite high up when I was a kid—Staff Sergeant, maybe. Where he was based now, or even then, I had no idea. Was he still in Winnipeg? If so, Lyle Street Station, perhaps, or maybe Princess Street. Street names had whirled round my head back then: the ones I had to know, the ones where friends lived and then, more vaguely, the ones my parents or the news mentioned. Maybe Jeff Cordingley had retired, though he seemed of an age with Dad and Mr D and Mr D was still going strong at the Chev-Olds dealership.

Of course I could always check with the Main Street station—and, feeling round the horror inch by inch, I pictured myself doing just that. Steadily up the steps I went, into (I guess) a lobby and up to the main desk. I hoped I wouldn't find myself in a situation where, although there was a crowd, the desk sergeant singled me out straight away, drew everyone's attention to me with a kindly 'Yessir?' Say that didn't happen. The policeman leaned to me as I leaned to him, twigging immediately that here was something of interest. Our voices dropped. Staff Sergeant Cordingley? Sir, things have moved on. Superintendent Cordingley—and sure, he's here. Name, sir? And how do...oh, your father knew him. What's it about? Well...ok, but I don't know if he'll...look, take a seat, sir, just there.

I pictured the scene around me. People came and went, civilians and police. I found myself facing a spread of wall-notices: recruitment, neighbourhood initiatives, stuff about addiction and domestic violence with helpline numbers, charity events, details of the command chain in the Winnipeg force. Voices came from the desk and maybe some corridor to one side— questions, confirmation of something or other, maybe a laugh or two. Then the tall blond guy— ok, not Texan—mannerly, soft-spoken, apologising for not remembering me. Ah, right, a long time ago, huh? And how's your Dad? Oh, say, I'm real sorry. So, what can we do for you, Mr Parry? Somewhere quiet? Sure, just hold on. He disappeared up the corridor. The door closed and I imagined it sticking, even swinging open again. I could hear but not make out his murmured conference with...the desk guy? In constant use, the door, perhaps pretty dramatic use sometimes—that was why it didn't close properly. Mr Parry? Sir? This way, we're ok through here. Coffee?

I had no idea whether a senior policeman would offer a member of the public a coffee at that point or any. But I imagined him offering it and I accepted. And once we were seated in the interview room, I studied the coffee mug—yes, white, no sugar, thank you—as years before I'd studied that ridiculous pot-plant in Mr Vesey's study. Good taste, the mug nice and warm. But I wasn't about to wish I could vanish into it as I'd wished with Mr Vesey's pot. I'd come because I was at the end of something, not the beginning. I'd made connections...ok, they'd been forced on me but I'd taken them...fettled them, like I said. I sipped my coffee and started to speak and as I spoke I pictured the lobby I'd just left, the kindly guy on the desk, the door that wouldn't properly close. I'd walked into all that freely. My freedom and the coffee, I guessed, would be finished about the same time.

I stared at Mrs Butler's letter, seeing the words blur, the lines double. Still no sign of Mum. I'd skimmed the farewell paragraph but now I read it with care: 'That's all from me for now Jonathan but I as I say I hope that you come out of all that's happened stronger. "God bless and peace" to your Dad. You make a good life for yourself.

We've only got the one so as I say if you're coming over do please look us up Kevin would love to see you he always liked you. And remember don't pick "Hiawatha" for your party-piece or I'll have to have words never mind what my Arthur says. You take care love sincerest best wishes Dorothy Butler (Mrs).'

Before I finished my drink I was up for a fresh one. Settling down again, I felt as though I could gather the light from the standard-lamp and wrap it round me like a blanket. Mrs B. So kind. Hope you come out stronger. Make a good life for yourself. We've only got the one. And love. The word looked as uncommon as wanker. The drink spread through me, another blanket. My mind had done its turn all around the houses. Once again I pictured the desk sergeant saying 'Yessir?', leaning forward with a smile. An actor's life for me, I thought, as I had in Mr Vesey's study when I'd satisfied two other policemen with my gingerly curbed truth. There in the Main Street station, I did a laborious double-take, gesturing and shrugging. Actually, now I think of it, it's…no, it's nothing…nothing now…sorry to have bothered you…but thanks, thanks anyway.

A shadow loomed at the window. Mum crunching back.

*

Will re-read the last page or so and then again. When he finished he fished around for another snack and chuckled. So, he thinks he'd have got straight through to Cordingley...I'd love to see DeConinck hopping to it so quick for any Joe Whosis. Murray would likely say he had a funeral or something (Will could just imagine old Clance's chuckling words at that: 'So that's grandpa number four gone, hey, Rod?'). But Barysko, now, he'd have had him in toot sweet. And never mind any leisurely, coffee-sip revelations either: he'd have got the lot out of him like you'd upend a guy for his loose change. Will had seen him in action times enough. Hell, even if it was Mark, Barysko would upend him...though no...if this was Mark's story he sure wouldn't think of going anywhere near a cop. Or maybe he would, if he'd already fixed it so that some poor schmuck was in the frame, nice and watertight: a soak like Tafler, say. In that case, Mark'd do the truly fine citizen bit: this is burning my conscience, officer, I couldn't live with myself if I didn't tell you what I know. Will could see how Mark would play it: have Barysko think he was turning himself in and then, at a critical moment, do the full dismay routine...oh, no, sir, not me, sir. If it was a movie, the inversion of Barysko would be slowed right down, Mark's eyes glinting as he followed the bounce of the man's dimes and quarters across the floor. Shoot, at least Jonathan got as far as thinking it through, even if he got no further. Yes. Ok.

Closing his eyes, Will repeated 'Ok' as near as possible to how he'd just thought it. You could

99

admire with that word and you could condemn. So how was he trying to make it sound now, and for whom? He opened his eyes, blinked hard and was about to carry on reading when he stopped and wrinkled his nose. Was the furnace on the fritz after all? First that needling noise and now...man, what was that smell? Bad as hell, too, if it was coming right through the door. He went out and dashed upstairs. Pointless to sniff around the furnace straight away: get an awful smell in your nose, it needed a serious cure. Unhooking his jacket, he stepped out again, to the front this time, and walked up and down the yard. Deep nose-breaths. Stand still, spin it out a bit. Man, the mercury was dropping. To fill the time, Will strained to see if he could hear the next volcano-rumble from the Balzers. Saturday night, after all...Patty was surely heading out, if she hadn't already...and to a Hallowe'en party, most likely...worse and worse, eh, Walt? But there was nothing save distant traffic, one car going past, the chirrup of trick-or-treaters nearby. Slowly he went back in and descended the stairs. And we only had the thing checked...hold on, was it me arranged it? Or Mags? One of us for sure, we never let the winter come on without—but the furnace was fine, its odour the usual mix of heat and metal. Will pushed open the rumpus room door. The smell was waiting; after the outside cold, it hit him so hard his eyes teared up, and he knew. This guy's apartment, the pile of rank laundry that the three of them had searched for and not found. Taking off his jacket, he stared at the bulky folder. Was it that? Something unspeakable pressed somewhere he hadn't reached, re-energised by the turn of the pages? That's crazy. But he went through the folder, caught a couple of phrases, 'non-face', 'one night the pain', and flicked on. Nothing. He sat down again, again wrinkled his nose. He took up his glass, sniffed, then leaned to the neck of the bottle. Whiskey, plain and simple. He pulled a jacket-sleeve toward him. Just warming polyester with an edge of the cold he'd been out in. As he lifted his head, rankness burst afresh on the rumpus room air. Like a struggling swimmer, he took great, almost panicky lungfuls, then sat still and breathed thinly, as though scared to. Was the smell easing down…?

Oh, come on, he muttered at last through his edgy breath, the mother's crunching back from the Derksens. With some little difficulty he found his place.

11

At the end of December I left Mum's fridge to its hum and got back just in time for a rare old party at Ray's rambling pile in Malden Park. I was fond of Ray—well, he'd indirectly introduced me to Laurie. And they certainly were good buddies. Laurie and I saw in the New Year in a way whose wonder I never thought possible…not for me, anyway. It wasn't just the loving and 'connection' sounds so facile but I can't think of another way of putting it, not now, not with time hurrying. Still, I owe it to that New Year to try. We made a delicious wholeness…no, that sounds like pastries from the oven. Alright, we were two become one, which isn't much of an improvement on 'connection' though a bit more specific. Oh, well, what they go on saying about clichés goes on being true. Folk despise them but use them because they can't better them. And I never thought I'd have the need to pin such feelings down. I suppose I could use one of Jim Kloes' love-maxims but it wouldn't fit me like it so surely fitted him. Anyway, whatever I found with Laurie that night, it kept me on my feet at the city ice-rink next day. Another first.

And the next few months were kind of a golden age. The Master's was going great guns and Jim and I got deeply into our comfy house-sitting (but without parties: we realised that we wanted to protect our domain from the grosser intrusions of the world and laughed at our martinet ways—which didn't prevent our partying elsewhere). Laurie couldn't believe how spick-and-span we kept the house and nor could whichever girl Jim had plucked for the moment from what seemed like a permanent, certainly permanently adoring, following. He reminded me a bit of how I'd been seen when I started high school in Winnipeg: a mascot, though twinkles and lurve were in his gift, not a whiff of the Mersey. Maybe he'd unearthed some accounts of Dark Age intimacy, modernising them—or maybe not?—to keep his ladies keen. But he wasn't all macho with it, just couldn't be, and perhaps that's what they liked best of all.

I loved the teaching I was given. Enthusiastic, sullen or just there, the students I was tasked with introducing to Design or case studies in Art History confirmed me in the feeling that this, and the whole college world, was where I belonged. Postgrads were assigned a member of department as mentor and part of that involved their dropping in now and then to watch us teach: 'You're a natural,' said mine, Tony North, at the end of one session, on the basics of alignment and how it shaped space—a session which, even setting aside the ever-jamming slide carousel, struck me as a dog's breakfast from start to finish. He was even more complimentary after observing sessions I was really on top of but, in a weird way, I was glad he saw a fiasco. It confirmed that I could never be less than a natural—or I told myself it did and, in view of what came later, that was something to hang onto. For dear life.

Spring break came round, Laurie got a week off and I finally spent time with her folks in Kenora. I'd met her mom and dad already when they visited their girl now and then: affable souls they were, too, Mrs Becker all good-natured fussing and admiration for the Queen, Mr Becker hearty but without the backslaps or need to hold forth on golf or the ills of the world. But the spring break trip was when I was on show to a wider audience. We got on fine...fine-ish...mostly. Uncle Gunther, a mechanic retired and widowed, was hard work. Though born in Canada, he was fiercely proud of his ancestry and seemed to see me as a symbol of all that had gone wrong since Germany lost the war...well, both of them. Ever and again he'd quiz me in a way that reminded me of my ring of interrogators when I started high school in Winnipeg. For just a moment, anyway: their wide-eyed admiration was hardly his thing. He asked me about English pop music, culture, politics. Though nothing was openly declared, I soon realised that all this was intended to plume his thesis that one of his fatherland's conquerors was just a fey decadent, unworthy of triumph in war or peace. More than a touch unfair, this. Since I hadn't lived there for ages and was only a boy when I had, my answers were inevitably patchy, and where they weren't they drew on much the same news sources as were available to him; but his manner suggested that my responses were wriggly, duplicitous— ah, what was I but a scion of perfidious Albion? At the same time, though, England's key ally got off scot free. Gunther loved America, crossed the line whenever he could, had wonderful friends down in Michigan and beyond. The subtext here...well, wasn't so sub: take the land of the free out of the equation in 1917 and 1942 and my fey forebears would have been screwed.

His manner wasn't harsh. This was no reverse Nuremberg. But nor did he try to match his sister and brother-in-law's affability. After the second such talk, I wished that, just for a moment, I could cast aside my status as guest and point out that I hadn't invented England just to get up his nose. Laurie and the rest tried laughingly to get him down from this hobby-horse. They could, I think, have tried harder…but, well, that's hobby-horses for you. Even when he wasn't at it he'd be doing the watching-you-boy routine, narrowed eyes and sidelong glances. Compared to him, both my Sids, Kettering and Builth, were the warmest-hearted souls out.

His caper, though, wasn't the whole story of my stay. I went here and there with Laurie, met her friends, went to a drive-in movie for only the third time in my life: *Tentacles,* a poor, no, destitute man's *Jaws*. What John Huston, Henry Fonda and Shelley Winters were doing in it, God knows. Maybe their agents lost heavily in Vegas and this was the Mephistophelean solution to the debt. Anyway, after about ten minutes, Laurie and I passed the time otherwise.

All of that said, though, the Kenora trip came not too long after another nixed attempt to bring Laurie to Winnipeg. This time Mum really had said 'Do what you like' but that, really, was worse than a flat no. In the event, I'd covered it with some excuse—Mum suddenly getting the chance to have the lounge redecorated at a knock-down price—which Laurie, I'm sure, didn't buy at all. Only much later did I connect all that nonsense with one day in Kenora when, getting some light groceries from the 7-11, I returned to the kitchen to see her and her mom at the end of their back yard. Her mom had maybe just asked a question. At any rate, she looked quizzical, her head cocked. After a second, Laurie shook her head. Another second and her mom did likewise, as if to say, now, that's not good.

When we returned to Windsor, I got firm word that another Teaching Fellowship was secure for the following year...and also found a different girl staring searchingly into Jim's eyes from the one he'd been with when we left: a friend, it turned out, of the guy who came to protect our prof's exotic fish. On the work side, I began dropping into conversation, in the department and at parties, with people who might be able to help me along once the Master's was done. God bless Mrs Butler: a good life looked like it was truly shaping up. Each day sped me further from my imagined confession to Jeff Cordingley, that station door which didn't close.

Laurie and I laughed about Uncle Gunther's offensives and more besides. Perhaps the buzz wasn't quite as strong as before; perhaps her friend Debs was now a tad distant with me (though she had plenty on in her life, being a love-magnet like Jim). But I didn't dwell on it at the time. Life couldn't all be closeness and skating and laughably bad movies. We both had our work—which for her now included an imminent promotion. Besides, out of the blue I was offered a contract for intersession teaching, May into June: a prof had fallen ill and 'We guess,' twinkled Tony North, 'that you're a safe pair of hands.' So I had to get weaving with all of that.

A fine May, it was—with, I hoped, the promise of a better summer. For a fleeting space, I toyed with the notion of going back just to give Mrs Butler a big hug and demonstrate that I'd kept faith with her words and couldn't recite a line of 'Hiawatha.'

Then, almost ten years to the day we'd arrived, Mum revealed that she was going back to England. No—that's me jumping the gun, making it sound like the department secretary collared me as soon as I'd had that intersession talk with Tony North and said, 'Hey, Jon...call from Beefeater-land.' In fact the revelation was seasoned by weeks of feints and prevarications. Once I knew—well, even before—I realised that it had long been on the cards. Dad was gone so it was unsurprising that her thoughts should turn, as you might say, to Gornal Wood, no doubt set on their way by the rellies' heavy show at his funeral. But by now my notion of family had thinned to nothing and that, I'm sorry to confess, included Mum. It irked me that, as with everything around Dad's funeral, it was another case of finding things out by surprise or at least sideways. Thinking about it, I should have guessed something was up from her reaction to my renewed attempt to bring Laurie to Winnipeg. At the time, of course, I was all caught up with ego things, anger at her manner, a hurting sense that sauce for the goose wasn't sauce for the gander: she'd found Dad...wasn't I allowed to find anyone, whether or not it was Laurie? It didn't occur to me that she might actually see the whole thing as a tedious irrelevance.

Then, too, the few letters I'd had from her during the spring dealt in the kind of enigma that draws you to probe further, only to be met with a heavy sigh. She wrote sparely and without enthusiasm of what she'd been doing so that I found myself waiting for a line beginning 'The thing is, Jonathan,' while having no clear sense of what the thing might be. After her latest letter, though, something that my golden spring had buried came back to me from the previous Christmas. In one effort at a happier mealtime chat, I'd tried to buck her up by mentioning her school's festive pageant:

'Another rousing success this year, Mum?'

'I suppose.'

'Oh, I'm sure it was.'

'Francey Martin reckoned so.'

'Was she helping? Training her up as your lieutenant, eh?'

A sigh, cutlery set down: 'She did all of it, Jonathan.'

'You let her go solo?' My look of surprise didn't tease out any words: yes, I guess her silence meant. I gazed past her to the crackers on the sideboard. I'd bought them in the hope that, however briefly, we might trick ourselves into the mood of jolly-ish times gone by. They were still in the box.

'Look, Mum, I was thinking, if the school's doing something next Easter and you, or you and Francey, need help with the set, I can always—'

'You'd have to ask Francey.'

'Oh…right. But you were happy, yes? With what she did at the Christmas thing?'

'I didn't go. Can we drop this?'

The day spring semester ended, Laurie gave me a ride to Kenora, where I spent a night at her folks' (and avoided Uncle Gunther, who was seeing one of his fine old buddies down in Ann Arbor) and then caught the bus to Winnipeg. Again, time was tight: Intersession was starting in ten days. We'd set off from Windsor way before daybreak with the aim of reaching Kenora by mid-evening and took the US route, heading through Michigan, Illinois, Wisconsin and Minnesota and then back over the border. At least the pay-off would be a bus ride of under four hours from Kenora to Winnipeg on the Trans-Canada.

It might have been our early start or the bad hold-up just outside Detroit. But things just weren't as buoyant and mirthful as on our previous Kenora trip. Past Detroit was Ann Arbor and I made some crack about Uncle Gunther and his buddies ambushing us at the city line with another 'Damn the English' quiz for me. Laurie started to offer a smile but closed it off with 'He's a good man, Jon.'

'Oh yes, I know, I know.' I felt as I had when I'd promised Mum I'd make a pilgrimage to Gornal Wood and take in all the rellies. We played tapes for a bit, then switched on the radio. The stations of each state came and went. Much later I gave it another go, when we stopped in

Wisconsin for a major rest-break. Just past Madison we pulled into a gas station that could have come straight out of her beloved Hopper painting:

'Look,' I said, 'not a single attendant going bald in high-waisted pants.'

'Yeah, I don't know about that painting anymore. Too creepy.'

By the time we approached Duluth we'd had enough of tapes, station jocks and silence but I had nothing jokey or serious to offer. The dilemma didn't last long:

'Your mom happy with the lounge, Jon?'

'Lounge?'

'Her big redecoration. Why we couldn't go. Why I couldn't meet her.'

'Oh, that...well, she hasn't said...not in detail...her letters have been pretty...you know.' Oh, give it up, I told myself, my response dwindling to 'Sorry.'

'All I asked is that you were straight with me, Jon.'

'I know.' At the time I assumed she just meant the fib about the lounge. Only later did I appreciate that past tense. Maybe she thought she'd said too much or said what she wanted too early. Her next comment was a touch perkier, ending with 'shame you'll miss it.'

'What? Polish Constitution Day?'

'Oh, you know Ray.'

Indeed I did: he was an inveterate thumber of almanacs in search of a themed excuse for his parties.

'Actually it was yesterday, May 3rd. But his Polish business buddies, they said, aw go on, stretch a point. So it's next weekend.'

My love of Ray's parties, the fact that I'd first met her through one: for a little while this brought back the old warmth, the buzz of our first few dates. But as we drove through Parkland and came up on the Duluth-Superior Harbour, my mood pushed me back to Christmas, when the fridge hummed and I was where my life wasn't. Laurie, Debs, Ray and his Polish buddies, Jim—who'd also become pals with Ray and at whom Debs had inevitably set her cap—would all be carousing and trying crazy polkas as the party rolled on. What would I find meanwhile?

Thank God for male obliviousness. Mr Becker was as pleased as ever to see me, even joked that 'You won't have old Gunther pinning you to the floor.' Mrs Becker was friendly but distant. She stared at me a lot. When at last I went up to bed, I blanked the mother-daughter murmurs I could hear from the kitchen, though I did catch what might or might not have been 'Mommy's boy'.

What I found back at Crescentwood were more surprises. Not only had Mum passed on her trademark pageant and shown complete indifference about Francey Martin's efforts: it turned out she'd been working just two days a week throughout the spring and sometimes not at all. More stuff had gone from the house, enough to make life there seem provisional. Here and there I discovered discreet tags on a few other pieces, marking them for charities.

Her manner, though, was as enigmatic as her letters. She took to speaking in a weird happy-sad tone. When I arrived I'd been bursting to ask what she planned to do but that reawakened my troubled notion of confessing all to Jeff Cordingley. There was only one thing at the logical end of that speculation and this reality: cold fact, no room for manoeuvre or hope of going back. I hadn't wanted cold fact in that pretend interview room and, really, I didn't want it now from Mum's lips. So I hid in the idea that, in her own way, she was slowly reshaping her life, that while she didn't want to banish Dad's memory, she'd decided at last that it would be healthier to build up a life that reflected the person she was, not someone's widow. New furniture would naturally appear. The part-time work arrangement was only temporary: of course she needed a chance to redirect herself—who wouldn't? Yes, Dad had been dead a while now, but who knew when someone would be ready to move on? These things took the time they took. Despite all the signs, she really was pulling out of the rellies' orbit. I left without pressing her on anything.

My Intersession class was a far happier hiding-place. It was full-on, six weeks solid, but I loved it. It removed—no, blasted clean away—any lingering doubts I might have had about what I should do with my life. What with the evenings of preparation, though, and the weekly work-assessments, I saw very little of Laurie. Perhaps I wouldn't have in any event: her promotion came through, bringing much new work with it, not to mention training sessions which, a couple of times, spread over a whole weekend.

But in the middle of my Intersession course we made a pact. Like a married couple carving out a date night, we set aside a Saturday evening into Sunday. Our laughter seemed as fresh as when we'd first met; our mutual choice of food and drink couldn't have been bettered by any lifestyle sage. Our loving rang all the changes. In ecstasy I looked up as she rode me, massaging her with fingers and tongue-tip. Candles burned everywhere, throwing us in shadow-shapes against the walls and curtains of her room, drawing how she curved as she bent to me, how I curved as I eased her to my face. We just knew that, as always, our resting would be afterglow and anticipation in a blissful mix.

I arched my back: 'Baby, yes,' cried Laurie, slipping her hands under me.

But it wasn't that. I was far away from her, from us, staring at two shadows that had reared up behind her. I say reared up: they were there so suddenly that they could have been paint fired across the room. One was bulky with sagging shoulders and something shapeless on its head. The other was small, neat of outline; something protruded from what must have been a pocket, a V-shape with a thin, tangled shadow tied to either point. They didn't move and nor did I.

Laurie rolled to my side: 'Oh, Jon, I'm sorry, did I do something?' It was a good minute before I lowered my back. Then, as if this were a schlocky movie and I was the villager who spots the monster on the hill, I raised a shaky finger. She raised herself and looked round. There was nothing. The other shadows rose innocently as before, only darting a little at a window-breeze.

'I know you're loving that teaching, sweets, but maybe it's getting to you.' I said nothing. 'Hey, you trying to freak me out? Ok,' she added in my silence, 'a game, right? Crazy stare, finger—you're Scrooge!' Still I couldn't speak and when she got off the bed and found her wrap, her 'I'm getting a drink' was tetchy. That set the mood for breakfast. I could have lifted it, I guess. If I'd really tried, I could have lifted it when we were in bed. But by saying what? Mum, Mum, nasty shadows, Mum? Or, remember I told you about that awful holiday I had in Dawlish before we came over? Well, a bit before that....

Instead I pushed what happened away and wrapped myself twice as tight in my work. Maybe she did the same. We met now and then for drinks or a movie. One time, out for an evening ramble in the last week of Intersession, I found myself in Malden Park and thought I'd call on Ray. Turning his corner, I thought I saw her car heading for the opposite end. Maybe it was hers. Maybe, despite her insistence that she and Ray were buddies only, I wanted it to be: like the night of the shadows, a sign of how things were waning. I walked past Ray's house. I told myself I wouldn't mention it.

*

No. No, Mags never left washing down here. Stuff went straight in the hamper and then, when the lid stuck out, in the machine. Will pulled his chair away from the wall, sniffed. Wasn't damp, was it? They'd had the whole place done out, a guy his sister Jayne's husband knew, Smeets had used him as well, thorough, pricey too but you get what you pay for. He bent to the skirting-board. Not as bad as before, the smell. Kind of thin, the equivalent of that needling sound from the furnace. A thunder of knocks on the front door made him jump. Ah, he'd better go up one time or Mags'd get to hear how hubby had been a real meanie to the neighbour-kids. He went back upstairs, trying to remember what she'd said about a bowl of candy someplace. When he came back down there was only the after-whiff of the chaperoning dad at the door. Man, some guys and their colognes.

*

At last, no more enigmas. The phone call was direct and clear. So at the start of July I made another trip—train this time—to find the house pretty well empty with just necessities remaining. I was on the sofa again. As from the following week, she said, she'd be staying with

115

the Derksens till her flight to England. And there was another letter for me, far different from Mrs. Butler's.

Uncle Kettering Sid was the writer, though I could easily imagine him ringed by the rest of them as they stood just outside a halo of light like the one from the now-departed standard lamp. Mum said he was ailing seriously but now, incredibly, tee-total. Perhaps the combination of hurrying mortality and new salvation sharpened his words. At any rate, what I had to do, he insisted, was get myself back home for good with my poor mother. I'd reneged on the Gornal Wood ceremony and hadn't been back since, even though I'd promised ('Had you not, Jonathan?') to do so. It was a crying shame that I'd apparently educated myself out of any feeling for a lonely widow still stuck in her grief:

'They have been golden to you, Jonathan'— that phrase again, Auntie Irene's, delivered with Nicky in tow when I'd told Mum that I couldn't make Gornal Wood—'Now it is time for you to pay your poor mother back for them both.'

As with Mrs Butler's letter, I took myself off to read it thoroughly—and indulge far different emotions. His precision angered me, the fastidious avoidance of all contracted phrases. It must have taken him hours to fashion it: a very different proposition from Mrs Butler's healthily dashed-off sentiments. But it made me smile, too, and damn near laugh out loud when I got to 'You too can make a life for yourself here with your mother. This is still a wonderful country for anyone with enterprise, maturity and, above all, a care for those who should mean the most to them.' Ridiculous from start to finish. Britain in the 70s? It was just waiting for someone to press the flush. 'Give my love to Rosemary and the Mounties,' he'd made me promise that Erkeley summer. Now, it seemed, the assumption was that I'd done so. Like a Boy Scout I'd dob-dob-dobbed and must march back to nothing.

Equally vexatious were the other voices echoing round his words. Bevvo, Gordy, Mr Vesey—I could hear their variously-pitched contempt as I read and re-read them. Once I'd finally done with the letter, I sought mom out. She was sitting with a pot of tea in the half-denuded kitchen. I poured myself a cup:

'Where will you live?'

'At Builth for a while. Sid and Irene have moved to a bigger house now Nicky's back with them.'

'Back?'

'He was a no-good, that husband.' Her tone caught Auntie Irene's melodic censure.

'What will you do?'

'I'll find something.'

'Teaching again? Retrain back there?'

'Look, Jonathan, I've not been put on this earth just to make sure Nativity plays go off with a bang. Leave me be, leave me be. You and your questions, on and on.'

At that moment, there were two of her before me: the drained widow who saw no further than being sheltered in the bosom of the family, and

117

the bright, talented woman who was kissing herself goodbye. I was angry with her and, momentarily, very sad.

'More to the point,' she said, 'what are you going to do?' And she looked down at the envelope from which she'd handed me Uncle Sid's letter. I closed my eyes, kept them closed a long while.

I kept his letter for a long while too. The sheets were larger than letter-size and had an absorbency which would have made fountain-ink useless. For ages they were perfect for cleaning nibs and brushes.

*

'So that's a no,' said Will aloud. 'How about a letter to your Uncle saying so?' He shook his head. Here he was again, getting under the feet of the story, wanting it to be other. To be his in some way? Why would he want that? He'd no real idea what those questions meant or why they made him shiver. Pushing them away, he wrapped himself in what he'd just read. Of course no letter to Kettering Sid, no straight answer to his mom in that bare kitchen. Where inward stuff was concerned, this guy was not a finisher. But then, would he himself have had the nerve to write to this Sid? Could he see himself writing some intervention on Uncle Gary's behalf during that Lloydminster hoo-ha, or to brother Mark telling him it was high time he got his ass out of Antigonish and made a visit?

118

Will worked his lips. Lloydminster again. Mark again. If a clan reunion could be engineered without him, that'd be just fine. Couldn't be, though. Even if no-one told him, he'd just know and blow in right in the middle of it. Yet they should meet again, the two of them. Hadn't laid eyes on each other since—that evening at the Erkeley, he nearly told himself. Setting the folder aside, he pictured the smoking-room guy he thought he'd be for its duration: smiling, nodding, filling slowly up with a good tale like a slap-up meal, knowing that his own house and life were waiting for him when it was done, cosy and just plain there. Him and that guy, they weren't in synch. Couldn't be? Something was opening up, there was a blur, a drift. 'You shouldn't be here,' he'd whispered to Mark on that Lloydminster evening. Mark's grin, his swoony tilt and fake-dumbo voice: 'Oh, and you should, big man?' He took up the folder again and hunched forward.

12

Tears came into her eyes. For a moment, she let them, then wiped them away and bent her head. The mood was Christmas with the hum of the fridge: everything was sterile, I felt alone. Well, it was a kitchen again.

'Shit,' she said. 'Shit, you stupid Laurie Becker.'

'It's not like that.'

'No? No, Jon? How do I know? How do you know—?'

'It's just her. Nothing to do with me.'

But Laurie was shaking her head.

'But it is, Jon, of course it is. She goes back, you finish your Master's, then you go back. Or maybe, what? Finish it over there?'

'Laurie…'

'Mom could see it's tough for her, all right. She wouldn't want me or any of us thousands of miles away. But she could tell.'

I thought of my times in Kenora, of coming back from the 7-11 to see that intimate dumb-show between mother and daughter in the back yard, then that other time, hearing the murmur from the kitchen the night before I caught the Winnipeg bus:

'I'm not a Mommy's boy. Mommy's boys don't'—I had to swallow hard. It was nearly out, nearly there like black, unmoving shadows on a wall. Mommy's boys don't get handy with a bottle-neck on a patch of rancid ground. Mommy's boys don't grab the trophy while their so-called friends stick to boring old punch-ups. Jonny Parry is our friend, he kills coppers.

Now, of course, I realise that Mommy's or non-Mommy's boys do anything if the situation's right. Even at the time I guess I knew. Lamely, I ended by saying that Mommy's boys don't come all the way to Windsor when they could study just round the corner at home. At that she just shrugged, reminding me that Ontario wasn't Mars. By now her tears had gone and she was staring fiercely at me. If we'd been in public, a passer-by might have thought that I'd just groped someone I didn't know.

There was just one more thing, for my own satisfaction. I wasn't going to say anything but... well, to the conquered some kind of spoils:

'Is it Ray?'

'Oh for shit's sake.'

'Well, I was walking round his way a while back and thought I saw—'

She turned away at a noise outside: Jim coming through the side-gate, back from a meal with his latest.

'I'd better go.' Smiling tightly, with a brief glimmer of fresh tears, she leaned up and kissed my cheek. 'You're a good guy, Jonathan. Hope it all works out.'

'See you around?' But she was gathered into herself, bag on arm, car-key at the ready as the kitchen door opened, and didn't answer.

'Hey, Laurie-Laurie B!'

She made some noise, of greeting or goodbye, and pushed past Jim. He stared after her then turned and, without taking his eyes from me, pulled off his jacket. We stood in the kitchen, hearing her door slam, the engine rev and die away.

'Oh, daddy,' he said at last. 'Oh, my man, my man.'

And out with the whiskey, Jim plonking a serious tumbler-full in front of me. I date my true taste for it from then. A whimsical lover but when it's in the mood it doesn't spare affection.

*

Late in summer, having reluctantly taken out a loan, I went down to Toronto. I'd booked hotel rooms for Mum and me, a three-day stay before her flight. I'd also figured out a way to see the main sights with minimum hassle, ending with the still-new CN Tower ('This Needle Will Guide You Home From Space,' one leaflet cheerily asserted. 'Bye Bye NASA'). Early next morning I waited for the Winnipeg plane and then got her settled at the hotel, after which we embarked on what proved to be a busily vacant ramble. Under other circumstances, I'd have got a real buzz from the St Lawrence Market, relished the sun on my face in High Park, been transported—as I had been twice before—by the Royal Ontario Museum. Previously the museum had filled my head chock full with all kinds of ideas, new designs and riffs on old ones. But Mum just walked through everything like it was a short cut down a mall. By our first lunchtime I'd mentally scrubbed the pièce de résistance, a tall ships cruise on Lake Ontario. As for the CN Tower—another trove, I was sure, of shiny ideas for my work—we simply went up it and came down again.

On the last evening, I took her down to Spadina for a slap-up meal, or in her case, sighs and fork-fiddling. After a summer of hints and clues and play-acting, here was a final surprise: I'd seen her tuck into Chinese time enough when

I was at home—restaurants, takeaways—but now she said she'd never liked it, she'd only made a show for Dad's sake. Her tears flowed freely. People turned to look and a few tutted as though I were giving her a hard time.

Next morning, we drank endless cups of coffee in the airport restaurant. Vacations were beginning or ending all around us. Some of the men's summer-wear reminded me of Mr Walden, Dad's old employer, and I fancied that at any moment he would emerge from the crowd, remembering us, again offering his condolences, asking us how we'd been doing and what was next. Circles completed. The plane's number and destination appeared on the flight board. I looked at Mum's stricken face, her quivery shoulders, and reached for her hand. That much at least was called for.

Suddenly wide-eyed, she stared past me: 'Good grief, some of the people they let in here.' I looked towards the entrance. A huge group—adults and kids, two or three families, I'd guess—were leaving. Skirting them on their way in were two figures who paused and looked around. Vacationers they weren't. One, elderly and rotund, seemed to be held together with herringbone tweed and twine. The pockets bulged on his ruinous coat. The other one's pockets bulged, too, but they belonged to a blazer. He was much younger, and his thatch of hair ended in sideburns, thin and straggly efforts like a couple of misaimed moustaches. I recognised the old one's face at once. I'd have recognised the other's too. But he didn't have one.

'Not by the doors,' hissed Mum. 'This bunch here getting trays. Behind you!'

I think I vaguely caught a suggestion of Hell's Angels gear and miniscule hot-pants in the servery line. But all the coffee was now back in my throat and I just made it to the washroom. While I was in there the boarding-call for her plane was announced but that didn't hustle me out any quicker. As I opened the outer door a figure flitted past, or maybe it was just a trick of the hard light on all those restless bodies in the restaurant, the faces full of hello and goodbye. For an instant something flashed at me, badge-shaped. *Sapience and Duty.* I watched it go or thought I did: all was noise and painful colour. When I focused again, a toddler was slapping its open hand against the glass of the entrance door, till its mother swept it up. No herringbone, no badge.

By the time I got back to the table Mum was hopping up and down. We raced to the Departure Lounge entrance and her name was called just as we reached it. Everything broke up in my gaze—bodies, gestures, surfaces—as though the whole world had been planted before one of those mad fairground mirrors. Our kiss and hug were perfunctory. I think I called out that I'd write soon; I must have done. The only clear image I have now is of Mum hotfooting away from me with a concerned official setting the pace.

I'd booked myself one more night at the hotel and I kept it together long enough to get outside and hail a taxi. Never mind bus or subway: I couldn't have brought myself to negotiate fare-change and keep an eye out for my stop. As I got my key from Reception, the clerk did a double-take:

'Oh, and mail for you, Mr Parry.'

Back in the room I tore at the large blank envelope. Inside was a greetings card, old-fashioned, a coach-and-four crossing a bridge. The coachman had a boy up beside him. Much effort had gone into the pose and features of the pair, a bit like on those old cigarette cards where luminaries of sport and movies have tiny bodies that swoop up to outsize heads with familiar, well-loved features. The coachman was ruddy-faced, wisps of hair fringing his hat-brim. His hand was arrested in mid-whip-crack, which pulled open one of his pockets. Thick and dark, the neck of the bottle was, tightly stoppered. On his further side, the boy leaned forward to reveal a leather jerkin whose pocket was also in use. The elastic of the slingshot looped out of it onto his knee. They were looking at me—at least, the coachman was. The boy's face was again not there. It might have been a Christmas card except that there was no snow and nothing inside. No printed greeting, anyway: just 'Johnny, Johnny, Johnny Canuck' in a smudgy hand.

'Yes? Oh, Mr Parry...sir, I'm just checking in new guests right now, could you phone down again when...pardon me? Your mail? Sir, I can't say. I've only been on...must have been Mr Rames, sir, I spelled him off at eleven...he's back on at six, maybe he saw...I have to go, sir, pardon me....'

A shower, a coffee, a long time staring all around the room. I fought back the urge to switch on the lights and fling open the wardrobe but I'd kept my eyes closed when splashing my face in the bathroom, trying to slap reason back into my head. What the mirror might hold was too much. It was no good. I had to be where people were...no...being with people was just a touch more bearable than staying put with who knows what clicks and whispers, what shadows playing along the walls...or standing still. Getting myself down to the harbour, I booked on a tall ship after all. It was pretty crowded and, from mast-bolted tannoys, the tour commentary poured down on our heads, urging on us the delights of Hanlon's Point, Algonquin and Ward's Islands and, inevitably, what the guide called the 'pretty damn humongous spear' of the CN Tower behind us. I tried to focus on each clump of trees, each sandbar, at times each wave. They weren't human, had never been human in another time and place, and that was some comfort. Hunched at the rail, I finally steeled myself to look round. Shorts, tee-shirts, sunshades, white hats, cameras held above or resting on generous bellies—and 'Johnny', cried into my ear. I thought I'd faint but a woman's voice said 'I'm so sorry' and pushed round behind me with 'Johnny, Johnny, I'm over here!'

Downtown had changed while I was on the boat. Stepping off, I knew that I'd never again see it as it had been. No buildings, cabs, walk-lights—just endless thickets of doorways and alleys from which anyone, anything, might come at you. It was as strange as a holding cell to a man whose world had been a tree and a pond. Better to take my chances with the hotel room again, where an odd sound might well be the air-conditioning on the fritz and anyway I could have the tv on, loud.

Mr Rames was small and had an elegance which his hotel-issue suit couldn't smother, perhaps accentuated by the way he touched his chin with his third finger while pausing to form a sentence. No, he regretted he did not see. Around eight-thirty that morning, perhaps a little before. The mail hadn't long come in and he was busy at the pigeon-holes when a voice said 'For Mr Parry' and he turned to find... yes, sir, that envelope, the very one. No, sir, just Dolores and her vacuum over by the information-stand. No one else. Any guests around were at second breakfast, probably. Perry, he thought the voice said and up and down he went through the lists, top to bottom, bottom to top, till he found Parry and took a chance. Sorry, sir. Was it maybe bad news? Was there someone he could phone?

The minutes of that night were sharp as razors. I pretended I was on the back seat of a Greyhound bus, checking all approaches, windows and aisle, keeping the world at bay. There was someone I could phone. As soon as I got home late next afternoon, I showered, changed and, as best I could, simmered down. Then I found my address book and put through a transatlantic call, blind to the cost, badgering the operator as though I were an efficiency goon.

'It's close on midnight here, Jonathan.' Mrs Butler sounded groggy—and initially scared. Mr Butler, it turned out, was away at a crown-green bowls tournament. But her natural kindness came through soon enough.

I tried to speak as nonchalantly as I could, but already I was thinking how I would feel when the light of day faded at my end. Jim was away—left the day before, I think. Working—and partying—like a Trojan all summer (but still finding time for an episode with Laurie's friend Debs, brief by mutual consent), he'd finally grabbed time for a trip home to PEI. Our lovely, comfy house would be no more than an arrangement of dark doors and stairs. The kitchen blind was thick but didn't reach all the way down the window, which meant that, even if the rest of the house was dark, anyone suitably placed—anything—would see the spilling light. I was in menaced space.

Talking quietly, brokenly to herself, Mrs Butler repeated my instructions: 'Right, I've got that. I can't say what my friend knows but if there's something she doesn't, I'll see what I can do myself. Give me your number.' A pause. 'And your Directory Enquiries is no go for all this?'

'You can never get through,' I rushed.

'Just like here. Nothing works. All right, love, I'll call you tomorrow.'

'If you could make it today? I'll be up'—could be all night, I didn't add.

'Ooh, lovey, your today isn't our today. I'll do my best.'

'I'm really grateful, Mrs Butler.'

'Dorothy.'

'Dorothy. Oh'—I scrunched my eyes—'and thank you for your letter. Fantastic. I'm sorry I haven't written back. I would do, I will, I mean I wouldn't bother you on the phone like this, only—'

'Sounds like something's grieving you, love.'

'Mum's coming.'

'To see you? Oh, that's really—'

'Coming back to England. Well, back by now. I saw her off yesterday.'

'Here? A visit?'

'Permanently.'

I'd meant to keep the news about Mum separate, a more normal-sounding topic to round the call off. But it obviously struck Mrs Butler, as it might have struck me had I been her, that my request and Mum's departure were connected. I felt bad about not clarifying things but I wasn't in a state to manage niceties; and anyway, the misunderstanding led to words which I could do with hearing right then:

'Now, I did wonder if that was on the cards. Something she said when she wrote to me in the new year. You're a big lad, Jonathan, but I'm sure that just having her over there was a boon. The way our Kevin talks sometimes, you'd think he was still a kiddy or we were in Timbuktu. I have to say, I think it hits you boys more, the changes. I can see now why you've phoned…an extra bit of reaching out. It'll feel strange for a while, love, but don't let it weigh you down. It won't always be dark at seven.'

Builth, I told her. Staying with my Uncle Sid and Auntie Irene. After that? She'd said she didn't know, not yet. Sorry? Oh, I'm sure she will phone, I said, and not at some daft hour. She'll be in the same today as you, Dorothy. Chuckles. After she rang off, I held the receiver for an age, as though she were still comforting me, as though the connection was still live and I mustn't break it. It won't always be dark at seven. The saying even got me a bit of sleep.

It had to be a delivery pizza and some of the friendlier remnants from the fridge next day— and the day after that. The waiting had me in knots. I got uptight when I had to forsake the phone for the bathroom, which of course made things worse: our landlord on his prof's salary and no extension cord in the house. On the second day Mrs Butler phoned around four in the afternoon. Her friend had come through with all the info and, as I'd asked, she herself had phoned the Hunters and Forbeses saying she was an old friend of my family. I'd been wondering how Bevvo and Gordy were doing, she told them, but I didn't have their addresses or numbers. Ever so sorry to phone out of the blue, she was…but would they mind passing my contact details on and giving her their sons' for me?

'Not great luck, I'm afraid, Jonathan. I mean, they were good, considering—said they'd get onto it at once and asked me to phone back. Got through to their boys, too, and they didn't hang about either. That Gordy told his lot no. Bit of a dusty answer, I thought...wouldn't have hurt to pass on a hello to you but, well, folks is folks. A bad influence, he told them you were, which I can't believe.'

I ignored that: 'Bevvo?'

'Took your number, apparently. Bit more civilised, I suppose.'

I'll say it again: bless Mrs Butler. Our chats hadn't come cheap for either of us but she'd been so sweet, so natural about it all, as though she lived on my street and I'd only asked her to pick up some groceries. Write to her, I instructed myself; send a gift.

Later that same afternoon, relieved at something done, I went across to the campus, got into my office—a bit of default space off the Design studios but it had a door—and dug out some notes for the start of the new course I'd be teaching. Strictly Art History this time round, beginning with the origins of Impressionism. Under normal circumstances I'd have been a bit peeved: I'd had to do a paper on the Impressionists in the third year of my BA and they didn't enthral. As things were, though, their disregard for sharp line and form were just right for how I felt. The blurry, the vague: I could hide in that. Reading the notes did me a power of good and the time just slipped by. I didn't even jump when Ted the night janitor rapped on my door and gave me the chucking-out thumbs up. I'd been minded to rush home as if through a thunderstorm, not looking at anything but my feet hitting the sidewalk. Instead I strolled, even lingered at what was called The Green, a triangle of grass and trees near the prof's house, formed by the way the side roads ran. I allowed myself to stare at the trees, even finger a leaf or two, and marvel at how the slow dusk threaded their branches. It won't always be dark at seven, I whispered to myself. Clearly I hoped those words would trump 'collateral damage' as a way to ward off the dark.

The spaces of my world struck terms again. The house went back to liking me. In a day or two I picked up with some old colleagues, went to a party, had some drinks and energetic chats at O'Maggio's and the Sidebar Motel. Twilight shadows stayed just that; night footsteps belonged to living people. Having found it on a scrap of paper, I even phoned Uncle Sid's new number in Builth, breezing my way past Auntie Irene, making solicitous with Mum, promising I'd be over without tying myself to when. Now and then, remembering that Bevvo hadn't nixed Mrs Butler's request completely, I stared hard at the phone in passing. Had he called one time when I was out? Ah, but taking my number meant he was curious: try once, try again. I wasn't about to flop down and stare moodily at the dial like a stood-up girl.

And Mum had gone and I could now step completely into the life which our kind old neighbour wanted for me. I told myself. It took a while, though, to get over my last talk with Laurie. Some things just won't be spooked away by burbling about collateral damage or how it won't always be dark at seven.

A week or so after Mrs Butler's good efforts, I was woken early by the phone.

'Hello.'

'This is Bevan Hunter.' Naturally older, the voice, but I'd have recognised it even if he'd called to me on a hurrying street. Even so, the words threw me for a moment, but I understood that a point was being made. 'Bevvo' was way back then. Years and distance gave him no obligation and me no right to use it.

Nevertheless, 'Bevvo!' I said, 'ah, thanks for ringing. I'd have called you but my folks' friend said you didn't—'

'What do you want?'

The voice was trying for a gravity it didn't possess. I imagined a newly-promoted policeman leading his first interview. Underneath, though, was there a residue of friendship in the voice? Was it hostile or just neutral? I gave that up. No time to faff with nuance: I was really thinking about what had to come next. At once what I wanted sounded foolish. But I'd got it all planned, even written it down. If I could get this sorted, I could find an explanation for the airport incident—for everything. Like a market-researcher, I started on my notes.

'And why would Gordy or me do that?' His voice remained steady but with more grit—calculated?—as it went on. 'Why would him or me leave a card in a hotel in a place we don't know, on the off-chance that someone we haven't seen or thought about for years was staying there?'

'It was the inscription. How many people would know that?'

'About as many as saw you getting floored in the playground after it first came out you were running away to Canada.'

'Hardly running away, Bevvo. My parents couldn't leave me behind, could they?'

'Christ, might have been the making of you. Too late for that, by the sound of it.'

'Hang on a minute...the sound of what? I'm doing all right with—'

'If Gordy or me wanted'—now he really tried for old beyond his years—'at all wanted to get in touch, do you not think we should have used a friendlier phrase than Wiznuk's on the card? Do you think we should have reminded you of him?'

The rest of my prompts went out the window—not least because he was starting to sound like Kettering Sid had in his guilt-spraying letter, all that fussy wording. More, he was starting to sound like Mr Vesey. Contemptuously, I wondered if that's how he'd ended up: likely-lad Bevvo as an ineffectual headmaster or something, a *Chef enseignant*, safe behind an office door, having failed to control les enfants de Coutances. I would have let the thought heat my words, but then he added, 'Assuming that you need reminding of Wiznuk' and that threw me right back:

'I hadn't thought of him till I got that card.'

'Had you not?' The words came slowly.

'No, and while we're on the subject'—what subject? I was scratching around and wasn't at all happy when I remembered Gordy's reported words to his parents. But if we were into point-scoring…

'I wasn't a bad influence.'

'Come again?'

'Gordy told his folks I was. I can't imagine how either of you would—'

'Were you not?'

'When?'

'Can you not remember?'

I was about to lay into him for his prissy finishing-school talk but 'remember' circled me back and I saw something to clutch at:

'You haven't thought of me for years?'

'Good God, I've had better things to do, me and Gordy both. But since this is the last time we'll speak, just admit it and then all three of us can agree on one solitary thing.'

'Admit what?'

'What Gordy said and why it's twisted your knickers.'

'I've told you.'

'What you think he meant.'

'Oh, come on, I was a good mate...the homework I helped you with, going out at lunchtime when I could've got busted with you pair.'

'Out to...?'

'You and him and your bloody smokes, you know where we went, always.'

'So say the name.'

I leap-frogged that: 'All right, he always won, Wiznuk, him and his goons, in the playground when you two weren't there. And I ran away. That evening. I spoiled your cool. Yes, I put my hand up, that was all bad.' Incredibly, I nearly burst out laughing. Good grief, if my cowardice in school was a bad influence on the likes of Bevvo and Gordy.... But I'd dangled bait. If he saw that I had, I reckoned he'd keep at his 'now listen, sonny' routine. 'But more than all that,' he'd begin and we'd be back to what Gordy hadn't come out and said. And if he didn't see...well, either way, I wasn't volunteering anything else. Let the black shadows rear up as they wished on this morning, let them drape themselves huge and unmoving over this sunny room.

There was silence. I waited for the click, the dialling tone. Instead—and who knows, this might have been a strange little nod to his old manner, the old days—he just sighed and said mildly, 'Anyway, this is costing me a bomb.'

'Say my name. Bevvo, say my name.'

'Oh, flake off'—now the dial-tone.

Jim came shuffling in, sleepily fighting the arms of his dressing-gown:

136

'Phone?'

'Yes, for me…sorry.'

'Time is it?'

'Just gone seven.'

He'd only got back from PEI late last night. Though he wasn't one for mouthfuls, I expected some modest kvetching. But he just sat down on the arm of the sofa:

'Problems, Dr Jon?'

'Oh, bit of old hassle.'

'From?' He tilted his head, concerned.

I mentioned Bevvo, giving his proper name in full. I was with a proper buddy now so the useless *Chef enseignant,* or whatever he was, had to be held at arm's length.

'Didn't know you still had any contacts from'—he cocked a thumb over his shoulder—'way back when, save that nice neighbour lady.'

Mrs B, I thought. A gift for Mrs B.

'Ah, he was just someone. Out of the blue, really. Looking for confirmation about some old thing. Schooldays, you know.'

'You were sounding pretty antsy. You sure that's all it was?' Before I could speak, he added, 'Thought it might've been Laurie and you were trying to start her up again.' He got up. 'Coffee?'

'Yes. Great.'

As he turned for the kitchen he said, 'Me and you, Dr Jon, we're not of the same cut with the damsels. When it comes to saying anything half-useful, I'm all advised out in a minute. And before you ask, I don't know what Laurie's doing now. You know that me and Debs'—he drew a

137

finger across his throat. 'But the way you've been…man, you must move on.'

The kettle went on, mugs clattered. I pushed the phone-stand away from my chair. *Didn't know you still had any contacts from way back when, save that nice neighbour lady.* Oh, it might be that I do, Jim, quite apart from the loser on the phone. Though when you say contacts—

'Next to no milk here, Dr Jon!'

'I'm going out, I'll get some.' I forgot what I'd just said. *Man, you must move on.* With Jim's help? Ok, he was no Mr Reflective about love— lurve, rather, which was surely coined for him— but it was about anything but that. Could I tell him, somehow? Find some middle way between my dumb-show at Laurie's apartment and the full Jeff Cordingley? No, that was self-defeating. How do you tiptoe round absolutes? Honey, I'm afraid your dog's a bit missing. Madam, I'm afraid your husband's a bit dead. Or your son is. Mrs Wiznuk. Ah, come on, I told myself: I can fettle, I'm handy at that…change the angle of light on myself, bad to at least half good…if he hadn't toppled, let go the bottle-neck…on at me all the time, he was, like Wallings' midges at Tafler. Mrs Butler being out of the running— time, distance, generation, how in all innocence she'd end up telling Mum about our call—who else had been so kind to me apart from Jim? And wouldn't that be enough, the Erkeley spoken of at last, words upon the air, an effort made? Wouldn't that still the shadows, stop harsh lights playing tricks among tables and serveries at airports—or anywhere?

'Hey, Jim,' I called, 'are you…oh, thanks'—as a mug was pressed into my hand—'are you round this evening?'

He squeezed his face into an apology: 'Seeing the man, Dr Jon. Meal at his house.' The man was Steven Porter, slated to be Jim's thesis supervisor. A jolly bear: in temperament, a cross between Burl Ives and Jim himself. He'd probably be happy to re-arrange things but I didn't want block any stage of Jim's progress, however briefly. Besides, I'd need time. So when Jim said, 'But tomorrow night, my friend, I'll be at your disposal. The Sidebar, O'Maggio's, or we swing by the liquor store for a bottle of heaven.'

I absolutely agreed.

'Good stuff. And I can always rejig it with Rachel. Ok, me for a shower now I'm up.'

'Rachel?'

He turned away, laid a hand on my shoulder: 'Drink your coffee, Dr Jon.'

*

Will looked up as though surprised by some fleeting form. Nothing…and no weird sound now, no rank smell. *Honey, I'm afraid your dog's a bit missing.* No, not yet, he whispered. Don't go back to all that yet.

*

'Let me at those old-time Frenchie daubers,' I sang, striding for the campus from the post office downtown.

A box of stationery doo-dads, bookmarks, little note-y pads, nicely bedizened with maple leaves, Mountie hats. An envelope properly padded. Mrs B would love it all. I'd taken time, in the downtown library, to write a careful letter, all positives emphasised. Yes, the work was hard, it was bound to be, but yes I was making the most of life, '*Just as you kindly advised me.*' A nod to her running joke, too: '*No, I haven't learnt "Hiawatha" by heart. I doubt if I could say a single line. Tell Mr Butler I'm sorry.*'

I was ready to dive back into the thick flowers and raggedy clouds of Monet and the rest. I felt like a wild preacher, my mind wheeling from this to that assertion. But my thoughts had to start somewhere, so I called them in, picked my place.

Like a kid, Bevvo was, scarcely better than Nicky's Craig in his pomp, yelling 'Jonathan, Bonathan, the silly old Ponathan' when I'd stopped him breaking yet another cherished toy. What, really, was the point of that call? Except to say without saying that he and Gordy were indeed damaged goods. They'd gone on somehow but he needed me to know that I'd done for more than one kid that Erkeley evening. But why not out and say it rather than making me play that bait, that leading comment about my uncool cowardice? He didn't bite, though: didn't speak his truth, his and Gordy's.

Crossing the boundary road to the campus, I bristled. Like Bevvo and his insistence on no more phone calls, I wasn't lingering on all that again. They'd had plenty of time, those two, to do their worst, to seek out their own Jeff Cordingley, Frisco cop or gendarme, and start the ball rolling. Who wouldn't, if the guy they were shielding were as contemptible as Bevvo made out on the phone? They weren't grotty kids any more, baffled and fearful about spilling the beans. Enough. Enough with what Bevvo didn't say. Now for a new start, a new circuit round the houses. No, not new but charged with a new exhilaration, the prospect of speaking to Jim, the declarations I'd made in my letter to Mrs B.

Here we go. Bevvo and Gordy really hadn't known, I insisted to myself, and sure didn't now. He said he hadn't thought about me for years. No, 'we', he said. He and Gordy were obviously in regular touch, letters and maybe the odd phone call filled with how-you-doing, how-I'm-doing, job and family and France is this and California's that. Jonathan the silly old Ponathan? Not a look in. No, Bevvo's phone call, it was really just spite for spite's sake. The manner, the questions like grown-up sighs, the ever so portentous silence. And his 'Had you not?' when I said I hadn't given Wiznuk a thought—that was just a nasty reminder of when I was other than now, hitting the deck yet again as Wiznuk capered about and his goons…ah, now, his goons…as you'd carry a jug full to overflowing, I held that phrase steady as I walked on.

In my office, I forgot about the good old daubers and instead took myself off on a grand excursion, almost a weird treat, further and wider than anything involving Jeff Cordingley's kindly eyes in a Winnipeg station. Round the houses? I went round the whole damn world. It makes me laugh now. Or would. But laughter's gone to join love.

Cadman and Bell...Wiznuk's goons. Really, it wasn't beyond the bounds, was it? At the airport, one or other, at a nearby table. Probably still thick but alive enough to catch the accent, recognise me—I was hardly Methuselah, was I?—eavesdrop, hear my hotel's name (had I mentioned it? Well, Mum had said something sniffy about her room—no pleasing some people—so it must have come up). Stuff what most people thought about coincidences. Hadn't someone said that, if you took the story of how the Great War began to a film producer, they'd show you the door? And what about that priest whose bishop or whoever ordered him off his ship when it reached Ireland from England? On the ship went and met its famous iceberg. Just last week, some kids a few doors along, heartbroken at the disappearance of their cat, were taken to the pet sanctuary for a replacement and found their Tiddles in a cage, not a scratch on him. Cadman or Bell—who'd run cluelessly off that evening in the opposite direction—had clocked me at the airport, heard what he'd heard and decided to ride the happenstance, create some dumb fun like putting cling-film over a toilet bowl. Honestly, the way some people fill their layovers. And that handwriting on the card wasn't some ghostly kid's from across the years. It was how one or other of them wrote now. As for the card arriving while I was still at the airport, well, no disrespect to the clerk I first spoke to, or elegant Mr Rames, but it was a big hotel and they were rushed this, that and the other way. In fact, thinking about it, the first guy's words were a bit pat when I phoned down from my room. Was he really up to his neck in new guests? As for Mr Rames...yes, he definitely sounded defensive, as though he had to say anything but 'I just didn't do my job.'

Yes...the card got there sometime before I returned from the airport and it was probably the cleaner with the vacuum—Dolores, did Mr Rames say?—who ended up dealing with Cadman, or Bell, to spare her superiors' blushes. Actually, stuff Cadman and Bell. It didn't have to be one of them. None of us was so old that we couldn't remember something of the sights and sounds from school. Tribal stuff in the playground can stick long after any lesson. Who exactly had heard Wiznuk yelling 'Johnny Canuck, Johnny Canuck' before his drongos did their same old same old to me? Well...who in the school hadn't heard, one time or another?

And my vision at the airport? None of the hotel guys' concern, of course, or Cadman's or Bell's or whoever's. *I have to say, I think it hits you boys more, the changes*: Mrs Butler was right in what she said when I told her Mum had gone back, though not in a way she'd have understood. Look at it: Mum and Dad and I hadn't been more than adjacent passengers on a longish journey. Like the Titanic priest, Dad had been obliged to step off. And yes, Mum's going had indeed hit me: no longer would I feel the chill of her loneliness from miles to the west. Life was at last fully open to me. I could, in the words of that poem that came to me in Mr Vesey's study, live untroubling and untroubled. But first, at the moment of Mum's departure, my mind had to feed briefly on old agonies to clear itself. So...early morning, gallons of coffee, the unending restlessness of the airport restaurant, the glare of lights that possibly brightened and dimmed of their own accord—who wouldn't hallucinate? And who wouldn't hallucinate in the throes of sex with someone who was already pondering a parting of the ways? Well, Jim wouldn't, of course, but Laurie had been a big thing for me, a new thing. Without knowing it, I'd picked up that she was deliberately unloving me. Already, the cold of afterwards was creeping in and with it the old, lonely past. Plenty of scope for the mind's underside to play tricks. To plaster two appalling shadows on her wall.

I firmed all of this up: expert fettling, though I say it myself. Like a sculptor, I was, teasing out details, refining. Having a good old arm-stretch to celebrate, I noticed my watch. The hours had flown but I wasn't the least bit hungry. My grand excursion had fed me famously. Still, I'd drop into the Arts café for something to take home.

The July - August summer school was going on a bit longer and there were one or two short conferences around the campus, so places were still open to catch the dollars. I'd make the café before it shut. Once home, I'd probably find I could eat a horse.

A noise made me turn: janitor Ted working his way through the Design wing. Without waiting for his usual rap on the door, I packed my bag and promised the Impressionists a proper stint the following day—till I remembered that a pal had phoned from Sarnia, the Luxembourg guy who'd founded Arundats in our Honours year, inviting me to a party. That was ok. There was nothing stopping me from an early start tomorrow, Monet and the lads plus perhaps a quick nose at schedules for my own studies, before I caught the bus. As for my heart-to-heart with Jim…well, what was the betting that he knew about the party too but, like me, had clean forgotten? But whether he knew or not, if he was putting mysterious Rachel off, it wouldn't be hard to inveigle him. And, thinking about it, did I need that heart-to-heart now?

I smiled, feeling the old bite of work-hard-play-hard setting me up for the coming year. Seeing Laurie about by accident would probably start not to hurt. We might get to be friends, although I didn't really know how that would go, if it did. I put such thoughts aside, reflecting instead that it was a shame to deprive old Ted of his out-you-go routine by leaving now; but there'd be enough late nights in the office before long. Closing the door behind me, I looked about. Where was he? Probably in the gallery, lingering over some of the raunchier undergrad work. In his shoes, I'd do the same.

As I reached the main door it was just swinging to. Ted was taking his time with the lock-up, but why wouldn't he? My building and the Drama studio next door were his domain at this hour and he was a dependable guy. He'd obviously tired of what the gallery had to offer in the way of education, or shocks, and had scooted out for one of his darts, as he called them, his roll-ups, just like…no, not a bit like Gordy…or Bevvo either.

'Night, Ted,' I called into the dusk. 'Think it was just me in there.'

Ah, he must have been right round the back. For all his bulk, he could move—certainly had during last Freshers' Week when a posse of engineers had rushed the studios, intent on liberating paints for the Engineering Soc. stalls and some war-tribe idea they had. He'd bested them all on his own-i-o. A quick scoot to the Arts café—the pastrami-and-mustard sub looked like it would last till I wanted it—and I was on my way.

I could still see the colour of the leaves when I reached The Green, even make out their different hues. Gazing at them, I wondered when Jim would be back. Way late at the very least, or Mrs Porter might make up a bed for him: Steven, too, was partial to a bottle of grain-heaven. That was ok. I had a notion to set the seal on the evening, all I'd sorted in my head. I'll touch a leaf, I thought, hold it a moment between my fingers. Clock its location so that afterwards, day or night until it fell, I could top up my happy voodoo if I wanted, remind myself of how far behind me he was now, that kid squirming under grave eyes in Mr Vesey's study.

As my fingers touched my selected leaf, I heard a commotion. At first it was hard to place: sounds play like wind around house-fronts. There was a thud then, metallic, like an overturned garbage can, and I knew it came from round the back of my prof's house. A posse of cats? The newly recovered Tiddles in a bundle with our prof's cat? Or the Tiddles kids trying to forestall its latest escape? Crossing the street, I unlocked the side gate and headed into the back garden. The security light wasn't on. Not kids, then, or even cats…that light was hair-trigger…

… but it flashed on now and had somehow got turned right down on where I stood. I felt like I was showering on the sun. Someone playing silly buggers while I was out, getting over the side gate or the back wall by the garage—both pretty damn high—to do pointless damage. What if the light-bracket had been pulled out of true? Left-field expense for my house-mate and me (for sure our prof would reimburse but we couldn't know when) and my first instructor's pay of the new year wasn't due till the end of September. But the light laid off me then and, softening, crept slowly over the lawn to the back wall. Its pace made me feel like it was still and I was moving backwards, like I was down by the Detroit River while the walkway lamps glided past.

I've often thought about all that since: the gate opening, the near edge of the garden, the light going on, my tenant-fretting, the picture of lamp-posts on the move. So clear, the sequence, my emotions. Sometimes it feels as though nothing has been that clear since, as though nothing could be.

Carnival weirdness. That was my first thought. Like an elephant on a stool, its trainer poised with a whip to make it lift one leg, another, rise in the air, beg to the cupola-space of the big top. On the wall, a little way from the garage, puffed out at the shoulders and torso, gathered tight at the rump with legs tucked in, Tafler sat and didn't move a muscle. He didn't sway towards me or away, not even when he began fishing in a pocket—that same pocket in that same coat, pulling me back into the airport restaurant and, through a blizzard of years, back onto the Erkeley at the moment when he claimed the stopper in Bevvo's hand. But now the tramp's exertion was a trigger. From beside the garage, just beyond the spread of light, a hand reached for his free arm as if in fear he might fall. Like a conjurer's sausage-string-from-a-hat routine, a long-bodied bottle emerged from the pocket in which he'd groped and there was the wet *thuck* of uncorking. Tilting his head back in the light, his hat now brushed by the moon, the tramp drank his fill, biffing the cork down with the heel of his

148

hand. The cloth of the pocket bulged like a running wave as the bottle slid home.

More noise now but quieter, stealthier. By the garage a shadow flexed and twisted. Inch by inch, the owner of the steadying hand came into view, closing the distance from the tramp, settling beside his tucked-in legs. Head bowed, the revealed figure swung his legs out from the wall and biffed it with alternating heels. Or I imagine it was biffed. But sound had stopped and I was watching a silent film, like some casual footage of the seaside or a Bank-Holiday bandstand, with a kid letting his limbs go free, just happy to be...the feet stopped...maybe their owner knew the next word in my head. Alive. Now a sharp clinking, the bottle against something else in that cavernous pocket. The tramp hunched and began to cough, a real lung-scruncher. I guess. The sounds had gone off again. What blew through his fit was the night breeze only, the faint medley of engines from the roads beyond The Green. No matter: those tiny bursts of noise were all the pair needed to say. The boy turned towards the man and again his hand reached out, thin-wristed, holding the tramp's shoulder till the agony was gone.

This was no peevish concern, no don't-you-show-me-up-what-did-I-tell-you? This was affection. They'd come a long way since the one with the bottle lay oblivious under his tree that summer evening with the other in the hole just yards away. Did the other one come for Tafler at the police station, slide into the holding cell moments after the tramp had done what he felt he had to do—lead him gently out in the freshness of his death before all the rattling at the door, the bursting in, the swearing over inert flesh and tatters? The tramp now still, the other one turned and looked at me. *Sapience and Duty* was badged clearly on his breast but there was no shock flash like there had been by the airport washroom. I thought he might have pointed to the badge, as in some garish depiction of Jesus and his exposed heart. But he just held my gaze. Well, I say that. As at the airport and on the card, he had nothing to hold it with. I could picture the face, though, behind the blankness. His thatch straggled down, a lock or two brushing those sideburns caught in their eternal wispiness. Below the chin, the stripes of the familiar tie, the blazer and all the rest. But between thatch and chin there was a kind of glow where his face had been. That face had hissed, taunted, set his goons on me, rocked with the step of his feet, with his 'C'mon, c'mon' that bottle-neck evening. A face made for primal delight and I'd taken it away. Beside him, the tramp stared at me too, thumping his chest to coax more soundless phlegm.

Another clink from the tramp's deep pocket and this seemed to be a sign. Wiznuk took him gently by both shoulders, turning him round till the ruins of him faced the back lane. There was a low glug, the wine or whatever it was sloshing in the bottle, as Tafler dropped from sight. Pete Wiznuk sat on a tad longer, watching and not watching me, till very slowly he lowered his head once more. For a moment he reminded me of a confessor who had done all he could with a wordy, twisty non-penitent. A swing of the legs and he too was gone. I heard a last *thuck* of the cork. One for their road.

I ran to the back wall, got on the garbage can—which hadn't, in fact, been knocked over—and peered up and down the lane. Returning, I was blinded by the light at its usual strength. Getting beyond it, waiting till it shut off, I saw that its bracket was fine after all. Out of nowhere, the prof's cat came and rubbed my legs. I'd forgotten my brief theory about cats in the garden…and I'd forgotten to get any tins—Jim never remembered—so it would have to make do with dried food. I'd like to say I scooped it into my arms, cuddled it, grateful for anything that looked like love. But I let it scoot into the kitchen and station itself by its bowl while I braced myself for the empty house.

13

Will had to start that bit again. He remembered about the old guy like an elephant on a stool and the kid drumming his heels, something about the security light being ok after all and the cat wanting its food. And of course there was lots of Jon-ness. He went through it a second time, willing himself to get it clear, keeping out of his head that earlier piece of Jon-ness that had ambushed him, when the guy was debating how to give housemate Jim the fettled truth. Once

151

he'd re-read it, he sat still for a moment; then he let those particular words back in: *How do you tiptoe round absolutes? Honey, I'm afraid your dog's a bit missing.*

Annie's dog. He traced a finger along *braced myself for the empty house.* The answer to her prayers at eight years old, a yappy ball of wire, fox terrier or German pointer. Pointer, that was it. The whole family had trooped off to the breeder's to take delivery. A griffon dog, the breeder had called it and immediately Mark had gone off on some jag, half-blustery, half-scared, that it was a fantasy creature, part-eagle, part-lion, only the breeder had disguised it to get it off his hands. But hey, no problem...it would burst into its terrifying glory while sitting by the table at Sunday lunch or while Annie was fussing at it with chews or ribbons. Or maybe anytime, with a bit of encouragement.

Boy, there were edicts all round that dog. His sister would've made a far better cop than him. She was the main walker...and dad was allowed, of course, though you could tell from his look that he was humouring the apple of his eye, that he'd rather be seen dead than dragging that swatch of rag-rug along. Jayne and Louise were allowed on occasion, but never together and only if Annie wasn't in a sister-strop with either or both. She always accompanied the one she favoured, reasoning that, as twins, Jayne and Louise needed each other to make a full character and were only half in control on their own. (Poor girls. Louise was sweet as pie. Jayne had her savage moments but nothing to what Annie could dish up.) As for Mark and him, they were banned outright. That was partly Mark with his griffon-gryphon routine but mainly because 'you guys'd just hurt the poor dear, likely use him with your cruddy pals for a football.'

Will frowned. Yes, we stayed home that afternoon. Mark and me. The rest had gone off to one of Jayne's swimming galas. I wanted to go too but Mark said no way was he going and presented that look like a cat when you try to get it off a chair—claws out, cling on. And I was the older brother so I had to be the interim dad. Man, that was one duty I could have done without. The Lloydminster evening was bad enough even with the adults around. Or because they were around. Ah, he was one resourceful asshole.

Truth is, I never liked being in the house alone with Mark. Soon as the car engine died away his eyes would get that twinkle and you knew the word 'mischief' would pop up like dollar signs. We'd had some narrow escapes. Things put back or rearranged in the nick of time. Somewhere at the back of my mind, I was just waiting for the day when the two of us would find ourselves alone with Natosi. The Blackfoot word for 'sun', Annie said. Sometime during the long, long days when she was wearing mom and dad down, she'd already settled on that as the name, whatever dog she got.

Away went the car and out came the twinkle. I was reading a book, maybe even for school, but Mark's eyes seemed to flash right through the pages. When I looked up, he was tilting his head towards the basket that Annie had installed for Natosi in an alcove of the kitchen. Basket: the thing was a palace, all rugs and soft toys, on a platform that dad had rigged up to stop all her wheedling.

Hey, no, I said. Mark, leave it. More than 'no' had been issued to us before they all left, Annie doing her stormy face routine, lots of 'don't so much as think' and 'I'll know, buster, I'll just know.' She nearly insisted on staying home with us but, when it came to it, Natosi's well-being still didn't quite match her horror at having to hang out with her dreadful brothers. It was left to mom to repeat Annie's gist in her own gently warning way and to dad to glower at us as, sometime before, he'd glowered at Uncle Gary the Lloydminster scammer.

You'd understand it, or maybe you would, if our ages were the other way round. If Mark were big brother and I just bowed to his authority. As it was I knew, we all did, that he was his uncle's nephew, that his twinkle always had to go somewhere. So I partly indulged and partly limited damage. If anything looked fishy, I covered. Looking back I should have fixed him long ago, told him not to be a dork. Not waited till that afternoon.

'I'll take him,' I said, 'and he stays on the lead.' We lived on the edge of the city then, so it wasn't long before we were away from the streets and working along the border of one of old man Mathieson's fields. That was craziness in itself.

154

Old man Mathieson had a huge spread but always managed to be everywhere at once in that yellow half-ton of his. Such cuss-words as we knew we'd learnt from him.

'Ok,' I said, 'along to the ditch and back and that's it.'

'Sure,' said the twinkle. 'I only wanted us to get to take him for a walk.' Butter wouldn't melt.

Natosi pulled a bit to start with but then settled to the rhythm of my feet. Brother followed on, grabbing at wheat-stalks, probably hoping that a few pulls would mean ruin for old man Mathieson that year. The sun was bright, prompting some nonsense from Mark about the dog's name, how we were meant to bring him out, show one sun to the other: 'Destiny,' he shouted. He loved coming out with stuff like that, picked up from his sci-fi crap.

As I got near the ditch I thought how quiet it was. My footsteps, Natosi's rustle but no careless tromping behind. A minute later I was on the ground with the lead loose in my hand. When I got to my feet I saw brother's head and shoulders opening a distant swathe in the wheat, heard his cry:

'C'mon, Natosi! C'mon, you gryphon! Take to the sky! Annie in one talon, Mathieson in the other! Do what you're born to do!'

Running after him, I thought I saw another swathe, a smaller one, feinting and circling. For sure I heard whines of bewilderment and fear, till a revving engine drowned them out and there was old man Mathieson's half-ton coming smartly along from the far end of the ditch. Staring full at me, he pulled up, cut off the engine. Back lunged Mark, nearly knocking me down again as he yelled 'We're out of here' and sped past. For a moment I thought, no, no, I'm going to walk along to meet the half-ton, explain and apologise, tell old man Mathieson that somewhere in his sea of wheat a dog was lost, crazy scared. The hell with that, said my feet.

Hours later everyone was in the kitchen and Mark was giving it the full aggrieved:

'What you need, Annette, is a decent lead, that's what you need. Will and me, we were doing you a favour. The hook just snapped like a twig.'

'You jerks! I knew I should've stayed back.'

'Well thanks for the gratitude, sis. All you guys out today, when was poor Natosi gonna get his exercise?'

'So where's the lead, Mark?'

'Oh, mom, who knows? Old man Mathieson, he was coming for us fast.'

'And what have we told you about going onto his land? You know what he's like.'

'It's science,' Mark pushed on, 'it's been proved. Sidewalks squish up a dog's paws. They need earth.'

'Makes sense.'

'You shut your mouth, Jayne Apland!'

'Annette!'

'Ok, Annie, Jaynie, everyone, enough.' Dad was weary-loud—maybe ready to indulge Jayne on any other occasion, what with her swimming

156

gala win and all, but not inclined to have her erupting now when his eldest daughter was fit to be tied. 'Well…if he's scared he won't stop crying and Joe Mathieson will hear him and bring him back. That's if the name-tag didn't come off with the hook'—and here he levelled an old-fashioned look at my mouthy brother. Then, of course, the slow turn of his head my way:

'And you, mister? What have you to say?' Some big brother you are, is what the words said.

'I'm real sorry, Annie. It was stupid. We were just'—all I could fall back on right then was Mark's at-the-ready bullshit—'trying to do a favour. Give him his exercise.' Which I had been, even as I knew that Mark and exercise, his own or any other beast's, were most times strangers.

I walked out of the kitchen then, leaving Annie to be consoled by mom and Louise, who was in Annie's good books at the time; leaving dad to gaze into space, maybe, and think, kids, who'd have 'em? Or, when's that William going to pull up those socks? Jayne skipped past me on the stairs, giggling low, swinging her medal. Moments later, Mark came into our room.

'Some fun, huh, big man?' he said. I gave him dad's slow look at me and now it was his turn to hit the floor, my baseball bat like a crowbar across his neck.

'This is the last secret I keep,' I told his cherry-red face. 'I'm sick of it. You frig about in future, pal, you don't get cover from me. In fact, I don't want to know. In double-fact, you don't frig about.'

For the first time ever he looked petrified. The Lloydminster evening came back into my head, all his sass and dumb doings. I still had my hand round the bat neck. I nearly didn't sling it aside.

Early that evening there was a phone call and a while later old man Mathieson's half-ton pulled up outside our house. Dad opened the door and Annie gave a wail of shock when she saw Natosi hobble in. He'd done himself some mischief out there in the wheat. 'Oh, that's nothing, honey, that's nothing,' said mom before she'd really seen him—getting a quick barrier up as she always did when chaos was brewing.

Old man Mathieson stood on the doorstep like a shaft of granite.

'Evening, Joe,' said dad. 'I believe you have business with my sons.' He summoned me from the lounge and Mark from our room, where he'd been holed up since I gave him that overdue view of the future. Did Joe want to come in? They could have the lounge. Thanking dad, old man Mathieson shook his head.

So dad stepped aside, I went out and, to be fair, old man Mathieson took the hand I offered. Soon came a shuffle down the stairs like some invalid walking for the first time in an age.

'Thanks for bringing him, Joe,' I heard dad say before the front door closed on Mark and me.

Mindful of womenfolk within, old man Mathieson kept his profanities short and low. Mainly he was concerned for the dog. Stuck in a huge field like that, who knows what else might have happened to it apart from whatever it was that hurt its leg? Blubbing like a kid, it was, when he finally found it. Just as well he was there, wouldn't we say? Pet like that, young, where's its homing instinct? It might have set off away from the city, and then me and my brother would have been royally screwed. Or one of his dogs might have found it—'They ain't fuckin' poodles, my three'—and that would have dragged the farmer into it further than he was.

I didn't hang my head but I made sure Mark hung his. Again I repeated the baloney about the exercise, the snapped lead, and apologised for the trespass.

'Well, all right.' The man was sermonised out, content. 'Last time on my spread, boys, you hear? Or I might be minded to shoot something 'sides the crows.'

Mark fled back upstairs. I went into the lounge, where dad was waiting with a cocked eyebrow.

'It's ok,' I said.

'Better had be, William.'

And luckily, it was ok in the kitchen, too, where mom was telling Annie and Louise to hold the poor thing still and, after it gave a gut-wrenching yelp, said, 'There, it's out. Louise, first aid box, please, and'—she raised her voice—'the boys can donate next month's odd-job money for the vet's bill.'

'Yayyy.' Annie's voice carried clear throughout the house. Mark must have heard it. If he was smart, he also heard that he owed me big time.

'Yayyy, indeed,' murmured dad. 'I'm not asking you to stand guard, William, but'—he pointed to the ceiling—'don't be making like you're the kid.'

For a week or so I kept the lead at the back of our wardrobe until, starting to feel like we had a dead body in there, I took it with me on a trip downtown and binned it.

Natosi grew old without another scratch on him.

*

Will sipped slowly. Of course that wasn't the end of Mark as Mark. For sure he didn't quit but there was never anything as blatantly out there after Annie's dog. And anyway, dad quietly doubled his watch on his younger son. But Mark found subtlety as the years went on. Or maybe he got to understand that subtlety mattered to others, manners and the done thing and all that, and he exploited gaps and misinterpretations. Where once he'd cry 'You gonna make me, big man?' or 'Sis, don't act even dumber than you look', now he'd creep up and do the full sidelong thing: *Aw, now they feel bad. Aw, I know you didn't mean it.* And his favourite, *You got that wrong.* Sometimes he'd whisper; sometimes, like an acoustics whiz, he just knew how to level his voice so no-one else would hear. He kept the swoony thing going, a trace of the old goading kiddy-speak. Maybe that was just a logical progression, a bigger-league version of his performance that Lloydminster evening.

But it wasn't only that. He got into refinements: the whispers and acoustic-tricks went public when required. He was the one holding the whatever-it-was—car-key, document, instruction—after you'd stumbled back empty-handed and baffled, just knowing you'd organised things right: 'Boy, I saved your bacon' or some such would ring out and there he'd be, holding the thing aloft, invisibly conducting the sighs and headshakes around him at your scattiness. Did Mark hide the car-key or whatever it was, even occasionally, to present himself as saviour of the hour? Will was sure of it and it saddened him because it showed a core sneakiness which, despite all, he'd hoped wasn't in his brother's make-up. Sure, sometimes he'd challenged Mark about it, only to get the kind of laugh that the Cheshire cat would give out if it could, or a long, wrung-out explanation...

...oh, yes, all the explanations over the years about why Mark hadn't, why it wasn't, how it could not have been him. If his younger self from that awful afternoon could have heard him, he'd have been truly impressed at what his crap about Natosi's lead and dogs' paws had morphed into. Louise, Will thought it was, once said that if you could electrify Mark's explanations, the entire province could go off-grid for a month:

'Those politicos in Ottawa had better watch out for you, Mark,' mom had said more than once and everyone laughed, except dad, who just

161

tightened his lips like he had a smile to offer but only if anyone looked his way.

And except Will himself, who thought again of his baseball bat. And what about how Mark had gone off-grid? Like telling precisely nobody it was Antigonish now, not Fredericton? And man, what he'd put Holly through. What the hell had the guy been thinking of? More, what had he himself been thinking of, trying to play fixer?

'She was lonely,' came that plaintive telephone bleat once again. She was also married to Mark's on-the-road boss. And then, of course, the how-long-you-got explanation, topped off with 'Anyway, Willie, what makes you the angel of angels? Don't you get bored with Mags?'

'Come on, Mark, your kids are only—'

'Aw, big man, you want come scoop 'em up so bad daddy don't infect 'em?' Then the swerve: 'Holly's never liked you, you know that? She told me.'

'Right, Mark, that would have been in the motel room when she was visiting with you and Lynn Ewings.'

'Wow, jokester-boy! I'm rolling on the floor here. Gonna come and try to be dad again? Whup me good like you always didn't?'

Like I most certainly did, thought Will now, and he pictured again the baseball bat at Mark's neck. But in this version he didn't sling it aside. Roars became gargles, thumps and clutches slackened, and as he pressed down their childhood room dissolved and he could smell the rankness of the pond, hear Tafler's thick voice at

162

its lullaby of Wallings and midges, the cries of a faraway fight nearly done.

He was on his feet, leaning against the pool-table, hearing the creak of the leg that had suffered from when the kids went a-sailing upon the Spanish Main. That smoking-room guy he'd imagined himself to be at the start of the tale, he was drifting even further away. He found it harder to keep hold of him. What would the guy have said at this point in the tale? Will tried to hear the words as if spoken by his mimic father-in-law, ripe and round: 'Well thankfully, the closest I ever came to this Parry chap's doings was when my brat of a brother played silly arse with our sister's dog. Funny old thing, it was. Four-legged mop.' And he would give—no, deliver himself of, that's how they did it in those old novels—a comfortable sigh, the kind that said 'This is splendid' and 'Anyway, do carry on with your tale, old bean.'

But Will's shoulders just sagged and his breath came in a hiss. Yes, he'd kept a long, long secret too. But it was just a dog. And nothing had happened. So was he a prophet, then, did he know it would go that way? From the moment he'd tried to push Mark back in his place—for the millionth time—by saying he alone would walk Natosi, wasn't he a sort of Jonathan Parry? He thought of himself and Mark running from the half-ton, the old man getting set to bawl them out, his riot act when he came by the house. He pictured another ending. Forgotten, Natosi breaks out of his wild circles and runs blind, away from habitation, smack into Mathieson's three dogs—into worse. Yes, worse, say it turned out that way. No phone call, no mad farmer on the doorstep, everyone in the kitchen later than really happened, maybe into the night, Annie like a banshee, dad putting off his gentlemanly ways, hauling him and Mark outside and cussing, cussing hard, like what Mathieson came out with was just cuteness. Would he have spilled the beans to the family then about what happened? Or days later, when there was a knock on the door and a perfect stranger was asking for dad and looking real awkward and saying sorry a lot? His tag was still on, sir. He's in the back of the truck. What's left of him. Real sorry.

But it was just a dog. But it was just the same. No harm done. But harm was on the loose with the dog till chance stepped in. Will stood up straight. I should have fixed you long ago, Mark Apland.

He had to speed away from where he was. Back in his chair, he got pen and paper again and wrote: *This folder, all hooey. Parry made it up. A cruddy life, natural depressive, might have topped himself anyway but wanted to count for something even just in words.* He stretched, flexed his shoulders, added *Yes!* How did his words make him feel? No, forget emotions, just do the job. Work backwards from when they'd found Parry in his apartment. Who was he really? His ID and all that had been dealt with: no blip in the system apparently, but their system wasn't the Almighty. Was there something about him

164

that no-one had picked up? Nationality. Ok, English and he had his 'landed' papers. Why hadn't he gone for dual citizenship or naturalisation? He obviously never got round to it. But why not? This was his paradise country and England was the pits. Wouldn't it have sealed the deal on all he'd said about reinventing himself, the new life that belonged to him alone, not to his mom or his awful family?

Will tried to coax back the image of the smoking-room guy, chase off his darker memories of his brother. He'd avoided the word so far but *Fantasist!* he wrote now. In his mind, Jonathan Parry took shape as one of those old-style remittance men. He has siblings, plenty of them, and all doing just fine in the mother country; but his folks are tearing their hair out. He doesn't or won't fit. There's a position in the family business: he blows it. There's something an acquaintance of his dad's gets him in on: he doesn't even show up. What do they do?

Dispatch him. Maybe they know someone over here, maybe it's family. One of his folks...Will flicked back to the start of the folder...yes, one of them said about being in Winnipeg after the war and wishing he'd stayed. Say the truth was that one of them was here all along. Sweet salvation for ma and pa, a foot in the door right there for the useless son. But it doesn't work out: the Winnipeg door shuts and whichever relative shuts it can't believe their relief. So Parry has to hit for himself. He can't go back and he can't survive on money sent from home. Or maybe he could but home warns him the transfers will soon dry up. So…a bunch of crap jobs, one after the other. Maybe he even does some roving farm-work like he said he was set to do if the cops came over the water. Yes, right, like a teen blow-in could do that. Ah, but he isn't a teen, this remittance-Jonathan, he's all grown up and everyone's washed their hands of him.

But with all of that, he's not a dumbo— dammit, look how he writes. And yes, the university owned up to his being a prof. So somewhere in the scramble, with the transfers from home ended and who knows what-all future ahead, he managed to study. And fair play, he found his niche and all he wanted. What was that he said? Will leafed through the pages till he found *with a Master's lined up to protect me a bit longer from the cold winds of the world.* Yes: he just wanted a hole his size. Will pictured the station on any particularly lively Friday night. The drunks. The hookers. The pushers, the crazy racers. Ninety-nine percent of them knew damn fine where they fitted and couldn't care less that it wasn't where society thought it should be. But every now and then you'd see it, on a blotchy face, behind the hard make-up or below the skewwhiff bandana. That look, saying, what is all this? I shouldn't be here. Not in the city or on the planet. I bailed out too soon from the spacecraft. I should be in paradise. Can't describe paradise but I'd know if I was there.

They were often the quietest ones—even weirdly grateful, like the busting and bringing in were the first things that made any sense. Terry M had a nose for them, could pick them out from the biggest melee. Almost shivering there, like the cold winds of the world were at them good. For sure he'd pick this Jonathan out if he was there because…because what? Some grifter had landed him in the shit. What else?

Will remembered what he'd thought when he opened the folder, how he'd appreciated the care the guy was taking with his great long last words…and later, when he could not believe that anyone would spend the end of their life cooking stuff up. Fooled you once, Apland, he said to himself: shame on you. Looks like I can be the smoking-room guy after all with his port-and-stogie contentment. Ok, Jonathan, if that's who you turn out to be: you got to be a prof, way to go, but—Will smiled at a scrap of court-speak—all the foregoing is null and void.

But his thoughts slipped through a crack, then through another. He was thinking about the new insulation in the garage, courtesy of Terry M's buddy: how glad he was it worked a treat, how a little later he wasn't so sure it was fine. Terry M. How he'd behaved in this guy's apartment. Yes, Smeets's theatrics had been justified. There was a vibe there, he'd said, and Will had felt it and no-nonsense Terry hadn't disagreed. Ok, Terry had done the whole man-you're-full-of-it routine when Smeets had gone on about the smell. Handed down from a time before our time, was how Smeets had put it. 'Lookit,' Terry had said, 'the guy just let the laundry stack up.' But it was Smeets's flight of fancy that bugged him. He didn't deny there was weirdness in the air. Will remembered how Smeets had looked when they arranged the patrol-swap for today. What he'd felt still lingered in his eyes, clouding their usual let's-go-guys sharpness. For all his grand-standing, Smeets knew not to push it way too far. If he did, well, he'd have no patrol-buddy, wouldn't be any use as a cop. And Terry M, yes, he rated Smeets, even if he did so through comically clenched teeth, even though he said stuff like, 'Give it a rest, Asimov' or 'Shit, out with the crystal ball.' If he didn't rate Smeets, would he have aided and abetted their Abbott and Costello shtick at the scene of so many crimes? But Terry's feet never left the ground. He could read anyone and anything like a book—not just the lost aliens among the Friday night crowd at the station—but for sure he wasn't one of life's spooky-vibe hunters. Right now he was out trick-or-treating with his own kids, except that he wasn't. Will knew he'd be standing back down each yard path as his kids scared the fake-bejesus out of each householder and came away with palms full of candy for their pains. Hallowe'en, Terry maintained, was money-making bull. If his kids said, dad, let's skip it this year, he wouldn't argue. But in that apartment, he'd felt the weirdness too.

Hooey. *This is all hooey.* Will read through what he'd written. The way Terry M was trumped everything he'd just confected. A smell handed down from a time before our time, Smeets had said. Setting the paper aside, Will wrinkled his nose. Like slow-rise water it was coming back…but maybe just in his nose. He recalled the pantomime Jonathan had watched from his prof's lawn, the bottle produced, swigged and put away, the godawful coat and hat, the blazer. The decaying clothes. He found his place in the folder again, again read *But I let it scoot into the kitchen and station itself by its bowl while I braced myself for the empty house.* 'Sorry about that, Jonathan,' he said to the neat lines. 'Disbelief goes with the job. I'll take your word.' The smoking-room guy began to fade. Mark did his swoony tilt routine. Will didn't care. Now he knew and now he went on.

14

Ornithologists do it. Naturalists in general. Train-spotters. Neatly-ruled little books with dates in the left column, then descriptions of what they see. The bird-watchers and naturalists use Latin. And, I should think, there's other stuff about sightings: when usual, when last, when likely again. If something unexpected turns up, that's a carnival, that's what they're in it for.

That's all I know about birders and naturalists. I was never interested and anyway, where I grew up in England wasn't much interested in nature, though it was a draw for any starling that needed fresh soot. But I remember the train-spotters, especially when everything went diesel round our way. It can't have been too long after that when, one Saturday, Bevvo, Gordy and I took the train from Coseley Deepfields to Birmingham. No more chuff-chuff or smoke through the windows. We pretended we were on some hover-glider out of Buck Rogers or Dan Dare. But at Coseley and at each station down the line—Tipton, Dudley Port, Smethwick—blokes in car coats and flat caps were massed at the far end of the platform, notebooks and pens at the ready, squinting at incoming engines. I can picture the look on their faces, a baffled fascination, joy and sadness mixed, as though they didn't know whether to praise this new stock more than mourn the old chuffers or the other way round. Bevvo and Gordy got a bet going: ten Park Drives for whoever saw a spotter blubbing first. I didn't join in...thought they were being rotten. That was largely because, back home, we'd just suffered a visit from Nicky and the appalling Craig and a couple more of my treasured toys had gone west. If some of the spotters were upset because something much-loved had gone from the world, I could understand that.

That old memory decided me—plus, of course, the need to track what they were up to...the toper, the faceless thatch. I bought one of those black-and-red account books and stayed faithful to it: the dates, where I was when they appeared, details (brief for sanity's sake) about what they did and, in the right-hand column, how long or short it had been since the last time. I read

170

through it again before starting to write this, to get back as fully as I could the course of their game. Actually, I thought of breaking off round here and leaving my spotter's book to tell the rest of the tale. But that might have implied that I hadn't budgeted my time and it had run out on me. As it soon will. But at least I've kept enough back to finish this.

Their game. At the time I bought my spotter's book I tried to get a fix on it as I'd tried with the airport, the card, the shadows on Laurie's wall. Were they playing it or was it playing them? Was something beyond what I'd done forcing them to show me their unquietness and wouldn't they have to go on showing it till...well, till they didn't? Getting to the heart of that, I thought, would give me some leverage, like understanding why a bully bullies. Such attempts made for more trips round the houses. As far as I could, I kept them short. I knew I'd have to steel myself for them. At other times I tried dispassion, seeing the pair as tortured souls who'd erred before ever I did anything and into whose line of haunting I'd unwittingly stepped. That made for brief sympathy with them but really it was the same kind of noodling I'd indulged in about their first interventions, and it soon sputtered out.

One thing, though, was for sure—here I was, alive, healthy but as unquiet in my way as they were in theirs. Transcendent equality. You've got to love it. And anyway, I came to realise that if they were in control and if their game could be squashed into a couple of hours, any sports manager would pay top dollar for the plan.

The spotter's book got off to a slow start. I wrote down what I remembered of that evening in the back garden since that was the first time they truly performed for me. After that, there were fleeting glimpses at the very edge of my sight and once I thought I saw Wiznuk's thatch among school-wear mannequins in the Army and Navy store. I nearly laughed but checked myself; any laughter might have to be paid for.

After that they backed off—long enough, anyway, to allow me to start the new academic year and weather wobbles of another kind. Our prof came back, cracking wise about expecting to find the fish or cat kaput, and Jim and I had to find somewhere else. We'd been sort of looking around and should have tried harder; but Jim had been happily bouncing about in his Jim-like way and I'd obviously had other things on my mind. I guess that, after our charmed year in the prof's house, we thought we'd just fall into something: another house all to ourselves or a two-bed apartment, fully serviced, spick and span, five minutes from campus, non-existent.

As it was, everything good to just-about-tolerable had been taken and we had to split up. His bedsit was a bit less disgraceful than mine but we agreed that both housed insects yet to be classified. He fared better than me, as I knew he would: the old irresistibility meant that, for every night he had to spend among his scuttling livestock, he spent two or three in more convivial surroundings—clean, nicely scented, an assortment of teddies and Tiggers gracing the pillows like Laurie had. Still, we kept the faith and met when we could at the Sidebar Motel (where, we were pleased to see, Arundats was still going strong with its fortnightly celebration of Honours-year hassles and triumphs). I loved those meets and not just because it was Jim and they got me away from the books and the latest discovery of mould in my kitchenette. Early fall was just starting to burnish and release the leaves and the walk to and from the Sidebar was almost as enchanting as my walks from campus to the prof's house had been, before the night of the commotion anyway. Passing days brought leaves more thickly underfoot, a perfect hiding place for sounds other than my own feet, stalking sounds, rustles before ambush. But no—they still lay low, tramp and rat. Maybe they figured that my rubby-dub bedsit was punishment enough on their behalf. Anyway, my time in that place was good training for later.

Suddenly there was a miracle. One of the Art History profs had just moved to Lakeshore, out of the city, but kept his old house on for rental. A block or two over from where we'd been last year, it was terrific: corner turret, porch straight out of a Rockwell painting. At a party there one time, a profs and grads do, he'd given a bunch of us the tour. It was magic inside, too.

But currently it was tenanted by folks who were going for gold in the yahoo stakes. Neighbour-complaints to the police, it seemed, tripled in one week alone. Their landlord had to make a move. Within an hour of the eviction, Jim and I were in his office. Why—why, sure. You guys...model renters, I hear. Thing is, though, it'd pinch the wallet for just the two of you. I'm not too old I can't remember when I was where you are now. Though if you want to advertise for a third and tough it out in the meantime...

Paul Farwell was a Drama with English grad. He was an Arundats veteran, too, which was where I'd introduced him to Jim, though I'd got to know him when I was helping with set design for a couple of Honours-year productions he was in (for which, I have to say, the cast and director's gratitude was a world away from Mum's watery thanks for my efforts at her schools). I'd been to his apartment a couple of times. It was a beauty, a stone's throw from the Odette Business School, still fairly shiny and new itself. His landlord was some kind of entrepreneur, on the move all over the world but one step ahead of the law wherever he landed. Paul had the apartment till the following August, he thought, but something had started to crumble in Cape Town or Paraguay or somewhere and suddenly there was a phone call from the rackety owner: awful sorry but could Paul be out in a fortnight? His immediate alternative was playing house uneasily with an on-off girl-friend ('I'll take her off his hands,' Jim had grinned one Sidebar evening, to which I'd replied that that would hardly solve the problem of where Paul should lay his head in peace). After Jim and I had clinched the deal with the Art

History prof, I found Paul in the Drama department, grimly trying to work his way into the character of Clov for what must have been proposed as an ironic Christmas production of Beckett's *Endgame*. Paul always looked worried, his eyes larger than they needed to be, as though he feared or had just heard bad news. Now they widened so much I thought his face would split. Would he like to join us? Would he ever! When? When was as soon as. Jim and I bade farewell to our bug heavens and Paul tried his landlord's last-known number. (And fair play, he received an inconvenience cheque a few weeks later and it didn't even bounce.) On the evidence of his old apartment, Paul was more house-proud than either of us. He was in for sure.

And still in were the Impressionists. At the start of that second year, I had what I can truly call a blast teaching them to my undergrad class. Slides, blown-up prints, I deployed the works. But it paid off: Monet and the rest kind of taught themselves and that set things up for a comfortable roll through all the other topics. Forever I'd associate them with the hour of dusk—precious in memory—before I reached a hand for that leaf on The Green, heard the commotion from over the street. I'd long realised, of course, that the footsteps in the Design wing that evening, the swinging doors, had nothing to do with janitor Ted. But I was still looking for some totem, some keepsake from the time when, as though I were all of thirteen again, I confected my singular notion about Cadman,

Bell or whoever, the airport, the card. So I ditched the topic I'd had in mind for my dissertation—Mondrian and the imperatives of the line, all a bit dour—and ducked down, so to speak, level with Monet's fields and Pissarro's avenues.

'Bit cautious, Jonathan,' said Tony North, who'd observed my teaching the previous year and was now to be my dissertation supervisor. 'I had you figured as an adventurer.' I went away, did some thinking and added Mary Cassatt, the Impressionists' Pennsylvanian contemporary. That expanded things, showed what an impact they'd made. But who didn't know that? The inquiry needed some turbulence. After more thinking on long downtown rambles, I introduced Cassatt's notorious co-student, Thomas Eakins.

'Ah,' said my supervisor, 'Eakins. The Anti-Impressionist. Now this could go somewhere.' As best I could, I made sure it did.

I guess I'm heaping up all this good stuff here as a stay against confusion. Autumn was wearing on, the nights were shortening. For a while now I'd been looking over my shoulder. Now I started to look left, right and dead ahead. A long straight street, and there were plenty, a curving avenue at twilight—who knew when their perspectives would show the stout tippler and the rat? I think I'd absorbed the spirit of that dreadful bedsit. That had given me grief in their name and now, edgy and watchful, I'd taken the grief over. I sensed that, the more my fortunes rose in the world to which I belonged, the more revenge they'd store up. You could almost say that, simply by being withheld, revenge had begun.

St Michael's Day, Michaelmas, is the twenty-ninth of September. I read somewhere that anyone called Michael was entitled on that day to a mad half-hour. As the weeks went by, and when I wasn't stuck into teaching or study, I gave in to the occasional Michael burst—much to Paul's baffled amusement and Jim's deeper concern.

Paul was a spot-on mimic: part of his training, maybe. Something would catch his ear and he'd savour it at random, anywhere, like an epicure of the spoken word. One time the tv was on as he was getting ready to go out: some dreary hagiography about the Royals. Footage of a speech by Edward Vlll included a reference to his mother, Mary of Teck; so 'Mai matha…the Quin Matha' echoed ebulliently round the house and out through the front door, Paul as besotted by the gap between the words as by the words themselves. He became the abdicating King again, a day or so later, by the freezer section of our local supermarket. That same night, Name-Badge Nancy, our favourite assistant at Centennial Sub 'n' Fixins, found herself briefly ennobled as the Quin Matha as she made change from our order.

Perhaps inevitably, Paul tried to chivvy me out of my dark half-hours in the same way. Fair do's, he never ascribed them to anything like artistic temperament; I never had one. His routines would take me back in time to the days before Dad started poring over maps of the world, narrowing his attentions to Canada and calling Mum to his side. By now, of course, my Black Country accent had been overlaid with a warmer, easier music; but the ground-tone was still detectable and he graced it with that long-unheard local patois:

'I ay gorra clew wot's up with aer Jonno but 'e ay roight up theer'—a tap of his head—"e ay roight in all this werld.' Or 'They shud'a brung back that Nash'nal Sairvice, mate, sort this one owt no messin', 'stead on all them books un' dairty pitchas.'

It could have been Bevvo or Gordy messing about before my fall from grace. It could have been me, tickled all over again by some paper-seller's bark outside Bilston Market or a crowd of yobs dispersing far from me through the main gate of Hickman Park. I can't say that his efforts hurried my moods off any quicker; but they guaranteed that warmth awaited me once I perked up. True, it was the warmth of lost innocence so it was transient and anyway illusory. But it had the same colours as Monet at his most reflective, and that got me back into my daily life.

Paul's routines amused Jim no end but he didn't pursue that mood when we were alone:

'Come on, Dr Jon, what is it?' he asked one time. 'Bad news from home?'

He spoke truer than he knew. When he pressed that question, I remembered my brief

178

resolve to tell him all and how my round-the-houses theorising had changed my mind. Slowly I shook my head but, of a sudden, it felt as though the words of confession were shaking themselves into place, ordered and ready. I looked at Jim with my mouth open as though I were one of those cartoon characters who overshoot the edge of a cliff, pedal their feet for a second and then look gormlessly to camera before, chased by speed-lines, they drop like a stone. Everything was about to change. Never mind a shadow like Jeff Cordingley proffering not-half-bad coffee while the business of the station went on around the interview room. Here was the only proper friend I had, would ever have. I opened my mouth, at which Jim anticipated:

'You still lonely, man?'

For a moment longer I quivered at the point of telling all, surrendering the world I knew. Then I sighed and, as so often before, sheltered in someone else's assumptions. My nod was as brisk as my headshake wasn't:

'Lookit, Jonathan, you might have heard anyways but Laurie's been transferred. Going to manage the Credit Union at Thunder Bay. I guess it makes sense…a sight nearer Kenora than she was here.' He bowed his head a little, but I heard what he rushed out then: the house near Malden Park up for sale, Ray joining her by Christmas.

'So that's that, cut and dried,' he continued.

'Well, I hadn't really thought about her.'

Jim cocked his head: 'You want to see a good old PEI tell-it-to-the birds look?' One eye nearly closed, the other was fierce as fire. 'I've said it before, man. You gotta move on and now there's no choice. Listen'—he beckoned my face to his as though we were conspiring in the Sidebar—'Now, look, just a suggestion and you can tell me to screw off. But I've seen how she looks at you....'

I went out for three weeks with Nancy Boudreau. Not once did I forget and call her Name-Badge Nancy. Like Laurie, she had nothing to do with college life, but unlike her she'd had nothing to do with studies. She could have done, she told me; she was valedictorian for her graduation year back in Mount Uniacke, Nova Scotia. But it seemed that her family were full-on achievers: older brothers and sisters who became variously a biochemist, a photo-journalist in Quebec, a person of consequence at the UN and an advisor to the federal government. Come her turn, as she put it, 'I just wanted out. Don't get me wrong, I love them and all, and maybe I'll do something. Sometime. But I just needed to do some thinking.' She grinned: 'I'm still at it.'

She was coy where Laurie was comfortable, occasionally diffident and old-fashioned: a lights-out-for-love girl. But Centennial Sub 'n' Fixins was a hoot, she said. Just for the heck of it she kept a little book in which she marked down all the marriage proposals she'd had, all the offers of a wild weekend:

180

"Cept from you.' She pursed her lips in a schoolmarm way, then twinkled, nudged me. 'What is wrong with you?'

At that moment, probably, I was thinking of my own notebook: unused for a while but that surely wouldn't last. As for what I'd nearly said to Jim but not…if the tramp and the rat had their own notebook, I'm sure that my latest failure of nerve was smartly marked down.

It could have happened. I'm convinced I'd have let it and damn the torpedoes: Name-Badge Nancy and her funny-voiced beau—'2 gevva 4 Evva', as a bit of English graffiti used to say. Her whole family would love me, she said, in a way that convinced me there'd be no francophone equivalent of Laurie's Uncle Gunther carping about *l'Albion perfide.* One Friday near the end of November, however, she was suddenly not there behind the counter when I went to collect her. Al, the manager, motioned me through to the back:

'All happened so damn fast,' he said. 'Phone call here after she arrived. Her mom and dad were just after leaving Halifax, some fucking clown on the 101…ten cars, twelve maybe, made it onto the CBC news.' He put a hand on my arm. 'Mr and Mrs Boudreau, they're hanging in there but…shit, I've got her home address and phone someplace.' He looked round his small bomb-hit office, then through the door: a late surge was thronging the counter. 'Look, Jon, can you call by tomorrow? If I got them…ok?'

181

If he did have them, he never found them. I scoured the papers from the Halifax *Chronicle Herald* on out. All that CBC showed afterwards was a clip of a conference with a Nova Scotia police chief, in which he spoke of boy racers, the fatal mix of alcohol and crazily souped-up cars: 'You treat 101 with respect,' he concluded. One time I was passing by Centennial Sub when Al spotted me and called me in:

'This isn't the home phone,' he said. 'Some contact for one of her brothers, I think.'

The number was no longer in service. Nancy never returned.

*

Will traced the elegantly-looped writing on the whiskey bottle, smiled at the word below the name. 'Classic.' Everything was classic these days. Didn't need a thing to exist five minutes and you'd think, the way they ballyhoo'd it, that it got put together by Adam and Eve. His mind drifted off to a mix of straplines from tv ads for drink: *Nothing feels like it...nothing tastes like it...when good friends get together...any time any place anywhere.* What was that other ad...that crazy thing? Oh, man, man, his father-in-law had it, must've been on a film from way back, a bootleg in his Brit movie collection—part of how he got so good at taking off Peter Sellers and Kenneth Williams and all. What was it? Stout? *Beer at home means*—some true-blue English name. Yeah...yeah, *that's the beer, lots of cheer*.... From way back. Would have been on English tv, Will guessed, round the time the Parry family were getting ready to up sticks over there. He imagined it blaring out, cheesy and ignored, the evening Jonathan left the house to meet Bevvo and Gordy at the Erkeley. Just think if he'd been detained, if Pa Parry had said, no way are you meeting them, we need you to stay in and look through this or that form about your schooling to date, or his Ma had started in about the clothes and stuff he'd have to leave behind. Will tilted the bottle, smiled at the easy bouquet that always seemed to go straight to the top of his nose. He turned his head slightly. Was that other smell still around? No? He chuckled. Maybe Tafler and Wiznuk had managed some quick freshening-up in whatever passed for their hereafter. Turning back, he caught again the picture of himself as the smoking-room guy. He was still fading—just eyes and a hairline, really, behind the smoke from his cigar. He could have been tiptoeing backwards, as you might if you'd been running hell for leather and suddenly found yourself at the edge of a cliff, like Jonathan said he'd felt when he almost spilled the beans to Jim. But Jonathan had gone off the edge and was set to fall, except that, at the last second, he'd found his faith in silence again and got himself yanked back. Right beside the smoking-room guy, Will now saw, was himself as himself: cop, dad and other half, fat-chewer, Balzers-negotiator, drinker of this whiskey right now, nice and warm in his hand but about to sustain hurt, as Uncle

183

Gary fondly described the act of boozing. Will watched the two figures, smoker-guy and cop, reversing into the dark. Setting down the glass, he reached out and gave the air a punch. Who for? He imagined thuds and groans, pictured Mark in a heap beside the gammy leg of the pool table, the tramp and the rat going tits-up off that back garden fence. Tightening his lips at Jonathan's latest loss and the fear growing behind it, he resumed.

*

Mrs Butler, Jim and Paul were the only family I knew. I don't know where else to put that so I'll say it now. Maybe, though, it belongs right here: another token, another leaf to touch on The Green, another Monet field at a suggestive hour of day.

At the beginning of December, about a week after I'd tried the number for Nancy's brother, they started up again. It was rather more, now, than small commotions in the corner of my eye. The one's badge would flash between evergreens as it had done at Toronto airport. Sun or gloom, the other's invisible waddle would now and then cast a dark shadow—recovered, you might say, from Laurie's wall—as I walked along. I'd hear laborious wheezes and what sounded like *nn-gah* as he kept pace.

Mainly it was a time of sounds. *Johnny, Johnny* returned upon the air, edging smoky breezes. Added were *Laurie, Laurie* and *We've seen Nancy's folks, Johnny, they joined us for tea,* followed by a wet giggle. Bottles clinked, were uncorked and corked: *Mister Tafler uses Bevvo's stopper,* said the rat, *did you know that, Johnny?* Maybe it was my imagination but Tafler did seem to try and mute the sounds, like a souse in an audience who just knows he won't hold out to the interval. But how do you restrain bottles and corks? In my last lecture before the Christmas break, however, he got serious. The only peace I found was when I clicked up each new slide about Jack Nichols, Goodridge Roberts and Canadian Art of World War Two. The bottle clinked and sloshed in the usual way but then its agitations grew louder, louder, till I was sure he'd decant the lot into my ear. Smelling of all the dead winters between the Erkeley and now, the bottle brushed the side of my head, back and forth, slow, while his wheezy *nn-gah* burst out like *Boo!* Trying to twist clear, I found myself swaying from foot to foot as Wiznuk had that Erkeley evening.

'Festive season started already, huh, sir?' I recognized the voice of the class clown, a kindly soul but no way marked for glory in Fine Arts. Female giggles trailed his question.

'Something like that,' I said in a slur. I think I intended to sound that way, humour the moment. I ducked out on the pretext of hunting an extra slide or two. The sloshes and clinks and *nn-gahs* pursued me. I felt a last brush of the bottle; then, disruption complete, all subsided. In one of the side-rooms I willed the clock forward but it didn't want to know. Only when the class clown called loudly, 'I guess he's out of it somewhere. Hey, Merry Christmas, Mr P,' did I realise, relieved, that time had moved and was up.

Tafler's routine signalled a new momentum. Now and then, along with the glimpses, the clinks and whispers, they'd centre themselves between me and the day. I did at last start to see them full on, singly or together, far down a street or where an avenue began to curve. They were the bad guys, stock still and ready to draw on the main street of a Wild West town. But I could see, too, how someone might call them the good guys and give me a level, soul-searching look. I didn't dwell on that.

They didn't have to go wild. As in early autumn, when they'd begun by not really beginning, so now they dabbed the brake, knowing my vigilance would do the rest. I was the coveted island and they could regard me from their calculated distance, come ashore a little further each time and depart again. Before long, though, my vigilance became second nature, like just knowing exactly when to take a pill. There was even a strange relief in all this. No longer did I have to waste effort in deliberately looking left and right. As though they knew that I knew how things now were, they didn't drag me blatantly to their next level, whatever that might be. But I knew it was there and, misty beyond it, others too. As an extra buffer, I got friendlier with the whiskey. Each time I poured one I remembered when my taste for it was truly awakened, the evening Laurie said goodbye and Jim parked that seriously full tumbler before me. 'Another token,' I'd think, regarding each glass for a moment. 'Add yourself to Monet and that leaf on The Green.'

But Christmas got itself taken care of. One of Paul's brothers lived in Humboldt, Saskatchewan. He was a lawyer, married with kids and, Paul said, a lawyer's house to match. All the family were converging from all over. What were my plans? Did I want to swell the party?

'Might be his last Christmas there,' Paul chuckled, 'before he gets run out.'

I looked a long time into his happy-worried face: 'Is business not good?'

Jim, who was also in the kitchen at the time, guffawed, twigging something of what turned out to be a long-running Farwell joke. A German town, Humboldt was; the rest of the family were forever ribbing brother Chris that, sooner rather than later, Teutonic patience would snap at the slack ways of an Anglo lawyer. For a moment I thought of Laurie's Uncle Gunther, then realised that any Farwell grilling I might get would come from another angle altogether. Possibly I'd be held responsible for the Sex Pistols—not to mention Vauxhall Vivas, whose shameful style and vague reliability had been much in evidence while I was still in Winnipeg. That disposed of, I thought about air-fares. I assumed we weren't thinking of a road-trip. Windsor to Kenora had

187

been gruelling enough and they were in the same province:

"'Ere, ower Jonathan, am yow gooin' head-walkabout again?' Paul cocked his head as he filled the kitchen once more with the long-ago tones of Bilston and Sedgley.

'I'd have to hustle,' I said. 'I mean, the money. And won't all the flights be booked—?'

Paul clapped a hand on my shoulder: 'In his line, the brother tends to accrue favours. Don't worry about it.'

That evening, Jim and I went to see him in that so unseasonal production of *Endgame.* Nicely warmed by whiskey, I was untroubled throughout. I even joined in the bursts of surprised laughter—including when Paul, as a sublimely hangdog Clov, parried Hamm's 'What's happening?' with 'Something is taking its course.' I was surely getting to know that something. Round noon next day, in some sort of shape after the cast party, Paul and I saw Jim off at the bus station on his trek to St Eleanors.

*

I could tell you where everything is in Humboldt—and every prairie town like it. The line of stores on Main Street staring out the hotel and bar opposite, usually The King Edward or The Queen Victoria. Starting diagonally opposite the hotel and spread out down two blocks, the farm machinery dealerships—Ford, John Deere, New Holland—dwarfing all around them. Adjacent, new and used car lots with, at that time of year, promotions on snowmobiles. Just up from the Main Street stores, a sleek one-storey library whose automatic doors, in Humboldt anyway, delivered the subtlest, most comforting swish I've ever heard. A block behind the hotel, the elementary school, with the high school in a snowy mist beyond.

Chris Farwell was a tall and genial man. His face was as relaxed as Paul's wasn't and, though he joshed his younger brother about planning to play Mr Dressup for a living, he was fiercely proud—the whole family was—of Paul's acting talents. For some part of his studies, Chris had been in the southern States, which accounted for the phrases which peppered his speech: 'Well, bless your heart,' he exclaimed, turning round and round the seasonal hamper I'd had made up. Beth, his wife, was a self-professed sun-bum in summer and ski-bum in winter; they were in fact off to the Rockies, Canmore, at the start of January. At seven and nine respectively, their children, Lara and Dwayne, were already getting the hang of the practice slopes. Chris and Paul's younger brother, Rob, hadn't long started a Meteorology course at the University of Alberta; shy and deferential, he nonetheless took every opportunity to collar me about English pop. To my relief, I found that he thought the Pistols, the Stranglers and the rest were just great—a vast improvement, he said, on 'the stonewashed jeans garbage' of the West Coast. At that, Gordy came sloping into my head; I handed him Rob's words

189

on a plate, as it were, and, speechless, he could only turn and slope off again. Marguerite, their sister, was affectionately dubbed 'The Traitor', but she took it in gracious part, as did her Bostonian husband. Their kids, triplets, two girls and a boy, had the looks and manners of subjects from a John Singer Sargent portrait, which rather contradicted their shared skill, at all of ten, as hotshot poker players, thanks to Grandpa's crash-course tutelage the previous summer: a state of affairs that caused Marguerite to roll her eyes and husband Neil to whisper, out of her earshot, that he was pulling them out of school and sending them to Vegas: 'Life of Riley here we come,' he winked.

As for the senior Farwells, the mum looked like I imagined Mrs Butler would in a few years' time and made me welcome from her first look; while the dad, far from grilling me with any Old-World New-World tetchiness, treated me royally to tales of when he was stationed in wartime England. He'd developed a taste for the beer, he said, but even more any stout he could get hold of. It was a Christmas rite, I learned, for Chris to lay in a crate of Guinness. When it got to D-Day, however, and coming ashore on Juno Beach with his fellow Canadians, Mr Farwell politely clammed up. Naturally I didn't press him. Dad had made it onto and back from Gold Beach and I'd long known the drill of respectful silence.

That the house still had plenty of space, even with fourteen people variously rattling around or taking their ease on specially reserved chairs, showed how well Chris had done and how, contrary to the running joke, his Germanic clients weren't about to give him the old heave-ho any time soon. But there was no side on him or anyone. It was a treat. Briefly, I imagined the kind of atmosphere that would prevail in an English household of comparable income and comfort—*Now, I'm just trying to place your accent* and all that—and, tramp and rat notwithstanding, I gave thanks yet again for the Atlantic.

Apart from Chris's house, the elementary school was the first building I went in. His kids were part of the school pageant: among other things, first row centre in a mass of ukuleles giving us a jingly song called 'I'm Gettin' Nutt'n for Christmas', almost in time. We were invited to join in the chorus and I tried to lose myself in the simple tale of this poor kid blacklisted by Santa. And failed. The line 'somebody snitched on me' triggered discomfort like a rash. Trying to escape, I fell into the thought that the whole thing could have been one of Mum's extravaganzas back in Winnipeg—at which moment I saw her at the side of the hall, a tweed arm raised to her left, a blazer cuff to her right, in the old *Ta-daa!* routine. What stopped me screaming was the farce of it. Mum was barely there, a phantasm cobbled together by a sorcerer's apprentice and his daft mate. You could see kids' artwork right through her on the wall. That moment, though, meant change. Up till then, I'd known there was trouble ahead but only as if the words were on a sign in country fog. Now I properly understood that the pair of them could do what they liked when they liked. But what a goofy way to change gear. My urge to scream turned to a loud chuckle and, having no clue how much time had gone by, I readied myself to join in with 'I'm Gettin' Nutt'n for Christmas'—too late, to judge from the glares and tuts directed my way. The ukuleles had vanished: now, a small choir of older children were singing what I later discovered was a lullaby, specially written by the Music teacher, about Canadian servicemen far from home at Christmas 1914. I whispered apologies, but the disapproving faces had turned away. That'll learn you, I told myself, remembering the last time I'd prepared to sing my head off, when, from the row in front, Bevvo and Gordy had dismissed me.

I didn't for a moment think that Mum had died. Still, Chris had said I could phone her any time while I was there, no problem.

'Sorry about laughing at the concert,' I said when I asked if I could put a call through later. 'I didn't mean it. I was thinking of something else.'

Chris laid a hand on my shoulder: 'Pay it no mind, Jon. But'—the hand stayed me a moment—'maybe ease off a little on the booze, hey?'

Mum was still living in Builth with Auntie Irene and Uncle Sid, though she'd made some noises—as far as you can in terse, chilly letters—about moving across to Kettering. Kettering Sid, it seemed, was dragging his feet at death's door. I waited until everyone was heading for bed before using the wall-phone in the kitchen. If I'd tried her earlier, it might have been just my luck to get an earful. I imagined making an attempt to match her tinny outburst with my jolly Christmas face while everyone milled around me. What I got wasn't much better but at least I knew it came from a living, breathing human and, while I was at it, I could get Christmas greetings out of the way: I'd only remembered to buy and post a card the day before Paul and I left for Humboldt.

Of course I paid for that chuckle back at the concert. I was insufficiently respectful of the tramp and rat's party-piece from the side of the school hall. Besides, the Christmas festivities involved a lot of happy clinking: glasses, bottles and, on one messy occasion, a yard of ale (though, mindful of Chris's words, I passed on my turn with that). Familial high spirits tuned out Tafler's racket for me, to his undoubted displeasure. As a result, I was just going into the kitchen on Christmas Day, answering someone's call for more paper napkins, when the badge flashed and I had Pete Wiznuk in my arms, legs wrapped round me, hands threaded at my neck. The non-face scrutinised mine as searchingly as if it were fully featured. The smell of turkey, roasties, veg, scented candles fell away. Bing Crosby and Nat King Cole shut up. Inches from me, thick lines of blood, black and molasses-slow, traced their way under his thatch, making it look as though someone had whacked his head from behind and, cartoon-like, the cracks were slowly working through. Once more all smells were summery-rank: the Erkeley undergrowth, the stagnant pool, soil from gouged hollows, unspeakable drink—and, as Wiznuk tightened his grip, the outbreath of flesh eleven years dead. Mad to get him off me, I slammed him into the kitchen door, which bounced back through thin air. I staggered, lost balance and caught my head on the counter. The last I heard was a clatter of utensils and Chris saying, 'Oh man, we dispatched the wrong guy. He's found a way to booze on the serviettes.' The last I felt was hands under me and an exploratory dab round my head. After that, all was dark for hours—save for a summons that came at me out of the tall, wide silence.

*

'You sure? That was some crack you took.'

Paul's concern was echoed round the pre-supper room.

'No, it's…I'm fine, thanks. It looks worse than it feels. A breath of fresh air'll be just the ticket.'

'Just the ticket,' echoed Chris's Dwayne, sounding exactly like me at his age. Paul gave me a that's-my-nephew grin.

'Well, ok,' said Beth, 'but you bundle up now. It's crazy cold out there.' Chris's mum told me to mind that bandage when I put my toque on.

'Flashlight hanging by the door,' called Chris from the kitchen and it was pushed into my hand.

'Not that you'll need it, with fairyland out there.' Still grinning, Paul turned into a nonspecific royal. 'Bat thet was shorely sam bamp of knollidge you sustained.' One of the triplets burst out laughing, then got confused. Should she go with her mother's shush or the smile I offered her?

Ridges and tides of snow, with more coming down. Winking lights just visible behind blinds and drapes, charge leads running down front paths and through grilles of cars. Outside was surely fairyland but one nearby street, dubbed Candy Cane Lane by the locals, wore its festivity with especial brio. Electric reindeer changed colour on roofs, burglar-Santas hefted themselves up the sides of garages. Across dormer windows, stars of the east shot and shot again.

But Candy Cane Lane wasn't the way I had to go. So silent it was as I walked to the elementary school: the silence of space. Compared to here, southern Ontario felt like one big town and England was just so many rats in a barrel. Paul was right: with all the sparkle around, I didn't need the flashlight to start with. I didn't really need it at all. I knew my way. Or rather, my way had been plotted in accordance with the summons that had sounded as I lay in the dark.

Between the elementary school and the high school was a park. I'd noticed the railings on the night of the concert: a manicured Erkeley, it seemed, even under snow. Kids' swings and teeter-totters were draped in white, climbing-frames looked like the bleached skeleton of a ship. In the middle of the park I sank deep and was grateful for the waterproofs Mrs Farwell had insisted I borrow. The lie of the snow made a wide furrow here and I knew I was in a gulley, maybe for running or pitch-and-catch. Checking the depth, I kicked away the snow and played the flashlight about. Bits of frame and swing slid past its beam. I turned it off and stood still. Amid all the turmoil before and since, here was another still, clear moment. I thought of my return home from campus back in the summer—a hundred years ago now, it seemed—and the old-wives'-tale impulse that made me reach for the leaf on The Green. I was all calmness then. For a flimsy moment, you might say, I'd actually found the place I'd imagined down in Mr Vesey's plant-pot. So it was now.

The snow was getting up. I could feel the tick of my watch. Gradually, at what I guessed was the gulley's far end, they grew out of the flurries. No bottle, no cork or slurp, no ratty leap into my arms again. They had their own light. In it, Wiznuk's non-face puckered. With a weird dignity, his features appeared one by one until I was staring once more at the bottle-neck savage on the ground behind Tafler's tree, feeling all I'd pushed away from me on my dash to *The Jolly Waggoner*. It was like a religious interlude where two deities return to confront a foot-dragging acolyte. Why do you still wish life were otherwise? Foolishness. How things are defines you. Yesterday is today and hereon in.

I got the message. Of course I waited to hear *Johnny, Johnny Canuck*, but I suppose there was no need for that now. That was a voice from a card in a hotel room, one of the whispers on the biting wind a few short weeks ago. Wiznuk's features sharpened as if something were inking them in. For a moment he looked exactly as he had just before he fell into his hole. Then the face sank back below his skin and I was looking at a portrait out of charnel-art: grandfather and grandson called to the eternal home before their time. Victorian abominations. My only family.

Snow blew into my face. By the time I'd blinked it away, they'd gone.

*

As he'd ignored all the faint knocks after his token gesture with the candy bowl, all the muffled voices and their 'Trick or Treat?', so Will now ignored the ringing of the upstairs phone. Over and over Jayne pushed past him on the stairs, jiggling her medal, exulting in Annie's distress; over and over he waited in the shared room for the opening door, the twinkle, 'Some fun, huh, big man?' He'd thrown the baseball bat into the corner. In his hand, the bottle-neck shone with the sun of another time and place, which were now his, too. After, he cleaned it with care and disposed of it far from the Erkeley.

15

Again life stopped and started.

Often I felt like two people. One went into the world and did the living for the other, who was stuck in an endless moment of knowing. Yesterday was today and hereon in. None of their pre-Christmas feints and excursions had said it so loudly.

For all that, a pact had apparently been made on the night of the gulley. I didn't understand it at the time but, looking back, I see that I was allowed some run of normality for the rest of my degree, some space to enjoy, while I could, the world I was made for and the comfort in which I lived. Perhaps, on some unimaginable level, they were impressed that I hadn't yet gone under; perhaps, despite what came after, I really was meant to regard my mother's school-hall apparition as a chuckling matter. 'Now women,' Jim had once said with a wink at the end of a Sidebar evening, 'have the divine right to say this is that and that is this.' Maybe those two citizens of the dark lived by the same rule.

Whatever, I completed my dissertation creditably enough. My exploration of the Impressionists—and Eakins, their non-acolyte— must have answered Tony North's hope of boldness:

'He was full of admiration,' Tony said, when we were back in his office after my viva, before we turned our attention to the celebratory party which (precipitately, I'd thought) he was arranging at his house the following night. Admiration? He'd given me a right grilling, that external examiner, Senior Conservator of Paintings at the Royal Ontario Museum. Never mind that he was an old acquaintance of Tony's; I would have been much more comfortable with another Tony North from a local department, Carleton, Guelph or wherever. The man, whose name I forget, looked like Laurie's Uncle Gunther, which hardly helped. But his informal feedback, Tony said, was congratulatory, 'and that alone,' he added, 'says PhD to me. Fact is, he'd like you to visit him at the ROM, take in an exhibition or two, see if anything appeals. Ok, if you want to stay European, fine; but he reckons, and I agree, that you have the kind of mind to do terrific work in anything.'

'Edward Hopper,' I nearly said, in a moment of mourning. It passed, but only after names and images had rattled through: Laurie in her dollar-get up at that charity do in Malden Park, Kenora, Uncle Gunther again, Ray, her cry of 'Baby, yes!' Her wall, the black shadows. Ray again. Instead I thanked Tony for the vote of confidence, said I looked forward to seeing the external's written report and added that the Royal Ontario Museum sure was an inspiring place.

'No, just your good self,' he called as I left his office. I paused. Had I said something, asked something? Apparently so. 'It's all in hand,' he chuckled, 'so you and those two desperadoes of yours and that's just fine.'

Ah, the party. Anything I should bring? That must have been what I asked. Well, it was kind of Tony, as Paul's brother had been kind when he put his hand on my shoulder, brushed away my apology for my oafish turn at the concert. But I wasn't planning to be coy with the whiskey the following night so there'd be one bottle at least in my party bag. No: one whiskey and, despite what Tony said, one wine for the host and hostess. Then judicious top-ups from the drinks table.

'It's Master Parry the Master!' Jim had a great time at the party, attaching himself to groups around the room and then, pretending he'd only just seen me, making a beeline across and pumping my hand. That his own viva was only a few days away didn't faze him at all. There was no reason why it should. He'd done splendid work: an award had already been mooted and several universities were interested in bagging him for a doctorate. Happy to let Sara, his girlfriend, do the rounds of any guests they knew, Paul stuck close to me. His own viva was a little way off but it was, by his own admission, a lower-key affair. Practicals had made up much of his Drama assessment: directing, one-man shows, staging and analysing a play by a friend of his. His dissertation, on the element of danger in the plays of Joe Orton, was more compact than Jim's or mine, but I'd read and enjoyed bits of it. Orton: he'd died the summer we came to Canada, murdered by his boyfriend. At his funeral they'd played the Beatles' 'A Day In the Life.' 'Complete

200

waste of money—they've got different voltage over there': as I sipped my whiskey and watched Jim gearing up to make another beeline for me, I remembered Mum's verdict on my purchase of *Sergeant Pepper* a week before we left. I should, she'd said, give the album to Kevin Butler. Nice, I thought, if Mrs Butler were to materialise right now, glass in hand, Drambuie or something: 'Well, congratulations, Jonathan,' I heard her say, 'and here's to you, you've done great, love, keep at it, we've only got the one life.' I imagined Mr Butler, too, somewhere nearby, collaring Tony North or Jim: '...first time I read it,' I heard, 'I thought, now that's a proper poem. Read it, have you? Bet you have. The start of it...scribblers today, they don't come close: *On the shores of Gitche Gumee / Of the shining Big-Sea-Water.* Cracking stuff, lads, cracking.'

Kenneth Halliwell, Orton's boyfriend was, increasingly jealous of Orton's success. I pictured him that summer getting madder and madder while, in a world as incomprehensible to him as his to me, Dad drafted and redrafted the latest letter to Mr Walden of Manitoba Power and Mum started again on her lists of what to send ahead and what to take as air-luggage. *Hey, let's come back here tonight, man,* echoed Gordy in my head. *Mooch round the Erkeley after hours.* A hammer, Halliwell had used, nine blows. The anonymous flat in Islington he'd shared with Orton, the Erkeley, probably umpteen other places: something in the air that summer. People at their tether's end. Halliwell had overdosed after—Nembutal, Paul said. If I'd been a different person, I might have got hold of some myself, done the sporting thing in memory of tramp and rat.

But if I'd turned into a different person later on, I might have come unstuck about Jim or Paul, hating how their lives could flow on as they'd planned: Jim's in Windsor or wherever else was ready to roll out the carpet, Paul's as actor and assistant director at the Westmount Theatre, Montreal, all set for the end of July after he and Sara had visited their families and had a vacation on the Gulf Islands. Of course I didn't, couldn't hate them. Never mind Auntie Irene's outraged defence of Mum and Dad: those two guys had been golden to me.

'Jon? What's up?' I didn't know whether Paul had gone to talk to someone else and then come back or whether he'd been watching me all the time. Either way, he was as worried as he routinely looked. 'You ok?'

'Me? Oh, fine, fine.'

His eyes wrinkling up, he clapped my back.

'You did it. You got there. Good man. Hey, and Chris said again, any time you want to take another shot over to Humboldt....' Reflexively I set my drink down and pushed it away. Paul saw: 'Hey, no, no, have your drink. He was just worried about you, they all were. Me too. And'— he gestured at Jim, who seemed to have abandoned beeline thoughts and was chatting to a girl who, in the usual run of things, would probably be his next—'that crazy horse. But you did it, hey, Jon? Jon?'

Yes, I'd done it. Still…I wasn't thinking at that moment of any pact with tramp and rat, but I knew I'd run all my luck in that warm and hospitable world. By the time Paul's words had wormed their way through to me, Sara was back at his side:

'A toast,' she said, 'to the bloke from the Black Country.' Bless her, she was no mimic. She clapped a hand to the side of her face: 'That sounds nothing like it, hey?'

'Absolutely not,' Paul laughed, and repeated her words as Bilston would have expected them. For the last time, in that affectionate correction, he made a picture of what I'd been.

*

'Yeah, well, I can see that.' Leaning back, Tony North steepled his fingers. 'It's been—what?—six years here?'

I nodded, wishing yet again that he'd replace the print that adorned the wall behind his head, Ensor's *Pierrot and Skeletons*. There was Pierrot, chubby-faced, arm extended, with those skulls crowding him so close they might have been the bedizened collar of a cape he was trying to throw off. Maybe Tony had put it there deliberately to shoo off any students who dropped by to moan. Then again, it didn't matter. Summer was passing and soon I wouldn't see it again.

'Six years of O'Maggio's and the Sidebar,' he was chuckling now. 'Yes, you've done your duty. Well, look'—he leaned forward—'what say we call it fieldwork? You and your brain and the big wide world? Ok. And I'll see if I can put in a word somewhere. And once you're gone, keep me posted, yes?'

'Oh, man!' I'd never heard Jim so mad. For a moment I thought it was because he'd be left in a hole with the house-rent but of course it wasn't that: he was off too, having chosen Dalhousie from all those clamouring for his doctoral talents. He'd only had confirmation that morning and now, to try and deflect him, I made some lame joke about his homing instinct: soon he'd be in Halifax, just 'a mighty spit over the water', as he'd put it, from PEI. But he wasn't having any of that.

'This is you,' he cried. 'This is your world, the books, the teaching. The curiosity, man. How did this one paint this and how did that one pick up on it. Who got a movement going and who said, bullshit, let's go that way instead. This is your buzz. More than all of us, me, Paul, anyone you'd name. You could be a prof right now, man. And you're walking away?'

I repeated Tony North's words about fieldwork, changing ground, the big wide world.

'But, Jon, that's not you. Ok, maybe you'd survive, probably you will, but...what? What you going to do? Work a cream separator in Alberta? Lobster-man in Cape Breton? What?'

'Tony said he'd put in a word for—'

'Ok, so, teaching someplace. So you may's well stick around and do your doctorate and then teach full-time the way you're good at. Or get him to phone Dalhousie if Art History's on their books...get your bona fides together, didn't take me long, I'll help you. Hell, phone Dal yourself. You and me, man....'

I didn't allow myself to relish the prospect, even consider it. The thought of what would follow if I yielded—probably worse than a bloody face pushed at mine on Christmas Day—put paid to that. I thought nothing else right then, but I sure felt a slow freeze in my bones. At last Jim gave up on my silence and, with 'You are one dumb fuck, Jonathan,' took off with a slam of the kitchen door.

As it turned out, I was the last to go of the three of us. Jim left round the start of August, still a bit mad, maybe still a bit hungover from the monumental toot he and I had with Paul, passing through one final time from his BC vacation to his theatre job in Montreal. Wisely, Sara had flown on ahead. It was left to me to wind things up with our prof-landlord, even, as the month wore on, play show-home man to prospective tenants for next year. I saw Tony North a few times—good as his word, he was putting out feelers—and some other folks. For a week or two I was called in to trouble-shoot a summer school on Abstract Expressionism: for sure not my neck of the woods, but even less, it seemed, for the course instructor, a supposed specialist. Mainly, though, I just kicked around the neighbourhood. Thinking this, remembering that, I felt as though I were starting to curate a bunch of years on which the door was firmly closing. One night I saw Debs, Laurie's old work buddy, in the Sidebar. She was with a crowd of people and gave me a tight little smile of way-back recognition. I started to move her way but the smile gave way to alarm and I veered off.

I thought of when I first came to Canada, my notion of taking off for farm work, the littlest hobo, if the police came over the water. Was it such a silly idea now? If I was going to leave everything behind...and I wasn't frail, wasn't leery of being outdoors if outdoors wasn't kind. Ok, it was the wrong time of year for a full season but harvest was coming up and maybe there'd be lots of winter work on the really big spreads out west. I was sure I could arrange to leave most of my stuff somewhere, maybe with Tony, on the vague promise that I'd be back. The day after I'd finished my trouble-shooting stint with the Abstract Expressionism course, I headed off to the library to look at the want-ads in *Ontario Farming* and *The Western Producer*. Passing the Returns desk I was waylaid by the Head of Art, who'd been present at my viva and who now said he was sad to hear from Tony North that I was, as he put it, lighting out:

'It would be a fine thing to have someone like you on standby for the coming year, just in case one of our new appointees proves himself another Mr Davenport'—a reference, this, to the Abstract Expressionist expert who wasn't. 'But I know, Jonathan, you have to live. Pity all our posts are taken: I'd have you in like a shot as a Junior. A third of the folks in this university don't have doctorates. But don't forget us. Next year might be a different deal.'

Egg production, fruit and sheep, machinery repair, stud hand...even someone hoping against hope for a cattle-whisperer in Westmoreland, New Brunswick. My mind was a fog. Still, I wrote down some contacts, telling myself that I wasn't being a dumb fuck, reminding myself that I'd had the best of the world I'd been cut out for, that anything more would be pushing it with tramp and rat. Arriving home to start phoning, I found a note wedged in the letterbox. I took it in, read it carefully, tore it up, pieced it together, read it again, drummed my fingers on various surfaces, had a whiskey, read it again, looked at the first number on my farm list, lifted the phone, put it down, had another whiskey and just sat. Next day I did as the note said, presenting myself in Tony's office:

'So there you have it,' he said. 'The Principal's an old college buddy of mine. Extra provincial funding out of the blue—how miraculous is that? They need someone straight away. If you give it a year, two, who knows?'—he smiled broadly— 'You might be set to come back to us, hey? I can get all your transcripts sent through, no problem. Big beautiful Alberta, Jonathan. You'll love it out there.'

I saw Tafler rattling his bottle in disgust, the rat summoning his face to gurn hideously at me.

I thought of their laughable conjuration of Mum at the side of the Humboldt school hall. Emotions collided and came out as nothing, fear and contempt forced a draw. I took a deep breath and took a punt.

*

From the Detroit to another river, the Red Deer, down either bank of which its city spread. The Community College was bright, well appointed. Everyone was fierce proud of the Kings Hockey team who, I was assured, could win everything in sight. My lodgings were spartan but functional. I didn't dare risk more. Here I was, teaching again, albeit not how I ideally wished. But overdoing personal comfort—that would have sent my diabolical kin up the wall.

And the teaching itself was a fearful prospect. As part of my workload, I was assigned First Nations students. Guiding them through Warhol and Lichtenstein was presumptuous enough. Presenting myself as an authority on their own art was surely a disaster biding its time. As it turned out, though, that year was the most stimulating I would ever know—which chuffed and terrified me at the same time. How could I hide such deep satisfaction without tramp and rat picking it up on the wind? More than once over the previous months I'd wondered whether I still needed my spotter's notebook. Now I kicked myself at the very idea of chucking it and, more practically, made damn sure I had the thing with me at all times. As it was, they stayed in the shadows again: a clink here, that might have been a rope against a flagpole; a badge-flash there, that might have been the ubiquitous crest of the unstoppable Kings Hockey squad.

I soon realised why. They'd been biding their time again, looking to the world to do their work. The deal was that this first year would be probationary. If I got through it, I could stay on till whenever. But whenever retreated. Towards the end of the year, certain words, mimicking the pair's tricks of old, made feints and darts into everyday thinking. Short-termism, cuts. Unemployment. 'Pogie', cosy-sounding slang for welfare cheques, was on more and more lips. As quickly as it had come, the provincial funding that got me holding forth about Plains Cree murals vanished.

My students got up a petition, in the face of which the Principal sighed sympathetically and ran a finger round his collar. At the year's end I was let go. And I let go myself. I fell off the map. I'd been in fairly regular correspondence with Tony North and—since he'd passed on my details when they contacted him—with Paul, going great guns in Montreal, and Jim, going great guns at Dalhousie but happy to lay them aside for at least a paragraph's reminder that he still thought me crazy as a coot not to be there with him ('or at least some damn place worth your talents'). When I left Red Deer, I had neither forwarding address nor intention of writing to them when I landed wherever. By then, I have to say, something of the Kenneth Halliwells had come into my thinking. I was envious of Paul, of Jim, of the maps they were making in their lives, their freedom to steer as they wished. Although it should have done, the notion that cuts and unemployment might hit them too didn't come into it. It would have spoiled the picture I was painting, as I'm sure something similar would have spoiled Kenneth Halliwell's rage at his lover's triumphs in Theatre-land. Well, whatever…I just had to let go of my friends.

As for tramp and rat, they'd no doubt watched from the shadows while the Principal had apologised, blamed the times, proffered good wishes. No doubt they'd shared silent thanks that economic vagaries had allowed them to conserve their energy, spared them the faff of bleeding at me or wheezing *nn-gah* in my ear. They'd known it would happen, I'd say, before the economy knew itself. So now they could watch me take the path into wilderness…which I did, having sold or disposed of everything that wouldn't fit into a biggish carry-all, in the middle of July.

August was long and sleepy. September was golden and rainy by turns, then the weather began to tighten. From England came news of a new political dispensation, with references to handbags and speeches in which *No!* figured a hell of a lot. In a reversal of my boyish plan to hide in the big nowhere if the English police came after me, I worked my way east. Sometimes I took the bus, mainly I hitched. In each new town I scanned the want-ads or fell into bar conversation, shelving my diffidence. I had to.

I dished pizza in Brandon for three weeks, during which Nancy and Centennial Sub 'n' Fixins were much on my mind. In Dolbeau, Quebec, a warehouse needed refurbishing as a farm dealership. I was ribbed as *le grand coup anglais* but the site foreman was a good-hearted soul and arranged for me to stay with a cousin during my month's stint. The cousin execrated me if I as much as looked like I'd get my wallet out for rent. And I made in onto a farm: Upper Derby, New Brunswick, where it was all hands to the construction of new barns ahead of the winter. No room with a cousin here, but I'd got the right clothes to bundle up in the draughty bunkhouse. Kettering, the farmer's name was, which I'm sure gave tramp and rat a chuckle in the ether. Still, his first name wasn't Sid and he didn't stand over my bed in the dead of night, reminding me how I'd disgraced the family name with my treatment of Mum. Even with work-gloves my hands turned hard and raw—just as I'd thought to make them all those years before, ready to vanish into anonymous work. Farmer Kettering figured me for a good worker. For a little while it looked like I'd be kept on over the winter as part of a rump-team, but there were mutterings elsewhere, references to wives and kids and needs, and suddenly I wasn't.

Winter was still New Brunswick but a deep basement in Miramichi. This time my employer was sitting right next to me in a bar—or that's how it turned out, when my enquiries about work made his eyes gleam. Newly in post as manager of a department store, he was looking for a way to cement his reputation. I was it. The years, it seemed, hadn't buried my accent as deep as I'd thought. Anyway, he heard it loud and clear, loved it and told me to come see him next day at Rideau's, Harkins Mall. So it was that I became a mall-mascot: nothing of the romance of my mascot days in Winnipeg, but I didn't expect that. This was a time of no dreams.

He'd got it all head-swimmingly planned, Ian Baillie, I'll give him that. I had a crash course on the store's chain of command, its merchandise, new lines, what was on each floor and of course the upcoming seasonal campaigns. From the end of November I was Advent Al, cruising Rideau's in a chequered get-up, swooping on customers, grinning and Gawd-strewthing, part-schmoozer, part-mobile help point. Without a twitch I turned into Santa, giving his jolly spiel a Black Country inflection: 'Are you that guy from Slade?' asked one perceptive parent, which pleased me no end.

Looking at the store on my way to and from my Rideau's Rubies grotto, I was taken with the layout, the meld or clash of colour, how the use of space was at once beguiling and functional. For a moment, a doctoral topic took shape unbidden but there was a clink, a wheeze and a sharp stab to my neck and I let it go. Still, even though I'd thought the chill distances of a farm suited my soul best, I loved the place's energy, the buzz. It was a happy counterweight to the basement digs I'd managed to find, which were worse than the place I'd landed in at the start of my second Master's year, till those hellish tenants did Jim and me the huge favour of getting themselves evicted from that fabulous house. It was below the bowels of a clap-board Gothic pile and its ceiling seemed to curate all the footsteps of Miramichi. There was a live-in caretaker…drink-in, rather, since he apparently did nothing but reel up and down the stairs at odd times, when he wasn't knocking on my door, staggering in, overstretching the welcome to the new tenant. Consciously I Canadianized my accent; I didn't want to go through all that old-country guff with him. Once he invited me into his place, a swamp without water, and held me there long into the night playing songs on an old reel-to-reel tape-recorder—by him, he said, and a variety of country bands he'd been in between Charlottetown and here. When he felt that conversation was flagging, and he seemed to need conversation even while the tapes played, he cried *Hwaall!* and lurched into a new topic. Insisting on sitting next to me, he'd clap his hand playfully on my knee. As the night went on, it stayed there longer. At the time it just made me uneasy. Now I think I should perhaps have seen it as a prediction of what was to come in the distant elsewhere.

Santa dispatched, I became January Joey, mouth full of yowzas for the Sales and forthcoming promotions. Ian Baillie was over the moon. December sales had been a dream, which he kindly imputed to my presence. 'You and me,' he said more than once, clapping me on the shoulder as I was about to don trilby and cravat. One time he said, 'Jon, I'm going to need an image man for permanent. Someone who knows the right note to strike all through the year, who can make the store say "Folks, from a tank to a peanut, we are all over your desires"— you hear me?' He stepped back and I'm sure he was about to do that *I have a vision* thing from movies where someone cups their hands round their eyes and looks to heaven. But just then he was called to the phone.

I did hear him. But image man…like my fascination with the store, that would awaken what I should no longer be. Again my mind would embrace projects and topics. Again tramp and rat would make like a high-voltage fence. It was a matter of luck that I took to being Advent Al and the rest…surprise, too. Given my natural personality, it was another kind of self-estrangement, a disappearance into nowhere. But despite Ian Baillie's confidence, I knew that his sales figures would have soared anyway. It was Christmas and people buy, never mind how. Besides, January brought another kind of chill. Head Office issued a directive about province-wide cutbacks. Ian Baillie had to let me go. I wouldn't after all morph into Springtime Stan or whoever. He was genuinely cut up about it, insisting that I keep in touch with him: things would be on the up again and when they were he'd have me back on the shop-floor like a shot.

Forbearing to say that he should look to his own job, never mind anyone else's, I shook his hand.

Ian Baillie, Farmer Kettering, the site foreman's cousin who wouldn't hear of my paying rent...they were all great guys. It was such a shame that, under the terms of the new life, I couldn't get near their friendship. Mind you, getting the bullet from Rideau's also meant release from my cave. *Family trouble,* I scribbled on a note with my name and apartment number, pushing it with two weeks' rent under the caretaker's door. I could hear a song from inside, something about that old boxcar and lonesome winds, but I was up the stairs before the door opened.

Something under two hundred and fifty miles, Miramichi to Halifax. To Dalhousie. I'd got the money for a comfy ride: hell, I'd lived like a monk. I pictured Jim's face across from mine in somewhere that looked and felt like the Sidebar. I imagined him asking how I was, what I'd been doing. I heard my silence as I didn't know where to begin or, really, what to say. I imagined him starting to talk of his doctoral work, guessed at the string of girls who'd fallen under his unique spell. He got awkward. He couldn't help himself:

'Look, man, when you giving up on this hobo nonsense? The Art guys here, you would not believe the stuff they do....'

At the bus station I picked Thunder Bay, change Jonquiere, change Kirkland Lake, change Geraldton. Maybe any one of those would do for a spell, or I might scoot well north

215

of Winnipeg and try elsewhere in Manitoba, Grand Rapids, Flin Flon. Or I might just switch from bus to bus the way that forgotten people ride the subway.

*

Will drummed his fingers. All was gloomier beyond the reading-light. He could hardly make out the near side of the pool-table, the plastic bucket with all the baseball stuff. The light was as bright as before. It just felt as though all beyond it was drifting into its own kind of sleep. Following the smoking-room guy, he thought, and smiled.

The smile hardened. Unwelcome words strayed back. *Sidewalks squish up a dog's paws. They need earth.* Boy, his brother would have done just fine. Advent Al? He'd have played it to the hilt, and Santa, and January Joey. As for the job cuts, he'd've wangled things his own sweet way. Some other poor schmuck would have had to evaporate: he'd've made sure of that and gone on to be Springtime Stan, Summertime Sid or whatever. That Ian Baillie, he'd've lopped an arm round his shoulder, goggling in admiration and just yay far from handing him his own job: 'You and me,' Will heard Baillie say. 'You and me, Mark. World's our oyster. Let them try to lay you off, my friend, just let them try.'

Holly and the twins. Will pictured them. When had he seen them last? He wondered if they were any happier now or at least managed

216

to look it. Mags had phoned Holly after the whole Lynn Ewings thing. Got about as much change out of her as Mark had given him. But no spite: she just sounded all fallen in on herself, Mags said, as well she might. *Holly's never liked you, you know that?* Was that true, Mark's hit-back? Oh, boy...Mark and truth...waste of time. Will's smile softened again. Whether Holly liked him or not, he'd see they were all right, her and the kids.

*

The backwash of days. Jonquiere became Kapuskasing, Kapuskasing became Thunder Bay; then into Manitoba, where I ducked south of Winnipeg and surfaced in Brandon again; then into Saskatchewan, Estevan, which soon became Weyburn, became Regina. I only remember most of the places now because I wrote them in my spotter's book. My return on this westward tide is largely a blur. I got work here and didn't there. There were days of worn shoes and blank stares at motel and rooming-house walls. Compared to all that, the jobs I did going east, especially at Rideau's, seemed like dreams come true.

They were with me pretty well all the way west. Apart from brisk attacks like the one when I savoured the spaces and colour of Rideau's, they'd hardly broken cover on the road east or in Miramichi. Now they were regular pals, one taking my arm on the street, both staring back at me in an anonymous room. You might have said they were helping me fill up the notebook. I only know how much time passed between Jonquiere and Regina because I dutifully noted all sightings. As if rewarding my efforts, they rang some changes. Tafler got himself a new bottle, smart, kind of hourglass shape. Other times it was a liqueur bottle with a seal at the neck, reminding me of Christmases back in England, Mum's tipples, de Kuyper, Drambuie. Wiznuk's badge shone out from a variety of jackets, on one occasion a hunting effort, cinched at the waist, but dark check rather than red. Well, hunting fitted. Another time, he affected light linen trousers...must have been the start of warmer weather. All this, I suppose, was meant to enforce the law laid down from the far end of that gulley in the Humboldt park: *yesterday is today and hereon in.* They could afford to entertain me by changing with whim or season. They had forever.

The westward tide took its slow time. I saw out all the seasons. Far from any department-store theatrics, the following Christmas was a crash-out on the floor of a fellow shifter and polisher at the Soo Line Museum, Weyburn, which—luckily for me—had arranged bumper events and exhibitions and needed seasonal muscle. I remembered Paul's kindly words at my viva party, or rather his brother's words, kindly conveyed. *Any time you want to take another shot over to Humboldt.* At around two hundred miles distant, and given the stretches I'd put in, the bright and welcoming home of Lawyer

Farwell was just a step along the street from Weyburn. But Christmas again? After how that previous one panned out? I might find far worse scenarios than that freezing standoff in the park gulley or Wiznuk wrapped about me, an undead monkey sharing his blood. And how might I react? Would Chris have to turn from kindly to professional, call in appropriate authorities, reach a certain decision? Tradition or not, this Farwell Christmas might be minus Paul, minus that joking compassion from happier days. I might even find myself back in Weyburn pretty damn quick, a guest of Souris Valley, the mental refuge. Refilling my glass in the variegated fug of my co-shifter's apartment, I figured that, all in all, I was wise to avoid courting whatever would come if I were to seek a bit of goodwill among the crackers and lights of Humboldt.

But finally, getting on for two years after Red Deer, there was Saskatoon and *High Office Initiatives*. Desks, they sold, and filing cabinets, swivel chairs and flip-charts, lamps with wayward necks. I was a gofer, packing and unpacking, going out on deliveries with a guy who claimed to be a great-nephew of Lester Pearson and talked incessantly about the Saskatchewan Roughriders, for whom he'd trialled, he said, some years earlier. Slithery Jake, he was known as, on account of the way he left any seat, easing down it as though it were a plane's emergency slide and springing himself upright at the last possible second. One time his exit from the van got a round of applause from construction workers out on Circle Drive.

'Shit,' Jake would say, 'I had the height, I had the supples. Guess that Bob Woloschuk was what the Riders wanted in a running back.' Now and then he would illustrate the Roughriders' error by shooting off with a sturdy parcel and getting back to the van while I drew a leisurely breath.

It could have been so different. There was another job, trimmer and litter-sticker round the city parks, short-term. Just think, if I'd gone for that, I'd have been on the road again by autumn, on to Alberta, BC. More barn-building, maybe, more malarkey in a department store. What happened—what, I see now, was coming like Christmas—would have taken quite another shape in another place. But the end would have been the same.

The manager of *High Office,* Don Rydell, was a rather different kettle of fish to Ian Baillie. Both were personable but with Ian it was a trait. Don tended to mislay it. For him, Scandinavia was where office design was at. He must have been doing good business to have designers and master-carpenters, here and in Regina, drop everything else when he needed them; but they paid for it when he parked the bonhomie:

'Look, guys,' he'd yell down the phone, 'those sliding drawers. I can hear them clunking in and out. I need more Oslo, guys, I need more Copenhagen, come on, work with me on this.'

Mostly he was fine with me, though after a while he started giving me sidelong glances as though I'd escaped from the Foreign Legion. In response I lobbied to go out more often with Slithery Jake. But one day he beckoned me into his office. I was ready to insist that I wasn't stealing brackets or dowels for any home DIY but he motioned me to sit, offered me a coffee and spoke of computers.

'Ah, he's been itching like a crazy to get into all that,' Slithery Jake said later. This was when computers were just seriously coming in and it turned out that Don had been in heated discussion with *Spindog Heaven,* the record store next door, to buy their premises and set up how-to stations, staffed by demonstrators, along with an array of state-of-the-art machines. But *Spindog Heaven* was doing good business too and nixed that. So it was that he'd invoked plan B—mobile demonstrators going hither and yon—and this, it seemed, was where I came in.

'I had you figured, Jonathan,' said Don that day, tapping his nose. 'You ain't just a hauler and a heaver.'

Reflexively I pulled out my dog-eared token: a letter to whom it may concern from the Principal at Red Deer, bigging me up in grand if unspecific manner. I'd never had use of it in my long, circling time on the road. I just liked it about my person, like a gift whose strange specialness is that you can never open it.

'Knew it.' Don slapped the letter with the back of his hand. 'I'm getting some other guys in, Jonathan. Briefings. I'll keep you in the loop.'

Sometime later Jake was treating me to Roughrider stats in a shiny new van, along with a guy called Peach Irving, a tech wizard from Stony Plain, Alberta. Another Peach Irving rode with another couple of guys in another shiny van. In the meantime I'd gone on an intensive course at the University, backed up with instruction from Peach. I'd brushed up against computers at Windsor. The Art History prof whose house Jim, Paul and I had rented had buddies in the new Computer Science department and I'd heard on the wind of Intel, Zilog, C programming language. Now I saw what was coming, what was happening already. I saw how bits and bytes, space and line and colour could marry. I was hooked.

And doomed. And defiant. They wouldn't stand, I knew, for any regression. Let him sling beer or fiddle with aluminium sidings. Let him pack parcels, drop them off, get signatures, return to Slithery Jake's evaluation of Brent Schwartz as a linebacker. Suddenly I didn't care. All that popping up alongside me on the road from Miramichi, that low-level chaperoning as though I were some ingénue out of Jane Austen—too cosy, I thought now, too much win-win for them. I guess that, deep down, I rebelled…between that first talk with Don Rydell and my first day on that course? The moment I produced that Red Deer letter? Who

222

knows? Do your worst, I muttered to myself as the shiny van roamed Saskatoon, keeping appointments at City Hall, the Library, the Lions and Shriners, church halls.

They did. A few times, I was allowed to be creditable second-string to Peach. Once I led a demonstration myself. But all too soon I turned inside out and became a liability. They came at me like a four-handed plague, pinching, biting, burrowing under my skin. At crucial moments I made like a blank screen and, despite Peach's 'Come on, man, we're there'—even his assured recap of the whole demonstration—deals with lucrative clients fell through. I became third-string behind Jake, paperwork-jockey. Blackouts meant that the paperwork rarely made it back to *High Office*. God knows how or where I lost it. Well, they know, tramp and rat. Luckily Don was high-profile, otherwise folk wouldn't have been dropping in so often with sheaves in their hands: 'Don, I found this cleaning up in the bar, in our lobby, at my concession stand. Your name here…looks like it shouldn't go walkabout.' Returned to in-house duties, I found I couldn't pack or unpack to save my life. Purring copiers suddenly jammed, once irreparably, when I went near them with a single sheet of paper. One time, Don was sealing the deal with a school secretary about a new desk for her principal. I happened to walk by, at which two of its legs buckled and it pinned her to the wall. Bruises and a torn jacket: 'Pay no mind,' she tried to chuckle, 'I get worse from the kids every day.' But she didn't, couldn't mean it and when Don looked at me now there was fear in his eyes. Finally, he had me in for what he called 'some needful up-fronting', and I knew that, yet again, the want-ads or a trip to Manpower Services were on the cards.

I knew they'd win—but somehow that didn't capsize me altogether. Yes, I acted as they required. While they were destroying my future as a computer-whiz, that feeling of being two people intensified. I had to let it. But the feeling was different now. Before, worker-me earned the crust for himself and for the other, who was frozen by a reality that could never be changed, certainly not changed back, as if he were stuck in a tight corridor with just one door on which, mockingly, were written *Entrance* and *Exit.* During the *High Office* catastrophes, though, worker-me managed—with, yes, some dispassion—to look back over the months and see a picture whose fullness offered clarity if not solace: himself as a mouse with a long tail, heading for new places, new stop-gaps and idle days while, certainly after Miramichi, the paw came down when it would, the grin became ever more pussycat. And now, as the demonstrations ended in chaos and the latest copier jammed, the other me unfroze and stepped up. He absorbed the day-to-day shocks for worker-me: my shiver before I opened strange doors, my dead stop on streets. He kept worker-me's eyes from screwing up, his head from ducking when he scooted across an intersection and horns parped and the latest driver roared 'WhattheChristyadoin' pal?'

'Life is real, life is earnest'. Worker-me looked at protector-me. We swallowed hard, nodded in unison, accepted, like it was a lesson drummed in by a hundred Mr Veseys. 'A Psalm of Life', that line comes from. Longfellow. That book the Butlers gave me back on another planet. I'd started but never finished 'Hiawatha' and only happened on 'A Psalm' by accident—back in Windsor, must have been, hunting some captions for a lecture on American Wilderness Art. I didn't use it but it stuck, as if it knew it would become a necessity. The next bit of the poem is something about how the grave isn't the goal of life: dust to dust 'was not spoken of the soul.' At some point, worker-me and protector-me concluded, we must have lost ours. Maybe Wiznuk glooped it up long before, during his kitchen-terror that Christmas day in Humboldt. Or maybe it leaked out much later, once tramp and rat had settled into their appalling complacency, popping up, changing bottles, sporting summer kecks. Maybe till then it felt it still had a place in this body, near this heart.

And protector-me kept the spotter's notebook up to date, fastidiously tracked their game. Yes, game alone: I'd long dropped that daft notion of them as writhing spirits working their fare in purgatory. They'd surrendered their souls too, which made us truly equal…which in turn gave me a kind of comfort and, in some corner where they didn't bother to look, kept defiance at a flicker. Protector-me even cheekily wrote 'doctorate' at the back of the book, as if it were a whisper of other possibilities that, even if they couldn't be taken up, still had their own life…like someone who'll never be truly fit might scribble 'will tackle Everest.'

*

All very well, though, to think like that. How they finished me at *High Office* was a lousy trick—though not half as lousy as Waskesiu, their flourish at the end of my time in Red Deer. Yes, they'd largely let me be during that year and yes, it was surely because they knew that year was my only one. I suppose Waskesiu was their way of saying that their silence wasn't sleep. Or that it wasn't enough for me to turn from the university prof trail at Red Deer and hunker down in modest digs. They had that other matter to deal with: my heart…all that came and went so easily with the Jims of the world.

I should have put this with the other Red Deer stuff, but the right words wouldn't come then and maybe they won't now. I thought in fact of leaving it out altogether, just quietly taking it with me. But why shouldn't you know it, whoever you are, reading this? If you've got this far, you'll be well tuned into their inhuman shows. Why should I withhold this one, a doozy as it is?

Dawn Koralewski was a secretary in the Arts division at Red Deer College. Her family had history with England, her Uncle Hieronym having been a pilot in the Polish Air Force from

June 1942 to VE Day. Shortly after, he'd married an English girl and settled down:

'Heedingly?' asked Dawn in our first conversation. 'That how you say it?'

'Headingley. Part of Leeds.'

'I keep saying I'll visit them and the kids. Hah, I say "kids". Uncle H is a grand-daddy now. One time I started to arrange it…and what do you know? They landed on mom and dad, surprise visit. Plus Uncle H mutters about retiring back here, so I'd better get the skates on.'

Dye, I thought. But no, her hair was naturally jet-black. Her looks reminded me of Laurie, her manner of Nancy, but really she was different from both. A real Prairie girl, she'd laugh: her folks rode tractors and combines, except for those who bought and sold them. Pawlowicz, she said, another uncle, who'd done famously for himself as a dealer: 'Here, in Sask, in Manitoba. He was hoping to break Ontario but'—laughing again, she pushed the tip of her nose up with a finger—'my dear, they have their own contraption chappies in Upper Canada, doncha know?' Pawlowicz. I knew the name: it had stared down at me from a dealership in Humboldt, just along from the library with those sweetly subtle automatic doors.

A couple of coffees became a drink, a movie. Nothing was said on either side about going together. Perhaps something wise was holding me back. For her part, you might say that she was like Frivolous Sal in that old barber-shop song: an open-hearted soul, honest as the day. I did wait, nervously, for her to say, 'Look, where is this going?' but she didn't. It just went there, without fuss, and I laid any wisdom aside...

...which meant another trip round the houses. Despite what had happened with Laurie and Nancy, I thought that if I could fight through, feel and show deep love this time, I might just touch something that tramp and rat didn't know they still had. Tenderness. An understanding that, whatever they might think—if they did—I could atone by loving well, even if I had to live on what the Victorians, Paul told me, called a modest competence. Rat had been tender to tramp that night in my prof's garden, solicitous at his convulsions, concerned lest he fall. Couldn't he, they, turn some of that outwards at last? Understand that sincere love is the best penitence? It was all so much fiddling with the vision in the airport restaurant again, with the card at the hotel. But I made myself not think that.

'Waskesiu,' said Dawn one evening over a meal in late May. *Unemployment, cut-backs, pogie*—those words were already on the air, and some of the students had already taken me and other colleagues aside and said they hoped the axe would miss us; but it was a little while yet before the Principal would call me in and reveal matters to the satisfaction of tramp and rat. Still, I felt a kind of nothing at the edges of my life and perhaps I became a little light-headed at the thought that I might or might not be on a road that was soon to fork. Perhaps, even, I felt a flicker of the defiance which would later warm me for a happy while at *High Office Initiatives.* So when Dawn mentioned Waskesiu that evening, Prince Albert National Park, friends of hers with a Winnebago and the vacation days she'd saved for June, I said yes without thinking:

'But I've never been in a canoe.'

'Easy as falling off a log,' she grinned. 'You do have logs back over there, hey?' Her detonation of laughter caused a number of other diners to turn round and a few to laugh. I would have joined in but from nowhere came the memory of Mum's tearful performance at that Chinese restaurant on Spadina the night before I put her on her plane, the way those other diners had looked round, some of them tutting as if I were being a brute. But Mum's tears vanished from my mind, along with all that chill disapproval, as I caught the end of the reaction to Dawn's mirth and managed a few chuckles myself. I could say that the ambushing memory was a warning, but if I took that line with everything I'm writing now I'd still be drivelling on about the airport washroom and the flashing badge and the card waiting back at the hotel.

Anyway, the trip to Waskesiu didn't happen...or so another of Dawn's jokes briefly prophesied:

'Bad news,' she said when I joined her for coffee next day. 'My friends can't make it after all.'

'Ah...oh, well.' For a moment I was back under Mr Vesey's beady eye: *So, no worries*

229

about canoeing, Parry. Happy reprieve, eh?
Heavens, you're a poor specimen. Dawn's hand
on my wrist jolted me back to the now: that and
her smiling eyes:

'But good news…they're letting us have their
Winnie to make up for it.'

460 miles, Red Deer to Waskesiu: a snip
compared to the eternal haul from Windsor to
Kenora. My second time in Saskatchewan, then,
and a far different proposition to Humboldt
snow, a swell of ukulele-buoyed voices insisting
they'd get nuttin' for Christmas. In the western
summer I could hardly imagine freezing at one
end of a gulley while, from the other end, my
masters revealed in dumb-show my life to come.

We started in the murk of a Tuesday dawn—
already warm enough—and by late afternoon we
were pushing open the door of the Park's Visitor
Centre. I hadn't done any driving since I
chauffeured a sloshed Jim home from the
Sidebar a few days before he left for Dalhousie,
but I did now. *Up the lazy river,* I found myself
thinking, partly in sardonic anticipation of the
canoe lashed to the roof, but mainly because the
open road felt just like that, what with breeze and
cruising speed and the vast fields of oilseed rape
running its child's yellow up to the highway,
unspooling like the soundtrack on a roll of film.

Prince Albert National Park wasn't Cannock
Chase or even Dartmoor. It was miles and lakes
and miles again, a quiet demand for respect, even
awe. By the time the ranger had taken all our
details, checked and double-checked our route

and confirmed where we'd be on which night, the light was starting to get low, so we slept in the Winnie with a fresh and early start in mind. And yes, my canoeing would have erased Mr Vesey's moue of contempt...just about. I certainly managed more than just rocking my shoulders in time with Dawn's and making paddle-in-water noises. In some way or other, I helped get us up Waskesiu Lake, with overnight put-ins at Paignton Beach and the Narrows. And I didn't get in the way of reaching the Bagwa, a circular canoe route taking in maybe four lakes, one of which, Lily, was where we made our longest stop.

All the time on our route we stayed practically naked. No, Dawn did. She was able to parry the mosquitoes with minimum spurts of repellent.

'Ah, they know my taste,' she laughed, and then, stretching the word as far as it would go, 'Bawwww—ring.'

But I was a foreign cut, prime tenderloin. They waited for me in clouds, till I wished I'd packed a radiation suit. Sometimes, though, they forsook me in favour of some side-creek, a bit of stagnation to enjoy. Only much later did I think of Jez Wallings and his Penzance-bred midges, picture them arrowing north-east along the Severn Estuary, clipping the border of Wales, homing in on the Black Country, the Erkeley, to make Tafler's life hell. Well, a lot of them waited for later, thoughts like that. A good half-dozen have occurred to me during this paragraph, but as I've said, I can't make room for them all. I have to get on. And there's less and less time to get on in.

I clung to my hopeful pledge. Real love, all the way round, would show the pair I could truly give myself, move them to set aside their shenanigans. Yes, well...like you can pledge to love as if you're an actor in a two-hour romance where there's naturally a lot of hurry-up involved. But they kept away, to the point where I didn't think of them the instant anything odd happened. On our second day at Lily Lake, I was lolling about in the canoe with Dawn swimming and sculling around me. It was late morning. We'd made love until, pushing me off with the giggly observation that we could have stayed home in Red Deer or just made the Winnie rock in the Visitor compound, so how about it, Jon, how about the great outdoors, Dawn got up and streaked for the lake. Following her, I ran out the canoe, but before that I had a look round to check that all was in proper shape at our camp. I knew it would be but on this trip I was more of a martinet than ever I'd been in the Windsor houses: I had the Park code by heart. 'My God,' said Dawn, 'he ain't only smart, he's a wife to boot.' And yes, maybe I was compensating for being the outdoors rookie and had got to thinking that real love must include keeping our successive patches of the wild spick and span.

Dawn circled the canoe, concocted a tale about nearly treading on the lid of the coffee-pot last night, just to get me going ('Guess I'll need a housekeeper upgrade, honey'), and then sculled off again. At that moment, there was a cracking noise from the further shore and its long grasses trembled. Thinking about it now, I'm amazed I didn't leap up and capsize. If I'd heard the same back in Windsor, on the edge of Lake St Clair or even on a nothing day in Malden Park, I'd have been struck to the bones. But it was as if the noise just moseyed across my hearing like a train in the distance or a garbage truck creeping up someone else's street. I attributed nothing dark to it. I pictured no flashing badge, no shadows to despoil the hot sky. Instead I just looked in the direction it came from with the dispassion of a crouching naturalist who senses that, in a while, he'll start to ache a bit. Turning and diving, surfacing and sculling on, Dawn noticed nothing.

And now, a little way in from the shore, the dry grasses pulsed and twisted. There might or might not have been a rustling, too, even the hint of some heavy tread. I smiled. If she'd spotted the commotion, Dawn might have hollered to me to get my ass over there with a long curry-comb and settle the whole mess down. Ah, me and my martinet ways. All very well keeping a temporary camp in trim, but you could do nothing about the unpredictability of the flora. Or fauna, I thought, as a nearby stand of grass looked about to break apart. Now, of course, sitting here, far from that expansive day, I guess that if she'd spotted something Dawn would have sliced her way back and told me to get the boat off the water tout suite. Words would have been said about my not hallooing her in the first place.

As it was, the grasses parted like the curtains at one of Mum's pageants and for a bizarre moment I expected to see a band of small people with ukuleles, drawing about them again the good cheer of a Humboldt Christmas. Something shone dark against the sun, a flank, and something else flashed above—antlers? An extra wave from grass-tips? After a moment in which the only sound was the splash of Dawn's back-stroking arms, whatever it was decided it had lumbered far enough. The flank turned and, like a drunk in a sleeping house, the creature thumped and crackled effortfully away.

Then I really did jump. From nowhere, Dawn was at the side of the canoe, rocking it in a playful threat to get me in beside her: 'Sweetie, I called three times. Where've you been?' I realised where. Lost in wonder. All that commotion and it didn't end in whispers or blood or Mum pinned ghostly against the waving grass with tramp and rat either side. It was just Nature going about its business—even though a remote lakeside seemed custom-made for the pair's terrible doings. But they'd heard my love-pledge, I told myself: knew I'd make good on it, were honouring it themselves. I could feel something in the stilled air: the world, their world, saying yes. I looked steadily at Dawn. I can love this woman. More than Laurie, than Nancy, lovely as they were. I simply can. At last she did pull me into the water and the air was filled with the shrieks and *don't-you-dares!* of a woman without complication, whose folks had spread out to turn

234

profits on farm equipment across the Prairies, to live and grow old a stone's throw from Headingly Cricket Ground in smoky old Leeds. Back on shore—with no thought to trembling grasses or how famously the mosquitoes were feasting on my skin—we made pleasure every which way till lamp-lighting, net-pulling time.

They kept away. Until I brought them back. Or maybe they hadn't really…oh maybe, maybe, a thousand maybes. Help yourself, take an armful. 'That was no bear,' she said. But not at Lily Lake.

For our last night we put in again at Paignton Beach. All was as lovely as ever. We took a last swim in the slow-cooling water, made love, took a break while I did my martinet thing, made love. As the sun dipped after supper I had a last check-round, making specially sure that the garbage bags were stowed safe in the trees. We retreated to the tent and, after a spell of dreamless sleep, I again felt her all over me:

'Oh darling,' I murmured, toff-like, 'you're too much. Again? Heavens, I couldn't possibly.'

'The hell with that,' she said, and I found that she had the whiskey bottle in her hand. 'Get up, Jon.'

Outside was chaos. The remnants of the fire were strewn far from its neat pit. The garbage bags were down from the trees, their plastic in tatters, the leftover-wrappings torn open, contents discharged wherever we shone our lights. Something had been at one of the oars, not to mention Dawn's book: *Changing,* as I recall, the autobiography of actress Liv Ullmann, very much the flavour of the time. I found it by accident, cover half-off, when my torchlight flicked out beyond the edge of the camp. Under other circumstances, I might have got even with Dawn for her jokes about my house-proud ways, murmured that there was something evaluative about the book's fate. But I didn't say anything, then or ever.

She was stock still by the fire-pit when I got back, whiskey bottle open in a little sling-bag at her hip. I made to speak, put my arm about her.

'Shh-shh.' Her response came in tight little spurts, as if, still though everything was, or perhaps because of that, she didn't want to risk drawing fresh attention to us. I let my arm drop and we listened. The usual counterpoint of night sounds came and went. Nothing of menace seemed to drop into them. But the air felt heavy as if trying to hold something back. I wondered if what I'd spotted and hardly cared about at Lily Lake had tracked us: no galumphing moose or elk but...I started mumbling the old litany...*if you run it'll outstrip you, if you swim it'll have you like a fish, if you climb it'll be waiting at the top.* I felt my legs starting to tremble as if fear was pressing my body to let me fall, play dead, just in case.

My mumbling must have been louder than I thought. Dawn pulled out the whiskey, took a swig, offered it over and wiped her mouth:

'No. That was no bear,' she whispered.
'What?'

Though I couldn't really see her face and didn't want to spook her with torchlight, I could tell that her expression had set.

'But look at it all,' I whispered. 'I mean, the mess, it's classic bear—isn't it? I'm really sorry, sweets, I must have missed a bag somewhere—'

'That was no bear, Jon.'

I looked round. A moment's relief at her words gave way to—well, to the old, old story. In the random strokes of my light, the camp was a horror-ground. I remembered how I'd played a torch round another scene, the swings and climbing-frames of that Humboldt park, no less desolate for being just down and along from houses, warmth, safety. We must have stood there for ages, trading the whiskey, listening to— what? Chickadees? Loons? I had no idea and wasn't about to ask her as though all was fine again. I said my little spotter's notebook was hardly meant for birds, but I thought about it now, visualised its colour and dimensions— anything to keep my mind steady. Finally I went back into the tent, emerged with a new plastic bag and started to gather up what I could.

'Oh, Jon, leave that.' For a moment I thought she was going to suggest we just light out now, tell the rangers we'd pay for the clean-up. 'Leave that,' she repeated, squeezing my arm, brushing past me. Folding up on the ground, she leaned her head to the tent-flap and slowly pushed inside. She could have been sculling a dry lake. A moment later, I heard soft sobbing. Never mind how scary that hour was: she needed tenderness more than anything. Easing in after her, I turned on the lamp, damping its glare with a face-cloth. I slid my arms round her, kissed her brow, heard her whisper 'That's so nice.' And began to talk.

I tried to stop. As well try to hold down a meal when a bug strikes. I tried to pretend to myself that I'd said it all for real, twice, to Jeff Cordingley, to Jim. That only doubled the compulsion. *That was no bear.* Of course not. The pair of them didn't have to burst through the long grasses of Lily Lake. Didn't have to dog my canoe-strokes with the old shtick. This was their best yet. Having laid the camp to waste, they were inside me now, speaking me like a river in spate. As for my love-pledge, it was dumped among the trees with a bag's innards.

As I spoke, the tent flap dragged a little on a slight wind, the lamp buzzed. No other sound than my voice. I can hear it now, steady, toneless, as though I were inviting someone to leave a message and then going *beep*. I can hear her silence, too, or maybe it wasn't really silence, maybe it was a string of little gasps and cries fighting my words. Anyway, when I got to the bit about running down the Sedgley Road to *The Jolly Waggoner* she pushed me back and there was the sound of two tidy gunshots, her hand striking either side of my face.

'What the fuck? I mean, what the fuck, Jonathan? This what you do where you come from, arms round a girl shit scared in the middle of nowhere, then all this? I told you, didn't I?

Second time we went out for real. I confided in you. That fucking trucker on the Coquitlam road, yeah, I know, more fool me that time of night, maybe any time, lucky I got clear into the trees, lucky he gave up looking, yeah, more fool me. So'—she pushed her face into mine—'you remembered that and saved it up, hey? The camp's fucked, you make like protector-man then you give me all this sick hooey about some sad kid nailing another sad— '

'No, no, not any sad...' I stopped. Tramp and rat were in her head, too, making her misunderstand. 'No, listen,' I said, though I could say nothing more.

'Listen shit! You get out. Out! And if whatever it is comes back it'll have you first and give me a head start and, hey, that'll make it quits for me with that insane trucker. Shit, he even looked like you. Now out!'

Nothing came back but the sunrise, by the light of which I managed to get the camp sort of presentable. My last bit of tidying was to hurl the Liv Ullmann book at the foot of the tent-flap. Childish, yes. Petulant. Exactly what some sad kid would do. But I don't think I was so utterly without hope as in that moment. I saw no future...well, none that would put up with fol-de-rol like love and pledges.

Whether Liv's clatter woke her or she hadn't slept, I never knew. In silence we did a final tidy-up, stowed our stuff aboard, paddled and portaged the long miles back to the Visitor Centre. In silence we waited while the ranger checked us out. I got edgy. Not because there was no talk, could be no talk, between her and me: given how I'd been made to shoot my mouth off the previous night, I accepted that. But someone had to say something about our Paignton Beach catastrophe, even if it meant dressing the real truth up as yet another near-collision between man and ordinary beast. So when the ranger asked if we'd enjoyed it all, I started to gabble but Dawn clipped my words with a brisk account of what happened: 'Just didn't seem like a bear,' she ended and I was about to put in my two cents about making damn sure that our camps were House Beautiful all the way when the ranger cut me off too:

'Now that'—he wagged a finger at a leaflet-stand—'is something. Had a bunch of folks through, oh, a couple of weeks back? Same thing. Can't remember if they stopped at Paignton. But one of the guys, a real old survivalist, said no, not a bear, man. Shoot'—he shaded his eyes against the sun-bleached window—'now you've said likewise...wonder what all else we got up there? Time for a serious look-see,' he added and blew out his cheeks.

Silence as the National Park receded, Christopher Lake, Spruce Home. As she'd planned, Dawn turned west at Prince Albert onto route 40 for the Battlefords. From there—like the Park code, I had it by heart—it was a short drop-down for the 40 on to the Alberta border, the 14, 26 and 13 to west of Wetaskiwin, the 2 south to Red Deer. Except it wasn't. At Hafford, a good forty miles east of the Battlefords, she pulled over and once again, though in a far different voice to the previous night, told me to get out.

'I can't do it, Jon. Not hours and hours with you, not now. And'—she drew a shaky breath—'it'll dead of night by the time we get back. Dark as Coquitlam,' she added in a whisper.

I climbed down, hauling my stuff after me. 'Someone'll be along for you,' she said. 'It's a busy route.' She held her hands tight in her lap as if afraid I'd suddenly catch one up and burble on about forgetting it all, starting again. But she did stare hard once I'd closed the door:

'Up till last night,' she said through the open window, 'I thought for sure you were the one.' Her smile was watery: 'Don't make like that with any other lady, hey?'

The Winnie shook up the haze as it disappeared. I didn't dare look around or even wonder if I was in a land of tall, crackling grasses. Thankfully, it wasn't long before a truck picked me up. The guy obviously needed to stay right on top of his time-sheet and hardly said a word, except to point out at last the Greyhound depot in North Battleford. There was an hour's wait before the Edmonton bus but at least it wasn't packed and I had a stretch-out on two seats nearly all the way.

So it was that I went north where Dawn had swung south. For a moment, when we pulled into the Edmonton depot, I was flipped back through the years. There was no great similarity, but the noise brought back Crewe Station, its

241

immensely, filthily curving roof, the shriek of the steam engines, family holidays from way back, one in Anglesey, another with a cousin of my Mum's who'd gone to live outside Dublin. That one was a disaster, though I can't remember why. Nor can I say why I pieced together as much as I could of Crewe station. Then again, as I'd watched the returning sun pick out the detritus at Paignton Beach, I'd felt all sense of a future leaking away. Maybe part of my mind wanted to rub that in by bringing back a past that was long gone and, probably, pretty featureless at the time. It was hardly enough to make up for what I'd done to Dawn, but sometimes punishment comes drip by drip...

...as I was reminded when the doors of the bus for Red Deer swished open and fresh Edmonton arrivals got off. Of course they were there, last down the steps, enjoying the restlessness about them as they had in the airport café. Of course one took a luxurious swig, bottle up like a ceremonial trumpet. Of course the other one flashed *Sapience and Duty* into my eyes, from the vest-pocket of his niftiest jacket yet, a real Fauntleroy number. His thickest, too—never mind all that depot-bound heat. Their tableau banished Crewe station and all at once I thought I heard that Laura Nyro song, 'And When I Die', which Jim and Paul would duet on in their cups, as bold as they were sozzled. Once again the singer pleaded for a coffin well upholstered to meet the fierce cold of eternity. Had tramp and rat lifted the lid of my head again, as they had under the lamp at Paignton Beach, and tipped the song in? Was it a hummable reminder of all that was left to bank on? I very nearly did start to hum it. That would have tickled them. So I didn't. Anyway, they were probably humming it themselves.

In my remaining time at Red Deer, I only saw Dawn from a distance. Some or other colleague of hers handled any admin involving me, no doubt at her understandable request, culminating in some of the paperwork around my departure. I spotted her, in fact, after that defining conversation with the Principal. She was heading back to her part of the campus world with a coffee and sandwich. Her world, set and safe. She didn't look round and I didn't want her to.

And a few weeks later I was dishing those pizzas in Brandon, thinking about Nancy, wondering where she was, grateful that I'd spared her—and Laurie—my turn as a gabbling dummy in the dark.

*

Silence: no ghost in the furnace, no further trick-or-treaters thumping onto the porch. But it was one of those silences that only starts when you listen. 'What have I missed?' thought Will and looked at his watch. He reckoned his own Hallowe'en band should be making their way back now, if Nanna wasn't fussing round them already. Best call, see how it all went...no, hear how Gram was the inevitable toast of the town, him and his special band, Hitchcock, Cushing, Karloff...Kenneth Williams, too, Will hoped, plummy and weird on the night air. Dr Watt...was that Williams's name in *Carry on Screaming?* He ran an aimless finger round the page he'd reached. The Battlefords had figured in Jonathan's life too, it seemed, in another piece of wreckage...as inevitable, that, as Gram's bullseye impersonations. He heard Kenneth Williams as himself, then through Gram's mouth. Where was the diff? Mid-chuckle, he caught himself and, after a second, wrinkled his nose. No smell to spoil his mood, nothing further from beyond the beyond. Huey and Louie must for sure be on a break, one changing his jacket, the other recharging the booze. Leaning over, he made to plug the rumpus-room phone back in but changed his mind. The snack bowl needed a recharge too.

Mmnneer, he tried as he climbed the stairs, *stop messin' about.* Jeez, he always fluffed that...*abaht, abaht,* it needed that...what was it Gram called it? The Cor Strewth Brit bit, like those loony rhymes, apples and pears and stuff. Like Jonathan had trotted out for his new buddies in Winnipeg, back when the paint was fresh on his escape. Man, he must get Gram to teach him the full Williams, the flared nostril thing, the downturned— He stopped. The light was flashing on the kitchen phone. Shoot. The phone had rung earlier but he'd been, well, alongside Parry in the Humboldt snow and then fixing Mark for good. It wasn't way late, but...had

244

something happened to the kids? Mags would have been with them. Wouldn't she? He couldn't remember if she'd said. Or had Gram been taken bad? According to Mags, he and Nanna had never had cross words, and he'd never heard one, but he could guess how things might have gone, Nanna worrying about the cold, wishing Gram's operation had come and gone—never mind next March or April—but not wanting to spoil things for the kids, a sentiment rousingly endorsed, no doubt, by the Battlefords' own Man of a Thousand Voices. Shoot, Gram would do his whole Hallowe'en show from a hospital bed if he had to. And Nanna and Mags exchanging anxious glances…so yeah, for sure Mags would have gone with them, one eye on the kids, the other on her dad. Oh, it was fine, all fine. What's the betting the phone message was from the kids themselves, taking their first steps towards *Gud Eveding* and *Mmnneer*? 'Mmnneer,' he repeated aloud as he pressed the button. 'Abaht, stop messing abaht.'

It wasn't the kids. It wasn't North Battleford. Will laid down the snack bowl and listened carefully. When the message finished, he opened the fridge without thinking, then an adjacent cupboard. He only realised the bowl was full when he saw stuff sliding off it and onto the counter. He skimmed off the top of the mound, put the surplus back, then turned and went slowly downstairs.

16

A little over a year ago, just into fall, I was a brief turn on Radio CKLZ Brandon during my second stint in the place. Something apart from my familiars had been tracking me west out of Ontario and found me dogs-bodying at the Assiniboine Hotel. And I was just thinking of moving on, too. Some would call this a miracle. For me, the only miracle now was that I was still going, still taking pot luck with towns and jobs.

Some way into my trek from Miramichi and Rideau's department store (which, I read somewhere, had since gone into administration), I sent Mum a birthday card. From Kapuskasing, I think it was. I hadn't planned where I'd be next but Thunder Bay must have been shaping up in my mind, so on an impulse I popped a note in, saying I could be reached there Poste Restante. I did that occasionally while on the road. Very occasionally. Foolishly, because such responses as I got were family affairs. There'd be just the one writer but I imagined a sheet of rough paper fleeting from Builth to Kettering and back again, gradually filling up with everyone's penny-worth, until the time was right to transfer the lot to Basildon Bond. But aside from localised details—a triumph here, a happy gathering there—the letters were much the same. Kettering Sid continued about his valetudinarian business. I'd never returned to visit Dad's grave and honour his memory. Why was that? When would I? Dear God, I was unnatural, a blight on Mum's soul.

246

What did I think I was playing at, staying over there, acting King Muck with my fancy ideas? Really, who did I think I was? In one letter, their apprentice censurer had a crack at telling me: *This is Craig,* announced an eruption of spiders in the midst of Auntie Irene's martial hand, *and I'd never foursake my mother. God help you in the army with me. I'd make sure you'd not last a minute. You are a dis-grace!!* With each letter, I told myself that was it: no more from King Muck. Then, slowly, I'd start to feel the beat of time. I'd struggle for a while, remind myself that they meant nothing to me, then either get a swift note over with or hold off till the next town. Often I'd use a postcard of somewhere I wasn't.

But nothing turned up while I was in Thunder Bay. Laurie certainly didn't. I'd forgotten she was there and, anyway, my finances were strictly cash-in-hand so I never became, in the usual bank-speak, anyone's valued customer.

I tell a lie. Something did turn up at Thunder Bay but not till I'd gone. Maybe I'd cut more of a distinctive figure there than I'd thought—maybe, after all this time in Canada, I was still an obvious Limey. Maybe I'd told someone particular that Brandon looked like the next stop. Anyway, something was dogged—fate or a momentary absence of chaos. Someone had a nose for my trail. I actually didn't bother with Poste Restante in Brandon, but the spectres of Builth and Kettering must have done because a reply to that birthday card for Mum arrived at the main post office. Much later, I pictured the whole bunch of them forming a circle round a map one evening and, after various discounted hypotheses ('Try Winnipeg?' 'No, he couldn't wait to clear out of there') or just through blind luck, stabbing a pin in Manitoba's second city.

For an age, though, I knew nothing of this. How could I? But finally, one of the postal clerks must have got sick and tired of seeing my family's reply unearthed, lying about, reburied, and called the local radio stations. And it was on the 'Afternoon Groove' with Herb Mann on 'truly wonderful CKLZee' that my name was announced and then yelled across the Assiniboine's Wheat Kings Lounge by Rudy the bartender.

'They want you to go down there,' said Rudy when I'd answered his summons, 'and they need identification.'

So, at the end of my shift and in the last half-hour of the 'Afternoon Groove', an assistant met me at the station, checked my ID and, finger to lips, ushered me into Herb's studio where she whispered in his ear and I sat tight during Kate Bush's 'Babooshka'.

Giving me the thumbs-up, Herb bit into the ending: 'Classy-song-classy-ladeee.' Despite the season, he was in barbecue gear, shades pushed back on his bandana'd head, a tee-shirt with *Take Off, Eh?,* a catchphrase from Bob and Doug McKenzie's 'Canadian content' send-ups on *Saturday Night Live.* On the back, I guessed, would be *Hoser!* Gold bracelets flopped round either wrist. Did he remember to keep them quiet when the mic was live or was rattling and clunking part of his style?

No chance to check any of that out. A moment later I was in a little slot labelled *This is Your Life.*

'You know how public-spirited we are here, folks,' barked Herb. 'You know how we get responsible 'bout as much as wacky.' He tilted back in his chair and gave the assistant saucer eyes: 'Man, oh, man—talk about wacky. Didn't we play "Jet Boy, Jet Girl", that Captain Sensible gar-barrrge, only last week? But'—on a rising tone—'just the once, hey? Just the once and no more?' The assistant's nod wrapped up that sub-routine. 'Now, seriously seriously se-ri-ous-lee, we are proud to do our duty when so called upon. Which is why I have here with me a letter from England in the U of K, courtesy of Canada Post—ou La Poste Canadienne, let's keep tout le monde happy—and I have here the gentleman to whom it is addressed. Now this letter, my friends, it's been loafing around for-an-absolute-age down at the Douglas Street Office. Shoot, friends, m' man Jimmy down there tells me it was hanging about so long it was starting to help out, make the coffee and I don't know what-all. So Jimmy—and yes, my friends, a humongous shout-out to all who ply their sorting trade at Douglas and everywhere in our Assiniboine River home—he phoned around all the stations. And'—hand-flings now—'I guess yours truly at CKLZ, the station with the digit on the pulse, has been the first to put out the word and unite man and missive, right here, right in your "Afternoon Groove" and'—a quick glance at the clock— 'with sixty seconds to go before a word from our beloved sponsors, Hopson's Seed and Feed. Now don't go away. Abba and the Eagles are happening right along. But ahead of all that, may I introduce the addressee of this determined old letter, Mr Jonathan Parry. So, Jonathan, my assistant, the divine Cherie Amour, she tells me you're from across the pond too. So—this is from the loving family, hey?' He handed it across as ceremoniously as the ticking seconds would allow. 'So—do they want to know when your next load of laundry's coming their way?'

I studied the handwriting, nodded, said yes. I would have said more and it wasn't nerves that stopped me. Damn it, I thought I was going to cry. Ok, so this was Herb's job, he'd do the same with anyone, but his manner and smile struck me as more than shtick. Who knows, maybe the letter broke up a grind of a day for him. For a moment I saw him alongside the warehouse foreman back in Dolbeau, his cousin who wouldn't take any rent, Farmer Kettering, Ian Baillie. As the seconds pushed toward the Hopson's ad, here was kindness. But he covered most of them by leaning across, patting my arm, saying 'Jonathan, it's cool, it's cool—not everyone has a bionic mouth like yours truly. Ask Cherie Amour here. But hey, you got a song request? We could slot her in tomorrow.'

'The Zombies? "She's Not There"?' How that came to mind and got me speaking, I've no idea.

But I could hear Bevvo: 'Nah, not their best. "Tell Her No", mate, that's the one.' In my head I told Bevvo no, then Herb was saying, 'A fine choice, my friend. Consider it done.' He pressed a button and a voice that introduced itself as Lou Hopson's gave a pacey rundown on next week's Seed and Feed deals.

On the way back to the Assiniboine, I found a coffee shop and, even better, an empty corner booth. Oh yes, I recognised the handwriting on the envelope, a neat tilt of loops, unbowed by the official stamps and scrawls around them. I opened it slowly, thinking that, well, at least this would be just the two of us, Mum and I. Hardly face-to-face but communing after a fashion as the Brandon afternoon went by.

Which meant I wasn't ready...the writer was actually Kettering Sid, whose words of sprightly admonition suggested that, far from hanging about death's door, he'd retreated from it, growing younger with every step. Or maybe he'd come to detest the tee-total life, if he was still leading it, and was taking it out on death through open spite. But death wasn't his target now:

'...and the couple down the way, they had the fright of their lives coming home last week from the pictures. There's your mother, your poor mother, weaving about on the Corby road. If one of them hotheads had come along, them ton-up merchants, she'd have been gone to the angels. That's how she is now, you little bastard, that's what your neglect has brought her to. Neglect, matey! God knows what end of the line place

251

you're in. But if there is a God He'd best make sure you get this. And when you do, just you get bloody home.' There was more like that, both before and after. *Get bloody home* popped up everywhere like spring weeds. Altogether it was an unbuttoned rewrite of that letter waiting for me at the near-empty house in Winnipeg when Mum was getting ready to up sticks.

I couldn't remember the last time I'd spoken to Mum: I pretty well avoided phone calls. It might have been a while back, which had finally guilted me into sending the birthday card. Or it might have been more recently, so the card had followed logically from the call, the other bit of a two-part package. She didn't say what if anything she was doing now and I didn't ask. She was still in Builth but a move to Kettering, which she'd hinted at before my Christmas call from Humboldt, was still a possibility. She didn't sound poorly, nor did she mention illness. She just sounded like someone whose life had stopped. We might have compared notes on that, but it wasn't possible. We just wouldn't have understood each other. That, I'm sorry to say, didn't bother me. Maybe, after all this time, it didn't bother her either. Ah, well…the pitfalls of duty contact.

But Kettering Sid was determined, yet again, that I should be bothered. For all that they were banged in like nails, though, his words meant only questions. *There's your mother, your poor mother, weaving about on the Corby road.* So had she moved to Kettering or was she just visiting? Either way, and if she was in such bad shape, wouldn't she have been better off staying in Builth with Auntie Irene, Nicky, the peerless Craig when he was on leave—something approaching a family? If she was in such bad shape, was Kettering Sid taking some kind of advantage, righteously insisting on her poorliness while having her nicely on hand to fetch and carry for him, however feebly? And her writing on the envelope when it was really his sermon—what was that all about? Her writing looked just as it did in her days as a top teacher. The switcheroo reminded me of a fight I got into with a kid in our street when I was nine, ten. Summer, it was, coming on evening, and he'd manoeuvred me into his gateway. I was scared, I remember, but even more, angry—you might call it a test run for the Erkeley evening. And it might have gone something like that but, as I stepped through the kid's gate, the neighbourhood hard nut flew at me from behind the hedge and laid me out on the pavement. One draws you on, another pounces. Pure Wiznuk.

In the last paragraph, Kettering Sid spluttered that he'd sent a previous letter and if I'd bloody got it I'd already know about Mum's state of health. That one had obviously missed its miracle. Maybe it was still lying in a sorting-room between here and the Maritimes or wedging open a postie's apartment window.

Next day I was down at the post office myself: not the main place on Douglas—I didn't want to risk running into the tireless, station-phoning

Jimmy—but a Drug Mart out on 18th. The telegram was brisk: *Last barmy letter received. What's this about health, Mum? Advise.* I arranged for any reply to come to the Drug Mart. As I walked back to the Assiniboine, I heard the last few bars of 'She's Not There' through the window of a parked car, followed by 'And that, my friends, is going out for Jonathan Parry, a friend in need. Man, I hope the news was good. He'll know what I mean, folks.' Again I recalled Herb's smile, his 'Jonathan, it's cool, it's cool'; again I thought of the occasional kindnesses I'd known in (by then) over a year on the road: how fleeting they were, how—in the absence of any other sort—I had to make the most of their passing shows. Such kindness didn't include Rudy the Assiniboine bartender, who wasn't unfriendly but now just wanted to pump me about the station episode, which he'd missed, and the letter. I dispatched the first with 'Nice guy, Herb' and the second with 'Oh, just family catch-up. I'd sent them the Assiniboine as my address but some klutz threw it away.'

In one way I was peeved at myself for sending the telegram. In another, though, I wanted to grab some kind of control over the present drama. Who knows what was going on over there? Setting aside Kettering Sid's carry-on—actually, that's exactly what I did, letting its pieces fall like Humboldt snow into the bin. If Mum was really ill, then I'd go so far as to make a compact trip back with only her health in mind. If she wasn't—if this was a new round in the game of get-him-back-just-to-show-we-can—then   I'd give Kettering Sid and the rest an unholy mouthful and still jump into a taxi for the airport—just earlier than planned. And if they sicked Nicky's Craig on me, well, I could get my dander up with one big memory of all the toys he'd ruined. That'd carry me quite some way.

So I stayed on longer than I'd vaguely meant to at the Assiniboine. There was no problem. It was a bumper time for conferences, everyone from the Manitoba Shriners to a humongous gathering of the great and good in Hockey Canada, and they needed all hands. It must have been round ten days later that Dale the under-manager beckoned me into his office: 'Yeah, this is him,' he said to a postwoman on the other side of his desk, who nodded at him, at me, and departed.

The telegram was sealed—an old-fashioned touch, I thought, but then, I'd never had a telegram before. In fact, the whole situation seemed like a tableau, stock-still boss, grave messenger. I took my time opening it. I said nothing. All Dale said, studying my face, was 'Oh, my man, my man'—just like Jim, I remembered later, when he'd come home to find Laurie and I leaving each other's lives. *Now will you come back?* the message ended.

Tramp and rat took a breather, kept a respectful distance on the flight to England. I passed much of the time by thinking of the months before the Erkeley evening. It's an old routine, I know: go back to how things were before the bad event, the nightmare; hide in them (well, I was a seasoned hider by then); wonder if there was something in that prior time that might have steered me past the Erkeley evening—even, more desperately, if there was something that might have prevented Gordy from suggesting we go there. All pointless, but no less seductive for that—reminding me of a line from Beckett that was much on Paul's lips in the run-up to that Christmas production of *Endgame*: *You must go on, I can't go on, You must go on, I'll go on.* I can't remember if it's in the play but I can still hear Paul at that patter like a dog at a bone. So it was for me now as, passing on the in-flight movie, I watched the sun spreading out on the clouds between Brandon and Toronto. You lose yourself in the useless what-ifs, knowing that all you'll get is a swimming head, but still you lose yourself more, more.

I certainly didn't dwell on that switcheroo fight when I was nine or so (though I should add that I came across that kid again a while later, minus neighbourhood hard-nut, and evened the score). But I did settle on a moment from a late spring. I was forever changing my bedroom around. It was something to do and part of me must have thought that, with each change, I'd find a more secure and Craig-proof place for the toys I kept up there. May, it must have been, a good two months before the Erkeley evening. I went for broke and turned my bed round, so that, instead of lying alongside the wall, I'd be right where the curtains met. Before, I always made sure that the curtains were pulled tight across each other. Now I left a gap, two, three inches, so that I could see the sky and the stars when our street stopped being annoying and fell quiet. Sometimes, even though I had to turn my head round a bit, I fell asleep with the evening star in view. I'd never slept that soundly before and I sure haven't since. It made a world—me, the quiet, the star—as good as, even better than, the retreat of academe. A few days later, Mum complained about having to squeeze past the headboard every time she went into the room. When I came back from school that day, the bed was hard against the wall again. Magic, I thought as we started our descent into Toronto where hours stood and waited before my night connection. It could have been magic, staying in that world with its evening star, living out the days in a dream. Roomier, too, than Mr Vesey's pot-plant.

Tramp and rat stayed well clear at Sedgley Parish Church, too, and at Gornal Wood Crematorium, where I stood on the other side of the chapel from the rest of them as Mum completed her trail from one continent to another, from Builth to Kettering, and back to Dad. Builth Sid, the sombre carpenter, had collared me just as I arrived at the church from my b&b far away in Stourton. I remembered how, when they all descended on Winnipeg for Dad's funeral, he'd been distant with me (well, that was his default manner) but also respectful. I guessed after that he'd been reabsorbed into the posse—that his sentiments chimed as loudly as anyone's with Kettering Sid's—but here he was, drawing me aside in a not unkindly manner, elaborating on the telegram they'd sent:

'She was going anyway, lad. Heart was done for after your Dad went. She tried to...well, she went after a few jobs.'

'Teaching?'

He shrugged: 'One was, maybe more. I think it was just for the look of it. She kept things close.' He studied me. 'I thought you should have come back here for your Dad. Still think it. But if you had your reasons....' Now he pressed my arm, the gesture surprising him as much as me. 'It was just you on your own, eh? I always thought that. Right from when—' But Auntie Irene was shrilling his name from the porch and he stepped back into himself, even clearing his throat like some tv character nearly caught with hand in till. 'Well, if we don't meet again, lad....' Pushing something into my pocket, he turned away.

Obviously that was not the time to tell him that I hadn't been alone since I saw Mum off at Toronto. And there wouldn't be another time. I watched him walk—reluctantly, I thought—to join his wife. With a back-cocked thumb he indicated that I'd arrived, at which she flicked her eyes skywards—a gesture no doubt copied by whoever might have been behind her—and shooed him inside. A moment later I followed, slowly, thinking of what I'd heard. At first I marvelled. Builth Sid had said more to me in five

258

minutes than in all my childhood years. Then I pictured Mum leaning over some application form in the kitchen or dining room at Builth, filling in this and that section just for the look of it—a faint, even rather grotesque replay of the antics that had filled our house that Erkeley summer. *She was going anyway, lad.* It had started in the year after Dad's death, when I'd willed her to become again what she could be, what she was, the top teacher, the full woman, all present and correct. Perhaps her manner with me—the withdrawal from her own life while she was still in Winnipeg, that mix of disinterest and irritation during our sporadic phone talks once she'd gone—was her way of saying there was nothing I could do. Not only on an envelope, it seemed, had she worked a switcheroo. She'd even worked it on Beckett's wisdom. You must go on. I can't go on. You must go on. I won't.

I wasn't planning to stay for the limp sandwich do after Gornal Wood and they weren't planning to let me. During the service and the cremation, they held themselves in, though Auntie Irene and Nicky couldn't help themselves and landed the odd glance. But I made sure I was first out of the Crem chapel—pushed out, really, by the final note of *Abide With Me*—and picked up pace across the grounds to where my taxi would arrive.

'We need a word wiv you!' If I could take one bit of revenge against tramp and rat, it would be to fill their heads with Nicky's voice. No more plaguing then—they'd scamper back where they came from, hands to ears, shrieking. I wasn't about to stop for her but another voice did the trick. 'Oi!,' it kept repeating, 'Oi!' I had to pull up then, had to turn. Call it appalled fascination.

Kettering Sid was stumbling along the path at the head of the posse. Nicky might have been ahead of him at first but now she'd dropped back to do the glaring with the rest. Pumped up to full height, Auntie Irene had adopted a walk to (presumably) make strong men quail but the effect was of a drag-artist trying to walk like a woman. Between her and Nicky was Craig, every inch the gauleiter, ready to play his part should Britain need to go all colonial again. Builth Sid, though, was some way behind.

As the yards closed between us, I saw how the veins stood broken and red on Kettering Sid's cheeks. Was this from his present efforts or was he off the wagon? Had that made Mum such a handy resident in Kettering—off-licence runs, quick nips into the supermarket? Had she been sampling the goods the night she wove her way along the Corby road? Whatever, he looked a state, as though Death was fascinated by him too and couldn't quite bring itself to yank the thread.

'Barmy letter?' he roared now, waving something over his head: my telegram, I guessed. 'Barmy letter? You article! You bloody, bloody article! We all saw her will—'

'—My Sergeant, he witnessed it—'

Add Craig's voice to the torment for tramp and rat.

'—and I'll tell you this much, chum'—now my telegram was closing on my chest; perhaps its bearer hoped it would magic into a sword—'you'll get nothing. Nothing.'

Nothing. It was the perfect legend for their escutcheon, like other families have Faith or Fortitude. And its power brought them all to a halt now. Beyond them, I could see our vicar standing by one of the columns where the wreaths and flowers were set out. Staring open-mouthed, he was surrounded by others no less aghast, presumably the mourners for the next farewell.

Now I got angry, though I kept it in. What had started with Dad's accident was ending with self-righteousness, the provincial preen, Mum used as a cheap excuse.

'I want nothing,' I said quietly, but they all heard. A horn pipped and I turned to see my taxi. As I stepped away, I got a good view of Builth Sid, several yards behind the rest. His face was inscrutable but that was a hell of an improvement on everything else I'd got.

'Goodbye, Uncle,' I called to him. It was the last I had to do with any of them.

In the taxi back to Stourton I thought of Builth Sid's words. *It was just you on your own. I always thought that.* Through my early years I'd seen him as a sphinx, a patch of silence at the edge of all the chat. Well, that's sphinxes for you: you can't tell what they're thinking. Or if? He clearly had been, though, as he watched me getting older, as he saw—what? An outline of aloneness around me, a shroud of frost? He'd guessed that I was the plus-one in our family, living luggage when we made the break to Canada. Maybe he thought he should have said something, anything, before then. But what would I have thought if he'd tried? And if I'd passed it on, wouldn't I have got him into some kind of mysteriously adult trouble, caused the traitor's *T* to burn into his cheek?

Still, he was bound and determined to betray them all today, to let it be known that over time he'd got the picture no-one else cared about. To speak once only before he sank back into the space the others allowed. Brigadoon Man. Bless him, I thought in my b&b room as I hung up my jacket and only then remembered...

...*We'd have come Jonathan,* said the letter with the condolence card I fished out of the pocket, *only Arthur got proper poorly round about last Christmas and the doctor said Mr Butler, you've been in the Black Country too long, time for bags of sea air so Kevin called in some favours (his very "words" you know the business world) and sorted us out a villa in Lytham St Anne's, made me chuckle "villa" it's a small bungalow honestly those estate agents and their chat but it's just right for us. Arthur's health's been up and down ever since, a bit better this summer just gone but with the weather (they say it'll be a "nasty" winter) we thought it best not to risk Gornal. We nearly came to Builth, July it would have been, but when I phoned I couldn't speak to your poor Mum and there seemed to be some confusion about whether she'd be there, I should've said to her come up here, would've if I'd got hold of her but as I say there was some confusion and we've had no end of trouble with the phone since, honestly if they can put men on the moon, they say we'll have a new phone in "two weeks maximum" I'll believe it when I see it. But you're welcome to visit Jonathan if this gets you while you're here and if you've time, address is above but we'll understand if not, you've got so much on your plate right now. Jonathan I hope all was sorted okay with that phone call stuff I did and those old friends of yours. Not that I'd style them friends I'd have thought they'd be happy you were trying to get in touch that Gordy sounded a right article not wanting to reply, but if the other one did it'd be no more than he should what's wrong with old time's sake? Anyway heartfelt good wishes from us and Arthur says "Have you learnt that Hiawatha yet?" and I tell him "Jonathan's too sensible for your nonsense" which makes him laugh which is the best medicine don't they say? You take care love, Dorothy (Butler, Mrs.) p s you've probably forgotten about it but this is on the paper from that lovely writing stuff you sent ages ago with that nice letter, I've still got a lot of the paper and envelopes which I only use for "best."*

My return flight was in three days, tied to a special deal. I'd thought about trying to bring it forward though I could ill afford the extra that might involve. Then again, 'address is above', as

Mrs Butler said, and I could do Lytham and then straight down to Heathrow. Given some of my accommodation on the road, culminating in my broom-cupboard at the back of the Assiniboine, a few hours dossing in an airport lounge would be no hell.

I found the owner, Tall Nige as he seemed to be known to all, and laid out my change of plan:

'You'll be lucky, my friend,' he said, and for a moment I thought he was talking about any refund for the two nights I wouldn't after all be staying. 'See these?' And he waved a hand over the day's headlines in the papers on the hall-stand.

'Oh,' I said. 'Right.'

'Nothing running. All the main lines, by the look of it,' he said, drawing my attention to a column in the *Daily Express*. 'Here, in and out of Liverpool Lime Street, look, well that's the one you'd be needing. Greedy buggers.' He threw the paper down. 'They want to try the hospitality trade, mate, no-one to give you a magic pay-rise there.'

Back in my room, I composed a thank-you to Mrs Butler, hoping that Mr Butler's health and the phone people would alike prove reliable, apologising that I wouldn't be able to visit because of 'present circumstances', whatever on earth I meant by that. As I wrote, I thought of how flimsy in all senses the business of writing a letter was, of sending words over an immense distance, waiting however long for a reply that might not come. Some people said that the very

264

act of writing a letter warmed them, that it made for a connection already. I just felt cold despite the cosiness of the room, a cold that deepened when I thought of what had happened at the Crem that day. Maybe if I hadn't felt that way, if Mrs Butler's phone had been working or the train-drivers weren't on wildcat strikes.... Here we go again. A thousand maybes. But maybe I wouldn't have had the idea which grew as I finished the letter and, cadging a stamp from Mrs Nige, posted it as I walked to The Stourton Arms for an indifferent supper.

'I'm going that way,' said Tall Nige next morning after breakfast. 'Going over to the Cash and Carry in Tipton. I can drop you off.' Which he did, at the top of the Sedgley Road. It was half-an-hour before lunchtime opening so I walked up and down near the Junction Inn, just enough to spot changes. From the traffic lights by the Inn you used to be able to see the signs for the Sedgley Gaumont and, next to it, Williams and Glyn's Bank. Both were gone now and I couldn't bring myself to find out what had replaced them. Despite being in the parish church the day before, I was unable to believe where I was…unable to believe, a little later, that I was drinking only the second pint of English beer I'd had in my life. I knew all the sneers about the North American stuff but it was what I was used to and the pint tasted like thinned sump-oil. Abandoning it, I ordered a double whiskey, Jameson's, dependable. Then I set off.

The top of the lane was just the same, though even from there I could see that the school was tattier. But the upper reaches of the Erkeley had gone. In their place, squat little cheek-by-jowl houses pushed downhill, the kind that would soon make the shanty-town detacheds below look all Victorian-sturdy. 'Sentimental journey, is it?' Tall Nige had asked as we drove in and I'd said something about looking up old friends and was ready with a name if he asked, which he didn't. I could never call the likes of the Timothys friends, not even remotely—*père* only existed in my memory as a gruff voice threatening all sorts if we messed about with his electrical goods and the only time I can recall speaking to *fils* was when I bought 'All You Need Is Love'—but as I walked down I wondered if they, or at least goofy *fils*, still lived in their shanty-detached. The miscalculations we make. It wasn't as if a century had gone by. Like Jeff Cordingley, like Mr Derksen next door in Winnipeg, Timothy *père* was somewhere round Dad's age, which probably meant he was still running his shop and nowhere near the grave; as for *fils*, acne and crooked teeth could well have given way to Jim-like good looks. For a second, I had an impulse to do what Gordy had suggested all those years, those evenings ago: pop up at the Timothy window, gurn at whoever was inside and leg it. Stupid. If they'd moved away, what would the new people think? If they hadn't— well, it was the middle of a working day, so would they or even Mrs Timothy (there had to be one) be there to rise to the bait? I pictured myself not legging it, standing frozen by the window as a Timothy or non-Timothy burst out of the front door and cried *What the bloody hell...*? I remembered that night with Dawn at Paignton Beach, how I'd poured everything out though it wasn't me doing it, and imagined doing just the same to an annoyed, then confused, then frightened stranger. I also remembered that Gordy had never said exactly which house it was and you'd think I'd have dropped the whole notion right there. But no: part of me was still up for picking any old house, gurning, loitering, confessing once more. I say part of me. Was it? They'd stayed well away since I left Brandon. Now the official reason for being here was over. Yes...Wiznuk had aimed his catapult, fired that stupidity into my head like the stone that caught Bevvo's ear. Toper and whisperer, they were about again. How could they not be?

Further down, stakes and plastic ribbons said that more little houses would be thrown up by and by. There'd be nothing left of the Erkeley by the upper end of the lane. But incredibly Tafler's tree was still there, below the ribbons, and so was the pond. Maybe some local civic group had managed to preserve them; maybe the little houses would have to pause and carry on past them to the boundary of the school. 'Mind you watch out for the Erkeley ghost,' Tall Nige had laughed. 'Old souse, he was, used to camp out there. Taylor or some such name. Kiddie-killer.' Stepping off the lane, I skirted the pond, opened my shoulder-bag and took out the flowers I'd bought the previous evening at Stourton petrol station. They were even sorrier now. By the tree I looked round: no-one about but I wouldn't have cared if there was. If they knew about Tafler they might have thought I was a relative of his, returned from the ends of the earth, determined to leave some remembrance in spite of the legend, laughingly rendered by Tall Nige, which had evidently chased his name into history. Or that I was a friend, a brother of the killed kiddie. Thinking of all that, I realised that the words waiting on my lips would have to do much more than I'd anticipated. As I lay the flowers at the base of the tree, I thought I saw something glint. The stopper, maybe, that Bevvo was set to add to his antiques hoard till the Lord of Erkeley staked his claim? Unretrieved by Bevvo at a later date, undisturbed all these years? In different circumstances, I might have investigated. But what different circumstances could there have been? And anyway, the words were pressing to be said.

'Sorry,' I whispered. Then, louder, 'I'm so very sorry.'

Stepping back, I looked up, expecting to see them a little way off, side by side in the dull air. Expecting, I guess, another version of how they'd appeared at the other end of that Humboldt gulley. Kinder. Happier. Somewhere in there, no doubt, was a renewed hope that what I couldn't reach by trying to love Laurie, Nancy, Dawn above all, would be granted me now.

Any or all of that must have been what did it. Compared to it, my fancy of gurning at the window of the Timothy house (or not) was, I see now, the best of good sense. It can't have lasted more than a minute: the thrumming, the wind tearing the flower-paper, scattering the petals, the thrumming louder, becoming the saw of a crow, the uprush of a soccer tribe when a goalie runs at a kick ('You fat bastard!'), fattening to a single wide note from a choir in a place beyond light and dark, splitting to a pair of noises, an almost snigger, an almost retch—turning at last to all that waits when, with time on your hands at the end of the night, you still forsake the bright lights for the short cut through the underpass, the wooded path, the alley.

Back at the b&b, I nodded as the doctor said, 'Well, if you're sure' and, thanking him again for his promptness, Mrs Nige led him away. I stayed sitting on the edge of the bed, hearing the door shut and nothing more. I couldn't have described what had happened hours before. I don't want to now.

I rallied for the flight home. The whole trip, though, had almost cleaned me out and I was waiting for the icing on the cake: Dale telling me kindly but firmly—as others had before and would after—that, hey, real sorry, but that's that for that. But the Assiniboine job was good for another fortnight. Rudy had taken off for a bar-job in Banff, getting into early position, I guess, for good money during the ski season. On the other hand, Mr Parbst, Dale's boss—whom I

269

might have seen twice in all my time there—had a nephew in Quebec who, for reasons Dale either didn't know or wouldn't reveal, had need of work, plus a buddy in the same boat. So that nepotism-and-a-bit soon saw me on my way west of Brandon. Still, despite the England trip, I had a little cash, something to keep me moving. Kettering Sid hadn't done for me altogether. A while later came that empty Christmas with my co-gofer at the Weyburn Soo Line Museum and then the slow roll towards my third time in Saskatchewan, *High Office,* and Peach, Jake, Don Rydell.

There I go again. Like Waskesiu, the England trip has slipped its place in the chronology. You should have read it, whoever you are, before Weyburn…before the *High Office* stuff, come to that. Well, yes and no. What left me mute on the side of the bed in Stourton didn't happen again. That's to say, once I was back in Brandon, the pair of them reverted to how they'd been before I flew to England: everyday escorts, nicely in place, unshowy save in the matter of a new bottle here or jacket there. They could almost have been a pair of maiden aunts whose favour I was courting in hopes of a nice legacy. But of course they weren't. As with the meeting in the dark snow of Humboldt, I'd had another roaring kick along the way things had to be.

Some folks say that a person might only need to lose it, really lose it, once in their life. Ever after, at some level, those round them, those who witnessed it, will be waiting for the next time…which is an hour hence or the twelfth of never. Of course, I'd waited like that before. And again the wait had been answered. But tramp and rat had dished up double, there at the Erkeley, and then some.

I should say that what left me mute on that Stourton bed never happened again in that way. The weeks passed, the months, the kilometre-markers, the brands of soda on the signs at the next gas station. But something like it did happen. So the England bit, I'd say, is in the right place.

*

Will turned over the last words for a long time. Then he thought about the flashing message light up in the kitchen.

'Jonathan, it's ok,' he said at last, taking an invalid's sip of the whiskey and setting it aside. He saw deep snow among pine trees, tamarack, sugar maple. A beautiful part of the world, where sister Annie had moved her family to. Mags and the kids, they loved home Christmases but already they'd been getting just a bit antsy about doing it someplace else this year. He chuckled. Moonlight in Vermont, eh? The whole clan together again. And why not? 'Course, didn't have to be moonlight. Could be late afternoon, which was near enough dark that you could say, what's the diff? A bracing walk, deep, deep into the forest. Not the whole caboodle. Well, they'd be into baking this, preparing that, and he could

271

just see all of the kids—small and not so small—
scooting about in that way they had just before
Christmas, starting to do something they'd been
asked, determined to do it, then forgetting in the
sheer buzz of it all. So not the whole caboodle
heading out to the forest with the moon waiting
to come up. Just two.

The hum of the furnace, the faint whoosh of a
car passing. Will's whisper: 'Jonathan, I can
make it evens. In your name, man.' His frown as
he tried for a moment to recall exactly what
Annie's place looked like. His uneasy shrug.

17

'Hey, Parry—message for you.'

I was late but it didn't matter. It was my last
day at *High Office*—about two months ago now,
and just over two years since I left Red Deer.
Hard to credit, really, but everything had long
been that.

Broiling, it was, right from dawn. I was late
but what was there to do save clear out my
locker, hang about for my final pay? For some
reason, Don Rydell wanted to hand it over in
cash rather than authorise the usual bank credit.
Maybe he had a little talk prepared before I
walked out into the world once more. Some part
of him, I sensed, had never given up on me but
he had a business to run—to save, you might say,
given my grand ineptitude instore and out.
There'd been some talk of my going with Slithery

Jake and Peach on one last demonstration call, on the understanding that I was just to smile and say a scripted word or two (one last use of my residual limey-appeal, I suppose). They were up for it, Jake promising on the q.t. that there'd be four in the van: 'Mr Daniels is ready for the ride,' he'd said. 'You just have a quiet sip whenever you're so minded—but keep the damn bottle in the bag.' In the event, I didn't go.

Outside my apartment on Cumberland Avenue, a bus sailed by. I let it. Umpteen blocks and then over University Bridge into town, but I didn't care, didn't mind the heat. Loose clothes and a slow walk would do me just fine.

When I got to the six hundreds, the lady from the apartment upstairs pulled up alongside me.

'Mercy, Jonathan, won't you be late?'

'It's ok, Mrs King, they…the manager has a big meeting on, told us all to be there by ten-thirty.'

'Oh…but I can still give you a ride. I'm going in that direction.' Lines crinkled at the corner of her eyes: 'The Bay, coffee with friends,' she smiled. 'Perk of being an old body.'

Smiling back, I studied Mrs. King's kindly, widowed face. Dorothy Butler hovered there a moment…smiling too, as she'd done that long gone evening when she and Mr Butler had presented me with the calf-bound copy of Longfellow; as I like to think she had during that phone call about Bevvo and Gordy or while writing the letter Mum had slid across the table to me that last Christmas in Crescentwood—who knows, even while she was writing what Builth Sid gave me outside Sedgley church. Mementos—Longfellow, kind words from an ocean away, one smile shared by a face from back then and a face from right now. More scraps from the family I'd missed.

'I really appreciate it, Mrs K, but I'm fine.'

'Are you sure? The day's set to cook a goose.'

'I'll take it easy.'

'Well, all right, but any other time…I'll be glad of the company.' Her wave, the car gathering speed, me stood there till it disappeared. I'd sent the Butlers a card the previous Christmas but hadn't given any return address. Well, I hadn't one to give: I knew I'd quit Weyburn with the new year and I sure as hell didn't want to go through that Poste Restante shemozzle again. I really had to write to Mrs B again, though, properly, whatever happened after *High Office Initiatives*.

Slowly I walked on, letting sights and sounds happen. The wide streets, emptying as the different clocking-on times came round. A high mesh fence to the right along the five hundreds: an elementary school, yard silent, a door swinging shut as some slowpoke ran to where he should be. Sometimes for minutes together, just the sound of my feet.

For a blissful while now they'd been on another vacation. For sure there hadn't been a repeat of the day I returned to Tafler's pond. Of course, it was Red Deer again: I'd got the bullet, they got free time. As I crossed University

Bridge, though, something made me wonder if they were loping back over the horizon. I stopped. Cars and trucks whooshed behind me—some heading out of town, no doubt, some headed for offices, workshops, Eaton's, the Army and Navy, the Bay (was Mrs King now in full flow with her friends?), the Bessborough, the Parktown Motel, where I'd met Slithery Jake a few times for some beers and more Roughriders stats. At that time I figured I'd be in this city for a while, so maybe part of me had been looking for a substitute, however faint, for the Sidebar in Windsor. As for finding anyone like Jim or Paul, though…well, in another time and circumstance, Jake, Peach—who knows, even Don himself—might have almost filled the bill. But then in another time and circumstance I might have been finishing a second thesis and, some time after that, Jim Kloes might have been lunging for me at another party, this time in a Halifax suburb: 'It's Doctor Parry!' I heard above the engines, the occasional horn.

I leaned over the parapet. For dog-day season, the South Saskatchewan was flowing strangely fast and seemed full of whispers. Whether tramp and rat were loping back or this was just in my head, I sensed that something else would shortly start to unfold. A memory came back from my last year at high school: the big play, *Dr Faustus,* for which I'd been roped in to dress the stage: thick drapes, musty books, a cardboard astrolabe, all that. It wasn't the first time that misstepper had been on my mind. I thought of a particular scene, where Faustus has another crack at repentance and at once Mephistopheles flips him a dagger. No, the dagger says—you stay with the devils or you deal with yourself. I thought of Bob Corey, a guy in my year, slight, a bit put-upon but able to handle it, who'd played Faustus's servant, whatever his name was. Wardrobe had given him a cloak and hat at least a size too big: bribed, it was said, by a couple of the school assholes. But that didn't stop him being the best on the stage, way better than his master. How he'd delivered one particular line must've made an impression on many besides me; folks were repeating it in awed tones for days after: *I think my master means to die shortly.* I repeated it now, looking down at the hurrying river. The flame of defiance that had reared up while I did that computer course to oblige Don, that abided even as tramp and rat trashed my IT career, that had never really gone out—it leapt now, leapt afresh, making me push away from the parapet so hard I nearly rolled over the hood of a car.

'Johnny Canuck,' I whispered to myself as the car's horn died away. Then, louder, 'Johnny Faustus.' Half scared, half laughing, I picked up pace downtown.

'You hear me, Parry?' came again. I'd hardly got in the showroom door. 'Phone message.'

*

Shoot. Will looked at his watch. Shoot. Phone. Maybe I'll just catch them. Squatting, he plugged in the rumpus-room phone. But the kids were in bed, Mags told him when she answered, worn out, happy as larks. Yes, they'd had a great time, and yes, Gram entertained the whole town with his daffy Hollywood ghouls and ghosties. He was in bed, too, tuckered out but none the worse for his exertions, and 'Mom and me, we're just sitting quiet.'

'Real sorry I'm so late calling, hon.'

'Whatcha been doing? Running some old stag movies?' Mags chuckled, her voice pure comfort. 'No, I was going to try you but I thought you might be out with Terry or whoever. But hey, thanks for phoning a while back.'

'Way back now, Mags. I wanted to make sure you'd got there ok.'

'No, while we were out.'

'What?'

'Mom took the call.'

'Who was it?'

'Well, you, honey. Don't you know your own voice? You said hi, hope all is good. Then you started frigging about.'

'With your mom? Never ever.'

Mags' voice dipped as she called 'He says it wasn't him' to her background. Then to Will, 'The voice went English, mom said, kind of wavery. Then it cut out and there was just static. Sort of. Like wind in the trees, she said. Like way into the woods.'

'What did this English voice say?'

277

'Nothing she could really make out. More just a limey tone, you know? Just blowing on.' Mags laughed. 'Could be the system's gone temperamental.' She turned away again—'What?'—then laughed louder. 'System schmystem, says Mom. Says we'll find it was Dad, spooking her from somewhere in town. Didn't see him stopping by a phone but the kids were so high I was pulled this way and that. Look at those huge spiders, Mom, look at those bats! He slid off for a while, too. Needed something from Gilliland's—so he said. I can't believe that store's still going. So I couldn't have eyes on him all the way. Anyways, whatever…if you did try calling when the phone was engaged…sweets, you still there?'

'She all right? Your mom?'

Mags laughed. 'Take more than a weird call to freak her out. Yeah, it's Dad, I'll bet. He played Mister Baffled about it when we got back—of course—but if he told the kids on the q.t. he must've threatened them with Dracula in case they squeaked. They were all up ahead of me on the walk back—great chance for a secret pact. But we'll get it out of them. No breakfast till they fess up.'

'Yeah, I was thinking, he's just got to get me right with all those Brit voices.' Will rushed his words. He pictured the flashing light on the phone upstairs. 'But what about that sound? The wind in the trees?'

'Will, my darling, if your father-in-law can do Hitchcock and Lugosi and all he can surely do nature. Man, it'll be such a let-down if it wasn't him. The wind came in fierce for real this evening. Some snow, too. So who knows? Could be the phones on the fritz. But I sort of hope not.'

'Yeah, Mrs Butler said the phone in their new place was kaput— '

'Mrs Who?'

'Nothing…nothing, sorry, just someone at work. Admin.'

'Oh. Right.'

'I was thinking about where to spend Christmas,' he rushed again.

'Land sakes, Will, think about picking us up first. Bus is in around three, ok?'

'Yeah, sure. Hey, love to all.' Without realising that he hadn't put the phone down, he said, 'The wind in the trees.'

'What? Oh, don't you mind about that,' jolted Mags. 'I'll get through Dad's angel-face routine.'

Will stared at the snack bowl. 'Yeah, just like brother Mark.'

'Is it ever…say, when did you hear from him last?'

She didn't probe his silence: 'Okay, honey,' she said at last. 'We're both bushed. Tomorrow round three.'

Unplugging the phone, Will heard the wind, saw a forest. Somewhere behind that was pre-Christmas happiness, Mags helping out with a drink to hand, Annie and the rest bustling, his two and the other kids capering about, helping but not. Out on the walk, he was trailing behind so that any words had to be thrown back at him.

Something about wishing they had a dog with them, maybe. That'd be rare fun. What you think, big man? Come on, keep up, keep up. Deeper and deeper through the snow, further and further.

Yes, it probably was Mags's Dad goofing about on the phone. But if it wasn't, that made no difference. Whatever happened, whatever he had to do, he'd take the hit. In the gloom beyond the light, the smoking-room guy he'd hoped to be sat perfectly still, so to speak, hands on knees, staring at him wide-eyed. *'You hear me, Parry?'* he read again, settling down. *I'd hardly got in the showroom door. 'Phone message.'*

*

I didn't recognise the phone number on the pad. But I recognised the voice when, locker emptied, hanging about to see Don—who, it turned out, was next door making another bid to buy out the *Spindog* guys—I gave it a try.

'Damn, I knew it. Where in the world have you been? Why didn't you keep in touch? I phoned Red Deer. They said they were awful sorry to have to let you go, but you'd just lit out. I'm real sorry I didn't try you sooner. Hey, I hope you haven't deprived the world of a new light on Eakins and Mary Cassatt but…maybe you've had to?'

Tony North's voice hadn't changed one bit: still as warm, whether serious or joshing, as when we'd had our discussions about my dissertation or bantered on the night of my celebration party. As he spoke, his office came back into view, my own snug part of the Art and Design block, the grave but impressed manner of my external examiner from the Royal Ontario. I could almost hear Jim's cheery assumption that of course I'd turn into Doctor Jon—that the whole world I'd hoped for would be mine evermore.

'Yessir,' Tony was saying now, 'been here a year. Going places, this university.' It had taken him a spell to adjust—hadn't I found that too? After Windsor, Sarnia, Hamilton…this world of wheat. Big sky country, they called it, and who could doubt that?

A pay-phone between the stores and the back of the showroom wasn't the place for any kind of conversation, least of all this one. Apart from that, his mention of Eakins and Cassatt implied that he wanted to hear all about me. I leaned into the wall.

'It's lucky you caught me. My last day here. So you like Saska—pardon me? Oh…well, you know, can't be helped. Staffing issues. The old story. Last in, first out.'

Passing by, the guy who'd hollered me sneered, 'Yeah, right.' Corrigan, his name was, small and twitchy, and he'd been complaining for a long time—even before I started to lose it— that he, not me, should be going out with Jake and Peach. I guess now he could, if Don agreed. But some people just can't resist a swift kick. I gave him my back.

'Jeez,' said Tony, 'I'm sorry. Times are plenty tough. Maybe goes with being the fifty-first state of Reagan's America.'

'So how did you track me down?'

'City this size, it's a wonder we didn't just collide. Anyway, it was a colleague here at the U of S. Art guy but big into IT. Just arrived but already he's working with a bunch of postgrads on…oh, hey Jonathan, this is no good, gabbing on a phone after all this time. And I guess you have stuff to see to. When'll we meet?'

It was fixed up. The Parktown Motel bar next night, eight o'clock.

'It'll be great to see you,' Tony said. 'More than that.'

'More?'

'Thing is, Jonathan…now we're actually talking…well, whether you were leaving *High Office* or not, I think I might have something for you here.'

His signing-off words were like a potion. I was vaguely aware of Don's return, the way the light came through his office window, the feel of the pay envelope in my hand. I rallied enough to ask what happened next door:

'Oh, the veteran hippy neighbours might be coming round. Then'—he gestured past my head to the showroom—'we'll grow and grow.' Frowning, he stood up and yelled over my head, 'Hey Corrigan! Never mind what's going on in here…lookit'—he pointed hard—'some guy's just come through the door, go on, about your work. Yeah,' he added in a mutter, 'like he'll ever

282

go out with the demo guys. Shit for brains.'
Sitting again, Don focused on me. His trashing
of Corrigan blended with Tony's mystery words
and again I sort of tuned out. He seemed to be
offering something mid-way between sympathy
and sermon and when he got to 'So you see how
it has to be,' I just nodded. The handshake was
firm, sobering me up a bit; the promise of future
reconsideration 'if you can, you know, get
through whatever you're in' was heartfelt. Well,
it would be: he'd part-paid for that computing
course I'd done and a lesser man might have
devoted our final talk to carping about wasted
money. Also heartfelt was 'Anytime you're
around, Jonathan. Just stop by. Man, what'll
Slithery Jake do without you?'

Outside, the heat of the day sent me back into
a dream. I floated through the downtown Credit
Union, handed over the cash and paying-in slip
like I was watching someone else do it. A Nutana
bus was waiting by City Hall. Blocks and blocks
away from home but I didn't care—in a different
way to how I hadn't cared on my walk in. A nice
district, Nutana. Peaceful, villagey. Jake, Peach
and I had found a good coffee shop on Broadway
whenever our demos took us that way and once
or twice I'd been to the one-screen cinema. I had
half a thought to stroll up and down, or even
linger in Safeway, just to get my feelings in some
order. As it was, I watched cinema and
supermarket going past and stayed on the bus all
the way to Avalon, where I cut left onto Ruth
with some vague notion of walking home empty-

headed but spent the rest of the day hanging round Market Mall. Around six-thirty—fed, watered, kind of happy—I decided that a bottle of whiskey was in order. I didn't really know that part of the city and, what with the heat and the mall noise, my daze was thickening again. How I got back to my neighbourhood I'll never know—just followed my feet, I guess. But I came to sharply enough when, checking my wallet on the way into the local liquor store—and wondering why I hadn't just pocketed my last *High Office* pay—I cannoned into an old guy and sent him sprawling. Luckily his booze was in a padded bag. Even more luckily, he was courtesy itself as, full of apologies, I righted him and dusted him down:

"S'alright,' he said, or something like that. 'Your age, I was just as hot-foot for my liquor.' He ran a finger round his collar. 'And this weather's got us all chicken-limbed. Mean as winter.'

Sometime around midnight, with half the bottle gone and a smaller one at the ready if need be, I indulged my last clear thoughts. Once I knew I was getting the heave-ho from *High Office*, I'd started looking around and come upon a bunch of work for the City, the kind I'd been tempted towards before Don, Jake and the rest came into my life. Parks and Recreation but all fixed-term—at this time of year, the emphasis was on getting everything tidy ahead of the snow. As I'd reckoned before, it was the kind of work that would lead to my exit from Saskatoon for the long, haphazard road. (A while back I'd thought about trying my luck in the States, never mind the hassle. I'd thought about it again, in fact, the time Don had me into his office for that 'needful upfronting', when I knew this very day would soon come round.) I'd resolved to drop in at City Hall the next day. But now, out of nowhere, Tony North had sprung up and, though I was glad I wouldn't hear the details till we were face to face—some kind of joy deferred, you might say—his words implied that he had more in mind for me than litter-sticking round the campus.

Here was the problem, a problem I'd had my head dunked in and the flush pulled when all was too good at *High Office*. Parry the hobo, fine; Parry the roving computer-man, a glitch but solvable; but Parry back in the world he was meant for.... I remembered how I'd felt that very morning as I looked down at the South Saskatchewan. Yes, that would bring the pair of them smartly over their horizon and the episode back in England, at Tafler's tree, would be as nothing compared to what would follow. Maybe I'd overbuilt expectations. Maybe Tony had heard of some temporary admin job and, happily surprised at reconnecting, thought he'd give me the heads-up. Maybe I should go to City Hall after all and, when he and I met at the Parktown, sound appreciative, thank him and then shake my head.

But Bob Corey's words came back, too, from that school production of *Faustus*. *I think my master means to die shortly*. The hunter hits a target. Fact bears him out. The quarry isn't still out there, rudely alive. It hasn't even dragged itself away annoyingly half-wounded, leaving a trail of blood to show a lousy aim. But the quarry has a mind, too—even a plan. Perhaps his end is not the hunter's gun. The hunter will say it is. But he'll never know if it isn't. Despite the lingering heat of the day, the urgent heat of the whiskey, I sensed something warmer inside. That defiance. That flame still going.

One more thing was needed. It had become habit, I guess, to see myself in two halves, worker-me and protector-me—like it had become habit to keep the spotter's notebook, and I couldn't let that go. I suppose the two-halves thing was a way of keeping tidy what life had become. Even exert a modest control? But perhaps, for that very same reason, my self-division would now be unwise. It had got me through sticky times for sure. Something told me, though, that it might not serve whatever was coming from that pair. I needed to be fully me. One pair of hands to fish out or pocket the notebook, one pair of eyes upon the shortening days, one mind to fear and work and fear. If Tony was inviting me back into that world, my true world, it would be dangerous to travel divided. Even more dangerous than before. What happened after I laid those flowers at Tafler's tree made the Humboldt edict sound like kids insisting that I was it and had to close my eyes and count to ten. Worker-me and protector-me might still do nicely side by side, good buddies in uncertain hours, but who knew if Mephistopheles' dagger might rear up on its own, push us far apart so we could only hear each other's cries in the dark? I smiled down at my drink, again saw Bob Corey in his ludicrously oversized hat and cloak, again heard his startling line. The knife, of course, might not be tramp and rat's to raise. But whatever was coming, there'd be more safety in a single skin—and maybe less pain? 'Well, let's see,' I spoke into the one-bulb gloom. 'Let's see what Tony says.'

By noon the next day, headache waning, mouthwash doing its work, I'd pushed hard enough. Was whole again.

*

Will stared into his own gloom. *This weather's got us all chicken-limbed. Mean as winter.* Yes, that would have been Ernie Lester he'd upended. That would have been the store where, a few hours ago, he and Ernie had passed the time of day and Ernie had called the day mean. He pictured the encounter between Jonathan and Ernie now, wove it into Mags's words about the weird phone-call to her Mom. Sure, that could have been Gram goofing about. And sure, his own professional training meant that he didn't run each passing coincidence into the ground, force a meaning upon it. But perhaps someone, something, was making a real serious effort to wind him in. If so, there was no further need.

They could spare themselves the energy. And he went back to the scene that had been gathering at the edge of his mind as he read the few last pages. The purposeful walk back to Annie's house through the snow. Calling Annie out...or waiting till she or her husband came out (John-Joe, Joe-John, he could never remember. Anyway, it always reminded him of John Fred and his Playboy Band, that stupid-ass 'Judy in Disguise' song). Yes, staying outside was best, not barrelling in on everyone and blurting it out. One-to-one, he could keep things cool, contained. 'Is he not back?' he heard himself saying. 'Well, man, isn't that just like him? No, he was there and then he was gone. And I'm the one with the flashlight. Okay, I'll go hunt around.' A reassuring pat on whosever arm it was. 'Nothing to worry about. Don't mention I was out here. No need to spoil the fun.'

Mags and the kids would never know.

Another reassuring pat: 'Yeah, he's a dork, alright. When wasn't he?'

Holly and the twins would be ok. Sure Holly liked him. Saying she didn't that time, that was just spite.

*

'So, Colin Brenna,' said Tony as the waiter placed fresh drinks before us. I'd just finished what I'd been rehearsing since I got up: a credible version of my life since I last sat in his office back in Windsor and he'd suggested that we call my sort-of-plan fieldwork. Not too short, not too detailed. Dawn was missing and for sure so was Waskesiu. I'd spoken fondly of the foreman and his hospitable cousin way back in Dolbeau, of Farmer Kettering, of Ian Baillie and Rideau's, of Slithery Jake. I made a chucklesome yarn out of Brandon and the rellies' attempts to track me down, adding an imitation of Herb Mann which, while far from accurate, made Tony grab a napkin as beer brimmed on his lips. ('Sounds like my brother,' he spluttered. 'My brother to the life.') I didn't mention Mum's death or my trip to England. Some instinct held them back for now.

'That sure was fieldwork.' Tony mopped his lips again. 'If I need a mini-barn or a costumed fool for my kids' parties, man dear, here's the provider. But'—he leaned forward—'maybe not, Jon. Maybe not. Hey, now listen.'

Colin Brenna was a new arrival on faculty. A man in a hurry, Tony called him. Based in Art and Design, he was an IT gun-for-hire, having moved that way via photography and film. The university had welcomed him—'Our President,' said Tony, 'damn near adopted him'—because he had a proven flair for wooing money. Film Board of Canada funds were trailing him from his last post, in BC. More was on the way from elsewhere. 'I would have thought Toronto was his next stop,' Tony mused, 'or even Hollywood. I can just see him fronting up production if they do more Star Wars movies. Have you seen either of them?' I shook my head. 'Love 'em, my kids do. But no…Colin's a pioneer. Of course he'll do

289

the Film Board stuff and whatever else—who wouldn't?—but he's all for spreading the IT word.'

'He didn't teach that computer course Don Rydell sent me on.'

'Oh, he wouldn't have. Not that he'd mind getting his hands grubby that way. No, that would have been one of the grads.' He looked enquiringly at me but I couldn't remember the instructor's name or whether I'd told him why I was on his course. I frowned. Strange that I couldn't. I must have told the instructor about *High Office*...surely? Or maybe tramp and rat, sensing that I was getting above myself, had stolen the memory and burned it.

Perhaps my instructor spoke to Colin. Or to one of the film grads who were already queuing up to be supervised by him. Tony didn't know, but someone suggested that Colin attend a *High Office* demonstration.

'I don't know how long we'll keep him' said Tony, who clearly liked the guy. 'Hot-shot graphics, design on the move, something he calls "Speak-as-Shown".' He shrugged. The twenty-first century was fast coming up, Colin had reminded Tony. The new world would, or damn well should, get braver. Tony was of course on the Art History side, more traditional, but people in several departments were warming to Colin's mission and Tony found himself commiserating with him when, over coffee about a week after he'd arrived, Colin said, 'I'm really not sure about the companies this place gets its kit from. Alan Turing, Tony, he'd call it old hat.'

So it was that, on a free afternoon, Colin and one of his grads checked out Peach, Slithery Jake and myself. For a happening prof, the venue and purpose of the demonstration he chose seemed inauspicious. Albert Community Hall, on Clarence, was a punt by Don. Show some of Joe Public's clubs and societies what was going on in our wowsa world, he'd said, and who knows? Maybe some, most, would get right along to *High Office* and buy a computer they'd use only a fraction of for their membership lists, schedules, dues owing.

I remembered it. There were Shriners, Lions, secretaries from this choir and that sports team, folk from movie and theatre clubs. One soberly attired man at the far back turned out to be a co-pastor of the First Mennonite Church in City Park but not before Jake had claimed he was Joe Faragalli, the Roughriders' new head coach: 'No surprise there,' he'd beamed. 'I hear he's a low-profile kind of guy.' Peach pointed out that there were low profiles and low profiles and that reticence was hardly a good fit for someone in Faragalli's position. Besides, how would he or anyone from the Riders know the demo was happening? And if they did know, if Don had got word to them, wouldn't they have sent someone relevant up from Regina—'Like, you know, a figures guy? Someone who's maybe done a course like Jon here?'

Jake wasn't having it. 'Maybe Joe has a connection in Saskatoon. Maybe he wants to get into this stuff for himself.' Even after Peach had gone over to speak to the man before we started, returning with the news that he was Co-Pastor Epp and made discreet use of a walking-stick, Jake simply drew attention to his eyes: 'Real deep crinkles, man. You can see them from here. Just like Joe's.' I remember that, too, how he couldn't quite let it go, not even when Peach threw up his hands and said 'So Faragalli's doing a secret life thing?' Ever the genial dreamer, Jake. He could weave a fancy from the merest straw. Yes...I could hear him shooting the breeze with Jim and Paul. The Third Musketeer.

What I don't remember was my performance that afternoon: another memory stolen by my dark chaperones. But guided by Peach and with Jake's happy vibes in the air, I must have done ok. So it was that, at the end, these two guys had come up, said they were from the university and asked for a card. Feeling about, Peach said he must have left his in the van but 'Hey, Jon, got one of yours?' I handed it to the older of the two...the President's damn near adopted son, as it turned out...

...who was buzzing, said Tony, next time they met. 'Old Colin, he was set to give me chapter and verse of your demo, but right then I was heading for a conference in Guelph— "Outside the Impressionist Box", remind me to tell you about it—so no time. I get back from there and Colin's taken off somewhere. Next

292

time I catch him for a drink, I ask if he's got a big order in at *High Office* yet. Well'—Tony opened his hands penitently—'sorry to disappoint your ex-boss, but Colin says he's been hunting around and can get the same quality stuff elsewhere for less. "But Tony," he says, "that was a proper show they put on. You should check them out." So he goes through his jacket pockets, in and out, out and in, and finally—voila!' Leaning across the Parktown table, Tony held out what had briefly been my life, with my name in black ink across the middle and, faint behind it, the sketch of an angle-poise lamp. 'Ok, maybe the card was random in itself—there's Jonathans, there's Parrys—so I ask him to describe you. "Accent," says he. "English. Been worn down but definitely there. Not hoity. More like that ELO guy, you know? Jeff Lynne." So now'—reaching again, Tony clapped my shoulder—'here we are again.'

I heard but didn't register his words. I was thinking about that afternoon, the hole in my memory of it. Peach and Jake must have clapped me on the shoulder too, taken me out for a drink. They were like that, even to the end, even when I was confined to the office and did my wreckage there. Pastor Epp, Jake's Faragalli routine, the two guys boostering us at the end—one of whom had brought about this evening, this table, Tony's wave which would shortly bring in fresh drinks—that was all clear enough. But my actual routine there in the hall? Ok, so I was boozing steadily at the time, but it was around middling then…the heavy sessions would resume later, would need to. Yes, tramp and rat had stolen my triumph as a housebreaker would lift a trophy in dead of night. Stolen me from myself yet again. I thought of what I'd pondered the previous day, again saw myself playing safe as the year got sleepy, clearing leaves and cutting back in Kinsmen Park, Kiwanis Park, Arbor Creek, thumbing through photocopied ads in the evening as chill became snow, *Winter Work in Montana, the Dakotas*—or going east again, maybe back to Brandon or Dolbeau, where that generous foreman might recognise me and where his cousin might still offer a roof against winter rent-free.

The drinks landed. I felt fire in my gut but not in anticipation of that next double. Dammit, had I thrown that other stuff so easily aside? My notion of the quarry with its cheating plan? The knife hanging contested, up for grabs, between me and my dark chaperones? I raised my glass as a condemned man might flourish a last cigarette:

'Here's to Mr Brenna.'

'Doctor,' corrected Tony with a smile. 'As you, sir, will be in due course. So here's to you too. And to Jay Williamson.' He chuckled at my questioning frown. 'Bear with me, Jon, I need the bathroom.'

*

Is he not back? Well, man, isn't that just like him? No, he was there and then he was gone. And I'm the one with the flashlight. Two, three times Will repeated the words he'd hit on. He gripped his glass so hard that it was only a spasm in the wrist that stopped him breaking it. What was all that blether? All that going back, getting Annie or John-Joe Joe-John proper anxious and then telling them all was cool? What if neither came out or someone else or no-one? What was he, a TV cop? The kind that always finds a parking space right outside the murder house in the middle of New York or LA?

'No, don't go back,' he said aloud. 'Not till way later...long after. Then you can simply say you thought he must've turned up ahead of you.'

18

Fall. I loved it here more than I ever had in south Ontario and that was wonderful. Golds, coppers, reds along the South Saskatchewan valley. You'd think the trees were rivers themselves the way the colours flowed and escorted the water on its way. Monet and the lads would have been in hog heaven down there.

Seven weeks since we met up at the Parktown, Tony North and I, and here I was in an office, my office, on a Friday evening, overlooking the university quad with that huge old building on the other side—Gothic but presentable with it. It could have been straight off a card, a card you'd love getting, not an arrangement of humpy bridge, flame-nosed

295

coachman, gawping oik with nothing to gawp out of. It was an old-gold evening. You'd think the turning leaves of the valley had been diverted for a brief hour from river duties so they could paint the air above the oval quad. The last such evening of the year, it turned out. Peace: pure, unlooked-for, fleeting peace. I was glad to sit in that chair, to gaze out and be nothing. A moment before I'd been pinned face down on the desk.

Returning from the Parktown washroom that first evening, Tony had proposed that double-toast to my future glory and Jay Williamson, whose loss, it turned out, was my gain. He was soon to be a big name, everyone reckoned: doctorate from City University New York, a few rookie years at the Universities of Maine and New Brunswick, now set to come here for a spell. Except not. Word had come through a couple of days before Tony phoned me at *High Office.* At about the twelfth hour, Williamson had gone with an offer from Boston which had apparently been hovering in the background all the while. Yes, he'd said to the University of Saskatchewan, sure, before saying it to his other suitor and leaving the department here in the gloop. So it was scramble, scramble—too late to re-advertise with the new semester breathing down everyone's neck, and too late for full interviews. All other doctoral types would have been snapped up and any likely prospect already in the department had their hands full for the coming year.

'I tell you, Jonathan,' Tony had said at the Parktown, 'I spent the whole day after I phoned you doing some truly fancy dancing.' He phoned Windsor for faxes of my degree transcripts, asked his old head of department to phone his current one with a glowing word. In between, he ran here and there, bigging me up to those who mattered and even some who didn't. It turned out that he'd even come west with his copy of my dissertation (at least one, then, still in existence). Over our fourth drink he'd enlarged on the idea of a doctorate, adding with warmth that my years out in the cold could be turned round and made to look good when the time came for me to start my studies and then, doctorate finished, apply for posts elsewhere. The field-work, he'd repeated at the Parktown—the warehousing, the bell-hopping, the Burlington Bertie workouts at Rideau's—all of it was grist to the mill. 'Bringing the life into the art,' was the phrase he used. I had no idea what he meant and maybe neither did he. But I instantly absorbed it like it was a headline on a front page.

'There's a new guy at the helm at Red Deer, a conference-buddy of mine from way back. For certain sure he wouldn't have let you go.' He'd phone him the very next day, Tony said. He'd be another booster. And where would the harm be in getting hold of his predecessor, the one who'd run a finger round his collar and apologised me out of my job? 'I know the moolah was tight back then. Your boss at Red Deer...well, a rock and a hard place with funding. But I'm sure he'll be

297

over the moon to know you've come good so I'll rush him too for the old bona fides.' Gazing absently at a coaster with the Parktown logo, I'd smiled at that and thought of the bona fides my old Red Deer boss had already furnished, that catch-all testimonial which, though truly battered, still clinched it for Don Rydell. It was no longer in my pocket and I couldn't remember where I'd put it. It would have been good, well at least fun, to present it to Tony as soon as he produced my *High Office* card. A swap-shop moment: two kids getting high on the upturn in one kid's destiny.

Now, on that old-gold evening with peace blessing my office at last, I thought of Tony's faith in me, the buzz of it, the drive. The idea that my old Red Deer boss would be over the moon that I'd come good...well I hadn't...at least, not the night Tony had flourished my *High Office* card. If he had thought about it, all Tony knew was that I had enough about me to agree a time to meet at the Parktown and stick to it. I could have fizzled out amid all the talk of Williamson the bolter and transcripts and bringing the art into the life. I could have slumped forward, a complete mess. But I didn't and the more he talked, the more I knew I wouldn't. Like Jim, he'd always been the man with the brio and the more he'd talked, the higher my flame of defiance burned. With each word, I grew a little more into my prospects.

Naturally he'd have oversight of my doctorate and arrange whatever shape it needed to take while I was lecturing. 'A couple of articles under your belt in the coming year,' he'd said, 'and hey, another exhibition at the end? Man, you could do all sorts with your time on the road. I know all the gallery guys here, still keep in touch with Windsor. We'll get the doctoral thing under way once you're steady—mix of residential study and distance, we'll figure it out. Guy I know at the U of Calgary, he'd be real interested in where you were coming from—Cassatt, Eakins, those who said *Oui* to Monet from this side of the pond.'

'Or *Va te faire foutre*,' I murmured and he laughed and proposed another toast, to the Dolbeau foreman and his cousin who'd been so rough-edged kind to me.

After that things had moved fast. His head of department read my dissertation double-quick and said yes. I swotted up on stuff in a fury and, when the semester started, shadowed one of Tony's colleagues for a week, stepping in for this topic, that practical. It all came back in a whoosh, the pace, the tone, the due pause for questions, the riding of someone's joke. Williamson's workload was shaved at the edges for me; obviously any grad work went elsewhere but he hadn't been given that much to start with. I got going on my own. A senior prof became my mentor; the head of department sat in on some of my early sessions. They nodded their heads.

So it was that, with an ease that stunned me if no-one else, I stepped into Jay Williamson's unworn shoes—and into that office. It was actually in the English department, way across

the quad from Art and Design: once word of
Williamson's deception had reached the estate
management they commandeered what would
have been his office for one of the university's
alumni-pestering crew ('Crazy,' said Tony.
'Image and Publicity should all be together in
Magnusson'—meaning the Gothic pile dead
ahead of my window. 'Still, we do have those
there telephones to yack on and, if you'll pardon
me, Jonathan, you look like some campus
walking wouldn't be so bad for you.'). Before
long, of course, there was another evening at the
Parktown, at which I got to shake Colin Brenna's
hand, adding 'I think we've met before' and
getting ribbed for what, given how things had
turned out, sounded like good old Brit
understatement.

'And of course this is the guy,' Tony had said,
clapping my shoulder, 'who did an IT course here
in the summer, so you better watch your back,
Col.' Colin beamed. I became his friend for life.
During that evening a part of my mind even
started riffing, albeit fuzzily, on new research
possibilities in Impressionism, Anti-
Impressionism and the roller-coaster refinements
of Apple and IBM.

Now I gazed out of my office window. Slowly
the world was changing from old-gold to the
deep purple which, in the words of that dreamy
song Mum was fond of humming, bathes garden
walls under the twinkle of starlight. Here again
was my old idea of shelter. Despite all my
turmoil on the road and before, the oaths I'd been

300

forced to take that I shouldn't, couldn't return, here I was thieving back the life I'd surrendered with Ontario, the life I sat on the edge of at Red Deer while telling myself—and being reminded if I forgot—that I could go no nearer. I imagined looking at myself from the outside, through the eyes of who I had been in Windsor, one of a bunch of sessional lecturers—here or anywhere, in any subject, doing their grad studies while hanging on to the system by their fingertips and hoping they'd get a full time post and become me right now. You jammy devil, I heard him say, heard them all say: look at it, turning up at *High Office* that day and someone saying 'Message for you' and the pad not trodden underfoot and the message still on it and even as you rang back, maybe, Jay Williamson on his plane to Boston. Your old supervisor in the same city, still in possession of your dissertation and, latterly, a dog-eared card that a wunderkind prof happened to give him over a drink they happened to have. Jammy, jammy. I thought of all that, of making up for squandered time when I'd been commanded not to. During the weeks since the Parktown drink with Tony, I'd even pestered the future, entertained the notion of my Windsor pals and Don, Peach and Jake, even Mr and Mrs Butler, pitching up for the ceremony when I got this shimmering, yet-to-be-shaped doctorate. I'd imagined a trip back to England after that, bumping into people I knew from school, people who, it amazingly turned out, had always liked me and wondered how I'd got on. In *The Jolly*

Waggoner I was bought drink after drink until, at some point, winks and nudges went round, the bar door opened and suddenly Mr Vesey was in my line of slightly blurred sight, frailer but still imposing, settling into a specially reserved chair across the table from me: 'What did I tell everyone, Parry, about avoiding Erkeley Walk?' he twinkled and we all had a proper laugh about how I'd fled the fight that Erkeley evening when that terrible thing happened of which, like the rest of the school, I was of course innocent.

I suppose that the idea of Mr Vesey sitting down in any pub, never mind *The Jolly Waggoner*, shows how far and high my thoughts took wing. Another go round the houses? Hardly: now I was circling the moon. That future wouldn't know me, nor would any other. I knew that, just as I knew the desperate heresy I was now committing—for which, once more with new, hot feeling, I'd just been punished in my very office. But still I'd stuck to the work. Still the defiance flamed high and, through it, I could make out the over-draped figure of Bob Corey in *Doctor Faustus*, uttering that prophecy about his master, reminding me that the quarry's end isn't always in the hunter's gift.

*

'Trick or Treat!'

Will jumped. The voice seemed to be coming from behind the chair. Only when there was a thump and a clatter did he realise: some passing drunk who, maybe knowing this was a cop's house, had bent down to one of the small rumpus room windows and bellowed and was now staggering off into the night. The sad echo of a yell confirmed it. Some guy hadn't got hammered enough or hadn't got laid and in the way of most Saturday nights the whole world had to know about it.

He rapped a thumb on *the quarry's end isn't always in the hunter's gift.* He had to admire this talky-thinky guy. Here he was doing what he'd been told not to, like it was himself and Mark and Old Man Mathieson's fields. And with it all a plan was getting clearer: get up his spooks' noses for a spell and then…well, all that about Bob Corey hit a touch deeper each time it came up. Sadder. He set the folder down. And what about you, Will Apland? What's your plan—beyond all that running back through the snow to Annie's and saying, oh, I thought he must've come back earlier?

He needed a break from the rumpus room. It was beginning to feel like Tafler's tree. Filling his glass, he went upstairs, pausing only to listen to the furnace. It was behaving itself. No tinny weirdness. At the top of the stairs he made to lean against the wall by the front door but stood bolt upright again. Reflected in the wall mirror was the kitchen phone's light, now flashing at the double. What was this now? He'd kept an ear out since phoning Mags. No other call. Hadn't the light stopped when he played that message? He hadn't really looked. So was the kitchen phone falling in with the furnace and that weird call to Mags's mom and doing its own spookiness? Was it just plain on the fritz? Or—Will breathed out slowly—was something drawing him to press the button again, right now? Oh no...not yet. It wasn't time.

So...he could scoot on through to the comfort of the lounge or bedroom. But he didn't want to. He didn't even want to close the kitchen door. All this upstairs, it wasn't just his, it was the family's. Given what he had to figure out, he felt that any rearrangement, any occupation of space beyond where he was would dirty that life up. Turning back at the top of the stairs he caught his arm on the knob of the huge walk-in cupboard and remembered that he hadn't put the folding chairs down in the garage with the other hibernating summer stuff. Setting his glass on the floor he slid back the cupboard door, worked a chair loose, unfolded it at the head of the stairs and lowered himself gingerly into it, checking the clearance between his feet and his glass. After the armchair down below it sure wasn't welcoming. Its single cushion had been thinned down with the years and the butts. But he needed that measure of discomfort, literally that edge, to focus his thoughts...

...which were all about checking Annie's place out before Christmas. He knew it was beautiful but dammit he couldn't remember specifics. Why was that? All he had was a Christmas card idea, house-in-the-woods, generic stuff. Was something stealing his memories too, like Jonathan and the name of that IT instructor and the time he'd aced it with that demo for the Shriners and such?

He screwed up his eyes and shook his head. Forget that...main thing was what to do. From here to Annie's wasn't a stroll down the avenue. He couldn't just light out, make a sudden and unjustified hole in the life of work and kids, of times and notes on the kitchen calendar. What he needed was something that Smeets was pretty damn smart at nosing out: a work thing, a conference, refresher training, something with one of those fancy straplines, *The Streets Today* and *Patrolling the Future*. He'd been on one or two himself, of course, but pretty local, Regina, Estevan, that thing in the summer, two days in Swift Current where delegates were housed with townspeople and he'd ended up with that awful couple uprooted from Vancouver who spent the whole time itemising everything Saskatchewan didn't have. Boy, he could have turned strangler after that. But Smeets managed to get himself all over everywhere, Stateside as often as here. Somehow he must square it with his family.

Will laughed. If he was a movie cop he'd all of a sudden sit as upright as the chair would allow, finger to chin. Wait, he'd say, what about that shindig advertised on the station board? Yes, something like, oh, *The Invisible Border: US-Canadian Cooperation and the Modern Felon.* Wasn't that New Hampshire? Right next door to Vermont, to Annie? And wasn't there still one place left? Sure, sure...and he'd take a swig and smack his lips. But real life wasn't that obliging. Right now it was just questions. Was there anything remotely like that happening this side of Christmas? Was it down east, at least in Quebec, preferably Montreal so he could drop over the border? If there was and Smeets knew already and had put himself up for it, would he agree to a swap and would Barysko and DeConinck agree the change? It was a bigger deal than asking Smeets for the patrol-swap today. And what if he found himself rostered for Christmas? Wouldn't he need to hold the schmoozing back to get himself out of that? Will took a sip and eased his back away a little from the chair. A whole forest of ifs. So what else?

Well, he could start to work on Mags about Christmas, choosing a much better time than on the phone back there. The kids would be up for it in a trice and they'd be his co-wheedlers. When was the last time they'd seen Annie's place? They must have been yay small. And what was worse than to show them a possibility and then say, sorry guys, maybe it won't happen? What was crueller? That underway, he could phone...no, write to Annie and move things along. Say in passing that he just couldn't picture the spread she and John-Joe Joe-John had. Mind like a sieve, yuk-yuk. Would a snap or two be ok to send? You know, whet the kids' appetites. That land you got, I'd just love to have them imagine how it'll be under snow. Will seemed to recall that John-Joe Joe-John was a crazy man for snaps, slides, home movies. They'd sent everyone photos of the place when they moved but...ah, it was probably just the house and anyway the photos were either long lost in the garage or in one of Mags's special tidy places that would need a night of ransack to find. No, he'd write to Annie and...he stopped, eased himself around in the chair again, took a slow sip...

...and started seeing that whole notion from after the plan was complete, after the fact, when the law was active. Maybe they wouldn't mean to say anything...but maybe, in the middle of all the searches, the questions, the just-routine-to-get-the-picture, Annie or John Whosis would say oh, it's probably nothing, but Will now, when he was arranging the Christmas visit, he asked for photos of the place. And this was to show his kids? Well, yes, officer, he said it was, just so they could try and picture it under snow. But ma'am, sir, he could get photos of Vermont under snow anywhere, show them those. Oh, I know but—what did he say, honey, in the letter?—he wanted them to see our land. Your land. I see. So not just the state in general or even Franklin County but your particular spread? Well, yes...to whet the kids' appetite, he said...you see? Well, yes, it could have been that, ma'am, sir, it could have been nothing only that. I'm sorry, officer, it was just a little...I shouldn't have brought it up. Pay that no mind, ma'am, sir. Still, just to fill everything in, I'll phone Saskatoon. Just a few more words with Mr Apland. Actually, he's Officer Apland, like you.

Oh, that's right…well, well… sure, sir, ma'am, it could be nothing at all.

Again Will laughed, but this was a different laugh to when he was fooling about with movie-cop coincidences. After all the time he'd been in this job he thought he'd picked up a trick or two from the opposition: dodges, feints, how to make things look or sound. Okay, so it didn't work with everyone they hauled in but every now and then someone slipped off the hook and it wasn't all down to a smart lawyer. Man, he thought he had picked stuff up—know your enemy and all that—but it obviously hadn't sunk in deep enough. Instead, here he was damn near making like—now who was that loser last spring? Terry M was on patrol with Rod Murray (and what was that all about? Well, technically it was about making the station bosses get their hands dirty all over again, connecting them with the beat now. But Murray was their famed locked-door-don't-bother-me guy, a bottomless well of excuses, and he'd just sat in the car like the car was empty while Terry did the nabbing). Some guy in a balaclava making free with a tasty household in Riversdale. Terry tried every damn which way and then back at the station Barysko did the same but that balaclava stayed put till the guy's representation showed up. Come the day in court, the balaclava protests that Terry M was crazy, it couldn't have been him because at that same time he was on getaway-car fatigues over to Market Mall. 'I kid you not,' Terry M had said. 'Spoke all solemn like a preacher pronouncing man and wife.' Will shook his head, hearing again the Franklin County cop he'd conjured up. Photos, ma'am, sir? He expressly wanted photos of your land? Will sighed. Shoot, how would that make him sound? Like the Riversdale bozo, that's how.

He finished the whiskey. Never mind all that. Never mind about knocking a hole in family life. He'd pick a time in the next month and get himself rostered round it and just blow and if Mags thought it was to do with a case then fine. And he wouldn't visit Annie. Two, three days, a motel—not too near, round Alburgh or Swanton—check out the lie of her land, hell, take his own damn photos. He'd be a figure in the trees, on the very edge of things, like Jonathan's pair had so often been. Maybe a trick wasn't beyond him after all. Meantime of course he'd work on the kids, on Mags, and make nice to his sister. Oh Will, he could hear her say, that would be just lovely. And you won't believe this, sis, but guess what…? But guessing what right then brought the winking phone-light back into his mind. Keeping his head turned from the kitchen he stowed the chair again and, taking his easiest breath since he heard that jerk yell 'Trick or Treat?', descended with his empty glass.

19

If I'd upped and insulted Mr Vesey in front of the two policemen that faraway afternoon, if I'd stood up alone in that final assembly and done to Bevvo and Gordy what I'd done to Wiznuk, it couldn't have been worse.

Intolerable, I was. Up until my stint as a big fat joke at *High Office,* I'd played their way and taken my lumps when I hadn't. But now, here I was at the end of all that hot twisty thinking on my last day there, when I'd strayed to Avalon and Market Mall and nearly done for that old chap's booze outside the liquor store. No more caution, no more what ifs. No hiding out as a parks litter-jockey till the falls of snow whooshed me east or west, north or south. I had my feet under a neat table in a cosy office and I was doing the work I was meant to do. If there was an early autumn cold snap and the campus heating packed up, I could spread my hands to what I'd done—in their eyes, how I'd sinned—and stay toasty warm.

God forbid that this should happen. Except that it had. And except that God didn't, couldn't come into it. Never mind, now, my vision of their leisurely trudge back over the horizon when I leaned to the troubled South Saskatchewan and thought for the first time of Bob Corey, when Tony North's phone message was waiting unknown. All those set-pieces—that night in my prof's back garden, Humboldt, my return to Tafler's tree. The effort that must have gone into them. The punch they packed then, the waste of time they were now. They must have thought so, from their perch, their cliff-top beyond time. Beyond forgiveness. Watching me as I said yes to Tony, as I was all gratitude to the Head of

Department, as I geared myself up to shadow a colleague and then go it alone, they must have felt like a nation's leaders summoned back from a well-earned vacation to deal with the ultimate catastrophe: an enemy of the state spurning the counsel that had been whispered, thrust, written in the blood of a dead schoolboy who leapt into his arms in a Christmas kitchen and pressed like a lover against his living flesh. An enemy goofing about with free will, if you please.

Perhaps those who live in dark worlds can be stunned as easily as those who live under the sun. Perhaps that's why they were slow off the mark. They made up for it, though, once they got going. As always, only I could see them. No-one was about that first time, a week or so after the autumn semester started, when I was walking home late down Cumberland Avenue. If someone had been, they'd have seen only a grown man apparently throwing himself over and over against the mesh fence of the elementary school where I'd heard the running steps of that slowpoke kid on my last journey to *High Office*. They'd have watched me hitting the deck and hauling myself up like a rag-doll, now flinging my arm out, now twisting my neck. They'd have called out, called others for help, but their words would have gone in one of my singing ears and out the other. The following day it was a rabbit punch as I was walking to Art and Design to check my mail. The day after, a crack to the head when I was about to call in a student for a one-to-one about a practical session. The pattern was soon established: one dose per day, concentrated wrath, the ultimate Milk of Magnesia, and far more chilling—more heartfelt, if I can say that about them—than their old routines of loafing about at the edge of my sight, modelling this season's blazer or even terrifying the air with *Nn-gah!*

Again, who could I have told? Told in the way I wanted to tell—not another uncheckable blurt such as had ended my hopes with Dawn on that isolated shore? But the question was less straightforward now, was shadowed by others. In another time and place, Tony North would without doubt have been my Jeff Cordingley, my Jim Kloes, But perhaps the time for revelation was past. If tramp and rat were into a new phase, so was I. Plan and quarry, I thought, quarry and plan. That comforted me but it also made me wonder exactly when quarry should turn trickster. And would they suspect? And could I hold out for as long as was needful? Tony had made that sideways comment about my condition, the fact that regular walks between my office and the department might not be a bad thing. In the mornings I'd sometimes give myself a good look-over in the mirror. The whiskey was surfacing. There was a slight redness round my eyes that looked as if, in the fullness of time, it would sharpen and stay put. My complexion had more of sallowness than prairie flush to it. I'd smile then. The fullness of time. Perhaps, as an alternative to that, I was ageing at a fair old lick inside.

It couldn't have been worse. Warm-ups, their daily doses were, reminders of what had happened on the day I stood before Tafler's tree, itself a down-payment. They started to come at night, come to my bed with anti-prayers, obscene whispers about Laurie and Dawn, gloating boasts about Nancy's dead parents, her disappearance from my life. One night, then nothing for a night or two, then two or three nights on the trot. Always at the same hour I'd feel the chill as the duvet was pulled back, I'd feel the two-body heft, slighter on this side, leaden on that. The fingers, the breath, the abominable busyness. *Did Laurie do that, Johnny? Did Dawnie let you do just like this? We scooped Mrs and Mrs Boudreau clean off route 101. Sometimes, Johnny boy, we do all this and more to them. You're not the only fish, Johnny, you're not enough on your own. They love it. Nancy, she'll love it good when we're ready for her.* Always Wiznuk's voice, always the brush of that thatch up and down my skin. Tafler was grunts and coughs and pauses for a swig. An hour, I'd say, each time. Then the merciful sense of death in retreat like a genie rebottled.

Fighting was no good. They were vampire-strong. Crying out was no good, it only doubled the attack. And just as I knew no-one could see them when I was hurled against the mesh of that school fence on Cumberland Avenue, so I knew that they alone heard my screams. Sometimes Tafler's breath would be ranker than I'd ever known but I'd say Wiznuk egged him on with that. Tafler was actually the gentler of the two, or the less monstrous—well, maybe the less adept. I don't know if they were too absorbed to control every last bit of me, but sometimes I could just about get through by tuning out Wiznuk's filth and grabbing at a scrap of memory. Laurie, Nancy, Dawn, lazy weekends and long afternoons, Waskesiu and the nights before Paignton Beach. Jim's endless sun. The way Paul owned voices. *Mai matha...the Quin Matha.* 'That Steiger' echoed Jake. 'The Riders picked him as wide receiver. Him? Couldn't receive a bar-check.'

Of course they couldn't overdo it. Of course it had the old cat-and-mouse appeal, this granting me permission to face another day. One Friday night, though, Wiznuk clean forgot himself. The pain was unbearable as he clambered up and down, his unholy whispers pouring in every which way. He jerked my head back, his no-face loomed over mine. *We love Laurie's style, Johnny. We might call her before her time. Dawnie's engaged, Johnny, did you know? Might have to get her guy out of the way on a killer road.* I was splitting apart but then, mercifully, came hisses and tugs as Tafler dragged him off, mutely asserting that, sure, it was the weekend but there still had to be enough of me left for future fun.

In the kitchen the following morning, I arranged myself around the shape of the pain. Before me was a big mug of coffee, the last of a farewell gift from Slithery Jake. *Rough 'N'*

314

Smooth, he called it, supposedly a top-secret blend awaiting endorsement by his beloved team. When I asked how he knew, he just tapped the side of his nose, leaving me to assume that, since his hope of making their squad was long gone, he'd sort of made up for it with some privileged boosting. 'If you need any more, Jon,' he'd said, 'just swing by the store. Once the Riders give it the nod, boy, the price'll go way north.' It seemed an unlikely endorsement. Pizza or sports gear, I could see it, though the main brands had probably been snapped up by other teams elsewhere. But it tasted pretty good—got me started each day and the more delicate the morning, the better it seemed to work. So yes, I thought, I might just swing by, or flag down the demo van that he and Peach still rode, which I seemed to see all over the place. Or how about another drink with him and Peach? I surely needed a connection that was off campus but still of this world.

At the kitchen table I did something I hadn't done for ages. Getting out my notebook (not spotter's book any more—what need for spotting now?), I turned it lengthwise at two blank pages and took up a pencil. Gradually I appeared as I had been in the weeks before Gordy's Erkeley notion, about the time I turned my bed round by my window and found how magical sleep and the night sky could be. I say gradually, but it didn't need too many strokes to show the goofy-happy face, the side-parting, the eyes guarding my tumble of thoughts, my devotion to music, my belief that my own company wasn't so bad, was actually pretty good—and resilient, despite being scribbled over by school, fights, family, the incursions of a world that was annoying, barmy, both.

Once I'd finished I centred the lost me on the table and gazed at him a long long time. Not bad, though I say it myself. I didn't really know why I'd done it and I don't now. A totem, however ineffectual, against those night visitations? An attempt, however doomed, to reach back to when I was just another bod among the millions and, on balance, happy enough with it? Or just something simple and pure, begun and lost in and finished for its own sake in a certain stretch of time? I think I'd go for the last. Doing it made me so content, though at one point, as I gazed, I nearly blurted 'It was all Gordy's fault for suggesting that', nearly turned as though tramp and rat were at my shoulder waiting to hear. That line might have been fine to fling up at them in the prof's back garden or across that snowed-up gulley in the Humboldt dark. But it was peevishness out of its time…not even worthy, I decided, of the face staring up at me. The so-young face. The face before it all.

I was so glad that I'd pushed hard and become one person again, worker and protector entwined. Not that protector-me would have been much use now. But that sense of wholeness sure did help me through the early weeks of autumn. After a while I stopped seeing my defiance so much as a flame—flames go out—

and felt instead what it had become, a steeliness which, in any other circumstances, would probably have been beyond me. It was as though the more abuse I suffered, the more resolute I became. You could say my work now was the nearest I ever got to a faith. I remembered the last days of catastrophe at *High Office,* how I'd mischievously written 'doctorate' in the back of the notebook, like it was a spell whose magic could be dreamed of though never roused. Now the doctorate was on the cards. No matter that they'd never be played. And what I was doing right now, the very thing I was meant to do, that was even more deliriously wicked. How much worse would things have been for me if I'd still felt myself double, tried to hold me to myself with shaking grasp, nerve and spirit cut in two?

I acquitted myself well. My students were happy. Tony conveyed to me the Head's approving noises and added his own. Both invited me to their homes, as did Colin Brenna and other colleagues. There were references to projects, intimations of possible grant bids. My time on the road had quickly become common knowledge and struck some like a tray of paints waiting for their canvas. I had a couple of long phone calls with Tony's friend at Calgary, my possible doctoral link, then met him in person. Yes, he said. Yes, indeed. Echoing Tony, he counselled seeing the year out with an article or two: 'If folks are already approaching you, joint authorship's the thing to get your chops in trim. Doesn't have to be what you write on later.

Doesn't have to be all print. Your field-work, Jonathan…I'll bet Dr Brenna is churning ideas even now. How about his name as co-author? Tap him up.'

Plan and quarry, quarry and plan. I admit that, in heady moments, it was tempting to forget them. But the reception I got in the department…like the prospect of the coming year, it was a teasing dream. And every handshake, every enthusiastic noise about future glories was, I knew, riling the pair a touch more. All very well preening myself on my reserves of steel. But they would up their game and I couldn't know how. Plan and quarry, quarry and plan. More and more, I knew I had to out-play them, I had to win. And still I couldn't know if they suspected where my thoughts were heading.

I kept going, got more comfortable in the world they would never accept. I ministered to my outraged body. And at last came that other Friday night—companion, you could say, to the one when Wiznuk clean forgot himself: that old-gold evening when I settled myself as gingerly as I had done the morning of the self-portrait, stared out from my office window at the last dusk of its kind I'd see and wept at the silence.

An hour it had lasted, in my office: their regulation time. As on that Cumberland Avenue evening by the elementary school, no one was around. Well, they'd have ensured that. Anyway, no-one else would have heard my cries. The pain was redoubled, my disbelief was as fresh as when they'd surfaced for the very first time. That chuffed them no end. It was as well I'd jumped the seasonal gun by wearing my long coat because everything else was in tatters by the end. On the desk, on the carpet, against the bookcase, they broke into me every which way, sometimes focused on that, sometimes just beating my head and face as they traded places. Just before I was let alone with the fading light they slammed me back down on the desk. I could sense Tafler stepping away and heard the inevitable cork. But Wiznuk leaned in, reached down, curled his fingers and made the longest speech I'd ever heard from him:

'A new dawn, Johnny'—his Black Country accent swirling the years away till we could have been back in school, his goons throwing me to the ground—'We weren't pissing about at Humboldt. Or when you dared show your face at our tree. A new dawn. This and more and worse. Morning'—his hand squeezing—'Noon'— harder—'Night'—hardest of all, till my tears, like my disbelief, ran afresh.

That deep purple, falling. It fell further out there through my window, over the quad, till the buildings opposite could have been the hardboard skyline I'd once constructed for one of Mum's school productions in Winnipeg. Winnipeg to Windsor, Windsor to here…and in between, what roads, what people, what empty rooms, what souring of time. What shattered atonement. What foulness in the middle of love. But here came a smile and I held onto it as the last of the purple leached away. Friday night again. The weekend. Time out, time to re-shape myself. And no janitor Ted banging on the doors here. I could stay all night if I wanted, but I knew I'd get myself home somehow, a tattered thing feeling along, skirting any lights. And, crazy though it was, skirting with something near happiness. I'd had my answer in that hour of hell. Quarry and plan. They didn't suspect.

*

It's got to be clean, Will told himself as, scribbling one of his figure-out notes on his paper, he set the folder aside and thought about snow, lots of it. A clean job. Not a mess of prints and skids all in one place, not like that Riversdale bozo would allow. But snow was mean beyond the cold. A traitor. If it was packed, it showed everything. Unless you got the miracle of a fresh deep fall right there and then, you might as well spread out your own incident markers with time and notes on—*I used my bare hands here...and just here, I finished it good....*

A clean quick job. He was in ok shape. Last medical was no problem at all. Even so, maybe he should take a few turns at the gym, build up a quiet schedule. There might be no need for it. Memory, though, told a different tale. The Lloydminster evening. Sometimes Mark was like a cat whose rage made it a tiger. Always and everywhere there's risk—which, as Terry M would say, you must not anywise take.

20

Mr Thorneycroft was our English teacher for my last year in England. Wildly eccentric, he used to wipe the board with his gown and then lean against it like Rodin's Thinker, only tweedy and ruffled, pondering his next question, which he would deliver while spinning round at us on one foot. It was in his class, I think, that we learned that poem about living unknown and out of sight, 'untroubling and untroubled', which came to me that afternoon when I faced those two policemen in Mr Vesey's office and willed his pot-plant to swallow me up.

It was in one of Thorneycroft's lessons that we also learned of 'God's own snorter', as he put it, when Shakespeare boozed the night away with Ben Jonson and Michael Drayton. Back in Stratford, it was, near the end of Shakespeare's life. 'A merry meeting,' twinkled Thorneycroft, quoting some or other account. 'Bollocks from first to last' was Bevvo's evaluation—and of all Literature, come to that. But I liked our chalk-shrouded dervish of a teacher and, though I never checked, I hoped that the story was true. So I was mightily pleased when, at the cast party for that un-Christmassy *Endgame*, Paul raised his glass 'To the Stratford Soaks' and corroborated it. 'My guess,' he said, 'is that Jonson was out of ideas for his own stuff and reckoned he'd pump Shakespeare. But old Shakes, he was onto that. He'd feed Jonson a notion, you know, *How'll that do you, Benny?,* and then get him a tad more tractored so he'd forget and have to ask again. Shoot, the Bard was probably mashing up his own stuff. *Hey, Ben, how's about twin Danish princes who set sail for Egypt disguised as Beatrice and Benedick? Some good, huh?*'

Jake, Peach and I on Saturday night in the Schofield Bar of the Bessborough Hotel—that was no Stratford snorter. But I'd wanted to reach out for a regular social such as thousands enjoy without a second thought and, the day after the office assault, happy coincidence fell my way. I knew I had to ride it. A new dawn, Wiznuk had hissed. It was time to get weaving. *Be wary,* says the Nurse to Juliet. *Look about.* That, Paul reminded me one post-bar evening, was after the lovers had enjoyed their one and only night. Now mother was stalking towards daughter's chamber. Tramp and rat didn't suspect. But how long would that hold?

And, that Saturday night, I sort of felt like Shakespeare on his mammoth toot: the furlongs cleared, most everything already behind. A bit rich, that comparison. But I don't have to care now.

I thought I might have to comb around for Slithery Jake. Saturdays were store sales only at *High Office* so the chances are he wouldn't be in and I'd have to fall back on the scrawled number he gave me on our last demo together. But there he was, late afternoon, coming out of the gate to the van-yard.

'My man, my man,' he called. 'Angling for more Riders coffee?' It turned out that Peach's other half was out of town for the weekend and they'd agreed to meet up.

'How's the Bessborough sound?' He widened his eyes. 'Blow the frost off a few cold ones where the rich folks go?'

Seven-thirty, we agreed. I could have hung about in town but I had something else in mind so caught a bus back to the campus and headed for the Faculty Club. Not exactly where rich folks met, unless you included an alumnus-made-good or one or two emeritus profs—certainly not where the likes of me would prop up its mahogany bar—but it didn't close till ten-thirty Saturdays and had a Reading-room annexe, mainly used, I gathered, by folks who wanted peace and quiet or just to sleep it off. Perfect.

A couple of sheets with the university's crest up top. I wasn't showing off. It was just that Mrs Butler had always been my champion across the water, and I figured it would chuff her and Mr B, burnish the tale of me now. I kept it concise and, even before I began, I knew how I'd end it: *...and who knows? Maybe we'll all meet one day on the shores of Gitche Gumee.* I hoped that they would take it as meant, a warm nod—warmer with the passing years—to that kind gesture back when the world was small and without evil, that calf-bound Longfellow. Certainly I hoped that they wouldn't read anything direful into it. If they did, though, there was nothing I could do. *I'll be over again,* I could have said. But that was a lie. In any case, and like everyone else, they would remain in another world, sunrise and sunset, the usual stuff going on in life. For how much longer in their case, of course, I couldn't know, so I made sure to enquire after their health, too, especially Mr B's. *I hope you're still enjoying your bowling, Arthur.* Afterwards I realised that I'd made it sound like alleys and skittles, not the serenity of a green. But I didn't cross it out. It didn't matter.

A few hours later there was no old-gold to be had in the sky but still, from the large windows of the Bessborough's Schofield Bar, the South Saskatchewan had pleasant enough colours to flow under. Jake was all animation; Peach smiled and, murmuring 'Good to see you again,' shook my hand. Having slipped me another pack of *Rough 'N' Smooth,* Jake leaned in and gripped our wrists: 'Man, dear, it's gonna be huge.' *It* was one of the last Roughriders fixtures of the year, in two weeks' time against Calgary. Peach, who, outside of computers, had always been on the quiet side, assumed a look of Buddhist acceptance as Jake proceeded to work through all the stats, the triumphs and failures, that had run through the weeks and months towards the Calgary meet. 'If we can do this,' sighed Jake in I-have-a-dream tones. 'If we can just clinch her. Man, we'll have our own stampede, never mind those Cowtown guys.' He fell silent. I smiled across at Peach and would have asked if anyone was riding with him and Jake on the demos these days, or did he have to absorb all this on his own, but Jake found his second wind and we were smartly into a breakdown of the Riders' likely squad. He was just starting on John Celestino's merits as Defensive Tackle when at last Peach sighed 'Oh, Jake, pick it up later' and asked me what I was doing now.

As with the letter to Mrs B, I kept it concise, which was just as well because Jake fought back in, regarding me now as Coach Faragalli—last seen, by him at least, before our demo in Albert Community Hall—might have regarded the latest hot-shot on the Riders' team. 'Didn't I say? Didn't I say he'd do all right? Man, oh, man, we're sitting us down with a real-to-goodness prof. Boy, if Don knew all this—'

'What would Don do?' We looked up. There was Don with two women.

'Well, hello, there.' Don took my hand and kept shaking it while he introduced his wife, whom we'd sometimes seen in his office, and his daughter, whose effect on Jake was instant. Unfazed by this happenstance, probably high on attraction, Jake started to re-run his happy amazement at my present fortunes, but Peach got in smartly, shrinking my account to a couple of sentences.

'I knew it,' said Don, elder statesman to Jake's Faragalli. 'You've found your place, Jon. That's good news.' Maybe he knew that Colin Brenna had considered but then passed on *High Office* as an IT source. Whether he did or not, I could sense in his bright eyes the hope of some collaborative opportunity. 'Now look,' he said, 'we've got to scoot,' and he gestured towards the

Thorton Banquet Room, adding that they were attending a business acquaintance's long-service shindig, or roast, or something. 'But I'm mighty glad to see that the Englishman has brought you two desperadoes up in the drinking world.'

'Hey, lookit, the venue was my—' All grins, Jake subsided amid the laughter. Don patted my back. 'Drop in sometime, Jonathan. Let's us two professionals catch up.'

After they'd gone, Jake took up the threads of John Celestino's fate. Later, he and Peach talked work. 'That Corrigan's gone,' said Peach and I remembered the little runt trying to earwig my very last talk with Don on that sweltering day. Jake added that it was hardly a loss, his total contribution having been sweet dick. The talk swirled on, a bit of office stuff, a lot more of the Riders, and I sat back. Hey, Ben, I imagined saying, here's a plot for your next play. English underling murders in self-defence and gets a life full of demons for his pains, till he resolves…yeah, resolves, Ben, aren't folk always doing that in our stuff? See, Ben, it's to do with hunters and quarries. Now your hunter, he goes in for his kill. Fact bears him out. But the quarry, he might not be just all squawk-you-got-me. Minds, Ben. Quarries can have them and use them and prepare them and…fettle a perfect outcome. Fettle, Ben. You know the thing.

They didn't come that night. Wiznuk's new dawn, I guessed, was taking some preparation. Or maybe it was prepared already and, as I'd felt before, the waiting was part of the hurt. Either way, I was glad they didn't work up a nasty postscript to the merry meeting. And it gave me a Sunday that, after a dose of the *Rough 'N' Smooth*, was nicely clear. Time to weave on. By mid-day I was back in the Faculty Club's Reading-room. Starting to write this.

*

Will turned back to the part about the self-portrait and allowed himself just a shake of whiskey. He pictured Jonathan gazing down at the recovered face gazing up from his notebook. He pictured his own face, in the snow and the dark, gazing down at the other. Perhaps eyes would meet a moment before it became clear this wasn't horse-play. You had to be careful with eyes. They could throw you right off, make you rage where you meant to forgive, kill resolution and drop apology in its place. What would those other eyes say? For a moment, no doubt, what the hell is this? Then, aw big man, and maybe, no, come on, no. Then more no, no. Then maybe, for the merest second, why?

Or was that just the movies too?

*

Old Shakes and old Benny. Old Paul. Magic guy. I saw him again, too, soon enough. Sort of. Coincidence's encore.

After the day in the Reading-room I had to return something to the Library chute and took the subway route from the quad. As I was coming back, something flapped at me from the entertainments board by the Student Travel place. *Les Promenades de Montréal.* Ionesco, *The Bald Prima Donna.* Sartre, *No Exit.* Weds 4th—Sat 7th November, 7.30pm, St Mathieu Street Theatre. Dir. Paul Farwell. There was even a small photo of him, in profile, looking looser and happier than his old frown could have predicted. Studying the poster, I imagined going to St Mathieu Street, getting word to him; the reunion, a quick breathless swap of our lives since Windsor. He might say...what?...maybe that it was Edmonton and then beautiful BC for the end of the run, 'And then, Jon, the usual Christmas tribal thing at Humboldt. Would—? I mean, if you don't have plans. Chris'd love to see you, they all would. What say? Should I wangle it?' As words flowed delightedly, I imagined another face looming at his shoulder with a grin to split the sun: 'Go for it, Doctor Jon! Man, you're back on track. Myself, I'll soon be done at Dalhousie and then, hey, maybe I'll come out here for a spell. All the best people are doing it, I'd say. You landed a Prairie lovely yet?'

I turned away. Yes I had and then I had to let her go. As I walked slowly on, I thought of Paul starting the Mathieu Street run and, while it was going, Jake and Peach haunting the Bessborough again, maybe the Parktown, Moxie's or that rubby-dub dive round the corner from the Army and Navy, and Jake proclaiming 'What'd I say? Calgary Stampeders, just pussies, man'. And before all that, very soon, Mrs B sitting down to write her reply from the nice little villa that Kevin had sorted out for them in Lytham, and saying, never mind all that Gitche Gumee chat, when are you visiting the shores of England, Jonathan?

All that world going on. Like someone on a train who, after talking a blue streak at you for hours, leans to the window, shields their eyes and says, ah, I think this is me. Well...maybe I've got that the wrong way about.

They didn't come that night either but there was a new chill on the bedroom air. Peach had said the coming winter was set to be fierce cold. As a nod to that, to the train, to the chatty body and I saying take care, all the best, I turned up the thermostat and lowered myself cautiously into sleep.

21

'Jeez, Jonathan, I'm so sorry.' Four nights later, Tony motioned for fresh drinks and leaned across. The Parktown again. Circles completed.

It had been all go that week. Bright and early Monday I posted Mrs B's letter. Then it was student appointments and a co-practical with a colleague and her group. After that it was a couple of places nearly at the city limits, where, discreet enquiry told me, I'd find what I'd need for the right time. In the days following, between lectures and seminars, it was the Reading-room, the Library, writing, writing. Waiting in the Arts café line, talking to this or that one, I felt that if I reached out my hand would go straight through everything. One of my colleagues hunting a joint grant called by my office and proposed a working lunch. Offering suitable nods and interjections, I watched as, on the other side of the table, he seemed to recede with each of his optimistic words.

Night-times were fingers laid cold on my face as I sank down, a sense that the bedroom was fifty yards long and that presences were deep at the end of it, fuller, bigger now, as though there were more than two. Each night the mercury dropped a notch lower.

By Wednesday evening, when I was turned out of the Reading-room by the Club manager— another janitor Ted, kindly, even the same hairstyle—I'd just finished talking to Dawn Koralewski for the first time, setting her straight on how to say Headingley.

Thursday was a gift. For a while now Colin Brenna had been engineering an event around 'Speak-as-Shown,' his kinetic graphics project, complete with IT insiders and media types from everywhere. In truth I'd always been as baffled as Tony by it but now I gave it praise indeed: the Art and Design and IT timetables were suspended for two days so that students could mingle with people called Alex and Bryony in ponytails or serious shades. I wished Colin well with his fest but, mindful that he might finger any colleague for unofficial stewarding duties, made myself scarce in a carrel on the top floor of the Library. Late in the afternoon, another stint done, I journeyed round the stacks till I found Biography and Memoir. Down a way from Paganini and Emmeline Pankhurst but a few spines shy of Louis Pasteur, I paused and stared a moment at the spotter's book (as was) in my hand. Then I slid it in, company for Ara Parseghian, Head Coach for the 1960s Notre Dame squad and the subject of a slim monograph in the *Football Focus* series. 'There you go, Jake,' I whispered. 'Ain't that the proper fit?'

Coming out of the Library I bumped into Tony. Happenstance again. But I'd have sought him out anyway. I was at the ready.

'I'm on mingling fatigues at Colin's bash tomorrow lunchtime. Care to tag along? I've been thinking, you should get your name across to some of those Film Board guys he's got in. Your time out in the cold, for sure one of them could find an angle. Put you right up there with Evangeline and Diefenbaker.' He grinned. 'Hush my mouth. Diefenbaker was Saskatchewan's guy. Got all three of his degrees from this place. Pardon my sacrilege.'

Evangeline. A Tale of Acadie. 'This is the forest primeval.' I had a momentary vision of Longfellow intoning his other famous poem to a rapt, select audience in the sitting-room of a nice little villa in Lytham St. Annes. But another part of my mind was on other fatigues. I think Tony was going onto something about my supervisor-to-be in Calgary…maybe that he was coming to town again soon and if so…but I arranged my face in a way that made him start and say, 'Jon, what's up?' I told him and they all vanished, Colin, Evangeline, Lytham, supervisor, the province's number one son.

'Oh, my man, my man.' Tony was all Jim Kloes, doling out the liquor after Laurie had brushed past him and out of my life. Sure, he said, Colin's thing had spelled him off his usual seminar that very evening…but even if it hadn't…. Of course the Parktown. Seven.

So there we were, the fresh drinks just arriving. Raising his, he paused till I'd started mine.

'May I…? How old was the lady?' And he shook his head, saying it was no age at all. I was sorry to deceive him but glad too, glad at the instinct which kept my mouth shut about Mum when we'd met right here for the first time all those weeks ago. I just knew it would serve its turn.

'Could I ask…what was it?' Builth Sid's face came into my mind, his brief, astonishing heart-to-heart that day outside Sedgley Church: *She was going anyway, lad. Heart was done for after your Dad went.* I didn't mind picturing him at all but I didn't want the rest of the pack at me. Vaguely, I said there was a history of heart trouble in the family, which was sort of true, really.

'So she lived in…Northampton, right?'

'Kettering. Not far. But the funeral's near where we lived.'

'Well, Jon, I hope she made a peaceful end.' I didn't know...very much doubted it. Well, I'd never been allowed to find out. But I got us past all that with a quick tightening of the lips.

'Look,' said Tony, 'no worries about a single thing. You do what you have to do. As long as you like. You're standing high here, Jon, not a one will take exception. I or someone'll get you to the airport, so let me have details.'

I thanked him but declined. All would be soon in hand.

'Well phone, dammit, when you're there and for sure when you're coming back. I'll meet you.'

I could only say yes to that. I looked at him while he took out a notebook and—'in case you forget to take them, you've got plenty else to fix up'—wrote out the numbers for the department secretary, his office and his home. Jim. Paul. That kind foreman and his cousin in Dolbeau. Ian Baillie. Jake, Peach. Hell, Herb Mann at Beautiful River City's CKLZee. So much kindness, unforced, as natural as a laugh for the hell of it. And now Tony, the last of the line...the last, as it were, to lean against the window of a slowing train, shield his eyes and say, ah, this is me. Afterwards, outside, I watched him walk away and was turning away myself when I heard 'Jon, call me while you're there. Never mind the time.'

Tony. Prepared for a call in the way Mrs B wasn't when I got that notion to run Bevvo and Gordy to ground. But she stepped up, bless her. The last picture I made was of the two of them, she and Tony. Man, said Tony, you should have seen him in Windsor days. What a hellion. His wink. Her face. Ooh, he never was, was he? Her laugh. Well, I said to him, I said to him more than once, we've only got the one life, you enjoy it, Jonathan, you make the most.

Darkness on Cumberland Avenue. The occasional gust, an over-revved engine going by. But no hands out of the gloom, no bloodied conversation with a mesh fence by a school, no *Ngah!* They sure were holding it back, building it up. Near my apartment I stopped and looked all the way round. This would be the last of outside. Another scrap for an album which, like that little book now keeping Coach Parseghian company in the Library, would shortly slide away along with Mrs Butler's long-ago smiles, Mrs King's offer of a lift on my last day among the desks and monitors, even that old gent's forbearance when I skittled him outside the liquor store.

All night I wrote. Murmurs rose and fell: the furnace, maybe, or voices from somewhere. Next morning, meeting Mrs King in the utility room, I didn't spin any yarn. Run-down, I told her instead, my sleepless night showing supportively about my eyes, my cheeks.

'Now, Jonathan, you don't want to line yourself up with a cold, certainly not with the winter they say we've got coming. Boy, when they take hold... '

'I'll be ok in few days.'

'Well just you holler up from time to time so's I know you're still in the country. Anything I can do, groceries or—'

'Thank you, Mrs K.'

Still in the country. That caring exaggeration rose and fell in my mind as I wrote on, as time fidgeted, sighed and folded in on itself. I shook myself and it was daytime; I started awake and it was night and the murmuring grew loud and soft, the sense of something at my back, over my body, pressed and faded and pressed again. Fragments bobbed up unbidden, tangled. A hallway opened out, the one in that fabulous turreted house where I lived with my friends for the second Master's year. The staircase rose, the panelling was as warm as abiding love must be. But the parquet was suddenly tarmac and Cadman and Bell, apishly obedient, were slamming me on it for the second time in one day. The Winnebago vanished in the haze and before long another engine sounded on the Hafford road. 'Dearie me, we were going to call the Mounties,' said Mrs Butler through an open window as their car pulled in. 'Oh, love, love, did you miss the Lytham train?' Laurie became Nancy became Dawn became one of the dinner-ladies who passed me after the news about Tafler broke: 'Guilt, see? He couldn't live with the guilt.' 'It's Doctor Jon!' cried Mr Vesey, urged onto a podium beside me by Tony and Jim and Paul and all the Farwells. The Humboldt gulley of snow changed into Gornal Wood and back. 'Let's come back here tonight, man,' said Gordy.

'Mooch round the Erkeley after hours.' 'Nah,' Bevvo said. 'Crap idea.'

But I held tight, kept writing in a straight line. The whiskey was at my elbow. The bed was waiting, nicely made. As for the other purchase, abetting the whiskey, I'd got rid of what it came in. When all was done I'd lie on the bed and scull back to that time before the Erkeley when I turned my bed round and, through a gap in the curtains, saw the evening and its star looking down just for me, promising peace without end. I was aware of Mrs King's car going out and coming back and once or twice surfaced properly to answer her knock. 'Oh, thanks, Mrs K, but I'm doing fine. Got all I need. Having a few, you know, hot toddies.' And an added chuckle. And warm wishes from the other side of the door. Of course I didn't ask her in. I didn't want to taint her.

*

There. I can't think of anything to finish with, except to say that it's early morning and it must be four or five days since Tony stopped me in my tracks, there in the dark, and told me to call him when I was where I'm never going. I'll leave it with Mrs K's knocks, unanswered now, her lovely concern. That can stand in for the good that came my way, the things that any sane person would prefer to remember while they could. Whoever you are, I don't know what you'll make of me. I can't…and I couldn't control it. It's

336

been a life. Maybe there've been worse. Never been near a church since Mum's service and hardly went near one before. Still, this can't hurt, can it? So…pray for me.

The bed waits. All is to hand. The party Tony threw after my Master's viva. I'll take that there with me, alongside Mrs K's kindly words.

*

~~No no I won't have it dear God I planned Bob Corey's line~~. I'd just closed my eyes after writing 'Mrs K's kindly words' and a hand on the back of my neck spun me round and their two faces were as far from mine as yours will be from this page when you read it. They hauled me into the kitchen and Mrs King was reversing her car with the trunk near enough against the window and it slid away, doors, aerial, hood. ~~She heard~~ I heard her idle and swing round for the road. I saw, in the space she'd left, the whole of their new dawn.

~~Bob Corey's cloak Ah Mephistopheles~~. Dear God. Dear God. All those faces looking at me. ~~Tramp and~~ And now Tafler and Wiznuk are out there, lining them up. Beyond all foulness, what have they done? Death splashed far and wide. ~~Ratty little~~ Wiznuk signals. The line ~~starts~~ curves forwards across the drive. All those faces. From all those times. I can't bear to look. I can't bear to recognise them.

No. No. One more deep breath and hold the line. They're not having it, I'm not a common kill. It's time for me to run again—off the Erkeley and

337

past the detacheds, the Timothy house, the flaky village green. Push on, push. Perhaps old man Timothy's son will spot me from their window and ~~know~~ remember that he'd sold me that last copy of 'All You Need Is Love' the day when Bevvo and I rode our bikes down every street in Bilston. ~~I remember how~~ ~~forget that~~. I can hear the storm door upstairs. Time to ~~stamp down~~ kick up the mud of Erkeley Walk, leap at the main road with cars and vans like dodgems round me, curses fading ~~far~~ uphill and down. Then race to the pub sign, *The ~~Happy~~ Jolly Waggoner,* that Black Countryman standing by his ~~work~~ livelihood, thumbs in braces, pipe in ~~hand~~ mouth. I can hear murmuring, many-voiced, on the stairs. ~~Minutes left?~~ A minute left? Do it, Parry, push, push. A last spurt to get me into that pub sign, under the waggon's canvas, as I should have done, that and nothing else, with the pot-plant the day two policemen smiled and wished me well and called me son.

22

'Bevvo and Gordy…'

Will turned the last page over and back. No, nothing beyond those names. Hell of a scramble after that calm bit about the bed waiting and all to hand. Those mad crossings-out when the rest had been so neat. And the writing gone to hell. But why wouldn't it? In any other circumstances, that last bit might have read like a faked ransom plea. But dear God...what circumstances could come close?

He reached for a treat. The bowl was pretty well empty again. Truly gutsy thing, writing on like that when all was collapsing. Plain stupid, some would say, but was it? 'Whoever you are, I don't know what you'll make of me.' Well, the guy had hauled himself past his polished finale and up to his last gasp. What I make of that, thought Will, is honesty. A kind of...yes, weirdly, a kind of courtesy.

Bevvo and Gordy. What was that with the names all naked and alone? A cry for those buddies who weren't worth caring about—yet surely were if they took the secret with them all through their lives? Were they the first two he saw in that unholy line? Ah, he'd have to puzzle it all again later, maybe root about in the overseas Missing files. Or maybe not. It wasn't the point here. The state the guy must've been in right that moment...Will shivered as though he'd been beside him and saw the names hit the page before the murmuring swelled and blew into the room. 'Boy, I do hope you got the jump on it all,' he said aloud and, topping up, raised his glass. 'Sure. I'll pray for you.'

Those words got him out of the chair. He stretched and drank. Where was that guy now, the one he promised himself he'd be, the Dickens guy, pleased to hear a tale about nothing that could touch him, just hopeful that it would last for two or three stiff ones? At the far end of a darkening street, poor klutz, turning away, the quicker the better, hoping that the next corner would bring a more welcoming bar, more genial company, a yarn that wanted him to do no more than shrug and say, well, life can get peculiar, no doubt of it.

He looked down at the folder, still open at the names. He'd drop it in tomorrow on the way to the bus station. Or...? Barysko would have clean forgotten by now that he'd left it for DeConinck to look over, neither of them would be in till midweek and old Clance took little notice of what came and went on the station desk—a self-awarded perk of his long service. So, time enough to copy it. He'd need to have a copy close, a totem, till after Christmas, after all was done. He could hardly drop it off somewhere to collect later. Any place like *High Office* was out, obviously, and troubling the station's Reprographics would be another Riversdale bozo move. Ok, so he'd do it himself, in stages, different places. Some at the City Library...till old Grace Popescul came looming with 'For exactly how many years, young man, do you intend to hog our Xerox?'—and possibly, God help us, 'You, sir, are the spit of a boy who used to run up humongous fines.' Some more up at the Uni. Library. Mags kept her visitor's card up in the letter-rack, just *M Apland,* photo pretty scratched. Hardly used it. Might take longer than midweek, but if someone set up a holler for the folder, well—he smiled—another of Clance's perks was chronic forgetfulness about tidying the Evidence store. He could himself volunteer to hunt for it. That'd push it towards the back of folks' minds: 'Oh, that guy's big book, Apland's on it.' And when it was all copied, a flourish in the Evidence doorway...it must have fallen down...I found it just next to....

So that was that. Bending gently down, Will closed the folder and was, so to speak, in the act of settling Jonathan on his bed—which is where, after all, they had found him—when it was up in his hands again and his mind was full of the bear that never was.

'Shit,' he hissed, 'shit, shit.' It took an age of leafing, back and forth, out from the start, in from the end. At last he was there, alongside Dawn and Jonathan in the Visitors' Centre on that miserable summer afternoon and she was doubting that what did for their camp was a bear and the ranger...now, the ranger said...yes, 'Had a bunch of folks through...couple of weeks back...same thing...one guy...survivalist...said not a bear.' Will shut the folder. Shit. So others had gone through the same thing, others who had nothing to do with Jonathan. He felt like someone who, passing a coat-rack, sees a thread hanging down from a cuff and, tidy-minded, pulls at it, only to find the whole thing unravelling to a gloop of stuff at their feet. Was this a dangling thread, set there deliberately? If so, how many others were there? Had he been right to doubt—God knows, more than once—while reading away? Had this limey chosen to depart this life for some other reason or none at all—or just so he could confect some memorable bullshit?

He couldn't believe that. He was too deep in. And did it matter now? Fool me once, shame on you. But what if your fooling turns inside out, offers a truth for me, a truth that's been waiting its time, complete with a way to act on it? You can fool on a hundred times, I can be fooled the same. Shame won't come into it.

Once again the folder was set gently down. The scribbled notes lay forgotten beside the chair. Jacket on, glass in hand, Will turned for the rumpus room door, the stairs, the future. Monday, back on earlies. More patrols with Smeets or Terry M or maybe both for hot calls. Smeets would for sure come back to this poor lone guy. By now he'd have a fistful of theories and the jargon to go with them. The city could save a pile by firing the coroner and the pathologists and getting him on board instead. What's the betting he'd have some fancy notion worked out about the smell in Jonathan's apartment? A smell from down the ages, he'd called it. Will could smell it again as he climbed the stairs, a real fierce go, but he barely shrugged. Old Smeets…he was probably beavering away the weekend with books on witchcraft and prognostications, hunting up the spooky word on smells, a new bunch of wisdom to make Terry M's eyes roll. Himself, he'd listen in, ready with the headshakes, the chin-scratches. Other times he'd do the same with other folks who had other tales to tell. He'd question, note, placate and, every so often, trouble Clance to check in his part of the day's catch from the wide and bursting river beyond the station doors.

'Worker-me and protector-me,' he said aloud at the top of the stairs. He'd for sure start to work on the kids about Christmas, bring Mags round if she jibbed, if she worried about being so far away, even for a short spell, with her dad's health as it was. For the rest, well, time with the kids, PTA stuff for Mags, dinner out here, late drinks there, the odd movie. The usual. But his copy of Jonathan's words would be his close protection, his guide. He'd take it with him for those fugitive days while he checked out Annie's place. For sure he'd read it again: there might be a trick or two he'd missed, something he could parlay into a move. Unlike Jonathan, he felt he could hold two of himself in safe balance, be there but not there for the daily round. It would be a mark of respect for the guy—a courtesy returned.

He opened the back door. It was getting light—and boy, was Ernie Lester right, back at the liquor store. The snow was thin but fast, scudding around. He took it in for a moment. Then, at last, he returned to the kitchen and, sipping slowly, pressed the message button again:

'Hey, big man. Long time no hear. You trying to keep a jump ahead of Le Revenu Canadien, eh? Now look here, it's been an age since we all got together and I thought, well, always me who makes the running but what the hell, Christmas

coming, Annie's gorgeous spread in Vermont, why don't we? Years since we got together, all of us, big man, years and years. Annie's cool with it, guess that weirdo husband of hers will be, too, but we don't have to bother with him more than basics. I don't know how often you bestir yourself to phone her—have you ever?—but her kids are all doing great. The two youngest are still at home. Pining for a dog of their own for Christmas. Hey, Willie and me, we'll take it out, I said. Cue conniptions at Annie's end. Man, she's never forgotten that. Poor ickle sad Natosi. In our kitchen, remember, the looks she gave you? And me bustin' a gut to save the day? Dogs and their itty little paws and all that suck-stuff? Anyways, I'm in a race with your machine here so get thinking about Christmas. Aplands in Vermont, eh? I'm gonna start crooning....'

Will walked slowly back through the kitchen and stepped out front, shutting the screen door behind him. For a moment he felt as he had when he—and, reluctantly, the other one—had faced Old Man Mathieson the day Natosi had been broken off his lead and treated like shit and later used...no, no, don't go back. All that's had its season. Now it's consequences up ahead: it's what has to happen. 'Jonathan,' he murmured, 'I've got this. Evens is the word. For you and me.' And for sure he'd look out for Holly and the kids. She might even feel relief.

The snow was still flurries but they were thickening up. Maybe the mother-in-law wasn't so premature, getting antsy about ploughs and warnings. Man, when had it last come on so early? The flurries started whipping around. You could see the house opposite, then you sort of couldn't. Will looked far down the block. The lights would be going off soon. A couple of flurries appeared to have taken a liking to one lamp on a corner. A blackness seemed to enter them, dance them about, bulk them up so that they became two...Will chuckled. A trick of bad visuals. Or maybe Patty Balzer had finally partied the night away, Hallowe'en no less, and Old Walt had trekked out to his welcoming station with Mrs B alongside, grabbing for his sleeve. Will craned his neck, waiting for the old familiar tune: 'Walter...Walter come on, now. Leave be. She'll be home when she's home. Let our girl have her fun.'

The End

About the Author

Michael W. Thomas has published eight collections of poetry, three novels and two collections of short fiction. His latest poetry collection is *Under Smoky Light* (Offa's Press); his latest fiction collection is *Sing Ho! Stout Cortez: Novellas and Stories* (Black Pear Press). With Simon Fletcher, he edited *The Poetry of Worcestershire* (Offa's Press). His work has appeared in *The Antigonish Review* (Canada), *The Antioch Review* (US), *Critical Survey*, *Crossroads* (Poland), *Dream Catcher, Etchings* (Australia), *Irish Studies Review, Irish University Review, Magazine Six* (US), *Pennine Platform, Poetry Salzburg Review, The Times Literary Supplement* and *Under the Radar*, among others. He has reviewed for *The London Magazine, Other Poetry* and *The Times Literary Supplement*, and is on the editorial board of *Crossroads: A Journal of English Studies* (University of Bialystok, Poland). He was long-listed for the National Poetry Competition, 2020 and 2022, and long-listed and short-listed for the Indigo Dreams Spring Poetry Prize, 2023. For more information, please visit: www.michaelwthomas.co.uk

Printed in Great Britain
by Amazon

32894258R00198